NOON IN CALCUTTA

Short Stories from Bengal

NOON IN CALCUTTA

Short Stories from Bengal

edited by

KRISHNA DUTTA

and

ANDREW ROBINSON

preface by

ANITA DESAI

BLOOMSBURY

First published in Great Britain 1992

This compilation and all the translations except
'The Little World of Shadananda' and 'The Conclusion' © 1992
by the editors Krishna Dutta and Andrew Robinson

Bloomsbury Publishing Ltd, 2 Soho Square, London W1V 5DE

A CIP catalogue record for this book
is available from the British Library

ISBN 0 7475 1157 8

Typeset by Hewer Text Composition Services, Edinburgh
Printed in Great Britain by Clays Ltd, St Ives plc

for the three Rays

– UPENDRAKISHORE, SUKUMAR, SATYAJIT –

inspired artists and storytellers

CONTENTS

How I cherish light and space! Goethe on his deathbed wanted 'more light'. If I am capable of expressing my desire then, it will be for 'more light and space'. Many people dismiss Bengal for being so flat, but for me the fields and rivers are sights that I love. With the falling of evening the deep vault of the sky brims with tranquillity like a goblet of lapis lazuli; while the immobility of afternoon reminds me of the border of a golden sari wrapped around the entire world. Where is there another land to fill the mind so?

RABINDRANATH TAGORE, letter, 1894
from *Chinnapatra* (Glimpses of Bengal)

During noon in summer, when I lay in my bedroom with the doors and windows closed, I don't know how – but at a particular time light would shine through a chink in the shutters and throw an upside-down image of the street onto a large patch of wall opposite one window. It was like magic: inside the dark room you could clearly see everything in the road outside, cars, rickshaws, cycles and pedestrians passing back and forth as in a picture. I have no idea how many noontimes I lay there and watched this free Bioscope.

SATYAJIT RAY, 1981
from *Jakhan Chhoto Chilam* (When I Was Small)

PREFACE

For most Indians, Bengali literature is associated with Shantiniketan, the 'Abode of Peace', the school and university that Rabindranath Tagore founded in the countryside, well away from Calcutta. Since it was removed from the city – and the official system of education – and had the reputation of a rural idyll where students read their lessons under the spreading trees, where no examinations troubled them, where the arts that were practised were gentle and pleasing, where festivals were devised to celebrate each season, and where above all presided the bard-like figure of the poet himself – 'Gurudev' as he was called, according him semi-divinity – Shantiniketan seemed in the popular imagination utopian, unreal and enervated. One pictured life there as set to the sweet plaintiveness of Tagore's music, interrupted occasionally by the song of a *koel* and disturbed only by a monsoon thunderstorm. So much of Bengali culture seemed to have come from there in the first half of the twentieth century, and it was all tainted with the suspicion that it was singularly out of touch with reality and the world, that it had a somewhat effeminate air, fit for young girls before marriage but not much else.

For me the illusion had an additional element, provided by my father's nostalgic memories of his childhood in East Bengal, of the myriad, meandering rivers, of the undulating paddy fields, of the boats and the boatmen's songs he recalled which enhanced the romance of that watery landscape for a child brought up in the arid monotony of north India. The romance was rapidly and drastically modified by my first visit to Calcutta, at age nineteen, an experience of a metropolis that made Delhi seem a village by comparison. Later I spent five years in the city and Bengal acquired for me all the grime and soot and shadows of a dark, disturbing reality.

A more balanced view and the necessary objectivity were finally achieved through the reading I did after I left Bengal, when I discovered that Tagore had not merely composed odes to the seasons and (as I felt) a tiresomely large cycle of melancholy songs, but an immense oeuvre of prose stories and novels about every political and social aspect of life in Bengal over many decades, in addition to his inspired and influential polemical writing on education, on ethics, on the environment and, again and again, on the nationalist and reformist movements of his time. Bibhuti Bhushan Banerji's *Pather Panchali* with its rich pathos made me see the poverty and hardship beneath the smiling green surface of lush paddy fields and brimming rivers. Contemporary novelists like Sunil Ganguli added the quotidian struggles of urban existence as known to Bengalis in Calcutta, and Mahasweta Devi's championing of the peasants and the tribals opened my eyes to the political and economic dimensions of modern Bengali life. The rather insipid romance of the old illusory Bengal began to seem as flimsy as a thoroughly washed and worn muslin sari, long past its useful life, torn into strips and showing through its rents glimpses of a much more interesting and disturbing world than I had imagined.

The stories collected here offer the reader a sufficiently diverse sampling of Bengali literature to convey the complexity of Bengali life and art. They make up a kind of nest, as of grasses and twigs gleaned from the landscape, but the nest does not contain a single, simplified egg-like image. It would be hard to find a label for a collection that includes both stories that recall an older, non-literary age – the age of oral story-telling and narratives that are part-fable, part-fairy tale and employ jingles and nursery rhymes – as well as sharp, satiric caricatures closely related to the cartoons that ridiculed the *babus*, semi-educated Bengali clerks, officials and 'men-about-town' who scrambled to imitate the semi-educated members of the British Raj, with all their consequent absurd and hilarious incongruities. There are stories that convey the charm of childhood memories and youthful dreams, and stories that dramatise the sad and dangerous traps into which these charming children and youths inexorably fall: the City, mammoth and overpowering, dwarfing the individual and reducing him to a speck of insignificant grime, or poverty that makes a hovel seem desirable and a drink of milk quite unattainable, or injustice that deprives drought-ridden cultivators of water and victorious soldiers of victory. No experience seems pure, private, every one is complicated by forces over which the protagonists appear to have little control.

That a collection covering a century offers such diversity is not in itself remarkable, but what will give the reader a jolt is the extreme nature of many of the voices, attitudes and events. Yes, there are the magical, jingling tales that never date. And there are the stories full of shifting images and impressions which Tagore's poetic, metaphorical writing makes one identify with the Bengali psyche. But there is also much that will shock and stun, stories that are like slaps and kicks to the reader's consciousness. These are not restricted to the contemporary work: the violence has always been there, like an unhatched egg in the nest; eventually it gave birth to Marxism that has all but edged out the other birds.

The history of Bengal in this century is a history of violence – from Lord Curzon's attempted division into West and East Bengal on a Hindu/Muslim basis in 1905, through the terrorism of succeeding decades, to the Partition of India and Pakistan in 1947 on the same lines as in 1905. We see it in operation in the riot-torn 'Farewell' and its legacy in the present-day fundamentalism portrayed in 'Rebirth'. Then there was the great famine of 1943/44 which left a memory of hunger that still lingers like a disfiguring scar, the war in 1971 that created Bangladesh and a new flood of refugees, and the armed peasant revolt in Naxalbari that sparked the educated youth of Calcutta and, brutally repressed there, survived to erupt elsewhere in India. Politics and political events being an essential element of Bengali life and thought, they enter into and saturate Bengali literature as well.

It was Tagore, the inventor of the Bengali short story, who made the polemical a literary tradition that has persisted, its tone increasingly insistent and uncompromising, until the early idealism, and the romanticism inherent in idealism, has all but disappeared under the cynicism and bitterness of later writers like Mahasweta Devi and Hasan Azizul Huq.

There is no dearth of situations from which violence may spring. The earliest stories here, 'The Raj Seal' and 'Natunda, Babu' concern the opposition of idealism and corruption within the idea of nationalism. 'The Goddess' dramatically presents the clash of tradition and super-stition with science and rationality; 'The Music Room' of tradition and the aristocracy with *nouveau-riche* upstarts and commercialism. At the end of it comes an acknowledgment that the violence, the fury – 'the madness' – already has a long pedigree:

Climbing the stairs, [Ray] found the music room still open. He peered in. The room was void, the love tryst had vanished. Only the bottles remained, lying about empty; and the still-flickering candles. The Ray forebears gazed down haughtily, and all at once they seemed to Bishwambhar Ray to laugh like maniacs. He recoiled, and as he did so, he caught a glimpse of himself in the mirror and saw – madness! He was no different from them; all seven generations in that room were touched by the same infatuation!

Later stories depict a society in which these charged confrontations have already led to damage that is irrevocable, embroiling castes and communities in an increasingly vicious struggle. In 'Primordial' a mutilated social outcaste makes criminal raids upon a rural society that has no way of accommodating them. 'Water' ends in the hopelessness of the struggle of the poor for the most basic necessities that are considered the exclusive property of the privileged. Meanwhile the middle-class works desperately at keeping alive an illusion of gentility in a house where even 'A Drop of Milk' is seen as an enviable luxury and a cause for both sacrifice and struggle, and in 'The Mourners' conducts a child's funeral with a casualness and callousness that has to exist where death is commonplace. Yet even the middle-class's minimal security and doubtful superiority are clung to with tooth and nail – to avoid sliding into the great black abyss of poverty that Amitav Ghosh exposes in 'Winter in Calcutta':

There was no place for me to sit, so I slipped back outside to the long verandah-like corridor. Raising myself on tiptoe, I leant on the low railing that ran along it and looked down . . . The ground fell away sharply from the edges of the building and then levelled out into a patchwork of stagnant pools, dotted with islands of low, raised ground. Clinging to these islands were little clumps of shanties . . . The pools were black, covered with a sludge so thick that it had defeated even the ubiquitous carpets of water hyacinth. I could see women squatting at the edges of the pools, splashing with both hands to drive back the layers of sludge, scooping up the cleaner water underneath to scrub their babies and wash their clothes and cooking utensils . . .

Our relative spotted me leaning on the railing and ran out. 'Don't look there!' she cried. 'It's dirty!' Then she led me back inside.

Although the middle-classes pretend to be concerned with dirt, actually their concern is with hunger, the shadow of famine which in 1943 was triggered by the disruption of war and allowed to spread by the indifference of government. In 'Homecoming', the village soldier who has fought for the freedom of his country, soon to be Bangladesh, returns and informs his wife:

> 'The battle's over now, you know – what's become of our country?'
>
> 'Our country has gained independence,' said his wife parrot-fashion.
>
> Alef was almost asleep but he revived abruptly with a choking sound: 'So now, I suppose we turn into kings and emperors? Do you think we will be so lucky?'
>
> His wife protested, 'Why? Why kings and emperors? At least we won't suffer any more.'
>
> 'Meaning?'
>
> 'We'll get food and clothes.'
>
> 'Is that right?' Alef opened his eyes as he spoke and looked hard at her. Her words did not seem to have sunk in. He said in a monotone: 'The meaning of independence seems remarkably clear to you.'

Readers who can find no equivalent of such brutal experience in their own safer, tidier worlds, might be able to see an analogy with Russian literature that helps to give such experience a universality. Bengali writers share with Russians a vision of the world in which great cruelty and degradation exist side by side with tenderness and innocence, where want and hardship appear to stamp out all traces of humanity from the characters, yet mysteriously manage to reveal a spirit, or soul, that seems indestructible, that is undeniably human and that manifests itself in moments of grace that can only be glimpsed, very rarely sustained. This juxtaposition marks Bengali literature as it does the work of Gogol, Gorki, Chekhov and Dostoevsky.

In both societies there is the preoccupation with superstition, religious or otherwise, only minimally affected by the introduction of science (with which certain Bengali writers display a particular fascination, as we see in the futuristic fantasy 'The Rise and Fall of the Gammans' and very many of the stories of Satyajit Ray, including his exploration of the ant universe, 'The Little World of Shadananda'). Another link is the allure of the city, which dazzles the minds of a traditionally rural people. Just as in the plays and stories of Chekhov, so much of Bengali prose and poetry recreates the glamour of the city, never borne out in practice but still a potent metaphor for promise, opportunity and a dimension to life missing from the grind of the agricultural cycle.

More importantly, there is the attraction in both societies of Marxism, born out of a common bond of oppression and suffering to which Tagore gave eloquent expression in his 1930 letters from Russia. But while the rapid spread of Soviet education enthralled him, he remained doubtful about Marxism as a solution to social problems. 'In the background of the picture of Russia that has taken shape in my mind lurks the dark misery of India . . . Many people here have asked my opinion about Bolshevik economics. My only fear is that in a scripture-ridden and priest-led country the natural bent of the ignorant mind is towards accepting a foreign dictum as biblical truth. Guarding ourselves against this danger, we must say that doctrine can be tested only by its application: the end of the experiment is not yet.' In both lands there has been the will to change the social and economic order, to bring about an equitable society, as well as the experience of being thwarted by the strength of orthodoxy and the ruthlessness of the patriarchy – whether in the form of priest or zamindar, commissar or magistrate, village elder or paterfamilias. If the family does not impose the same stranglehold in Russia as it does in India, the state replaces it and becomes indistinguishable. Both lands have known authority at its harshest, and in both the spirit of revolt is strong.

Four of the stories in the collection were written in English, the rest are translations from Bengali. There is the absent language to be considered. Can the English language convey thoughts, emotions and situations that are alien to the English experience? What about those that have grown out of the contact of the two languages, a contact which has infiltrated many English words into Bengali (and a few vice versa, such as bungalow), where they have taken on a connotation and flavour very different from their usage in English? And what of the sound, tone and rhythm of Bengali? It is difficult to characterise the latter when it takes on such a diversity of tones – from the innocent jingling and boisterous punning of the fairy tale and the fable, through the shifting, subtle allusiveness of the more introspective stories with

xiv

their wealth of metaphor and imagery, to the hard-hitting and abrupt and often coarse dialogue in many other stories. The translators have tried to convey these different qualities and it seems a measure of their success that instead of reducing it all to a bland, recognisable English that is international, they have maintained these individual voices, and retained the Bengali grain. Family appellations and regional rites and rituals of food and dress and worship need their own vocabulary, and it has quite often been retained, the meanings of the Bengali words woven into the text rather than left dependent on elaborate footnotes or a weighty glossary. This requires of the reader a certain effort – to break through the regional code to arrive at a universal meaning. That effort is essential, and if it is made the reader will find it possible to enter another world. The best literature is always a shared experience, and it takes both reader and writer to create it.

ANITA DESAI

INTRODUCTION

The painting on the back cover of this book, which dates from around 1917, has the title in English, 'Confusion of Ideas'. Its title in Bengali, 'Pranam Bibhrat', is subtly different: it means 'Confusion of Pranam' – the *pranam* being the traditional Indian gesture of prostrating oneself before the deity, or of 'taking the dust' from an elder's feet when greeting him or her. The two 'brown sahibs' in the picture, attired in western garb and attuned to western values (as they think), offer a deliciously hybrid salutation at the temple: neither a Hindu *pranam* nor a Christian prayer, neither a Bengali foot-touch nor a British hand-shake; instead it is a farcical melange of Bengali and British etiquette. In other words, a typical example of the behaviour of the Bengali *babu* – in the eyes of Rudyard Kipling and most of the British of the Raj.

But the irony in the image is Bengali, not British, the artist the leading satirical artist of Bengal, Gaganendranath Tagore. He was following the example set in literature by his uncle, the famous Rabindranath. Beginning in the 1880s, when he was already a poet, playwright, novelist, essayist and composer, under the inspiration of the western short story, Rabindranath had single-handedly created the short story in Bengali. In due course he wrote nearly a hundred of them. Satyajit Ray, Tagore's modern interpreter to the world, the supreme creative figure of post-Independence Bengal and, even more than Tagore, an artist steeped in the cultures of East and West, regards some of these short stories as 'among the best ever written'.

We have selected two of them for their utter divergence of setting, style and mood and placed them at the beginning and end of the book so as to indicate Tagore's all-embracing influence. No Bengali writer, indeed no Bengali artist in any medium, has been able to ignore Tagore, though many have tried to limit his importance, to deny that he understood the harsher human truths. Tagore idealises his characters, they maintain; he writes to reform society not to describe it; he is not a 'realist'. And yet careful study of Tagore's entire works always eventually disarms the unbiased critic – even one as pugnacious and naturally non-Tagorean as Ritwik Ghatak, the film director, playwright and uncle of Mahasweta Devi, who is perhaps Bengali literature's starkest writer. Just before his death in 1976 Ghatak said:

> I cannot speak without Tagore. That man has culled all my feelings long before my birth. He has understood what I am and he has put in all the words. I read him and I find that all has been said and I have nothing new to say. I think all artists, in Bengal at least, find themselves in the same difficulty. It just cannot be helped. You can be angry with him, you can criticise him, you may dislike him, but in the final analysis, you will find that he has the last word.

Tagore's story 'The Raj Seal' bears virtually no resemblance to the mystical poetry of *Gitanjali* which won him the Nobel prize for literature in 1913. Its subject is the Calcutta *babu*, in particular his twin incompatible urges to be both British title-holder and patriotic hero. Tagore wrote the story in 1898, a year which he began by delivering a paper at the Calcutta Town Hall entitled 'Kantharodh' (The Throttled) in protest against the government's Sedition Bill; then attacked the government for arresting a leading Indian nationalist on a charge of sedition; and finally had a go at Bengalis too, insisting that the presidential address of the Bengal Provincial Conference should be read in Bengali as well as in English (the usual language of Bengali politicians in that period), and at the same time severely criticising the servile mentality and orthodox mores of some leading Bengali landowners. As in life, so in the story Tagore spares no section of society; but his tone throughout is ironic, not hectoring, his criticism covert not explicit. Although the world of Raj politicking he depicts has long since passed into history, the story shows that Tagore was acutely alive to the risible and corrupt character of the politics that might easily replace the Raj, once his countrymen had a free hand in government.

Less elaborate, closer to farce, is the portrait of a *babu* in 'Natunda' by Sharat Chandra Chatterji, Bengal's most popular novelist. A Bengali writer and critic (Buddhadeva Bose) has called Chatterji 'Tagore Made Easy', 'like Dickens, the idol of his public', and Sharat Chandra himself is said to have rebuked a worshipper who once told him that he held him far above Tagore, 'Yes, Sir, I can quite believe it. It's readers like *you* I write for, whereas Rabindranath writes for readers like me.'

'Natunda' is an episode from *Shrikanta* (1917), Sharat Chandra's autobiographical picaresque, 'a sort of Bengali *Huckleberry Finn*', according to E. J. Thompson. It draws upon the author's childhood and youth, which were times of great poverty, as they were for the majority of Bengali writers. Though born in Bengal, Sharat Chandra spent ten years as a government clerk in Burma, which gave him the inestimable advantage of viewing Bengal and Bengalis from the outside. He began writing seriously only in 1913, when he was 37, but he quickly became the first Bengali writer to make a real living out of his work. It was soon a staple of stage and cinema, adaptations which were mostly execrable yet highly successful: 'That Sharat Chandra can brave the worst distortions is in him a curious quality which leads one to think that he is either very gross or very subtle. Perhaps he is both,' wrote Bose.

Sharat Chandra can be read in the kitchen, Rabindranath cannot be – though he can certainly be sung there: that is what a Bengali feels about the difference between the two writers. Sharat Chandra's critique of society is domesticated, comfortable, Rabindranath's radical, discomforting – as their respective stories illustrate. Both writers mock '*babu* culture', but whereas Sharat Chandra's narrator – an ordinary, fairly orthodox Hindu – is presented sympathetically, Rabindranath remains almost as detached from those of his characters who criticise the *babu*, as he does from the *babu* himself. It is intrinsic to each writer's personality that Rabindranath would later decide to write a novel (the well-known *Home and the World*) denouncing Bengali terrorism and would refuse to join Gandhi's non-co-operation movement in the 1920s, while Sharat Chandra would decide to do the opposite, and produce a popular novel supporting terrorists as patriots.

Tagore often gifted ideas for short stories and other works to promising young writers. One of these became 'The Goddess', published by Prabhat Kumar Mukherji in 1899. It is a story of conflict between orthodoxy and rational values, centred upon Bengal's favourite goddess, the terrifying-looking Kali, 'The Mother'. A young wife in a rich village family is ensconced as an incarnation of Kali by her devout widowed father-in-law, the village's zamindar. He has perceived her true identity in a vision. Her husband, the zamindar's younger son, who has been educated partly in a western way, cannot accept the vision, but does not wish to challenge his father outright. The girl, wrenched in two directions, is fatally confused.

The theme is a profound one, and not just for Bengal: many westerners, such as Christopher Isherwood and Aldous Huxley, have been drawn to Kali; Margaret Noble, an Irish convert to Hinduism famous at the turn of the century as Sister Nivedita, gave several packed and controversial lectures in favour of Kali worship in Calcutta during 1899: Tagore, in suggesting the theme to Prabhat Mukherji, may possibly have wanted to counteract such influential support. To this day the story remains controversial: when, in 1960, Satyajit Ray made a mesmerising film of it, he faced strong criticism from extreme orthodox Hindus. Tagore himself is said to have been not wholly satisfied with the story, possibly because he found it too short to allow a full and convincing revelation of the father's blindness to reason (unlike the film), or perhaps because he found Prabhat Mukherji's ending too brutal (it was softened by Ray). In general, 'Tagore interpreted life, Prabhat Kumar Mukherji (like Maupassant) unravelled it,' thought a writer of a later generation, Tarashankar Banerji, who was born in a zamindari family not dissimilar to that of 'The Goddess', in a village not far from Tagore's school and university at Shantiniketan. But Banerji, unlike Mukherji, did not come under Tagore's direct influence. When he began seriously writing in the early 1930s, unusually late in life, after a period in the Gandhian movement and a spell in jail, he introduced into Bengali literature such rustic characters as snake charmers, potters, witches and wandering minstrels, all on the brink of ruin as a result of commercial trends. He also described the decaying landed families, from one of which he himself had sprung.

'The Music Room' (1934) is among the most famous works in Tarashankar's prolific output of novels and stories. There is a pathos in the self-destruction of its central character, a zamindar who lives only for music and dance in his crumbling mansion, that transcends the man's feudal selfishness and the particular predicament of the Bengali elite. His ineluctable eclipse by his unctuous money-lending neighbour, who can never forget the fact that his family owed allegiance to the zamindar, is peculiarly pointed in today's India, but it speaks to a present-day British reader too. (Maybe there is a whiff in it of the final years of the sly, venerable Harold Macmillan vying with a philistine successor as Prime Minister.) Satyajit Ray, who filmed the story in 1958, says that he 'tried to show the inevitability of the old order being replaced by the new – but not necessarily better – system . . . There's no doubt that the zamindars were real connoisseurs of music, and sponsors of music.'

For the many admirers of the film, a comparison with the original story should prove interesting. The film is faithful in spirit but altered in several crucial ways (entirely approved by the story's author). In translating, so as to avoid confusion in a non-Indian reader's mind, we have taken the liberty of clarifying something the author left vague: whether the dancers (*baijis*) dance *and* sing, or only dance. In our version the dancers dance but do not sing – capable though such dancers were of doing both things. This resolves the story's uncertainty in favour of the film, in which dancer and singer are two different people. (Just how close story and film really are is indicated by an amusing story. After endless fruitless searching, Ray chanced upon a decaying mansion suitable for shooting, more than two hundred miles from Calcutta on the banks of the Ganges between India and East Pakistan, and informed Tarashankar Banerji. The family who owned the palace turned out to be the very family on whom Tarashankar had based his story!)

Coincidence is a close cousin of superstition, as are the supernatural, speculative, fantasy and fairy tale worlds that are a special feature of Bengali literature. Tagore wrote several atmospheric supernatural stories, but the leading writers in this general field (not counting Satyajit Ray) are four: Upendrakishore Ray Chaudhuri and Sukumar Ray, respectively the grandfather and father of Satyajit Ray; Rajshekhar Basu; and Rabindranath's nephew Abanindranath Tagore, the younger brother of the satirical artist Gaganendranath.

'The Adventures of Goopy and Bagha' was written by Upendrakishore in 1915, only months before his premature death, for his children's magazine *Sandesh*, which his grandson Satyajit now edits. Satyajit first read the story when he was about eight, around 1929; forty years later, partly to please his young son, he created a musical film from the story which has immortalised it. The film quickly became a classic in Bengal, and even outside Bengal where the words of its songs do not transplant; it is a favourite of, among others, Salman Rushdie.

Upendrakishore was a diversely gifted man. Besides writing and translating, he illustrated superlatively, composed and sang songs, played several instruments and was an internationally-known pioneer of half-tone printing. But perhaps his finest and most particular gift was his ability to appeal to children, epitomised by the language of 'Goopy and Bagha', which is so charming and limpid it can hold an adult reader.

The appeal of his son Sukumar's writing, at least in Bengali, is akin to that of Lewis Carroll and Edward Lear. Sukumar Ray is the divinely-inspired monarch of Bengali nonsense illustrating and writing, in the form of verses, plays and a few short stories. The story we have chosen, 'Drighanchu' (1916), in which a King demands an explanation from his terrified courtiers of why a crow chose to enter his court and say 'Caw', is among Sukumar's masterpieces. We have called the story 'Crowmagnum' in an attempt to capture the original title, a sonorous but bogus Sanskrit-sounding word meaning something like 'Beaky Dicky'. Though more easily translatable than most of Sukumar's work, the story contains four lines of nonsense verse, famous in Bengal, that are bound to be paler in English than in Bengali. These apart, we hope the quick wit of the original is unimpaired.

Much of Sukumar Ray's writing was satirical, but his targets tended to be so veiled as to leave the reader guessing. The slightly older Rajshekhar Basu, who wrote under the pseudonym Parashuram, was much more explicit. The Basu family, gifted in the sciences as well as in the arts like Upendrakishore and Sukumar Ray, were old friends of the Ray family; Rajshekhar's younger brother, who corresponded extensively with Freud, was the Ray family physician. Rajshekhar himself was by training a chemist, the founder of Bengal Chemicals and Pharmaceuticals. He gave wonderful names to toothpastes and lotions – all based on Sanskrit words. He also wrote a dictionary of colloquial Bengali still in constant use, and his summaries of the epics *Ramayana* and *Mahabharata* are greatly admired.

There are two films from Rajshekhar's stories made by Satyajit Ray. Both films delight the sensitive Bengali with their shrewdly judged but indulgent undermining of middle-class hypocrisy and gullibility – they are reminiscent somehow of the British television series *Dad's Army* – but neither film works all that well in English; humour being the part of a culture that is toughest to translate. The story by Rajshekhar chosen by us, 'The Rise and Fall of the Gammans' (1945), with its avowedly international setting, a last-ditch conference sometime in the future to procure peace between nations – does not suffer much in translation;

nor, despite the passing of the Cold War and the worst of the nuclear threat, has it much dated. In fact its ending seems ahead of its time, a Bengali pre-vision of Gaia, that persuasive modern myth of Earth as a living organism, to which ancient India gave earliest expression.

Abanindranath Tagore's 'The Sweetmeat Child', by contrast, harks back to a hoary triangle familiar in all cultures. It is based on a Bengali folk tale about a King who favours his younger spoilt wife and forsakes his older faithful one. The author was encouraged to retell it by his uncle Rabindranath, in 1896. He was already a coming Indian painter, and was soon to found the Bengal School, which would specialise in reinterpreting Indian myths, sacred stories and epics, often in miniature form, employing gorgeous colours. (Its less gifted adherents, working at Shantiniketan and elsewhere, would help to create the impression of Bengali effeminacy referred to by Anita Desai in her Preface.) The prose of Abanindranath's fairy tale mixes both the imagery of the painter and of the natural story-teller. It exults in 'sheer luxury', according to its earlier Bengali translator Bishnu Dey, a poet, while being simultaneously

> racy and colloquial, full of the air of the old Bengal village. Abanindranath revels in the tradition which our peasants and our women have carried on through the generations. Folktales, rituals, village arts, rhymes, the very turn and twist of the language of our people, all find an almost Joycean meeting-place in Abanindranath's abounding fancy and zest for life.

We could not fully reproduce in English all this, especially the extended references to Bengali nursery rhymes towards the end of the story, but we think the enchantment of the plot (and maybe the importation of magic into recent English fiction) will carry the reader over the occasional obscure or purple patch.

Manik Banerji/Bandopadhyay* derived his passion from village Bengal too, but from grim reality rather than from Bengali Grimms. Much of his output of thirty-nine novels, twelve story collections and over

---

* Banerji is the anglicised spelling of Bandopadhyay (the direct transliteration of the author's name in Bengali), by which he is known in Bengal.

two hundred scattered stories, was vitiated from the mid-1940s by his political allegiance to Communism, but 'Primordial', a well-known story written in 1933, was not so affected. Its picture of life and death in the lower depths is an assault on the reader's brain. Not that Banerji, unlike some other writers, was ever forced to live in squalor himself; he was brought up in a middle-class Calcutta household, but rebelled against it and against himself:

> I was hating expressions of sentimentality at the same time as being sentimental myself. I liked the genteel, cultured existence, did not entirely drop my middle-class hopes and aspirations. Yet I felt my mind constantly poisoned by the narrowness of that life, its meanness, open or disguised, its artificiality. Sometimes, I ran away from my own life to the company of the peasant-labourers – just so as to breathe. Other times, tormented by the hardness of their deprived lives and the raw reality of their ruthless existence, I ran back to my own life – just so as to breathe.

A greater writer, in fact second only to Tagore in this century, was Bibhuti Bhushan Banerji. His true fame rests on his novels, notably *Pather Panchali* (Ray's first film), but the quality of some of his short fiction justifies the inclusion here of two of his stories, fairly brief and contrasted as they are. His early life, first in a village, later in Calcutta, was desperately indigent, as anyone who has seen the autobiographical *Pather Panchali* and its two sequel films will easily appreciate. After 1928, when the serialised *Pather Panchali* enthralled Bengali readers, Banerji had a regular income. But, according to the writer Nirad C. Chaudhuri, who was a close friend of Banerji (helping him to get *Pather Panchali* published), he never much cared for personal wealth. Chaudhuri's portrait of him in his second volume of autobiography is wonderfully vivid and perceptive (and also reminds one of Anita Desai's comparison of Bengali and Russian literature), while not altogether flattering to his friend:

> . . . in his novels he showed an astonishing capacity for detailed observation of both nature and human character, combined with great humour and tenderness in describing what his observation discovered. His hard life had not embittered him, nor made him a cynic. His sympathy for ordinary people was unlimited, and he

was not repelled even by the squalor in which such people had to live in our society. Somehow, he could always make them rise above their surroundings; I would even say – far above the limitations of their world

– as our first story by Banerji, 'Bravo to the Boss' (1937), precisely illustrates. But –

[there] was a sort of hardness, which lay at the core of his outwardly soft nature and made him incapable of strong personal affection for anybody . . . I saw often that he could be totally indifferent even to those very near him. It may have come from his intensely egocentric nature or from the first sorrow of his life [the death of his young wife] which made him grow a protective callousness

– as our second story, 'Unaccountably' (1937), moodily suggests.

It takes place wholly in Calcutta, the first of eight stories in the collection to do so. In hardly five pages it somehow distils the special spirit of affectionate disdain native-born Calcuttans (but few outsiders) feel for that multifarious, monstrous metropolis. Even Tagore, whose dislike of Calcutta was well-known, was not absolutely immune to this feeling; Satyajit Ray certainly is not.

The half-century since Tagore's death in 1941 has not treated Calcutta well. The fighting in the second world war, though it stopped short of Bengal, disrupted the region and the capital city's economic life. It was one of the chief causes of the Famine of 1943/44, in which more than three million died and Calcutta's streets were littered with the corpses of villagers (an event that prompted Bibhuti Bhushan Banerji's novel *Distant Thunder*, powerfully filmed by Ray in 1973). Two years later, just prior to Independence, came a Hindu-Muslim massacre, the so-called Great Calcutta Killing of Hindus and Muslims, and then, in 1947, the mass exodus of refugees from East Pakistan (now Bangladesh). They overran Calcutta, and eventually settled in colonies in the suburbs. Some two decades later, in 1971, the influx was repeated, this time as a result of the war that gave birth to Bangladesh. In the meantime, the city's internal politics had been relatively stable, but from 1967, and particularly in 1970/71, the Maoist-inspired Naxalites – mostly young students from better-off Calcutta families –

battled viciously with the police, the army, the ruling party and each other, leading to many thousands of deaths.

These events find their way into several of our chosen stories, among them 'Farewell' by Samaresh Basu, undoubtedly the most popular short story writer to emerge in Bengal post-Independence. It was published in 1946, his first work in print. When his first novel appeared, he sold the fifty copies given him by the publisher to friends: his sole income from the book. In the next four decades he wrote over one hundred books of novels and short stories. The best of these far exceed 'Farewell' in sophistication but not, perhaps, in emotional power: brevity seems perfectly to suit this story of meeting, confrontation and parting of two total strangers – Hindu? Muslim? they do not know – in the violence of the night. Their wild oscillations between fear and intimacy are masterfully done. 'In reality human beings search for life amidst awful uncertainty,' wrote Samaresh Basu in later life. 'But however primitive their efforts may be, they are the driving force of human progress.'

He, like many of the writers in this book, had his roots in East Bengal, where he was born. The 1947 Partition, which split up such families, is a fertile source for fiction. It underscores 'Winter in Calcutta', an extract from Amitav Ghosh's 1988 novel *The Shadow Lines*:

> My grandmother, looking out of her window in amazement, exclaimed: 'When I last came here ten years ago, there were rice fields running alongside the road; it was the kind of place where rich Calcutta people built garden houses. And look at it now – as filthy as a *babui*'s nest. It's all because of the refugees, flooding in like that.'
>
> 'Just like we did,' said my father, to provoke her.
>
> 'We're not refugees,' snapped my grandmother, on cue. 'We came long before Partition.'

Though Ghosh was educated mainly outside Bengal and writes in English, it is Bengal and Bengali-speakers that he describes in his fiction. He has said of himself:

Many of my images have come from Satyajit Ray. They are part of my internal landscape, part of the way I now see Bengal in my mind's eye. It's a great fortune for me that Ray has made films about a particular milieu from which I happen to come as well, so that what he says about Bengal and what I feel about it are in so many ways totally intermingled.

The Hindu-Muslim relationship is one of the few aspects of Bengali culture Ray has hardly touched. It is subtly and movingly explored in 'Rebirth' (1988) by the Calcutta-based writer Abul Bashar. Rather than the city, he writes of the village life from which he hails, in this case a few days in the life of a respected Muslim thatcher of Hindu shrines. Communal feeling, so prominent in India in recent years, drives a wedge between the thatcher and his (Hindu) employer, against her better instincts. The probing of the psychology of both characters by telling use of detail, and the searching honesty of the writer, who has remarked that he is always aiming to find 'the life flowing deep down below our ordinary life' – make 'Rebirth' a classic of the Indian short story.

'Matilal, Padre' (1958) by Kamal Kumar Majumdar, achieves the same density of emotion, but in relation to Hinduism and Christianity, rather than Islam. It was the hardest story in the collection to translate (though actually one of Majumdar's easiest to read in Bengali), because of the author's brilliantly detailed descriptions and allusive imagery. 'He introduced into his best work an authenticity, an uncommon compassion and a brightness,' Satyajit Ray wrote of Majumdar on his death. In person, his conversation was uniquely eloquent; many people, meeting him for the first time, were overwhelmed by it. He could be extremely witty, as in this superb shaft at the ubiquitous Calcutta intellectual, the *babu* who by the 1950s *pranam*ed Marx and Mao rather than the British. Are the peasants and labourers in the villages aware of the concern for their plight shown by these Marxist *babus* in the cities? As Kamal Majumdar put it: 'Does the frog know it has a Latin name?' Majumdar's erudition (in French, as well as in Bengali and English) and his intuition were formidable. Interestingly, he once advised Ray, then planning a film of Tagore's novel *The Home and the World*, that the novel's central character Nikhilesh (who is really Tagore himself) was a 'Christ-figure': his own portrayal of padre Matilal is very much that of an Oriental Christian, not an Occidental one.

Religion is ritual and superstition, not moral force, in 'Water' (1984) by Mahasweta Devi. Born in East Bengal but educated in West Bengal partly at Tagore's university and in Calcutta, Mahasweta has been studying and living with tribal and outcaste communities in rural Bengal and in neighbouring Bihar since the 1960s. Her stories, published from the early 1970s onwards, are almost all documents of oppression, often employing a sophisticated juxtaposition of the flat, statistic-based language of government reports with the unfiltered harsh experience and unpoetic speech of the system's numberless, anonymous victims. Yet, for all her acute, analytical awareness of the economic and political facts of rural life, her focus remains the individual, not ideology. 'I have always believed that the real history is made by ordinary people . . . The reason and the inspiration for my writing are those people who are exploited and used, and yet do not accept defeat . . . Sometimes it seems that my writing is really their doing,' she wrote in 1986.

Her use of dialect poses a problem for the translator (as it does in Manik Banerji's and Kamal Majumdar's work, and in Hasan Azizul Huq's). Tagore, unlike Kipling say, avoided dialect in his stories, believing that it distanced the reader from the world he was trying to let him enter. We, in translating, have tended to follow Tagore's view, while making the language as colloquial as seemed convincing in English. There is of course no ideal solution: slang is notoriously cuture-bound.

The leading short story writer of Bangladesh, Hasan Azizul Huq, migrated in the opposite direction to Mahasweta Devi. He was born in West Bengal not far from the setting of Tarashankar Banerji's stories, but left there in the mid-1950s, finally settling at Rajshahi University on the border of Bangladesh after the 1971 war, as a professor of philosophy. His experience thus encompasses both Bengals, and this is reflected in his work. He is among those who admire Tagore but feel that he was not a 'realist', that he idealised his characters. Huq's writing, including 'Homecoming' (1973), is brutally devoid of romance, though not entirely bereft of hope. He is sceptically modern, sans illusions, yet not an out-and-out cynic: at the end of the story his wounded peasant-soldier expects little or nothing from the new government – but he compels himself to give his errant wife another chance.

'I have come to realise that I have no talent for writing about profound social changes or for revealing the true nature of class inequal-ities', admitted Sunil Ganguli, a poet who is also a highly successful post-Independence novelist, in 1977. 'I write about individuals, about their desires and weaknesses, their greed and their efforts to be free from it – in other words their attempts to rise above themselves. This seems to me the hardest task to master.' Not surprisingly, Satyajit Ray has been drawn to Ganguli's novels, moulding them into two profound films, *Days and Nights in the Forest* and *The Adversary*. He has written of Ganguli's work:

> Characters, incidents, relationships are all largely built up by means of sensitively observed external details – a fundamentally cinematic device . . . The dialogue is sparse and lifelike, with not a trace of high-falutin didacticism. If the surface appears simple, there is depth and density underneath; and there is lyricism too – for Sunil is a poet – to set beside the sudden, bold, wrenching scenes which strike one as much by their unexpectedness as by their conviction.

Many of these qualities find expression in 'The Fugitive and the Followers' (1972), if necessarily attenuated by the short story form. The spareness of the language, the absence of internal monologue or reflection by the writer, the namelessness of the pursuers, match the Naxalite central character's narrow radicalism well, and set off his occasional flashes of humanity to thought-provoking effect.

Ashapurna Devi, another prolific writer, manages something comparably strong with her pared miniature of Calcutta domestic life 'The Murderer' (c. 1970), though without Ganguli's political punch. The setting is quotidian, typical of her work, a neighbourhood like any of a thousand congested, shabby, middle-middle-class Calcutta *paras*, riddled with social and economic tension, with constant conflict between and inside its human residents. In fact there is no murder, it is a figment of the narrator's mind conjured by an overactive conscience.

'A Drop of Milk' (1953) by Narendra Mitra, 'The Mourners' by Premendra Mitra and 'Private Tuition by Mr Bose' (1978) by Anita Desai, all describe the same milieu as Ashapurna Devi, seen from different angles and in different moods. It is the world of 'small men, small schemes, big talk, limited means' (V. S. Naipaul on R. K. Narayan's Malgudi), who must practise the 'jungle-craft of gentility' (Amitav Ghosh); the world of the smothering, back-biting joint family, of the struggling private tutor, of the ill-paid office worker, the last of which has been portrayed with scornful brilliance by Nirad Chaudhuri (who briefly inhabited it in the 1920s) and with affection by Satyajit Ray in his 1963 film adaptation of Narendra Mitra's novel *Mahanagar* (*The Big City*).

Mitra, a writer of fine sensitivity, though constantly aware of the abyss below his characters, does not allow its presence to overwhelm them. His namesake Premendra Mitra is much more introspective, melancholy, given to despair, a truly metropolitan mind, and with a wider social range than Narendra Mitra: he enjoys a wider appeal than him, not just in Bengal but elsewhere too (and he has been notably filmed by Ray, Mrinal Sen and others). Of all the Bengali-language writers in this collection, Mitra is the one whose sensibility feels close to a writer like Graham Greene. 'Mitra has observed with cool objectivity how man's self-knowledge is blinkered by his self-deception', says a contemporary critic, Saroj Banerji.

The same internal conflict, but sympathetically and amusingly sketched, infuses bitter-sweetness into Anita Desai's story of a dreamy teacher of poetry condemned to giving mundane tuitions to bored and hopeless students, the story's gentle and poetic ending reminding the reader of the archetypal Calcutta story 'Unaccountably' by Bibhuti Bhushan Banerji. The daughter of a Bengali father and a German mother, Anita Desai first saw Calcutta only as a young adult, after early years spent in Old Delhi. She has written little about the city directly, except for her second novel which she disowns as callow and overwrought; but her better known works, both the novels and the short stories, are in many ways expressions of her Bengali temperament operating within an English literary tradition.

Amit Chaudhuri, the youngest writer in the collection, is another insider-outsider. His family is Bengali but he grew up mainly in Bombay and writes in English. His prize-winning first novel *A Strange and Sublime Address* was based on his visits to Calcutta in childhood and adolescence to stay with his joint family; 'Sunday' is an extract from it, originally published as a short story in 1988. It is told through the eyes of a child, like Satyajit Ray's 'The Little World of Shadananda' (1962) that follows it, and radiates a charm reminiscent of R. K. Narayan's first novel, also about a young boy (in addition to having a sensuousness not found in Narayan). 'I had no intention of telling a story, or of conveying any political feelings – I wanted to convey what it was to be alive in that place,' Chaudhuri has said. To Sandeep (his boy hero) and to Sandeep's uncle, as to the young Satyajit Ray and the adult Ray who made the poetic *Big City*, Calcutta is a zone of magic, a place where each day,

day after day, when the inevitable power-cut ceases and the street lamps 'glitter to life simultaneously', there is 'an uncontrollable sensation of delight, as if it were happening for the first time.'

This apocalyptic vision of the city could scarcely be more different from the common foreign vision of Calcutta as an infernal city. Calcutta, indeed Bengal as a whole, is nothing if not a place of extremes. It seemed to us right, therefore, to close the collection with two stories that are a vast contrast, poles apart in their view of Bengal: the one distant and detached, the other intimate, involved, indulgent. This latter story, 'The Conclusion' (1893, again filmed by Ray), is among Tagore's most lyrical stories and one of his very few with a happy ending, being a romance between a Calcutta-returned village graduate, a budding *babu*, and a wayward, illiterate village girl; while the former story, 'The Tenant' (1988) by Bharati Mukherjee, is a brittle, knowing, sexually frank picture of love's failures among today's US-based Bengali community: the kind of story that 'people who read Tagore and believe in Tagore culture don't want to accept', as Sunil Ganguli put it, speaking of a common Bengali reaction to his earlier work. New ground for a Bengali writer, one might think, truly modern, a break with the past? And yet, and yet, the deracinated and confused Bengalis, lured by the West but still bound by Bengal, who populate Mukherjee's story, impaled by her penetrating irony and observed by her omniscient eye – haven't we come across characters like them before? We have indeed: their ancestors are alive in Tagore's works written nearly a century ago, compressed, like seeds in a pod, into a story like 'The Raj Seal'.

KRISHNA DUTTA and ANDREW ROBINSON
London, October 1991

xxx

A Note on the Selection and Translation

This collection does not consist of the best short stories from Bengal ever written. If it did, it would need to include a large number of Tagore's stories; it would also be much longer than non-Bengalis would want.

It is, in the last analysis, an expression of its editors' tastes, but controlled by a range of other factors. Chief of these was our wish for diversity – of milieu, mood and period. We have consciously avoided weighting the choice towards stories of the rich, or of the poor, or of the middle-class, or focusing on the poetic, or the documentary or the ironic, the past or the present – any one of which would have been feasible. Without wishing to sound presumptuous, we have tried to gather a collection that describes a whole culture.

A second factor was translatability. Certain excellent stories will not translate well into English, either because the settings and emotions are too unfamiliar to non-Bengalis (one thinks, for instance, of Kali worship), or because the language used by the writer is too allusive, clever or personal – as in much of the writing of Kamal Majumdar, Rajshekhar Basu or Sukumar Ray; or because both difficulties exist (often the case).

Then there was the question of length. We wanted variety here too: our shortest story is only two pages long, the longest nearly thirty. Several worthwhile writers had to be left out because their best stories were too lengthy for the balance of the collection.

Finally, there was the stature of the writer. Given the language of the collection, the four writers writing in English virtually selected themselves. As for the others, more than three quarters of them were 'must's: a collection without them would have been rightly judged lacking. That left us with limited space for manoeuvre, especially as the book had somewhat exceeded the planned length. Some well-known writers had to be omitted, to our regret; we should also have liked a slightly greater representation by Bangladeshi writers, though of course many of the writers of West Bengal have roots in East Bengal, and

Tagore's stories belong to both Bengals. We abandoned the idea of having a second story by Hasan Azizul Huq with reluctance.

With the exception of Satyajit Ray's story, all the translations are our own. Our aim has been to make the stories written in Bengali read as well as those written in English, without distorting the meaning of the original. If we have succeeded, the reader should barely be aware of the difference. Hardly any previous translations of these writers, whether by Bengalis or by others, have been satisfactory in this respect: most have been dreary, when not inaccurate or semi-comprehensible.

As for the use of Bengali/Indian words, e.g. *pan*, *luchi*, *puja*, we have been sparing, and tried to introduce them in such a way that the non-Indian reader may half-guess their meaning from the context. It would be wrong to omit them altogether, equally wrong to overload the text with them as more academically-minded translators do: a balance is required, as in the use of colloquialisms in dialogue; and the acceptable line has surely shifted appreciably in recent years through the spread of Indian food, clothes, films and customs abroad, and through the polyglot writings of Salman Rushdie and others.

The transliteration of Bengali names and words in English is a tricky and unsatisfactory business. Rabindranath is pronounced 'Robindronath', for example, Satyajit – 'Shottojeet'; Tagore is an anglicised form of Thakur, Banerji of Bandopadhyay, Chatterji of Chattopadhyay. Many names and places mentioned here have no widely agreed spelling and we have adopted one that is commonly used or reasonably consistent and, if possible, not too off-putting for a non-Bengali reader. All Bengali words we have spelt without cumbersome diacritical marks, and have tried instead to use a spelling that reproduces the sound not the orthography of Bengali. This means that, rather than employing the conventional but confusing 's' and 'sh' to represent the three Bengali letters for 's', we have transliterated all three letters as 'sh', except where there is an established spelling, as in the word sari.

For permission to publish the stories, either in English or in English translation, we thank the contributing authors and the holders of their copyrights. We should also like to thank Anita Desai, Liz Calder, Mike Petty, Jenny Parrott and David Davidar for their support and interest in the book, the idea of which first occurred to us in 1986.

THE RAJ SEAL

Rabindranath Tagore

When Nabendu Shekhar tied the knot with Aruna Lekha, behind the haze of holy incense the marriage god Prajapati had a good laugh. Alas, the things that amuse Prajapati are not always funny for us human beings.

Nabendu Shekhar's father was someone with quite a reputation among the British. He, Purnendu Shekhar, had skilfully navigated his path in the world and successfully salaamed his way to that summit of social prestige, a Rai Bahadurship; even greater heights, more difficult of access and more laden with honours, had been within his grasp when, at the age of fifty-five, his gaze still avidly and dolefully fixed upon the misty peaks of a Raja-hood, he unexpectedly departed the world unfavoured, and the joints in his neck, fatigued by salaaming, finally found rest as his body was laid out at the cremation ground.

But energy, so scientists tell us, is conserved, it shifts only in form and location and is never destroyed; and so like the fidgety goddess Lakshmi and her motionless consort, the father's salaaming power transferred itself to the son. Soon young Nabendu Shekhar's head was bobbing up and down tirelessly at the doorsteps of the British, like a pumpkin carried by a swiftly flowing river.

In his childless state, following his first wife's death Nabendu took a second wife. But the traditions of the two wives' families greatly differed.

The elder brother of the new family was its guiding light. Everyone at home and in the neighbourhood revered his opinions on all matters. He was a BA and had a capable mind, but a fat salary and a position of authority did not appeal to him, neither did the whole business of contacts and patronage; the British kept their distance from him, and

1

he, likewise, preferred to keep them at arm's length. Thus, though his presence dazzled his domestic circle, he exerted little influence further afield.

Earlier, he had spent three years away in England. The courtesy of English people there had so captivated him that he had forgotten the humiliating condition of his country and had returned home suited and booted in the English style.

His family had been a bit embarrassed at first, but soon they began to say that no one wore sahib's clothes as well as their elder brother. In due course, the glory of English dress penetrated to their very hearts.

The brother's own idea when he came back was: 'I shall set the first example of how to be on equal terms with the British.' By always bowing and scraping when we meet them, he maintained, we simply make ourselves inferior and at the same time do the Sahibs an injustice.

He had brought back many cordial testimonials from important figures in England, and so in Bengal he managed to attain some slight position in the councils of the British. Accompanied by his wife, he partook of English tea, dinner, sports and humour. His success made his blood tingle and go to his head.

It was around this time, on the occasion of the opening of a new railway line, that some respectable native gentlemen, a favoured few, were invited by the company to travel along the new track with the Lieutenant-Governor. The elder brother of the family was among them.

On the way back a railway sergeant insulted the party by compelling them to leave their special carriage. The brother, dressed in his usual English attire, was about to get out when the official politely said, 'Why are you getting up? You may stay.'

The privilege puffed him up a little, to begin with. But as the carriage rolled on and the arid ashen-coloured fields of Bengal rolled by, the dying glow of the sun setting on the western horizon seemed like a shameful stain across the whole country; the mind of the lonely passenger, observing it unwinkingly, felt abashed. The thought of his Motherland cleft his whole heart and made his eyes sting with tears.

An old story came to his mind. An ass was pulling a temple car along the sacred way, and the passers-by, prostrating themselves in the dust

2

before it were offering their *pranams*. 'They are all worshipping me,' the foolish ass thought.

'There's only one small difference between that ass and me,' the elder brother told himself. 'I have at last realised that it is not my person the British sahibs respect, but the jacket weighing on my shoulders.'

As soon as he reached home, he called everyone together, lit a fire and cast into it all his English clothes, one by one, as sacrificial offerings.

The higher the flames leapt, the more excitedly the children danced for joy. From now on their respected elder renounced his sipping of tea and munching of crumbs with the British, and made himself once more inaccessible inside his domestic fortress; while the rest of the aforementioned degree-and-title holders donned their puggrees once more and went off to buzz around British doors.

This, then, was the family whose second daughter, by divine conspiracy, Nabendu Shekhar married. All the girls in it were as well-educated as they were attractive. Nabendu thought, 'I've struck lucky.'

The reverse notion, that they were in luck to have acquired him, he lost no time in substantiating. Various letters which various sahibs had at various times written to his father kept somehow popping out of his pockets quite by chance, upon which he would casually hand them to his sisters-in-law. But when he noticed the cutting little smiles that appeared on their cherry-shaped lips like daggers glinting in some gorgeous velvet scabbard, the unfortunate fellow became aware that he had misjudged his audience. 'I've made a blunder,' he told himself.

The eldest of the sisters-in-law, who was also the most appealing and accomplished of them, was Labanya Lekha. One day, an auspicious one, she arranged a small shrine in an alcove of Nabendu Shekhar's bedroom, consisting of a pair of English shoes anointed with vermilion, and then proceeded to place in front of it flowers and sandalwood paste and to burn two candles and incense. The minute Nabendu entered the room two of the sisters-in-law commanded him, 'Prostrate yourself before your beloved god, whose blessings will promotion bring.'

The third sister-in-law laboured long and hard to embroider a sacred scarf, a *namabali* – but instead of the usual names of the gods it bore well-known English names like Jones, Smith, Brown and Thomson. This she presented to Nabendu with due ceremony.

The fourth sister-in-law, not yet of an age for such things, nevertheless

3

said to her brother-in-law, 'Bhai, I promise you a rosary, so that you will be able to count the names of your sahib friends.'

Her eldest sister ticked her off: 'Look here, don't be so cheeky.'

Nabendu was inwardly annoyed, but he found it impossible to break away from the sisters-in-law, especially from the pretty eldest one. They were like nectar as well as thorns; they drew him to them and scratched him at one and the same time. He was like a maddened insect circling around them, wounding his wings but continuing to hover in blind intoxication.

However, destiny had willed that the lure of intimacy with sisters-in-law would eventually overcome Nabendu's lust for the company of sahibs.

The latter had reached such a pitch that when Nabendu wanted to pay humble court to the most senior sahib – the Burra Sahib – he would tell his sisters-in-law, 'I'm off to hear Suren Banerji's latest speech against the government.' Or if he planned to pay his respects to the sahib next in rank – the Chota Sahib – on his arrival at the station from Darjeeling, he would announce, 'I'm going out to visit Uncle.'

The wretched fellow had landed himself in a real fix, with a foot in both boats. His sisters-in-law vowed, 'We shan't let you go until we hole the enemy vessel.'

A rumour now reached Nabendu's ears that in the next Queen's birthday honours he would at last step into a Rai Bahadurship, would ascend the first rung on the ladder to heaven. Alas he did not have the courage to break the joyful news of the likely preferment to his sisters-in-law. That is, not until one autumn evening when the bright moonlight struck him and he suddenly revealed his passionate excitement to his wife. The very next day she climbed into her palanquin, went straight to her elder sister, and in a voice choked with tears poured out her troubles. Labanya listened and said, 'Calm down a bit, it's not as if Rai Bahadurs have tails – why be so ashamed?'

Aruna Lekha could only repeat, 'No Didi, I don't mind what else I become, but not a Rai Bahadur*ni*.'

The fact was, Aruna was already acquainted with a Rai Bahadur and had well-founded reasons for her objection.

Labanya firmly assured her, 'All right, stop worrying. Leave this to me.'

The husband of Labanya, Nilratan, was then working at Buxar, many hundreds of miles west of Calcutta, near Benares. Towards the close

4

of autumn Nabendu received an invitation from Labanya to join her. Delighted, without hesitation he set out. As he boarded the train the left side of his body did not twitch – which only went to prove that the superstition about a twitch in one's left side being a bad omen was just that – a superstition.

The climate of early winter in western India had made Labanya Lekha glow with health and charm like the radiant streaks of dawn. She sparkled and rippled with laughter like the billowing fronds of a bunch of *kash* grass beside some lonely riverbank. To the enchanted eyes of Nabendu a blossoming jasmine creeper seemed to be scattering dewdrops that flashed in the sunbeams of early morning.

The pleasure in his mind and the air in the west cured his usual indigestion. What with the delights of health and beauty and the thrill of his sister-in-law's ministrations he felt as if he had soared away from the ground. The river Ganges flowing past the foot of the garden, flushed with water, seemed to embody his own wild emotions as it swept swiftly on towards its unknown destination.

When, bathed in the rays of the dawn sun, he ambled back along the bank from his morning walk, his entire body felt gratified, as if embraced by a lover. And after that, when he attempted to help his sister-in-law cook, he allowed his ignorance and incompetence to stand exposed at every step. He showed not the slightest desire to attend to his faults; in fact each day he repeated them, earned appropriate rebukes and derived no end of satisfaction from them. Measuring out ingredients, lifting pots on and off the stove, preventing vegetables from burning – whatever domestic activity was required of him, Nabendu proved helpless, feeble as a new-born child. The laughter that greeted him, sometimes affectionate, sometimes contemptuous, he revelled in.

At the midday meal, prompted by hunger on the one hand and his sister-in-law's insistence on the other, not to speak of his own greediness, the deliciousness of the food and the delectability of the cook, Nabendu found it hard to restrain himself.

Even at cards, after eating, he demonstrated no sign of genius. He fiddled the pack, he looked at others' hands, he snatched and bickered – but he did not win. The fact that he could not accept his defeats brought him endless ridicule; but in spite of that, the reprobate was completely insensitive to reform.

Only in one respect did he totally change. He abandoned the belief that to be in favour with the sahibs was the ultimate goal in life, at least he did so for the time being. Instead, he basked in the glory of the attention and affection of his family and friends.

The atmosphere he was now inhabiting was of course new to him. Although Labanya's husband Nilratan Babu was a senior advocate at the courts he did not keep up contacts with the local sahibs, a fact that had provoked comment. He said, 'What's the point? When courtesies are not returned, whatever I give will not be repaid. What joy is to be had in sowing seed in the desert, however fair it may look? If you want a harvest, better sow in black soil.'

Nabendu too came to accept this attitude. He ceased to worry about a return on his former investments. Once, both he and his father before him had ploughed furrows in the hope of reaping Rai Bahadurships. Now he no longer felt the need to sprinkle water on this particular ground. After all, hadn't he already at great cost had a racecourse built in a favourite resort of the British?

The time of the annual Indian National Congress session approached. Nilratan Babu received a letter requesting him to collect contributions. Nabendu was contentedly playing cards with Labanya when Nilratan appeared one day, subscription book in hand, and said, 'We'd like your signature here.'

Recalling his allegiances, Nabendu could not prevent his face from falling. Labanya remarked, as if in desperation, 'Careful! Don't do it, your racecourse will be ruined.'

This made Nabendu brag, 'Why should I lose sleep over a thing like that!'

Nilratan reassured him, 'We won't print your name in the papers, don't worry.'

Labanya replied with an air of great deliberation, 'But think of the consequences. What if someone happened to – '

Nabendu interrupted impatiently, 'If my name gets printed will that diminish it?'

So saying, he took the subscription book from Nilratan's hands, abruptly inscribed a figure of a thousand rupees and signed. But all the while his mind was hoping: let my name not appear in print.

Labanya struck her forehead in a gesture of great concern: 'What have you done!'

The proud Nabendu said, 'Why, what's wrong with it?'

'But what about the guard at Sealdah station, the sales assistant at Whiteaway's, and the sahib who grooms the horses at Hart Brothers –

won't they take offence and be angry with you? Will they still come to your *puja* celebrations and drink your champagne, pat you on the back when they see you?'

'So what to all that,' said Nabendu haughtily. 'You want me to stick to "at homes" and die of shame?'

Some days later he was sitting sipping tea at breakfast, reading the newspaper when his eye alighted on an anonymously published letter. It expressed fulsome thanks for his contribution to the Congress and added that the support of such a figure as Nabendu Shekhar was of incalculable benefit in building up the Congress.

Building up the Congress! Oh late lamented Father Purnendu Shekhar! Was it for this that you procreated your miserable son on the soil of India!

Still, hand in hand with sorrow goes joy. Plainly, this fellow Nabendu, for whose influence both the British and the Congress were covetously and singlemindedly angling, could hardly be regarded as a nobody: the fact was now public knowledge. Nabendu therefore presented the item to Labanya with a broad smile. She read it with a bemused expression, as if she had no idea of who had written it: 'O my! Now the cat's really out of the bag! Too bad! It's really too bad! Who could be your enemy? Let his pen wither, let his ink become full of sand, let white ants eat his paper – '

Nabendu was benign: 'Don't curse him too much. I've already pardoned him and given him my blessing. Let his pen and ink turn to gold!'

Within two days the post brought Nabendu a reply to the letter in the form of a second letter printed in another newspaper, this one opposed to the Congress, edited by an Englishman. The letter was signed, 'One who knows'. According to its writer, those who were familiar with Nabendu Shekhar could never give credence to the scandalous report that had recently been linked with his name: for it was impossible that he should wish to turn Congresswallah; that would be as if a leopard were to try to expunge the black spots on its skin. Babu Nabendu Shekhar was a man of substance, the writer continued, not a job-seeker or a briefless pleader. He was not one of those who had gone abroad to England for a short stay to ape English manners and dress and try to bluff his way into English society before returning home a frustrated failure. Why therefore would he do such a – etc, etc.

7

Woe to the late Father Purnendu Shekhar in his abode of the dead! To think how assiduously you once cultivated your good name in the eyes of the British!

This was a letter fit to be displayed before a sister-in-law like a peacock's tail. Before anything else, it showed Nabendu to be by no means a worthless nonentity, but actually a substantial and significant figure.

Once again Labanya looked bemused: 'Who is this bosom friend of yours who writes like this? Must be some ticket collector, leather dealer or bandsman at Fort William?'

Her husband Nilratan said, 'You ought to write a reply, don't you think?'

Nabendu was lofty: 'There's no need, surely. One cannot respond to everything people say.'

Labanya burst into such peals of laughter they seemed to spill over the entire room like a fountain.

Nabendu was put out: 'Why are you laughing so much?'

This made her giggle so unstoppably that her blooming young body seemed about to disintegrate.

Nabendu felt completely drenched by this spray of mirth. In a rather injured voice he said, 'I suppose you think I'm afraid to write?'

'Not at all,' said Labanya. 'I was only thinking of that racecourse. You haven't quite given up hope yet, have you? – where there's life, there's hope.'

'You think that's why I don't want to write?' Nabendu cried angrily, and at once he took up pen and ink. But while writing, the warmth of his feelings did not find full expression, and so Labanya and Nilratan took it upon themselves to redress the balance. The process was akin to the frying of a *luchi*: Nabendu would dip his pen in water to cool it and in ghee to soften it and then roll his words as flat as possible; while his two assistants would promptly take these words and puff them up crisp and hot. Ultimately, Nabendu's letter asserted that an enemy within was far worse than an enemy without. Pathans and Russians were less of a threat to the good government of India than the arrogance of the Anglo-Indian governing class. It was this group that constituted an impenetrable barrier to the permanence of the bond between the Government and its subjects. Congress was anxious to open a broad avenue of lasting friendship between rulers and ruled, but the Anglo-Indian press had covered the path with thorns. And so on.

8

Nabendu was quite alarmed – and yet the quality of the writing pleased him. Such a fine piece would have been beyond him unaided.

For some time after its appearance, controversy raged back and forth in various papers concerning Nabendu's donation and support for Congress. Nabendu became a fearless patriot, so keen was he to impress his sisters-in-law. Labanya laughed to herself and thought, 'All right, but you have yet to pass through fire.'

Prior to taking his bath one morning, Nabendu was in the midst of trying to oil the inaccessible regions of his back, having already oiled his chest, when a bearer entered holding a visiting card printed with the name of the District Magistrate himself.

To encounter the Magistrate with a body covered in oil – it was unthinkable! Like a well-marinated *koi*-fish about to be tossed into the frying-pan, Nabendu fussed about in an agony of futile indecision. Then somehow, in a flash, he bathed, dressed and breathlessly emerged into the drawing-room. The bearer said, 'The sahib waited a long time and then left.' Exactly how much blame for this total lie should be attributed to the bearer and how much to the nearby Labanya would make a pointed exercise in ethics.

At any rate, Nabendu's heart sank and began palpitating distractedly like a fragment of tail chopped off a house lizard. The whole day, whatever he did, he felt bothered.

Labanya, with a great effort, suppressed her laughter somewhere in her innermost recesses and persistently questioned her brother-in-law, 'What's the matter with you today? You're not ill, are you?'

Nabendu managed to crank his features into a smile and produce a fitting response: 'How can I be ill here in your domain? Aren't you my very own heavenly physician, my Dhanantari sent by the gods?'

But a moment later his good humour evaporated and he began to ponder, 'First I made a donation to the Congress, then I wrote that letter to the papers, and then to cap it all, when the District Magistrate himself came calling, I kept him waiting – what must he be thinking of me?'

'Woe betide me!' thought the son of Father Purnendu Shekhar. 'Through the slings and arrows of Fate I have been made out to be someone I am not.'

The very next morning, sporting a watch-chain and an enormous puggree on his head Nabendu stepped out. 'Where are you off to?' asked Labanya.

'An urgent engagement,' Nabendu replied.

Labanya said nothing.

When Nabendu presented his card to the orderly at the sahib's house the latter said, 'You cannot see him now.'

Nabendu reached into his pocket and produced two rupees. There was a quick salaam and then – 'There are five of us here.' Promptly Nabendu proffered a ten-rupee note.

The summons came from the sahib. He was sitting at his desk working in his dressing-gown and slippers. Nabendu· salaamed, the District Magistrate jabbed his finger in the direction of a seat and without looking up said, 'What's your business, Babu.'

Nabendu fiddled with his watch chain and said in a submissive, slightly trembling voice, 'Yesterday you did me the honour of paying me a visit, but – '

The brows of the sahib knitted, then he raised his eyes from his papers and said, 'I paid you a visit? Babu, what nonsense are you talking!'

Nabendu sweated. 'Beg your pardon! It's a mistake, I must be confused,' he mumbled, and somehow made his escape. Much later, lying in bed, a sentence would keep running in his head like a chant in a nightmare, 'Babu, you are a howling idiot!'

On the way back in his carriage a thought struck him: 'The Magistrate did really call, but out of annoyance he didn't want to admit it.' Then he thought, 'I wish the ground would crack open!' But the earth refused to oblige him and he arrived home safe and sound.

He told Labanya, 'I went to buy some of the local rose-water to send back to Calcutta.'

Before he could say more, half a dozen peons in the uniform of the Collector's office presented themselves before him. After salaaming him they stood silently smiling.

Labanya too smiled: 'That donation to Congress you made – do you think they've come to arrest you?'

The peons now grinned in unison, revealing six sets of pointed teeth: 'Bakshish, Babu Sahib!'

Labanya's husband Nilratan appeared from a nearby room and said in an irritated tone, 'Why bakshish?'

The teeth gnashed gloriously: 'Bakshish for seeing the Magistrate Sahib.'

Still smiling, Labanya remarked, 'So the Magistrate Sahib sells rose-water now, does he? So much more soothing than his previous trade.'

The wretched Nabendu, desperate to reconcile rose-water and Magistrate, uttered some words which no one could follow.

Nilratan spoke sharply to the peons: 'No bakshish for you here. You haven't done anything.'

Nabendu diffidently pulled a note from his pocket, saying 'They are poor people, what's the harm . . . '

'There are much poorer people than they in the world,' said Nilratan, snatching the note from Nabendu's hand. 'I'll give this to them.'

Deprived of his chance to placate these demon followers of Lord Shiva – well, in this case, the Great Red-Face Shiva Sahib – Nabendu could only gaze piteously at the peons as if wordlessly pleading, 'Don't blame me, my friends, it's not my fault you know.'

The week of the Congress session arrived. To attend it Nilratan and his wife journeyed to the capital. Nabendu accompanied them.

The moment he set foot in Calcutta he was mobbed by Congress supporters; they danced around him as frenziedly as if the end of creation was nigh. There were eloquent speeches and encomia without end. The chorus was, 'Without heroes like you working for the country, the country has no hope.' Nabendu could hardly deny the truth of this, and so, all of a sudden, among all this hue and cry he found himself a national leader. When he entered the conference hall everyone rose to their feet and loudly shouted such queer foreign greetings as 'Hip hip hooray!' The Motherland blushed to the tips of her roots.

Her Majesty the Queen in due course had her birthday, but the prospect of a Rai Bahadurship for Nabendu had retreated and vanished like a mirage in the desert.

That evening Labanya Lekha invited Nabendu to her room, with great ceremony offered him a set of new clothes and with her own hands decorated his forehead with a blood-red *tilak* mark. After that, each sister-in-law hung around his neck a flower-garland of her own making. His wife Aruna Lekha, decked in a red sari and jewels, sat in her own room smiling shyly, looking radiant behind her veil of ornaments. Her sisters, pressing a particularly thick garland into her hands – which were hot with anxiety and chilly with embarrassment – tried to drag her to Nabendu, but she was unyielding; and so Nabendu's neck had to wait for its most important garland until the secret solitariness of night-time.

11

The sisters-in-law told Nabendu, 'Today we've made you a real Raja. No one but you could have received such honour from all India.'

Whether or not this genuinely consoled Nabendu may be known only in his heart or perhaps by God. We must remain extremely doubtful on the point. Rather we believe firmly that Nabendu will be a Rai Bahadur before he dies, and that the occasion of his passing will be suitably marked by obituaries in the *Englishman* and the *Pioneer*. For now though, let us give 'three cheers' for Father Babu Purnendu Shekhar. Hip hip hooray! Hip hip hooray! Hip hip hooray!

(1898)

NATUNDA, BABU

Sharat Chandra Chatterji

It was a shivering cold night. The day before had seen a heavy downpour, now the wind was as piercing as needles. A full moon was up, flooding everywhere with its light. All of a sudden Indra appeared. He said, 'There's some theatre tonight – want to go?'

The word theatre made me jump up. 'Pull something on then,' said Indra, 'and come over to my house, soon as you can.'

I grabbed some clothes and got out in under five minutes. Presumably, we were going by train. I thought we had to get to the station in Indra's family transport, hence the rush.

But Indra had other plans. We were going by dinghy. I was rather disheartened. If we had to go upstream on the Ganges we would surely get delayed. We might not even make it in time. 'Don't worry,' said Indra, 'there's a strong wind; we'll not be late. My cousin Natunda's here from Calcutta, and wants to have a trip on the river.'

Anyway, I got the oars ready, set the sail and sat waiting – and after a long delay Indra's Natunda appeared at the ghat. My first sight of him in the moonlight gave me a fright. He was a real Calcutta *babu*, in the prime of *babu*hood, complete with silk socks, shiny pumps, overcoat from top to toe, muffler, gloves and hat; he was taking no chances with the cold west wind. Somehow, with the most finicky care, leaning on Indra's shoulder and holding on to my arms, while all the time calling our beloved dinghy the most insulting names, he ensconced himself in the middle of the boat.

'What's your name?'

I replied with trepidation, 'Shrikanta.'

He made a wry face. 'I see – *Mister* Kanta, eh? I shall call you only Kanta. Kanta, you can prepare my tobacco. Indra, where have you put

13

the hookah? Let the lad have it so he can light it!'

My God! What a face the fellow had just made! Normal people don't look like that, even when talking to servants. Indra was embarrassed and said, 'Shrikanta, come and hold the helm, will you – I'll do the tobacco.'

I didn't reply but simply got on with preparing the hookah. He was Indra's cousin, after all, who lived in Calcutta and had just passed his Licentiate exam. But inside me I turned against him. When I handed him the hookah he sucked contentedly at it and asked me more questions: 'Where do you live, Kanta? What's that black thing you're wearing? A wrapper? Best quality, eh? Its stink should keep the ghosts away. Ouch! give it here for me to sit on – something's pricking me.'

'Take mine, Natunda, I'm not cold.' Indra took off his shawl and flung it over. His cousin picked it up, made himself comfortable and resumed smoking.

The Ganges in winter is not particularly broad: within half an hour our dinghy had reached the other bank. But just then the wind dropped.

Indra said uncomfortably, 'Natunda, there's a problem: no wind, so we can't use the sail.'

Natunda answered, 'Let the lad row a bit then.' Indra smiled faintly at this sample of Calcutta ignorance and said, 'Row? It's beyond anyone's capacity, like sawing wood against the grain. We'll have to go back.'

The statement made Natunda instantly livid. 'Why bring me here then, you wretch? Whatever happens, you must get me there. I have to play harmonium in the theatre – they've made a special request.'

'Someone else can play, Natunda,' said Indra. 'If you don't come, they'll still cope.'

'No! How will they? Can anyone in this land of bumpkins play a harmonium? Let's go, you must get me there.' The expression on his face made me seethe. Much later, I heard him play, and it was nothing to brag about.

Still, for Indra the thing was a calamity. Half-muttering I said, 'Indra, I suppose we could tow it.' I had hardly got the words out when the man gave me another shock. He gnashed his teeth in a way I recall even now. 'Go on then, start pulling! Why stand there like a dumb animal?'

After that Indra and I took it in turns to tow the boat. Sometimes climbing up, sometimes dipping down and often standing within inches of the ice-cold water, we plodded on. What's more, from time to time

14

we had to stop to prepare tobacco for the *babu*. He, however, sat stationary throughout, not lifting a finger. When once Indra asked him to hold the helm, he said he could not remove his gloves for fear of catching pneumonia.

Indra began to say, 'You don't need to – '

'So costly, and you expect me to ruin them!' interrupted Natunda. 'Carry on as you are.'

The fact was, I had seldom seen a more self-centred, miserly individual in my entire life. With his own eyes he could see our difficulties, but for the sake of some worthless whims he would not lend a hand. And that was despite the fact that we were boys compared to him. In case he caught cold and fell sick, or got a drop of water on his expensive overcoat or lost his comfortable position, he preferred to sit absolutely inert, while ordering us around with a stream of bullying chatter.

Worse still, a healthy breeze blowing over the river roused the *babu*'s appetite, and this was further stimulated by his tireless flow of exhortation. In due course the time reached ten o'clock, and when the *babu* learnt that it would be two in the morning before we reached the theatre, he was furious. At eleven, with a desperation belonging exclusively to a *babu* of Calcutta, he called, 'Indra, aren't there any villages round here? Somewhere we can stop and buy some puffed rice?'

'There's a big one up ahead, Natunda. You can get everything there.'

'Come on then – yes you lad – pull a bit harder, will you? – aren't you a rice-eater? Indra, how about telling your pal to pull harder.'

Neither Indra nor I bothered to reply. We went on as before and after a short while there appeared signs of a village. The bank sloped down and became flat at the edge of the water. We managed to pull the dinghy into the shallows and drew breath.

The *babu* said, 'I want to stretch my arms and legs a bit. I must get out.' And so Indra carried him on his shoulders and set him down. In the moonlight he paced up and down on the light sand of the beach.

The two of us set out towards the village with the aim of satisfying the famished craving of the third member of the party. Although we knew it would not be simple to procure edible food in such a poor and tiny place at such an hour, we had no option but to try.

The third party had not been keen to be left alone. As soon as he had admitted the fact, Indra had immediately invited him along. 'Join

15

us, Natunda, you may get a bit scared here – come and have a stroll. There are no thieves here, no one will take the dinghy. Come.'

Natunda had grimaced: 'Scared! Fellows like me from Darjjipara aren't scared – even of old Yama, Lord of Death! But Darjjiwallahs don't visit villages like Dirtypur. The stink gets up their noses and makes them ill.' For all his boasting, I had realised that what the *babu* really wanted was that I should stay behind as his guard and tobaccowallah. But I had become so disgusted by his airs that I ignored Indra's hint to this effect; I couldn't stick the fellow's company on my own. So Indra and I had set off together.

To keep his spirits up the *babu* from Darjjipara began clapping and singing a popular song: 'Chink chink lift the drink.' We could hear his effeminate nasal tones for quite some distance as we walked away. Indra was highly ashamed and mortified by the behaviour of his cousin. He said, as gently as he could manage, 'These Calcutta fellows can't stand the heat and cold like us, you know, Shrikanta!'

I acknowledged his comment but made none myself.

Indra spoke of his cousin's exceptional achievements, probably in the hope of arousing my admiration. Apparently he was about to pass his BA and become a deputy magistrate, so Indra said. Whether he ever did, and to which place he was posted, I have never enquired; but I suspect he must have been appointed – otherwise why do we hear so much nowadays about these famous Bengali deputies? Of course when I met him, he was a mere youth. People say that is the time when the heart is largest, the sympathy broadest. Well I cannot forget the sample of his qualities I received during the few hours I spent in his company, even after so many years. Luckily, such specimens are rare; were they not so, the entire world would long since have turned into a police state. But enough on the subject. As I shall now relate, God himself decided to punish this particular *babu*.

Indra was familiar with all the lanes, ghats and stalls in the area. He went straight to the grocer's shop, but it was closed, doors and shutters down against the cold, its owner in deep slumber. Words on a page cannot begin to fathom the depth of that sleep. Here slept not some dyspeptic indolent zamindar or harrassed householder anxious to disembarrass himself of daughters in marriage: here sleep came naturally. When, after the day's labour, people lay down on their charpoys, nothing short of burning down the house – certainly no shouting on their doorstep – could wake them: Lord Arjuna himself, the great

16

truth-teller, would have had to scorch himself for lying had he made his solemn vow to rouse that grocer instead of to slay Jayadratha.

The two of us stood outside the shop and yelled, besides trying various other stratagems, but after half an hour we had to return empty-handed. The ghat was empty! Every corner of it was clear in the moonlight, but there was not a soul to be seen. Natunda of Darjjipara had vanished. The dinghy was just as we had left it, but where was its occupant? We both shouted to save our lives – 'Natunda!' Our desperate cries only bounced back faintly from the high banks to left and right.

We had heard stories of tigers visiting this area during winter. And we knew that local cultivators were sometimes bothered by packs of hyenas. The thought suddenly struck Indra: a tiger had taken his cousin! My whole body prickled – how dreadful! The man's earlier uncivilised behaviour had been very provoking, true, but I would never have wished such a fate upon him!

Our eyes settled at exactly the same moment on a patch of sand where something lay glittering in the moonlight. We approached it and recognised an expensive pump. Indra collapsed on to the wet sand with a cry of 'Oh! Shrikanta! And my aunt's just come too! I can't show my face at home now.'

Soon we worked out what must have happened. While we had been at the grocer's shop trying vainly to awaken him, we had heard dogs howling somewhere not far off – they must have been making a vain attempt to inform us of the accident, as we now plainly realised. We could still hear them barking nearby. There could no longer be any doubt about it: the hyenas must be feasting on Natunda while the dogs hung back, barking for all they were worth.

Indra suddenly got to his feet and said, 'I'm going.'

I gripped his arm in panic and said, 'Are you crazy?'

Indra did not reply. He went over to the dinghy, picked up an oar and put it on his shoulders. Then he took a large knife from his left pocket and said, 'Stay here, Shrikanta; if I don't return, tell them at home what happened – I'm going now.'

His face was ashen, but both his eyes were burning! I could sense his resolve. His was no inflated bragging, to be punctured by a few timid words of caution. It was clear that nothing could stop him; he was like someone unacquainted with fear. As he was about to leave, I could hold myself no longer: I grabbed whatever came to hand and made ready to follow him.

17

Indra turned back to me, took my hand in his and said, 'Shrikanta, aren't you losing your head? How is this your fault? Why should you go?'

His voice brought tears to my eyes. Somehow I managed to suppress them: 'Is it your fault then, Indra? Why should you go?'

Instead of replying, Indra took the bamboo pole out of my hands and threw it away from the boat. 'It's not my fault, I know, Bhai, I didn't want to bring Natunda here; but I cannot go back alone, I have to go.'

So had I! I was no coward. I simply collected the pole once more, and without further ado we both cautiously set out.

'On sand, don't try running,' said Indra. 'If you try, you'll end up in the water.'

Right in front was a large dune. When we reached the top we saw five or six dogs standing some way off near the river's edge howling their heads off; there were no tigers so far as we could see, not even a jackal – only these dogs. Taking extra care we began to advance and saw something blackish in the water which the dogs were guarding. Indra abruptly yelled, 'Natunda!'

From his position neck-deep in water Natunda gave a muffled shout: 'It's me.'

We both took off; the dogs dispersed and Indra plunged in, reached his nearly-submerged almost-fainting cousin from Darjjipara and dragged him out. He was still wearing the second of the costly pumps, his overcoat, his gloves, his muffler and his hat, all soaked and so swollen up that he looked like a tom-tom.

After we had left him earlier, the village strays had very likely been drawn by the rhythms of 'Chink chink lift the drink', become captivated by the unfamiliar strains and by the unusual splendour of Natunda's garb, and been moved to give chase to the honoured stranger. Having run as far as he could, becoming desperate to save his skin Natunda must finally have jumped in the water; and then spent the subsequent half-hour of a chilly night immersed up to his neck, expiating his past sins.

To break the spell of his austerities and restore him to this world was no mean task. But, strange to relate, when he reached dry land the *babu*'s first words were, 'My other pump – where is it?'

(1917)

THE GODDESS

Prabhat Kumar Mukherji

The time is a little over one hundred years ago.

Night seemed never-ending during the month of *Paush*. Uma Prashad had just woken. His hand explored beneath the quilt, but his wife was not there. Searching the entire bed he found the sixteen-year-old creature in a corner, curled up fast asleep. He shifted towards her and very gently covered her body with the quilt. Then he inspected her feet to see if there were any bits still left bare.

Uma Prashad was a young man, about twenty years old. Of late he had given up the study of Sanskrit normal to his age and begun to learn Persian. His mother was no longer living, while his father was a learned pundit: a pillar of virtue, devotee of the goddess Kali, zamindar of the village, held in boundless regard by high and low. In fact many people believed Kali Kinkar Roy to be divinely endowed, touched by the power of Kali herself. There was not a soul in the village who did not worship him like a god.

Uma Prashad had had another new experience recently too: the intoxication of first love. Although he had been married five or six years, only now had he reached a certain intimacy. His wife was called Dayamayi, which means 'tender-hearted'.

He pulled the quilt back a little and laid his hand against her cheek. Her skin was cold, because of the winter air. With slow ceremony he kissed her lips.

The regular rhythm of Dayamayi's breathing was suddenly checked. Uma realised that his wife was awake. He said softly, 'Daya.'

'Wh-at?' she said, drawing out the single syllable.

'So you were awake?'

With a slight swallow Daya said, 'No, I was asleep.'

19

Uma Prashad tenderly embraced her. 'If you were asleep then who was it who answered me?'

Daya grasped her mistake and became embarrassed. 'I was asleep before, then I woke up.'

Uma Prashad questioned further, 'When is then? At what moment exactly?' He felt mischievous.

'What moment? Just then!'

'When?'

'Oh, I don't know,' said Daya, and tried helplessly to escape her husband's clutches.

The exact moment was something Daya did not really want to mention, but her husband was persistent. After a little more tiffing she surrendered. She said, 'You know, when you – ' and stopped.

'When I what?'

Speaking hastily Daya said, 'When you gave me a kiss – oh! satisfied? you crafty man!'

Quite a bit of the night remained. They began to chat. Most of what passed between them was of no significance. Regrettably, our grandparents' and great-grandparents' conversations were as inconsequential and negligible as our own. Though the scion of an illustrious and devout family, Uma Prashad was not exercised by any wish to educate his wife in the rites and rituals of Kali, the Mother; and so she remained in general ignorance.

Uma Prashad went on talking casually for a while, then said, 'You know, I need to go west to look for employment.'

'Why?' asked Daya. 'Why worry about that? Does a zamindar's son ever seek employment?'

'Here I have too many worries.'

'What worries?'

'If you understood what they were, then I wouldn't have them.'

This upset Daya. She began to wonder – what worries? But she could not imagine what they were. She decided to tease her husband: 'I know. It's because I'm not the wife you wanted, isn't it?' Daya knew that saying this would upset Uma Prashad.

In revenge he showered her with kisses. Then he said, 'Yes, you are my worry. Each day I don't get enough of you. Being together at night is not enough. If I go away and take a job we'll be together all the time, not just at night but in the daytime too.'

'But if you take a job how can you be with me in the day? You'll

20

leave me all alone and go off to your courthouse.'

'I'll go to the courthouse and come back so fast you won't notice.'

Daya pondered for a moment and decided this was possible. But there seemed to be many obstacles to its happening.

'You say you will take me, but will you be allowed to?'

'Do you imagine I'll take you from here? When I hear that you've gone to stay with your father I'll come secretly and whisk you away.'

This made Daya smile. Would such a plan work?

'How long will we stay away?'

'Years and years.'

The smile continued to play upon Daya's lips, then another thought struck her: 'Will I be able to leave Khoka* for so long?'

Uma Prashad brushed his wife's cheek with his own and said, 'By then you may have your own Khoka.' Daya blushed to the roots of her ears, but since they were in darkness, no one could see.

Khoka, just mentioned, was the only offspring of Uma Prashad's elder brother Tara Prashad. Uma Prashad in his time had been 'Khoka', the last such one this ancestral house had boasted. Since those days that particular seat within the family had been vacant, *khoka*-less; which was why its present small occupant was the cynosure of all eyes. His mother Hara Shundari was inordinately proud of him.

Abruptly Daya said, 'Why hasn't Khoka come yet?'

Every day before dawn Khoka would come to his auntie, his 'Kakima'. This was their routine. There was no shortage of maids in the house, but still Daya carried out many tasks herself, in particular the preparation of the shrine for her father-in-law's daily *puja*; this he entrusted to no one but her. Even so, busy as she was the entire day, Daya never lost sight of Khoka, not for a minute. If Kakima herself did not dry him after his bath, Khoka refused to be dried; if Kakima herself did not apply kohl to his eyes, then Khoka would not wear kohl at all; and if he were placed in any lap but Kakima's, Khoka would not take his milk. Late into the night Kakima had to stay in Khoka's bed in order to lull him to sleep, and when he woke at break of day crying 'Kakima', she would hug him at once. Naturally enough, all this exuberance and all these unreasonable demands brought him his just deserts from his mother, slaps and cuffs. Needless to say, these did not stop his crying,

---

*Little Boy; a common nickname for a child.

they only made it ten times worse. Then Hara Shundari in her anger would grab him and, still half-asleep herself, would deposit him before Daya's door calling out to her younger sister-in-law, 'Chhoto Bou! O Chhoto Bou! take your Khoka.' Without waiting for Daya to surface Hara Shundari would return. Often Daya would already be awake, but even if she was not, Khoka's plaintive cry would soon make her stir and she would quickly emerge, hug Khoka and pour affection upon him, murmuring 'Who's hurt you? Who's hurt you?' Beside the head of her bed she kept various kinds of sweets in a *pan*-box, including coconut drops: she would give Khoka one to suck and then, lying peacefully in his Kakima's lap, he would drop off to sleep.

That was why today, when Khoka did not appear, Daya enquired somewhat anxiously 'Do you think the little one's ill?'

'It's still dark,' said Uma Prashad. 'That's probably why he's not here. I'll get up and see.'

Uma Prashad left the bed and went to the window. The garden outside was a profusion of mango and coconut trees. The moon was still up, but it had not long to go. Daya came wordlessly and stood beside her husband. Then she said, 'The night's nearly over, isn't it?'

A bracing winter breeze was blowing into the room. Nevertheless the two of them stood side by side in the feeble light and looked at each other for a long while. They seemed as if starved of each other's sight.

Daya said, 'You know today my mind feels a little uneasy. Khoka's not yet come. I don't know why, but my mind's uneasy.'

'It's not yet his time. The days he sleeps late he comes late – you know that. There's another reason why you're uneasy. And I know what it is.'

'Tell me?'

'I told you that I want to go west to look for a job, and you aren't happy about it,' said Uma Prashad, and drew his wife closer.

Daya allowed a short sigh to escape her. Then she said, 'I don't know why, but I feel as if I won't see you again.'

Outside, the moon still shone with wan intensity. Hearing his wife's words, Uma Prashad went pale.

They continued standing together. The moon sank. The trees and shrubs retreated into darkness. They shut the window and retired to bed.

Chirps from the odd bird began gradually to filter in. Wrapped in each other's arms, they slumbered on.

22

Then, equally gradually, rays of sunshine started to penetrate the chinks in the window shutters. The two people on the bed still slept.

Quite suddenly, from the corridor outside the bedroom came the sound of Uma Prashad's father calling, 'Uma.'

Daya was the first to awake. She roused her husband.

Again Kali Kinkar called, 'Uma.' His voice had a tremble, sounding quite different from usual, as if he were in pain.

Father never calls this early, thought Uma – and why in this tone? Perhaps Khoka really was ill! He jumped up and opened the door.

He beheld his father in blood-red silk attire of worship, the sacred scarf printed with the names of the gods around his shoulders, a string of sacred beads hanging about his neck. What did it mean! Why so early a *puja*? As a rule his father first took his bath in the Ganges, then put on his *puja* vestments. This thought raced in Uma Prashad's brain.

The moment the door was open Kali Kinkar asked his son, 'Where is she? Where is Chhotobou Ma?'

His voice quavered. Uma Prashad looked about the room. Daya was up but she was in a corner, cowering.

Kali Kinkar's eyes too had found her. Immediately he went to her and prostrated himself full-length at her feet.

Uma Prashad was speechless. Dayamayi was thunderstruck.

Rising from his *pranam* Kali Kinkar said, 'Ma, I am blessed in this birth. But Ma, why did you not speak to me before, Ma?'

'Father! Father!' cried Uma Prashad.

'Son, make your *pranam* to the goddess.'

'Father – have you lost your mind!'

'Now I have found it, Son: before I was mad. Now I am recovered, by the grace of the Mother.'

Uma Prashad could make no sense of these words. He replied, 'Father – what are you saying?'

Kali Kinkar continued, 'Son, I am highly fortunate. Our family is now blessed. Ever since childhood, when I first received the mantra of Kali, I have worshipped her, and my devotion has not gone in vain. Mother has been merciful, now she has incarnated herself in my house as Chhotobou Ma. I saw it all last night in a vision: I received the divine command. My life has been rewarded.'

Dayamayi was a woman – but all of a sudden she became installed as a goddess.

*   *   *

23

Three days had passed since the incident. In the meantime the news spread far and wide. From villages all around the mansion of the renowned zamindar Kali Kinkar Roy people came to take *darshan* of the deity, to fill their vision with the sight of Dayamayi.

An elaborate *puja* in her honour was inaugurated. Lamps glowed, incense swirled, conch shells sounded, bells tintinnabulated: the whole paraphernalia of ritual. Within those few days many goats were sacrificed before her.

She, however, could only weep. Eating and sleeping had virtually forsaken her. The suddenness and strangeness of what had happened bewildered her, routing her senses and wiping out the memory of the time, only days before, when she had never appeared openly before her father-in-law and brother-in-law. Now, unveiled, she faced them, but the eyes that she turned upon them were as vacant as those of a madwoman. Her voice became extremely soft, her eyes red and swollen and her clothes were in utter disarray.

It was dead of night. In the worship room in one corner a ghee lamp dimly flickered. On a couch made of folded blankets covered with a silk cloth sat Dayamayi. Wrapped around her was a thick shawl. The door was only just closed and had been left unbolted. Inch by inch it began to open. With the care of a thief Uma Prashad crept inside, shut the door and bolted it.

He settled on the couch beside Dayamayi. It was his first private contact with his wife since that dawn three days earlier.

Dayamayi was awake. The presence of her husband made her sit up. Uma Prashad said, 'Daya, what is all this?'

Words of affection, the first such words she had heard from her husband in three days. In between, the endless 'Ma, Ma, Ma' of the flocking devotees had desiccated her heart and left it drained. These few tender words coming from the lips of her husband were like an unexpected shower of moonlight. She hid her face in his chest.

Uma Prashad unwrapped the shawl and hugged her tightly. In a voice choked with passion he said, 'Daya – Daya – what is this – what is all this?'

She said nothing.

For a while Uma Prashad too was quiet. Then he asked her, 'Daya, do you think this thing is true? That you're not my Daya, you're a goddess?'

This time she spoke: 'No, I'm nothing but your wife, I'm nothing but your Daya – I'm not a goddess – I'm not Kali.'

24

Uma Prashad instantly and ardently kissed her. 'Daya, tell me then Daya, we can leave this place. We'll go somewhere far away, where no one will come looking for us.'

'Yes, let us go,' Daya said. 'But how can we?'

'I'll arrange everything,' said Uma Prashad, 'but I need some time.'

'When? Please be quick: I may not live long,' Daya replied. 'I feel my life is leaking away. If I don't die, I may go mad.'

'No Daya – you must not think like this. Allow me seven days – be patient. Saturday, a week from today, I'll be back here to take you from this house. Hold out for seven days. There's hope, my darling sweetheart, my precious girl.'

'Achchha,' was all Daya said.

'Now I must go, before someone comes and sees me here.' Uma Prashad embraced his wife again and went away.

The following morning, as the *puja* of Dayamayi came to its close, a wizened villager, eighty years old and leaning on a stick, came forward. Tears streamed from his sunken eyes. Around his neck he wore the ritual cloth. As he beheld Dayamayi he fell to his knees, folded his hands together and said, 'Ma, all my years I have been your worshipper. Today I'm in great danger, Ma: help your humble servant.'

Dayamayi stared at the old man's face in absolute confusion. The priest said, 'What is it, Dada, what's the danger?'

The old man said, 'For several days my grandson has been feverish. This morning the doctor said there's no hope. If he dies my family will be extinct, there'll be no one left to light the evening lamp in my house. I've come to you, Ma – have mercy on his life.'

Kali Kinkar sat reading a scripture about the goddess Chandi. The sorrow of this ancient supplicant moved him; he looked at Dayamayi's face and said, 'Ma, please save this old man's child.' Then he turned to the old man: 'Dada, bring your grandson and lay him at the Mother's feet. Yama, the Lord of Death, would not dare to snatch him from this house.'

The old man was heartened. Leaning on his stick he rushed home.

Within half an hour he returned, with his widowed daughter-in-law carrying the boy. A bed was made for him at Dayamayi's feet and the dying child placed upon it. That done, the priest administered periodic drops of holy water, slipped into the boy's mouth with a sacred spoon.

25

The young widowed mother had once been a companion of Dayamayi. Seeing her afflicted face now, Dayamayi's heart went out to her. And when her eyes rested on the child they filled with tears. She focused her mind on the goddess and prayed, 'Please Lord, if I am a goddess, if I am Kali, or if I am human – whatever I am – let this child live.'

Everyone noticed her tears and they all said, 'Hail Mother Kali, hail Mother Dayamayi, what mercy lies in her eyes!'

Kali Kinkar renewed his reading of the book of Chandi with redoubled fervour.

As the day lengthened the child's condition gradually improved. By nightfall all could see that he was out of danger and could safely be sent home.

The news that a dying infant had been restored to life spread swiftly, even more swiftly than the news of Dayamayi's divinity. Next morning someone else turned up and appealed at Dayamayi's feet on behalf of a daughter who had been in labour for several days. Kali Kinkar responded: 'Why so anxious? Let the girl have some drops of holy water from the Mother. She will recover.'

The man went away with tears in his eyes and a pot of holy water on his head. Before the morning was out, word came that immediately after receiving holy water the girl had been delivered of a princely-looking son with auspicious signs.

Saturday arrived. Today Uma Prashad planned to abscond with his wife. The arrangements were all in place, the necessary funds collected. They would head not for nearby Murshidabad, Rajmahal, Burdwan or somewhere well-known, but further afield, where there was no risk of discovery. Boarding a boat they would go west, far off: exactly where, Uma Prashad was not sure. Perhaps Bhagalpur or Munger. Travelling expenses were all in hand, and the jewellery his wife was wearing – wouldn't selling that keep them in food and clothing for a couple of years? In that time could he not get a job? Surely he could. With enough effort was anything impossible?

Thoughts such as these preoccupied him all day. It became evening. For once, he decided, he would attend the evening worship. He had yet to see it. In evenings to come, when the courtyard of his ancestral house resounded with the sound of conches and bells signalling the start of *puja*, Uma Prashad would have moved way beyond the village. Tonight was Dayamayi's final service, her final *arati*: he must be there. In the morning, when the priest arrived to open the room, he would find the goddess gone. Uma Prashad wondered how the priest's face would look at that moment.

Evening deepened into night. The entire household slept. Uma left his bed stealthily and with quick steps made his way to the worship room. Opening the door he cautiously slipped in. The ghee lamp in the corner flickered. Uma Prashad sat down beside Dayamayi. She was slumbering.

He gave her an affectionate kiss, then he touched her to wake her. She came to hastily and sat up.

'Daya? So sound asleep? Get up, we must go.'

She seemed startled. 'Where to?'

'Where to! We're about to leave – and you ask where to? Come on, the boat's waiting; we're heading west.'

Daya sat silent and brooding.

'Get up, get up; you can think on the way. Everything's set. We must be off.' As he spoke Uma Prashad took her hand.

But Daya abruptly withdrew it and said, 'Don't touch me as your wife. I'm not sure, I'm not sure I'm your wife, not the goddess.'

Uma Prashad laughed. He pulled her towards him and tried to kiss her, but Dayamayi recoiled. 'No no, you may bring harm upon yourself.'

Her words devastated him. 'Daya, are you crazy?'

'Why then did they get better – those people? Tell me why? Is everyone here crazy?'

Uma Prashad tried despairingly to make her understand. He entreated her. He wept before her.

All she said was, 'No no, you will bring harm on yourself. Maybe I'm not your wife, maybe I am the goddess.'

Ultimately Uma Prashad said, 'If you were her, you would not have such a stony heart. How could my words leave you so totally cold?'

Dayamayi cried desperately, 'Oh, you don't understand!'

Uma Prashad sprang from the bed and paced the room in an agitation bordering on frenzy. All at once he turned on Dayamayi and said, 'Daya, did you not marry me?'

'Of course I did,' she replied.

'If you are a goddess, if you are Kali, then I must be Shiva, your consort – otherwise how could such a wedding take place?'

What could Daya say to this? She kept quiet.

Uma renewed the argument. 'Let us say you are the revered Mother

27

of All Creation – then who on earth but Shiva would have the power to wed you? I did wed you, you agree, and I have occupied my place as your husband. So I too cannot be an ordinary man, I too must be divine, I must be Lord Shiva incarnate.'

Slowly Dayamayi replied, 'Well, certainly I am your wife. I may be a goddess . . . or a human being . . . but I am your wife.'

It was music to Uma Prashad's ears. He clasped her tightly. 'Then let us go,' he said. 'We must go. The longer we stay here the longer you and I will be apart.'

'All right, let us.'

They started out walking the short distance to the river, to where the boat awaited them. But very soon Daya again came to a stop and said, 'I shall not go.' Her tone was extremely determined.

Uma Prashad pleaded with all his soul. But this time it was fruitless.

Daya said, 'If I am a goddess, you are Lord Shiva; let us both stay here, both receive worship here – why flee? Why hurt the feelings of all the people who come? I cannot leave, I must go back.'

Uma Prashad stood mortified. He said: 'You go alone, I will not.'

She went. Alone she returned to her divinity. Uma Prashad mingled with the midnight and vanished. The next morning there was no sign of him.

The faith of the people endured, except for that of the elder sister-in-law Hara Shundari, Khoka's mother. In the early days she had been a source of consolation for Dayamayi. When Dayamayi had lacked faith in herself and had said to Hara Shundari between outbursts of weeping, 'Didi, what's become of me?' Hara Shundari had replied, 'What's to be done, sister? Our lord and master has gone off his head. In his old age he's gone senile.'

Two weeks passed after Uma Prashad went missing. In the third week Khoka developed fever. As the days went by he became emaciated.

The doctor was called, but Kali Kinkar refused to allow treatment. He said, 'When the Goddess herself is resident in my home and incurable cases are being cured by her holy water, how can I allow a doctor to practice here?'

The elder sister-in-law wept to her husband Tara Prashad, 'Please, please let the boy see the doctor, otherwise he'll die. That witch of a creature cannot save the boy. She has no power.'

Tara Prashad was highly obedient. A father's word, a father's command: to him these were like the holy writ of the hallowed *Vedas*.

28

He told his wife, 'Be careful what you say, you'll do the boy harm. Whatever Ma says should be our guide.'

But his wife went direct to the head of the house and entreated him so wildly that he felt obliged to seek the Mother's advice. In all humility Kali Kinkar asked Daya, 'Ma, the illness of Khoka – does he need to see a doctor? Is it necessary? You must tell me.'

'No,' said Dayamayi, 'I shall make him well.'

Kali Kinkar was relieved in mind. And so was Tara Prashad.

Khoka's mother despatched a trusted maid to speak to the doctor; she gave him a detailed description of the symptoms. Could he prescribe a medicine? The doctor heard her out, then said, biting his tongue for shame, 'Please tell your revered mistress that when the Goddess herself has announced that the boy will recover, I cannot commit the sin of prescribing him medicine.'

Everyone now saw Khoka's mother cry out in despair, 'Please – someone – some medicine: give him some medicine. My boy is dying!'

They all replied, 'Shame on you, how can you think like that? In your own house the Mother of All is present.'

The boy's condition slowly worsened. Daya said, 'Place the boy in my lap.'

There he remained all day. He improved somewhat, but by nightfall he again deteriorated.

With all her mind and heart Dayamayi poured blessings on the boy, caressing his thin body with her hands.

Khoka did not live. As the fact of his death spread through the house Tara Prashad ran up distraught and cried, 'Witch! You've taken Khoka? Haven't you mercy even for him?'

The child's mother at first was stunned by her grief. When she became a little calmer she too scalded Dayamayi with her words: 'Goddess! She's no goddess! She's a fiend. Does a goddess devour a child?'

Kali Kinkar stared at Daya with brimming eyes. 'Ma, give Khoka back, I beg you Ma! his body is still fresh. Give him back, Ma, give him back!'

Dayamayi's tears flowed unrestrained. In her mind she summoned Yama, Lord of Death: 'Restore Khoka's soul to Khoka's body at once.'

When nothing happened she beseeched. But the Lord of Death was unmoved by the appeal of the Mother of All Creation: Khoka's body remained lifeless.

It was then that Dayamayi lost faith in her divinity.

29

That day her worship dwindled almost to nought. No one came near her. She sat abandoned, contemplating her fate.

Evening came. It was the time of the main worship, the *arati*. Somehow it was got through.

The morning after, Kali Kinkar entered the worship room and received a terrible shock. Using her sari Dayamayi had twisted a rope. The goddess had hanged herself.

(1899)

THE MUSIC ROOM

Tarashankar Banerji

By three o'clock in the morning Bishwambhar Ray was usually awake and pacing his roof. His old servant Ananta would fetch carpet, cushions and bolsters and then disappear downstairs for the hookah and tobacco. Bishwambhar would glance at these things but would not sit down. Head slightly bent, he would continue to pace just as before. Not far off, flowing past the foot of the Ray family's Kali temple, lay the luminous ribbon of the Ganges.

Above it, to the south-east, the morning star shone brightly. To the south-west, competing like a second star, burned the unwinking electric lamp atop the mansion of Ganguli, an up-and-coming local magnate. The clock on Ganguli's roof could be heard striking the hours. For two hundred years the clock of the Ray family had done this; now no longer. Nowadays it was habit that woke Bishwambhar Ray, or the cooing of pigeons. They began calling with the coming of the morning star. Then the breezes of dawn began wafting a wonderfully sweet fragrance. But spring no longer made the Ray family home festive: Ray no longer had the means to bid it proper welcome. For lack of gardeners the flowers had all withered. Only a few trees – *muchkunda, bakul* and other varieties – remained. They were devoid of shoots, like the family tree; both of them were decaying together like the cracked old palace. In fact several of the trees had fissures in their trunks. There was not a sign of spring on their outstretched arms. Maybe they were trying to catch it – who could say?

From the stables came the whinny of a horse.

Ananta settled the bowl of tobacco upon the hookah and, holding the tube in his hand, called out softly to his master, 'Huzoor?'

Bishwambhar Babu was startled. 'Huh.'

He eased himself on to the carpet and accepted the tube pressed into his hand by the servant. Below, the horse neighed again.

After a leisurely few puffs, Bishwambhar Babu said, 'The *muchkunda* flowers are out. I'll have them in my sherbet from today.'

Ananta scratched his head and said, 'Yes, Sir, but the petals are not yet ripe.'

There was a further restless whinny from the direction of the stables. Ray snorted with irritation. 'Does that Nitai spend all his time asleep as he grows older? Go and wake him up. Toofan is impatient. Can't you hear him calling?'

Toofan was the horse's name. He was all that survived of the Ray family's nine stables. Twenty-five years before, he had been the wild mount of Bishwambhar Ray in his fearless youth. In those days – even as recently as two years ago – strangers from far and wide, seeing a great white stallion with a heroic-looking, fair-skinned, turbanned rider on the highway, would ask the local people, 'Who is that?'

The reply would come, 'He is our Raja – Bishwambhar Ray. One of the greatest of hunters – thinks nothing of killing a tiger.' And then the visitor's gaze would follow the white horse and its mount with admiration as they swept into the distance. Soon they would be just a spiral of dust, a whirling eddy merged with the horizon.

Every morning at dawn the turbulent Toofan was taken out for a spin by Bishwambhar Ray – until the day, two years ago, when the Ganguli family took out a procession with drums to proclaim their new dominion in the village. Ever since, Toofan had been riderless and Nitai, the groom, had been seen tramping round, holding him by his reins.

Once Tara Prashanna, the manager, had ventured to say, 'If you give up the tradition, your health may – ' Bishwambhar's stare had cut him short. He uttered only three words, 'Shame, Tara Prashanna!'

Ananta was about to retire downstairs when Bishwambhar called out, 'Listen.'

Ananta came back.

'Nitai told me yesterday that Toofan is not receiving his full ration of grain.'

'The crop is not good this year, Sir, so the Manager said – '

'Huh.'

After a few more puffs Ray said, 'Is Toofan looking thin?'

Ananta smiled a little. 'No, well not really –'

'Huh.'

32

Another pause. 'Make sure he's properly fed, you understand? Tell Tara Prashanna in my name. And call Nitai here.'

Ananta left. Bishwambhar Babu reclined on his bolster and looked at the dawn sky. He let the tube of the hookah fall. One after another the stars were being extinguished. Bishwambhar mused, fingering the ribs of his broad chest; first one, then the next one. He had broken one the day he set out to break Toofan. What a beauty Toofan had been! What unruliness! Only music could control him. When he heard music his hooves never failed to respond. How he used to incline his head and sway!

Bishwambhar Ray got to his feet. Until today, memories of the past had lain buried in his heart like stars in the midday sky, hidden by the glory of the Ray family reputation. Today that glory seemed suddenly eclipsed by the shadow of nostalgia. Only one bright star could be seen: Toofan, constantly illuminating the world. For two years Ray had not been downstairs, now he had an urge to see Toofan again. He slipped into his wooden clogs and descended to the floor below the roof. The marble of the great verandah surrounding the inner courtyard resounded to the firm slap of his clogs. Flocks of titmice, disturbed by the noise, flew swiftly out of the blinds screening the tops of the pillars on either side. They were audible too inside the locked and darkened rooms. The room next to the stairs leading to the roof was for bedding. Fluffy bits of cotton lay on the floor. Beyond it hovered an unpleasant whiff. It came from the room used to store mattresses, durries and carpets. Something must be rotting there. From the room next to that the beating of bird's wings could be heard, and the tinkle of glass: presumably the cut-glass pendants in the chandeliers were aswinging. After that came the corner for the keeper of the carpets and chandeliers. It was vacant.

Ray turned to look east. These had been apartments for the Ray family's lease-holders. They had been a wealthy group, drawn from the various districts under the family's jurisdiction, each contributing between 500 and 5000 rupees per annum. When they used to pay visits, they resided in these rooms. Grand paintings hung on the walls of the verandah. Ray glanced at them. The first frame was empty, without picture or glass, the second lacked glass, and the third had vanished altogether. With a deep sigh Ray averted his gaze. Above his head, perched on the joists, the pigeons constantly cooed. The staircase lay at the eastern end of the verandah. Two years had passed since he had set foot on it. On his way he saw rooms stacked with papers, the estate record-offices.

The family history stretched back generations. Bishwambhar Ray was the seventh Ray. He smiled slightly in the gloom. He was thinking of the founder of the family who was reputed to have said, 'To keep Mother Lakshmi showering wealth upon us we must keep the blessings of Mother Saraswati* too. Ink on paper – that is the strongest kind of bond. Maintain the accounts properly – and Lakshmi will not become fidgety.' This ancestor had been a settlement official in the court of the Nawab of Bengal.

Paper, pen and ink had all been applied in plenty over the years. But Mother Lakshmi had flown the house.

At the edge of the verandah a dog was lying in the shadows. It began to bark loudly. Ray paid no attention and carried on down. The noise stopped. The dog wagged its tail and started to circle Ray's feet. There was no one to control it. Probably it was the offspring of some dog that had fed off scraps thrown by Bishwambhar Ray's ancestors.

He passed the entrance of the courtroom. To the right lay the cowsheds, to the left the stables. Beyond them was the temple. Ray called out, 'Nitai!' He heard his respectful reply: 'Huzoor!' The rest was drowned by an excited whinny from Toofan. Further off, an elephant trumpeted.

Ray went up to Toofan. The old horse stamped his feet and neighed like a child. He patted its muzzle and said, 'Young fellow.'

Toofan nuzzled his master's palm. Beyond, the elephant became agitated. It trumpeted frantically and tried to break its chains. Rahamat, the mahout, hearing the sound of his master, had come to stand beside his charge. In a tone of mock accusation he said, 'Huzoor, Chhotoginni will escape.'

That was the elephant's name. She was part of the dowry brought by Bishwambhar Babu's mother. At that time her name was Mati. Then the head of the household, Dhaneshwar Ray, had taken Mati hunting and returned singing her praises. Mati had grabbed a leopard in her trunk and trampled it to death. Seeing the affection lavished on Mati by her husband, Bishwambhar's mother had dubbed her 'co-wife'. Her

---

*Lakshmi – Goddess of Wealth; Saraswati – Goddess of Learning.

husband had said, 'She is indeed a wife worthy of a Ray. I shall call her Ginni.'

'Not Ginni,' Bishwambhar's mother had insisted, 'Chhotoginni – she's your Junior Wife, after all.'

Rahamat's words made Bishwambhar abandon Toofan and approach Chhotoginni. Behind him Toofan gave an aggrieved snort. Ray spoke to Chhotoginni: 'How are you Mother, my Lakshmi?' Chhotoginni twisted her trunk and proffered it to Ray. It was her request for him to mount; he always did so via the trunk.

He stroked her trunk. 'Not now, Mother, not now.'

Chhotoginni understood. She rested her trunk on Ray's shoulders and stood waiting peacably like a good girl. Ray said, 'Nitai, take Toofan out for a ride.'

With due hesitation Nitai replied, 'Toofan won't like to go today, Huzoor – not now he has seen you. If you would care to . . .'

Ray made no response. He patted Chhotoginni's trunk and said, 'Good girl, Mother Lakshmi!'

A sudden irruption of band music spoilt the deep calm of the dawn. Ray, startled, removed Chhotoginni's trunk, took a few paces back, and asked, 'Where is that band playing?'

'At the Ganguli family house,' replied Nitai quietly. 'His son is to taste his first rice.'

'Huh,' said Ray as usual.

Toofan cocked his head and started to tattoo the ground. Ray smiled gently and returned to his side. Behind him, Chhotoginni was shaking her shackles like a dancer's anklets.

Ray stepped through the main entrance of the palace and into the darkness of the interior. His mind went back to old times, how at dawn the music from the platform above the gate would make the animals dance – Toofan on one side, Chhotoginni on the other.

He climbed upstairs again and called out, 'Ananta!'

'Huzoor.'

'Call Tara Prashanna.'

Ray waited on the roof. When the elderly manager Tara Prashanna came and stood waiting Ray asked him, 'Is Mahim Ganguli holding *annaprashana* for his son?'

'He is, Sir.'

'He has invited me, perhaps?'

'He has,' replied Tara Prashanna with reluctance.

35

'Send him a gold mohur on a plate – bell-metal will do.'

Tara Prashanna remained silent. He lacked the courage to argue. But clearly the arrangement did not meet his approval.

Ray said, 'The mohur is with me. I'll give it to you later.'

The manager went away. Ray sat quietly. Ananta returned with a fresh bowl for the hookah and held out the pipe: 'Huzoor.'

Ray stretched out his hand as of old habit. Then he said, 'Chhotoginni's howdah, caparison and bell – have them made ready. Tara Prashanna must go to Ganguli's house to offer my blessings on the child.'

Three generations of Rays had accumulated wealth. The fourth generation had ruled. The fifth and sixth had enjoyed themselves and piled up debts. In the seventh, the time of Bishwambhar, the Lakshmi of the family had vanished into an ocean of debt. Bishwambhar was now like Indra, Lord of the Gods, but without Lakshmi his consort. What was more, he was without living issue. The judges of both the District Court and the High Court had given Lakshmi notice to quit the Ray family with her casket. All that was restraining her was an order from the Privy Council.

The last time the palace of the Rays had resonated with full glory was the day of its scion's sacred thread investiture. Then, indulgence towards all and sundry in the name of luxury and charity had reached a peak like the high tide at full moon. Afterwards, the ebb had set in, and the entire family had ground to a halt. On the seventh day of the ceremony the pomp had turned to poison: cholera had broken out in the house. Within a week Ray's wife, two sons, daughter and several other relatives had died. Only Bishwambhar had survived, to await death humbly, as the Vindhya mountains are said to have awaited the return of their guru, sage Agastya.

Well, not exactly. Ray may or may not have lived for death from that moment on, but he was certainly not bowed by it. That did not happen until two years later, the day the Privy Council gave its verdict. Even then, despite the death of his wife and children, the lights had still burned in Ray's music room: sitar, *sarangi* and ankle-bells had still been heard; and shouts of appreciation had still shattered the depths of the night; Chhotoginni had still worn her howdah for hunting parties, while Toofan had strained at his ropes in a fury of pique.

But the fact was, the Privy Council decision had confiscated the family's entire land and property. Ray's right to occupy the family house, and a few other perquisites were all that remained. Some squiggles of ink written on paper by the founder had enshrined these particular rights in such a way that no power could remove them. The arrangement took care of religious obligations to the family deity, Chhotoginni's food, Rahamat's salary and similar matters: they all owed their survival to these historic agreements. That was why rice of the variety 'fit-for-a-Raja' still arrived on the first of each month, and why every morning there was free fish from the ponds, and water-fowl too. The past was gone, but not in its entirety. The family mansion, though broken-down, was still known as the 'big house'; and local people still addressed Bishwambhar Ray as Huzoor – 'Master'.

To the *nouveau riche* Ganguli Babu the whole situation was intolerable. In the shadow of a moribund mountain, he had erected a golden shrine. The world took note of the former, but never noticed his shrine. Some antique elephant commanded more respect than his expensive new motor-car.

Mahim Ganguli had resolved that he would sweep away that decrepit heap of a house.

When the bell was hung around Chhotoginni's neck, she swayed with pride. The bell began to ring insistently – dong! dong!

The manager Tara Prashanna came and stood before Bishwambhar Ray. He was seated in the hallway to the inner apartments, a room he no longer used. Portraits of his ancestors, male and female, lined the walls. Each was shown in middle age, adorned by a scarf printed with the sacred name of Kali, a garland of dried *rudraksha* fruits around the neck, and a rosary around the wrist. Bishwambhar Babu sat gazing at the paintings. Seeing the manager he lowered his eyes and called out, 'Ananta, pass my cashbox.'

He took the keys out of the box and unlocked the iron safe. On the top shelf the casket of Lakshmi could be seen, shining. Two or three boxes lay beneath it. Ray took out a particularly lovely one. It was his late wife's jewellery box. He opened it. The interior was almost empty, the only ornament a crown for the parting of the hair. The crown had been used in the traditional welcome of brides over seven generations. All else had vanished, save some mohurs in a side pocket.

Some of these coins had been presented to Ray's wife at her wedding, others had been given to her by Ray himself in the early days. In that first year of marriage he had visited his estates and received the mohurs as gifts. He picked out one of the gold pieces and placed it in the manager's hand without a word. The manager went away.

A while later, Chhotoginni's bell grew louder. Ray went to the window to watch. The elephant's head glistened with oil, and on her forehead was the auspicious vermilion mark. She moved forward with gigantic, undulating grace.

That afternoon Ganguli's sparkling motor-car pulled up at the half-ruined entrance of the Ray mansion. Ganguli himself got down. Tara Prashanna hurried out with a cordial welcome, 'Come, come in.'

Ananta too had been watching events from upstairs. He quickly came down, opened up the private reception room and then retreated.

'Where's Thakurda?* – I want to see him!' said Mahim.

Ganguli's family had long worked as money-lenders on the estates of the Rays: Mahim's father Janardan had addressed the head of the Ray family as Huzoor. Tara Prashanna did not care for Mahim's brash tone, but he replied mildly, 'Huzoor is not yet up. He's resting after taking food.'

Mahim said, 'Go and wake him up.'

Tara Prashanna gave a wry smile and said, 'We cannot do that. If you would care to tell me your message, I will inform him.'

Mahim was impatient. 'No, I must see him.'

Ananta returned and offered Ganguli a silver tumbler of sherbet.

Taking it, Mahim questioned, 'Is Thakurda up?'

'He is. I've told him you're here. He asks you to come.'

Mahim finished the sherbet and said, 'Ah! What an aroma! What's the secret?'

Ananta lied and said, 'Spices from Benares, Sir. I don't know what kind.'

The moment he entered the upstairs room Mahim cried, 'There you are, Thakurda. We missed you at my son's feast.'

Bishwambhar laughed and said, 'Come, take a seat, Bhai.'

'I was very disappointed, Thakurda.'

Still smiling, Bishwambhar said, 'Forgive your old Thakurda, Bhai. He's an old man and his body doesn't always behave itself.'

'I will try to forget,' said Mahim, 'but you must step into my house tonight.'

---

*Thakurda – Grandfather or grand-uncle.

38

Bishwambhar said nothing and pretended to smoke.

'I've summoned a special *baiji* from Lucknow to dance for us. We won't appreciate her properly without your presence.'

Ray still held the tube of the hookah, and silently puffed. Then he remarked, 'My health has not been good, Mahim Bhai. There's a pain in my chest right now. I'm often laid low with it.'

Now it was Mahim who stayed silent. 'Achchha, then I must be off, Thakurda,' he said, rising. 'I have to go to town. I must escort some sahibs – they're all coming tonight.'

Bishwambhar said only, 'My apologies, Bhai.'

Mahim exited from the room. On the verandah he paused and suddenly blurted out, 'You ought to look after the house, Thakurda. It needs a lot of repairs!'

There was no response.

'Goodbye, Huzoor,' said Ananta.

The dance party at the Gangulis went off in a blaze of light. The canopy was decorated with various-coloured lanterns. Ganguli possessed a dynamo: electric wires were laid all over the place. The poles they required were concealed with leaves and flowers taken from the trees. Garlands of coloured paper hung everywhere. The guests were invited to spread themselves on sheets lying on the carpet. One side of the space had rows of chairs, while the other was kept for the ordinary listener. There was a place for ladies too.

By eight o'clock the space was full. The tabla and *sarangi* players were tuning up. Then the two dancers from western India arrived, splendid in their brightly-coloured baggy breeches, veils and jewellery. The hubbub ceased. How entrancing they looked!

The singing commenced. Seated on a chair among the distinguished guests was Mahim Ganguli.

The elder of the two dancers performed first. As her accompanist gradually explored the introductory section of the *ragini*, the party's attention began to drift. Conversations sprang up among the listeners. Things became really noisy among the special guests. The uniformed servants standing behind those seated on the floor, said 'Shsh, Shsh.'

Before the performance had quite finished Mahim called out 'Wah! Wah!' in his suavest tone. The steps of the dancer were slightly disturbed. The dance finally over, she sat down, exchanged a few words and a smile with the younger dancer and signalled her to rise.

Soon the listeners became lively with interest. It was as if the nimble footwork and captivating gestures of the dancer and the vocal acrobatics of the singer had undammed a cascade of enthusiasm. The applause became uproarious. Notes and coins poured forth from the distinguished guests.

After that – encore! encore! encore! The whole party was fully awake. When at last it broke up Mahim called the dancers and said, 'Everyone is thrilled.'

The elder of the two salaamed. 'You are most generous.'

Indeed he was. Mahim kept the dancers for five days instead of the expected three.

And on the day of farewell he was even more expansive. 'There's a big house here. Before you leave, look in there. Bishwambhar Ray is is the owner – wealthy, and a connoisseur of music. You may get to perform.'

The elder dancer replied, 'We've heard of his reputation, Huzoor. We'll certainly pay a call on him. I always intended to do so.'

Tara Prashanna was inwardly furious. He decided that yet again he was faced with one of Mahim Ganguli's devious tricks: an attempt to insult his master with a prostitute. He said severely, 'Babu's health is poor. Song and dance are impossible.'

The elder *baiji* pleaded, 'At least let us – '

'It is not possible,' Tara Prashanna cut in.

'It is our fate,' said the *baiji* sadly. They rose to go.

At that moment a voice called from upstairs, 'Tara Prashanna!'

The manager went up to Bishwambhar who enquired, 'Who are they?'

Tara Prashanna replied nervously, 'They have given a performance at the Ganguli house.'

'Huh.' There was a pause. 'You've sent them away?'

'Kindly accept my salaams, Huzoor,' the elder *baiji* said as she bowed low. Hearing Ray's voice, she had come up the stairs.

He was a bit irritated at her presumption, but not for long. The sight of her beauty softened him.

She gave the traditional greeting again and said, 'Please pardon the intrusion, my Lord; I have come unasked.'

Bishwambhar gazed at her. Her complexion was the colour of pomegranate seeds and her eyes etched with kohl, her glance was intoxicating, her lips were like rose petals, her figure was fine and her waist slender: the essence of the dance seemed concentrated within her, momentarily stilled. He felt it would suddenly speak, were she to stir.

With a smile of appreciation, Bishwambhar said, 'Please sit down.'

The *baiji* respectfully alighted on the carpet and said: 'Your obedient servant awaits your command to dance.'

Bishwambhar was about to respond that his health was not good. But somehow the idea made him awkward; perhaps he scorned the idea of lying to a mere entertainer.

The *baiji* continued, 'Everyone speaks of the great connoisseur in the grand house. Even Ganguli Babu – he called you a noble Raja.'

Ray's pipe stopped bubbling. He looked at the *baiji* with a smile and said, 'You must perform here tonight.' Then he called, 'Ananta!'

Ananta had been outside. He appeared immediately. 'Give them rooms. Open up one of the guest rooms used by the lease-holders.'

'Come,' said Ananta.

Though the *baiji* spoke no Bengali, she had no difficulty understanding. She rose, salaamed and said, 'Fate has smiled upon us. You are too kind, Huzoor.' She followed Ananta out.

Tara Prashanna stood dumbfounded. There was a lengthy pause, then he said, 'At Ganguli's house they received a hundred rupees per night.'

'Huh.'

The smoke bubbled through the hookah. 'Cash in hand, how much . . .'

Ray did not bother to complete the sentence. Again he sucked the hookah. Tara Prashanna said slowly, 'There's about a hundred and fifty rupees only, earmarked for family worship.'

For a moment Ray pondered, then he got up, opened the safe and once more took the box out. He picked up the bridal crown, the family heirloom, and placed it in Tara Prashanna's hands, saying 'Write in the temple account book that Anandamayi received a bejewelled crown, worth a hundred and fifty rupees.'

Anandamayi was the Ray family's name for the Goddess Kali.

And so, after years the family locks were prised open and the silent mansion echoed with activity again. The doors and windows of the music room were thrown open. So were the doors of the chandelier room. Light streamed into the carpet room.

Ananta dusted everything. Nitai and Rahamat helped him. The ancient maid who kept the family shrine cleaned the sceptre, the brass bases of the hookahs, the large platters and the censers of rosewater and attar. Tara Prashanna stood watching and directing.

Ananta said, 'Someone needs to go to the town, Babu.'

'I've made a list,' the manager replied. 'Listen and tell me whether I've forgotten anything.'

Ananta listened. 'It's all there except two items: some attar and a bottle of foreign liquor.'

'I thought there was a bottle somewhere.'

'There's not much left in it. He likes to have a drop now and then. If he asks for it today, there will not be enough, Babu.'

'But who will go? Will anyone on foot get back in time?'

Ananta said cautiously, 'What about Toofan – Nitai could take him?'

'If Huzoor gives the order,' said Nitai, 'then – '

'Achchha,' said the manager, 'I'll go and ask him.'

Bishwambhar Babu was lying down. When the manager appeared he immediately remarked, 'I was about to call for you. Better go to Ganguli's house and invite Mahim. And make sure some selected people from the village are invited. Go to Ganguli yourself.'

'I'll do it personally.'

'And put the howdah on Chhotoginni.'

The manager waited a bit and then suggested, 'Nitai needs to take Toofan to town.'

'Huh.'

Another pause. 'Let him go,' said Ray.

Not long after, Toofan's whinny was heard. Ray opened the window overlooking the stables. His eye travelled over the private road of the Rays, shadowed by deodar trees. He heard the beat of horse's hooves. Then he saw Toofan moving swiftly, tossing his superb outstretched neck, the beat of his feet shaking the earth.

Some time after that came the clang of Chhotoginni's bell.

Ray sat up. Looking out again, he saw the elephant advancing proudly. Slipping off his couch he began to pace the floor. His whole being was excited. A celebration! – after such a gap!

His ears picked up sounds from the music room – jangles and tinkles. They must be from the cut-glasses of the chandeliers. He went into the verandah. Ananta was there hanging lanterns on their wall hooks. Hearing footsteps near the door the servant glanced round and saw Bishwambhar Ray in the doorway. His eyes were on the

42

portraits that lined the room. Each ancestor was suspended there – from Bhubaneshwar Ray, the founder, down to himself, each one shown indulging his particular penchant. Great-grandfather Rabaneshwar was painted as a *shikari* with one foot on a tiger, a spear in his hand and a shield on his back. Dhaneshwar, Bishwambhar's father, was shown in his howdah, riding Chhotoginni. Bishwambhar was portrayed riding Toofan.

What storms had devastated those faces, Ray reflected. Rabaneshwar had been the family's first pleasure-lover. He was the builder of the music room. But he had lacked the courage to enjoy it. On the very day of the first concert, his wife and son perished. The candles in the chandeliers had been snuffed out half-burnt. Rabaneshwar had not dared to open the doors again.

Had the entire family perished then, it might have been for the best. Instead, out of loyalty to his lineage, Rabaneshwar took a second wife, his late wife's sister. He used to say that Anandamayi, the family deity, had commanded him. Their son Tarakeshwar had been the one who had opened up the music room and lit all the lights once more. It was said that in there, vying with a wealthy friend, Tarakeshwar once gave a *baiji* five hundred mohurs in bakshish. The story reminded Bishwambhar of Chandra – Chandrabai! One night, when the concert was over and the guests had all departed, he, Bishwambhar, had remained with her in the music room: the excitement was still absolutely fresh in his mind. She had been like a bouquet of blossoms.

Ananta stopped dusting. The look on his master's face made his hand unwilling to go on. Ray was flushed, as if a blocked vein had suddenly been released and made his bloodstream surge.

At dusk Ananta appeared with a silver tumbler of sherbet on a tray and set it down without a word. In one glance Ray inspected Ananta's uniform, gold-embroidered, with a sash at the waist, a puggree on his head and the Ray family crest on his chest. Silently he picked up the tumbler. Ananta retired. Shortly after, he returned and laid out a crimped and spotless dhoti, a *panjabi* fine-spun in the Mussulman fashion, and a silk *chadar*. Ray recognised them all: they had been specially made for his visit to a zamindar friend in Murshidabad five years previously.

'Everything is set?' he asked.

Ananta smiled: 'The candles are lit.'

'And the guests?'

'Bhandari, the landlord, has arrived with his son. The four footmen

43

sent by the landholding Brahmins are guarding the door.'

There was the racket of a motor-car below.

Ananta bustled away. Mahim Ganguli had arrived. A hubbub could be heard at the foot of the staircase. The guests were being welcomed, and a buzz of conversation floated upstairs. Soon it was joined by the diverse sounds of the musicians tuning up in the music room. Someone was tapping a *tabla*. All seemed ready.

Ananta came to the door and called, 'Huzoor.'

Bishwambhar was dressed and pacing the room. 'Huh?'

'The guests are waiting.'

'Huh.'

Several moments passed, then he ordered, 'Pass my shoes.'

With a slight hesitation, Ananta opened a corner cupboard, took out a bottle and glass and placed them on a table. The shoes followed: he dusted them. Another pause. Once more Ray started to pace. The volume of the instruments downstairs gradually grew.

'Huzoor!'

Ray said only, 'Huh.'

Still he paced. But now his tempo had increased. Ananta waited expectantly. Ray went over to the table and called out, 'Soda!'

Inside the great music room decorative cloths had been arranged on three sides for the audience's comfort. At the back, in rows, there were cushions. The candles in the three cut-glass chandeliers hanging from the ceiling were burning. The candles in the lamps attached to the walls flickered in the breeze.

Some of these lacked chimneys and had been blown out. Consequently giant shadows ran up the walls as if cast by some invisible melancholy.

Music had started but the pace was still languid. Plangent notes, like seedlings poking through the flow, could be heard here and there. The thirty or forty gentlemen present were conversing quietly amongst themselves. Four or five of them puffed at hubble-bubbles. The two performers sat in silence. Occasionally, the loud voice of Ganguli was audible. Dragging on a cigarette he eyed the lamps that had gone out and exclaimed, 'There's not much light in here, is there!' No one responded. He called out, 'Manager Babu!' When Tara Prashanna came to the door Mahim said, 'Look at all these lamps. Ask my driver and he'll fetch a couple of Petromaxes.'

The manager kept quiet. Only the elder dancer spoke – in Urdu, almost as if talking to herself: 'I wonder if such light would suit such a room.'

Hearing loud footsteps, the manager glanced behind him and respectfully moved aside. A moment later the doorway was filled by Bishwambhar Ray, followed by Ananta. The *baijis* both got to their feet. So did the entire party – even Mahim, who half-rose involuntarily, then abruptly sat down again.

Ray smiled a little and said, 'I have kept you waiting.' He took his place. Mahim picked up a cushion, then put it back. He pulled a handkerchief from his pocket, flicked at the cushion and said rudely 'Bap-re-bap! What dust!' Tara Prashanna sprinkled the attar. Ananta replaced the bowls of the hookahs and settled Ray's hookah in front of him.

The elder *baiji* rose to her feet and bowed gracefully, the customary *kurnish*. The musicians continued to play an extended, indolent, introductory *alap*. But slowly it began to acquire depth and direction. The audience fell silent. Ray closed his eyes and sat trance-like. His whole body swayed very slightly with each ripple of melody. One of the fingers of his left hand, poised, gave a light tap on a cushion at a precise moment – just as the tabla emitted a sharp beat; his eyes opened; and the ankle-bells of the *baiji* suddenly stirred. The performance began. It was the dance of the peacock. The gestures were those of an excited peacock on spying the first clouds of the monsoon. The dancer's neck was slightly angled, and her hands held out the edges of her gaily-coloured breeches like a peacock parading its tail. The restless ankle-bells seemed to tinkle almost surreptitiously.

'Wah!' exclaimed Ray, intoxicated by the rhythm.

Precisely as he spoke, the feet fell still, and the beats of the *tabla* ceased.

Mahim lent over to Ray and whispered in his ear, 'Thakurda, we're not exactly jumping for joy, our voices are all dried up! Krishnabai's leaving us cold, you know.'

Krishnabai gave a small smile, as if she had understood. Ananta presented Mahim with some sherbet. 'Not for me. All these late nights have given me a chill.'

Ray too smiled and beckoned Ananta.

Soon he came back with whisky, soda and glasses and stood at the door with the tray. After mixing the drinks he gave a glass to

Mahim and then looked at the other guests. They all averted their eyes. He proffered a glass respectfully to Bishwambhar Babu, who took it without a word.

Mahim had been eyeing the younger *baiji* for quite a while. Now he shifted a bit and said, 'Pyaribai, set us aflame.'

Pyari started to move. Her tempo was fast. Ray shut his eyes, and spoke only once in a suitable gap: 'Slow down a little.'

But Pyari's nimble feet moved to her own command, so rapidly that a million frothy bubbles seemed to fly about the room. Mahim shouted, out, 'Terrific! Terrific!'

Ray's brows became knitted. Mahim's ignorant outbursts were an affliction.

But he continued to sway to the music like a great spellbound snake. His blood was up – Ray family blood – coursing irresistibly through his veins. Pyari was gay and blithe as a butterfly. She reminded him of Johara from Lucknow; and she had a definite resemblance to Chandrabai. Chandra from Delhi, she had been a whole chapter in his life. When Pyari stopped, Ray was lost in his past. His reverie was broken by the clink and rustle of money. Mahim had given Pyari bakshish. He had broken custom. The master of the house must be the first to give reward: that was the ancient rule. Thrown off balance, Ray sat staring in front of him. Nothing was there: neither a silver container, nor any silver to fill it. He studied the floor in brooding silence. Krishnabai began another dance. A surge of feeling passed through the gathering like a wave. It seemed to suffuse every heart and soul, it was ethereal. The words of the accompanying song spoke of Kanai – Lord Krishna – and his flute. Hearing his music Yamuna, the river goddess, was so overcome she reversed her flow and flooded her banks, desperate to reach Kanai and embrace him. What a wonderful outpouring of music and movement! Ray was swept away. When the music stopped he cried out, 'Tremendous! Tremendous! Chandra.'

Krishna salaamed. 'Your humble servant is Krishnabai.'

From the other side of the room Mahim called out, 'Here, Krishnabai, here's your reward.'

Ray got to his feet. His slow footsteps passed in front of the assembled guests. The echo of his heavy shoeless tread reached the verandah, becoming fainter as it did so, and then ceased.

Mahim said, 'Pyaribai, let's have another.'

Krishna said, 'First let Huzoor return.'

'He'll come,' said Mahim, 'don't worry. That's probably him now. He's on his way.'

But it was not Ray who entered; it was Tara Prashanna. He carried a small silver plate, which he set down. On it were two mohurs.

'Babu's mark of appreciation,' said the manager.

But where is he?' Mahim questioned restively.

'His chest is giving trouble. He cannot return. Please listen to the music. He begs pardon of you all.'

There was some whispered discussion among the company. Mahim got to his feet, stretched contemptuously and said, 'I'm off then, Tara Prashanna. Have to fetch a sahib tomorrow.'

Tara Prashanna had no objection. Everyone else rose too. The music party was over.

The jewellery box of the ladies of the Ray family lay open on the floor. Inside it was empty. Ray wandered aimlessly back and forth, his head held high. No, the prestige of the family had not been diminished. He felt as if his blood were on fire with alcohol and excitement. Time and space were topsy-turvy. Absentmindedly he drifted from the room. He was drawn by the blaze of light from the music room. He went in. No one was there, except his ever-watchful ancestors. He stared through the gaping window. The earth was flooded by the full moon. The spring breeze brought him gusts of *muchkunda* perfume. Somewhere on the branch of a tree a cuckoo called endlessly, 'Piyoo-ka-ha! – piyoo-ka-ha!: where is my love? – where is my love?' Ray's brain was alive with music. He could hear Chandra singing a long-vanished raga, Behag – '*Shunu ja shunu piya*: listen, listen to me my love.' Looking up he saw the moon hanging high in the heavens. Footsteps sounded behind him. Ananta had come to extinguish the candles.

Ray forbade him: 'Let them burn.'

Ananta went away. Ray called after him, 'Bring my *esraj*.'

When the instrument appeared, Ray seated himself before the window, the *esraj* upon his lap, and commanded, 'Pour.' He indicated the open bottle standing on the tray. Ananta obeyed, then left.

The bow struck the strings of the *esraj*, and the resting palace was once more roused. As he played, Ray was transported. The *esraj* seemed to speak to him. He could hear its voice, sweet and poignant. The words of the song sang in his ears: 'I am a prisoner, sleepless in the dead of night. Beyond my doorway, watching, is a venomous sprite. My eyes

47

are closed, but sleep has not come. Slumber I feign; it is your beauty I pine. Oh my love! why did you play your flute at such a time?'

Ray put the *esraj* aside and stood up.

Softly he uttered, 'Chandra, Chandra!' It was her song.

From outside there came a soft call, melodious: 'Master.'

'Chandra, Chandra, come, come in. All my friends have left. Oh Chandra!'

Krishna entered smiling shyly, bowing. With honey in her voice she sang the last line of the song Ray had played: 'Oh my love! why did you play your flute at such a time?' Ray laughed and in the most delicate voice he could command sang, 'My love! on such a night, with ecstacy in my heart, how can I stay alone?'

He struggled with the cork in the bottle. Krishnabai stretched out her hand and said, 'If my Lord permits me.' With a smile Ray passed the bottle to her. Krishna opened it. She poured the drink and handed it to him.

Again came music from the *esraj*. Krishna's voice quietly accompanied it. She began to dance too. 'Oh my love! I do not want a garland made of fallen flowers; get me a bunch from the topmost branch. If you lift me up, I shall pluck it for you myself.' Her face was upturned, her arms outspread as she moved. All of a sudden Ray dropped the *esraj*, leapt up and gripped her feet, using his fists to make the feet dance to the rhythm. Her voice stopped. She pretended to fall and screamed. In an instant she was free. Bishwambhar besottedly and tenderly called out, 'Chandra, Oh Chandra, sweetheart!'

Song followed song. Drink followed drink. One bottle was finished already, the second well on its way. The *baiji* collapsed on the carpet, numb and dishevelled. But Bishwambhar sat on, as liberated by the liquor as Lord Shiva by his poison. He contemplated the fallen *baiji* and gave a short laugh. Having made her comfortable with a pillow beneath her head, he began to bow the *esraj* once more. Then the second bottle was empty. But the night was not yet finished. The clock on the Ganguli family house struck three – dong! dong! dong!

Up above, among the arches of the palace, pigeons started to coo. They broke Ray's trance. It was a sound he heard everyday, the signal for him to arise. He fondled the sleeping Krishna, murmuring 'Chandra, Chandra, sweetheart.' Then he went into the verandah and shouted 'Ananta!'

The old servant was on the roof, laying out carpets for his master.

Hurrying down he heard Ray say, 'Fetch my puggree, shawl and riding outfit. And tell Nitai to saddle Toofan. Quick!'

An astonished Ananta looked at his master. Ray was grooming his moustache. The sight was not unfamiliar to his servant, but he had not seen it for a considerable while. 'Perhaps you will freshen yourself first, Huzoor?' he gently suggested.

Not long after, Toofan's delighted whinny shattered the tail-end of night. It woke up Tara Prashanna. He looked out, and there was Toofan – and on his back Bishwambhar Ray. He could see Ray's close-fitting pyjamas and buttoned-up *achkan*, and the white puggree on his head. It was too dark to see his embroidered shoes and the fly-whisk and whip in his hand, but Tara Prashanna could imagine them. Toofan shot off at a gallop.

He dashed past fields in a whirl of dust like the typhoon in his name. The cool air of pre-dawn rushed over Ray's raging forehead. Slowly, very slowly the effects of the whisky wore off. They reached a village named Kushumdihi. A cart loaded with vegetables was trundling by. Two passengers were on board. They were probably headed for market. A fragment of their talk struck Ray's ear: 'Now that Ganguli Babu and his lot have bought – '

Ray jerked the reins and brought Toofan up dead. He heard more: 'After paying the rent there's nothing left for us. We were better off when a Ray was Raja –'

Ray glanced about him, bewildered.

He found himself back on Toofan. But where was this? He did not recognise the place. Then, gradually, it came to him: he was standing on his forfeited property. Abruptly, violently, he jerked Toofan round, whipped him once then whipped him again. Toofan ran like an arrow. At the stables once more Ray looked about him. A light glowed tentatively in the east. Darkness was nearly gone.

'Ananta!' Ray shouted. He gasped for breath, and as he did so he felt Toofan wildly shiver. Ray dismounted. He saw cuts on Toofan's mouth, made by the rein. His muzzle was covered in blood. His shiver was the shiver of exhaustion. Ray stroked the horse's head and muttered, 'Young fellow, young fellow!'

But Toofan's head did not rise. Probably the drink was still in charge as Ray cried, 'What's wrong, young fellow, what's wrong? – You're wrong, I'm wrong too. But don't be ashamed, Toofan dear! Get up, get up!'

Nitai had been watching from behind. 'Perhaps he is worn-out, Huzoor. When he has calmed down, he will get up.'

Ray turned in a trice and fixed Nitai with a stare. He handed him Toofan's reins, then with brisk steps entered the palace. Climbing the stairs he found the music room still open. He peered in. The room was void, the love tryst had vanished. Only the bottles remained, lying about empty; and the still-flickering candles. The Ray forebears gazed on haughtily, and all at once they seemed to Bishwambhar Ray to laugh like maniacs. He recoiled, and as he did so, he caught a glimpse of himself in a mirror and saw – madness! He was no different from them; all seven generations in that room were touched by the same infatuation!

He retreated to the door. Leaning heavily on the verandah railings he gave a panicky cry: 'Ananta! – Ananta!'

Ananta came running up the stairs. He had never before heard such a cry from his master. As Ananta stood before him, Ray ordered, 'Put out the lights – put out the lights – extinguish them! Close up the music room – close it!'

His words stopped. His whip flew from his hand. It landed with a thud before the entrance to the music room.

(1934)

THE ADVENTURES OF
GOOPY AND BAGHA

Upendrakishore Ray Chaudhuri

Can you all sing? This is the story of a man who knew only one song.
His name was Goopy Kyne and the name of his father, who ran a
grocer's shop, was Kanu Kyne. Although Goopy knew only one song,
no one else in the village could sing at all and so they all treated him
with respect and called him Goopy 'Gyne' – Goopy 'the Singer'.

Goopy knew only one song, true, but that song he sang without
pause; if he was unable to sing it even for a moment, he felt choked.
If he happened to be at home, his father's customers all fled. If he
went into the fields, the cows all broke their ropes and turned tail. In
the end, the customers stopped coming to the shop and the cowherds
stopped grazing their animals in the fields, for fear of Goopy. Then
Kanu Kyne picked up a hefty bamboo and chased his son away into
the fields; whereupon the cowherds set upon him with their sticks and
drove him into the forest. There he would be able to practice without
interruption.

In another village not far from Goopy's lived someone called Panchu
Pyne. Panchu's son had a passion for playing a big drum. When he
played he swayed from side to side, nodded his head and rolled his
eyes; he also grinned and frowned. The villagers would stare at him
open-mouthed and emit appreciative sounds expected of an audience –
in this case 'Aha! Ah! Arghh!!' – but when he gave his concluding
beats accompanied by several 'Hah!'s like the snarls of a tiger, they
would grab the chance of a quick getaway, falling over each other
in the attempt. From this he got the name Bagha – 'Tiger' – Byne. It
quickly caught on; soon his real name, whatever it was, was entirely
forgotten.

As Bagha went on playing he destroyed a drum a day. There came a

51

point when Panchu could cough up money no longer. But Bagha could not stop playing. What was to be done? The village people said to Panchu, 'If you don't mind, we'll club together and buy you a drum. The village maestro must have a chance to play.' And so each of them made a contribution and together they presented Bagha with a drum built to survive even his savage beating.

What a drum it was! Three and half cubits wide, with a skin of buffalo hide. Bagha was bowled over with excitement: 'I shall play it standing!' he said.

So from now on he stood and played the drum with sticks – for a month and a half non-stop, day and night, without making so much as a dent. By then his mother and father were going crazy and the heads of the entire village were spinning. If the playing had gone on any longer, it is hard to say what might have happened. But one morning the whole village banded together and, brandishing sticks, they paid a visit to Bagha. 'Dear chap, dear boy, we've brought you ten pots of sweets. Go somewhere else, anywhere you like, otherwise we shall all go bananas!'

What could Bagha do? He had to head for another village. But he had not been there two days when the occupants ejected him. Wherever he took himself he was soon expelled. In due course he began to roam the fields all day until the pangs of hunger drove him back to his own village; there, the moment he began to play people came running and shut him up with gifts of food, commenting, 'What a relief!' But after a while they stopped feeding and began threatening him with sticks the instant anyone in the neighbourhood heard the notorious beat. The poor fellow decided, 'No more! Better I live in the forest than live with these brutes. The tigers may get me there, but I'll be able to play!' So Bagha put his drum on his shoulder and set off for the forest.

Now he felt free to have some fun. Now, if anyone happened to hear his playing he did not chase him with a stick. Being eaten seemed a remote worry, since the forest was both tigerless and bearless. Only one ferocious beast bothered him; he had yet to spot it, but the sound of its cry made him quake with fear and think 'Goodness me! If I meet that it'll have me in one gulp, drum and all!'

The creature was none other than Goopy Gyne. The noise that was making Bagha tremble was the sound of Goopy practising. Goopy, for his part, had heard the sound of Bagha's drumming and was as terrified as Bagha. He had been telling himself, 'Stay here in this forest and you've had it, better escape right now.' He was in the process of creeping out of the forest on tenterhooks when he noticed a man with a huge drum on his shoulder, also emerging from the trees. Much astonished, Goopy asked him, 'Who are you?'

'I am Bagha Byne,' said Bagha. 'Who are you?'

'I am Goopy Gyne,' said Goopy. 'Where are you off to?'

'Wherever will have me, that's where I'm off to. These village asses don't appreciate music, so I've been living in the forest with my drum. But you know, Bhai, there's a ferocious beast nearby. I heard its call. If I bump into it I won't last long. So I'm getting out now.'

'Same here!' said Goopy. 'I too heard a beast calling and I'm running away. Tell me, from where did you hear its roar?'

'Over there, on the east side, underneath the banyan tree.'

'Achchha, that was my singing!' said Goopy cheerfully. 'No need to think of a beast. But the howl I heard came from the western part of the forest, underneath the balsam trees.'

'That was my drumming, I was playing right there!'

It dawned upon them together that each was fleeing the other's music. They roared with laughter! Eventually Goopy suggested, 'Bhai, I seem to be as keen a singer as you are a drummer! If we join forces we'll surely do better still.'

Bagha totally agreed. And so, after a short discussion, they decided to go to the King together and sing for him. He was certain to be happy to hear them, of that there could be no doubt: perhaps he would give them half his kingdom and his daughters in marriage?

The idea of their royal command performance made them immensely happy. Laughing and dancing with glee they reached the bank of a large river, beyond which lay the palace.

The river had a ferry, but the boatman wanted a fare. The two friends had recently come from a forest – how could they have any money? They said to the boatman, 'Bhai, we don't have money but we can sing and play for you. Let us cross over.' The ferry passengers, hearing them, were enthusiastic and said to the boatman, 'We'll all contribute and find you the fare. Take these two along.'

The boatman himself, seeing Bagha's drum, felt a desire to hear music, so he made no objection. With Goopy and Bagha aboard, the boat cast off. It was crammed with people: where was the room for a performance? By the time everyone had managed to make space, the boat had reached midstream. Then Goopy began to hum and Bagha began to drum – and in a flash all aboard tumbled over each other and became entangled. The boat swiftly capsized.

The danger was tremendous. Luckily for Goopy and Bagha, the drum was so big that by hanging on to it tightly they saved their skins. But their journey to the palace was over. They drifted all day in the current and finally, at evening time, they pitched up at the edge of a fearsome forest. To have gone there in daytime would have been frightening enough, let alone at night. Bagha said, 'Goopyda, I've really got the creeps! Now what do we do?' 'What can we do?' said Goopy, 'other than I sing and you play. If a tiger's going to eat us anyway, let's at least show off our skills.'

'Absolutely right! If we must die, let us go like maestros not like those village fellows, as feeble as ghosts!'

So saying, still in their wet clothes, they opened their hearts. The fact that Bagha's drum was wet gave it an unusually deep note. And the fact that this might be their last song made Goopy's voice deeper too. Drumbeat and voice combined, were the gravest sound anyone could imagine. The dark deepened towards midnight, but there was no let-up in their music.

Then they both began to sense something strange happening around them. Shadowy figures were perched in the trees, peering at them from high up, their eyes like fiery discs, their teeth protruding like long radishes. Bagha's hands stopped moving; they felt as if they had shrunk, along with his feet; his back felt hunched, his head sunk into his neck, while his eyes popped out and his mouth gaped. Both of them were shaking so much, their teeth were chattering so noisily, that escape was out of the question.

But the ghostly beings – the *bhuts* – did not touch them. They had overheard the music and dropped in to enjoy the concert, and also to book the musicians for the wedding of the *bhut*-king's son. When the music suddenly stopped they said encouragingly, 'Why stop, friends? Play on, play on, play on!'

Their words gave Goopy and Bagha heart; they thought, 'That doesn't sound too awful, why not play a bit more.' They went on singing – and all of a sudden the *bhuts* sprang from the trees and started to dance.

Such a sprightly hullabaloo is impossible to describe to someone who has not seen it for himself. In all their lives Goopy and Bagha had never had such a responsive audience. Soon the night was over. Dawn was near, the hour after which no *bhut* may remain outdoors. The *bhuts* said, 'Come, friends, come and meet our leader. We will reward you.'

Goopy said, 'But we want to go to the palace!' The *bhuts* replied, 'Go later, first come and play a little at our place. We shall reward you.' So the two of them picked up the drum and went with the *bhuts*. There is no need to go into what they played, but when the time came for farewell the *bhuts* asked them, 'What do you desire?'

Goopy spoke: 'We desire that when we sing and play, all shall be delighted.' The *bhuts* said, 'Granted; whoever hears you sing and play shall be unable to leave his place until the music is finished. What else?'

'We desire to have no want of food or clothes.' At this the *bhuts* produced a sack and said, 'Whenever you desire food or clothes, put your hand inside this sack and you shall have them. What else?'

'I can't think of anything else,' said Goopy. The *bhuts* enjoyed this remark and then produced two pairs of shoes, saying 'While you wear these shoes, if you desire to go somewhere you will suddenly find yourself in that place.'

Their worries thus spirited away, Goopy and Bagha took leave of the *bhuts*, slipped into the shoes and said, 'Well now, we desire to go to – to the palace!' That very instant the dreaded forest vanished and Goopy and Bagha saw that they stood before the main gate of a grand mansion. Such a vast and splendid building was way beyond their ken. It must obviously be the palace.

They were confronted with a problem. Several guards with terrifying expressions were on duty. They had already set eyes on Goopy and Bagha and the drum: grimacing, they challenged them, 'Who are you? State your business!' Goopy said falteringly, 'Baba, we have come to play for the King' – which only served to anger the guards further; they lifted their truncheons and shouted, 'Clear off!' Goopy's lip curled with contempt, 'Eh! We've come to see the King.' A moment later, thanks to the shoes, they were in the presence of His Majesty.

The King was having a nap in the inner apartments, the Queen fanning his head, when, without so much as a by-your-leave, Goopy and Bagha and the powerful drum suddenly intruded. Bolted doors and closed windows offered no obstruction to them, courtesy of the shoes. But even if no hurdles hindered their arriving, there were certainly hurdles in the way of their staying. The Queen had such a fright she screamed and fainted; the King shot up and started running around like a lunatic; everyone else was in pandemonium. Soon sepoys and sentries came running with swords and shields.

The tight corner confused Goopy and Bagha. If they had only said, 'We wish to go to place X', the shoes would have got them out of their fix. But words deserted them. Instead they tried to run, and before they had gone two paces the unlucky fellows were set upon. Shoes, sticks, whips, fists – every possible kind of blow, ear-pulling included, Goopy and Bagha received. Finally the King ordered, 'Take them away and produce them before me three days from now. Then I shall announce if they will lose their heads or be hanged or be fed to the dogs.'

Poor Goopy! Poor Bagha! they had come to the King to sing, hoping for some bakshish, and look what had befallen them! The guards tied their hands and beat them, and then dumped them in a gloomy cell. There, for a whole day, they lay, unable to move for pain. That was bad enough, much worse was the loss of Bagha's drum! Bagha struck himself several times in despair and blubbered, 'O Goopyda! Boo-hooh! O, Goopyda! I can take a beating, I'll even risk losing my life – but not my drum, never!'

Goopy was by then a bit calmer. He patted Bagha's head and said, 'Don't despair, Dada. The drum's gone, but we still have the shoes and the sack! We look pretty foolish – but we're not beaten yet. Never mind what's happened, let's have some fun now.' Bagha relaxed a bit and said, 'What fun can we have, Dada?' Goopy replied, 'Let's have some fun with food first, then we'll see about other kinds of fun.'

He stuck his hand into the boon-sack given them by the *bhuts* and said, 'Kindly bring us one dishful of pilau.' What an aroma wafted out! Such a pilau was not often found, even in royal kitchens. And what a giant-sized portion! Would Goopy be able to extract it from the sack? Somehow he managed, and then once again he spoke to the sack: 'Some fries, some spicy dishes, chutneys, sweets, curd, milk pudding and sherbet – and look sharp about it please!' In no time the cell floor was covered in gold and silver platters of delicacies. How much could two people eat? As they gobbled this unrivalled feast, their aches mysteriously disappeared.

Bagha said to Goopy, 'Dada, shouldn't we run away from here, before they feed us to the dogs?' Goopy replied, 'Are you crazy? We have the shoes – how can they feed us to the dogs? Let's stay here and see what happens.' Bagha was reassured. He could see that Goopy had some real mischief in mind.

Two days went by and the day of judgment set by the King was upon them. That night Goopy woke up early, put his hand in the sack and said, 'We desire royal costumes.' He pulled out clothes of superfine, not to mention superhuman quality. When they had dressed themselves, they rolled up the serving dishes in their old clothes and made two bundles, slipped on their shoes and said, 'Now we wish to take some air in the open fields.' A moment later they found themselves in a field some distance from the palace. They concealed their bundles in a corner, and strolled in the direction of the palace.

The King's men spotted them while they were still some way off, and ran to give their master the news: 'Maharaj, two Kings are approaching.'

The King sallied forth to the main gate in order to greet the visitors. When Goopy and Bagha arrived he hugged them handsomely and ushered them inside. They were settled in magnificent chambers. Innumerable servants, cooks, flunkeys and guards were put at their beck and call.

When in due course Goopy and Bagha had washed and refreshed themselves and taken some rest, the King appeared. From their dress he took his guests to be rulers of considerable stature. At last he could not resist asking Goopy 'Of which lands are you Kings?' To which Goopy replied with folded hands, 'Maharaj! You call us Kings? We are but your obedient servants.'

Goopy had spoken the truth, but the King did not really believe it. He thought, 'What modest people, how courteously they speak. They are as gentlemanly as they are mighty.' Without any further enquiry he conducted them to his court. There, this very day, he was to give judgment on the two persons who had trespassed into his bedchamber some three days before. The appointed hour had come, the guards had been sent to fetch the accused, where were they? Three days previously, they had been locked away – but when the locks were opened, there was no one there, the cell was empty.

There was a hell of a hubbub. The commander-in-chief furiously upbraided the guards. They, folding their hands, begged, 'Huzoor! The fault is not ours, we kept the doors locked and stood outside them every minute. They were not humans, they were *bhuts* – otherwise how could they vanish while inside?'

On this point all were agreed. Even the King, whose first reaction was to condemn the commander-in-chief and threaten him with execution, finally admitted that, yes, the two strangers truly must have been *bhuts*. 'My bedroom was bolted, how else could they get into it with that drum?'

Then everyone said, 'Yes yes, quite right, quite right, those two were *bhuts*!' And as they said this, their bodies shivered and sweated at one and the same time. Then they remembered Bagha's drum and called out, 'Maharaj! the *bhut*'s drum – what a vile thing! Don't keep it here any longer. We beg you – burn it immediately.'

'Goodness me! Is the *bhut*'s drum still here? Bring it here this moment and burn it!' the King ordered.

No sooner had he commanded than Bagha covered his face with his hands, yelled 'Ow! Ow! Ow!' and began to roll around the floor.

Goopy was in a real hot spot. If Bagha behaved like this at the mere mention of burning his drum, what on earth would he do if the drum was actually burned? Would he, Goopy, be able to stop Bagha from letting on that the drum was his? What a mess! It looked as if they would be found out and lose their lives.

At that instant Goopy's sole desire was to disappear with Bagha. But that was impossible; to attend court, one had to remove one's shoes.

Bagha's outburst had provoked absolute chaos amongst the courtiers. Everyone decided that Bagha was seriously ill, about to die. The royal physician was called, took Bagha's pulse and shook his head extremely gravely. A strong dose of purgative was administered and a hot poultice applied to Bagha's stomach. Then the doctor advised, 'If one poultice does not cure him, then another must be applied to his back and, failing that, two more, one on each of his sides.'

Bagha listened: immediately his writhing ceased. Everyone thought – what wonderful medicine that cures pain so fast! And despite the agony of the poultice, Bagha did feel somewhat relieved because his seizure had made everyone forget about setting fire to his drum. After this, he was taken with great care to his room and put to bed. Goopy remained beside him, fanning the poultice.

When everyone had gone Goopy said to Bagha, 'Hey, Bhai, did you have to yell like that? Don't you see what a pickle you've got us into?' 'If I hadn't shouted,' said Bagha, 'by now they would have burned my drum. I may have a smarting tum, but at least I know I've saved my drum.'

They chatted like this for some time. Meanwhile, in the court the commander-in-chief put his lips to the King's ear and said, 'Maharaj,

I would like a word, if Your Majesty pleases.'

'What is it?'

'That man who was rolling about on the floor, and the one with him, they are the *bhuts*; I recognise them.'

'So it seems,' said the King. 'I too thought they were familiar. We have a big problem. What's to be done?'

Whispers broke out all over the court. Someone said, 'Call the exorcist. He'll soon drive them out.' 'But if he can't,' countered someone else, 'those two could lose their tempers and create havoc. Better to burn them at night, while they're sleeping.'

The idea found general approval, but immediately a further difficulty arose: if the *bhuts* went up in flames, then so would the palace. There was a lot more debate and ultimately a decision was made: they would offer the *bhuts* a garden house; burning that down would be no great loss. The King added, 'That drum – it can be placed in the garden house too, then everything will burn together and preserve us from this peril.'

When Goopy and Bagha heard about the garden house they were thrilled. They knew nothing of the dastardly scheme behind it; they thought only of moving into secluded comfort, of being able to practise music to their hearts' desire. The house was indeed secluded and lovely. Though made of wood it was wonderfully designed. Just being there soonmadeBaghafeetbetter.ButGoopysaid,'Bhai,whystayhereanylonger? What's the use? Let's move on.' Bagha replied, 'Dada, such a fine place – we may never have the run of somewhere like it again; let's stay two days. Oh! if only I had my drum!'

Bagha went off wandering through the house, while Goopy took a seat in the garden and began to hum. Quite suddenly he heard Bagha shriek. He could not catch any of his words except, 'O Goopyda! O Goopyda!' But he was plainly speaking at the top of his voice. Goopy ran back and saw Bagha prancing around like a half-wit, babbling endlessly, 'Goopyda, Goopyda.' He was so overjoyed to have his drum back that he could not put his words in the right order. It took nearly half an hour before he was calm enough to say, 'Goopyda, look, look at this! In this room my drum – what fun – eh, hey!' Then he danced again for another ten minutes. 'Dada, after all this sadness it's come back! let's sing! let's play a bit.' 'I'm ravenous,' said Goopy. 'Why don't we eat, then we can sit on the verandah tonight and have a long session.'

59

The King, however, had fixed that night to burn them. His orders to the commander-in-chief were to spread a delicious feast in the garden house in the evening. The commander-in-chief and fifty or so men were to attend. When Goopy and Bagha dropped off to sleep after eating, fire was to be set in every part of the wooden building and all means of escape blocked off.

The food was truly outstanding. Yet Goopy and Bagha sat thinking – once everyone goes we can begin to play; while the commander-in-chief sat thinking – once these two go to bed, I can have the place set ablaze. He was keen to see sleep overtake them. From the look on his face they realised that he would not leave them until they went to bed, so Goopy, followed by Bagha, laid himself down on his couch and started to snore.

Shortly after, the two of them sensed that everyone had vanished, there was not a murmur to be heard. They waited a little longer and when the garden seemed totally empty, they crept into the verandah and struck up.

The commander-in-chief had instructed his men, 'Make sure the fire's properly lit at each door. Take care it's well and truly burning before you go.' He himself went to fire the stairs. Just as the flames had taken proper hold and he was thinking, 'It's time to be off,' Bagha began to beat and Goopy began to sing. Neither the commander-in-chief nor his men could move a muscle, and so they were all burnt to death. Meantime Goopy and Bagha caught sight of the flames; they at once grabbed the drum and the sack and used the shoes to decamp from the garden.

Very few of the men in the party survived the fire that burned their commander. When these few carried the news back to the King he was sore afraid. Several more men from his court appeared; they reported that having gone to watch the blaze, they had heard unearthly music and before their very eyes the two *bhuts* flew off into thin air. How the King trembled now! He could not attend his court. He rushed inside his bedroom, bolted the door against the *bhuts*, hid himself under a quilt and did not come out for a whole month.

Having escaped a fiery death, Goopy and Bagha happened to land in the forest where they had first encountered each other. Their dearest wish after such an adventure was to see their parents once more. Looking about him Bagha asked, 'Goodpyda, isn't it here we met?' Goopy said, 'Yes.' Bagha suggested, 'Don't you think the fact calls for a little musical celebration?' Goopy replied, 'It certainly does, Bhai. Why delay? Let's begin right now.' They started to play with full hearts.

And then a peculiar thing occurred. A gang of dacoits had robbed the King of Halla's treasury and made off with his two sons as ransom. The King's soldiers were following them in hot pursuit but they had been unable to catch up. As Goopy and Bagha began to sing the dacoits were passing through the forest. When the song reached their ears, they could run no further until it was finished; they were forced to halt. The music lasted all night long and still the dacoits could not budge! And so, in the morning, when the King of Halla arrived, he easily captured them. And when he learnt that he was able to do this because of the magic of Goopy and Bagha's music, he naturally fell upon them in gratitude. The princes too said, 'Father, such extraordinary singing you've never heard; let them come with us.' Then the King said to Goopy and Bagha, 'Come with me. I will give you five hundred rupees every month.'

Goopy saluted with folded hands and said, 'Maharaj, kindly permit us two days' leave. We should like to visit our parents and seek their permission to attend you in your capital.' 'Achchha,' said the King, 'we shall stay here two days. Go and see your parents and come back. Then we can return together.'

Ever since Goopy's father had driven Goopy away, he had been very sorrowful. When he saw him returning, he was overwhelmed with happiness. But Bagha was not so lucky. His parents had died some time before. When the villagers saw him coming, his drum resting on his head, they said, 'Oh no! That fellow Bagha's back, come to rattle our bones again. Throw him out!' Bagha said humbly, 'I only want to see my parents; I'll be off in a couple of days, I won't play at all.' Did they listen? They just gnashed their teeth, shouted that his parents were dead and then attacked him with big sticks; he had to run for his life under a hail of stones that wounded his leg and cracked his head, covering him in blood.

Goopy was on the verandah of his parents' house talking to them, when he saw Bagha hobbling towards him at a frenzied pace, his clothes in tatters and soaked in blood. He ran up and questioned, 'What's this? Why this state?' Bagha looked at him and grinned broadly. Catching his breath he said, 'Dada, I've had a close shave! Those blockheads nearly broke my drum.' He spent a blissful two days at Goopy's house under his parents' tender care. When their time was up Goopy bade

61

farewell, saying to his parents, 'Keep yourself ready; the moment we have leave again, I shall come for you.'

Several months passed. Goopy and Bagha settled happily in the palace of the King of Halla. Their names were spoken far and wide: 'Such maestros have never been heard before, and never shall be heard again!' The King adored them; he could not let a single day pass without a concert. Soon he confided in Goopy all his joys and woes. One day Goopy saw him looking exceptionally glum. He seemed to be brooding continually on some calamity. At length he revealed to Goopy, 'I have a terrible worry, I don't know what will happen. The King of Shundi wants to snatch away my kingdom.'

The King of Shundi was the one who had tried to burn Goopy and Bagha. The mention of his name gave Goopy a fantastic idea. He said to the King, 'Maharaj! Put your worries aside. At your command your servant will sort this business out, and have some fun too.' The King smiled and said, 'Goopy, you are a singer, don't tangle with war, which you don't understand. The King of Shundi's army is huge. What can I do against it?' Goopy said, 'Maharaj, if you permit us, we can try once. It can't do any harm.' 'All right, do as you wish,' permitted the King. Goopy was extremely pleased. Calling Bagha he went into a huddle with him.

They plotted and planned a long time that day. Bagha became highly excited. He said, 'Dada, I want to go through with this. But I'm scared of one thing; if we suddenly have to run away I might just forget to wear the shoes and get a sound thrashing like some ordinary fellow. Look, you can still see the marks of attention from those blighters in my village.'

Somehow Goopy allayed Bagha's fears and the next day they set to work. For several nights in succession they travelled to Shundi and wandered about the palace picking up information. The war preparations were certainly fearsome; if they ever hit Halla no quarter would be given. The prayers in the royal temple were equally ferocious. There were ten more days of rituals, then the army was set to head for Halla.

Goopy and Bagha saw everything. They closeted themselves in their room, bolted the door and spoke to the *bhut*-given sack: 'We desire a new type of sweet, superior in quality.' The sweets that popped out cannot be described. No one had ever consumed such sweets before, or even seen their like. Then, with the sweets in tow, Goopy and Bagha

62

perched themselves on the tallest pinnacle of the tallest tower of the King of Shundi's temple. Down below them the pre-dawn *puja* was in full swing; incense was swirling, conches were booming, bells were clanging without cease, and in the courtyard was a sea of worshippers. Then, from above their heads, with a whoosh the sweets came pouring down. Aloft, clinging to the temple pinnacle, Bagha and Goopy relished their game. In the darkness, in the smoke and dazzle of the ritual, no one could see them.

The sudden sweet fall silenced the courtyard momentarily. Then many people leapt up while many others shouted and tried to flee. A handful of brave souls picked up sweets and fearfully inspected them by lamplight. One finally shut his eyes and slipped a sweet into his mouth; he said nothing, instead he grabbed sweets from the courtyard with both hands, stuffed them into his mouth and began to prance and gesticulate. Everyone pitched in like a swarm of scrambling and squabbling birds.

Several people ran to tell the King. 'Maharaj! God is really gratified by today's *puja*. Today he sent his bounty from heaven above. And what heavenly *prashad* it is, we can't find words to describe its taste.' Even as they spoke the King hitched up the back of his dhoti and proceeded post-haste to the temple.

Alas, disaster! By then the *prashad* had all been eaten. The courtyard was scoured but not even a particle of the holy food could be procured for His Majesty's consumption. He grew wrathful and said, 'You call this fair? I offer the *puja* but you all eat the *prashad* leaving me none! Couldn't you save me even a tiny scrap? I shall impale the lot of you!' Everyone shook with fear and cried as humbly as they knew how, 'Mercy Maharaj! We have eaten all the *prashad*, we admit, but can it be finished for ever? Surely not! We gobbled it today, please forgive us; tomorrow you'll have it all to yourself, Maharaj!' 'Achchha,' said the King, 'all right. But mind you remember.'

The following day the King, looking forward to his *prashad*, was up extra early pacing the temple courtyard, staring at the night sky. Not far away, his courtiers sat anxiously in a circle, awaiting the blessed event. The *puja* was a hundred times grander than usual: they all thought to themselves, 'The gods should be even happier and send the King even finer *prashad*.'

Goopy and Bagha had been sitting atop the temple since midnight with sweets of the rarest refinement. They were attired in gorgeous raiment, crowns, necklaces, bangles and earrings; they looked as if they were gods themselves. Because of the incense nothing was visible, but the King was nevertheless staring impatiently upwards. With much giggling Goopy and Bagha launched the shower of sweets. There was a shout and the king jumped three feet in the air. Immediately, he pulled himself together and began to grab fistfuls of sweets with both hands. Having filled his mouth, he whirled about like a dervish.

A moment later Goopy and Bagha descended from the pinnacle of the temple into His Majesty's presence. 'The Gods have come, the Gods have come,' everyone chanted and began to bow, assuming that this was the correct thing to do. The King prostrated himself full-length on the ground and touched it with his forehead. Goopy said, 'Maharaj! Your dancing has pleased us mightily; come, let us embrace each other!' The King was in seventh heaven: to embrace the gods! – could there be greater good fortune than that?

The embrace began. The worshippers cried loudly, 'Hail! Hail!' Grabbing the opportunity and the King between them Goopy and Bagha called together, 'Now, take us to our rooms!' No sooner had they spoken than they arrived, King and all. The people in the temple were left gawping at the sky. When their ruler did not reappear they went home saying to each other, 'What a miracle! The King has gone to heaven while still a mortal. The Gods came down in person to take him there!'

In fact, the King had fainted in Goopy and Bagha's embrace and did not revive, even after his arrival. When, early the next morning he awoke, he saw the two *bhuts* sitting beside his head. He leapt to his feet and said shakily, 'Please, have mercy! Don't eat me! I will sacrifice a hundred buffalos to you.'

Goopy replied, 'Maharaj, you need not fear. We are not *bhuts* and we are not going to eat you.' But the King did not have much confidence in their words. He kept quiet and sat trembling with his head between his knees.

Bagha went to the King of Halla and said, 'Last night we kidnapped the King of Shundi; now what do we do?' And the King of Halla said, 'Bring him here!'

When the two Kings came face to face, the King of Shundi realised he was a prisoner. His fate was not to win Halla, but more likely to lose his life. But the King of Halla did not take his life, only his kingdom. He turned to Goopy and Bagha and said, 'You have saved me. Without you both my kingdom and my life would be gone. How can I repay you? I shall give you each half the kingdom of Shundi and my two daughters.'

On all sides there was wild applause. So it was that Goopy and Bagha became royal sons-in-law, received half the kingdom of Shundi each and were able to practise their music in total peace. The honour and happiness of Goopy's parents knew no bounds.

(1915)

CROWMAGNUM

Sukumar Ray

Once there was a King.

As he sat in his court one day, surrounded by flatterers and friends, nawabs and nobles, sepoys and sentries, from out of nowhere a raven flew in, perched itself upon a high pillar to the right of the throne, inclined its head, looked about – and gave a grave 'Caw'.

So solemn a sound, uttered without the slightest warning, set all eyes in court a-rolling and all jaws agape. The Prime Minister, who was clutching a sheaf of papers and was in the midst of explaining something, suddenly lost the thread of his speech and looked foolish. A boy who was sitting near the door burst into tears. The person in charge of the royal fly-whisk let it fall from his hand and flop on to the King's head. The King, who was just dozing off, suddenly woke up and said, 'Call the executioner!'

The executioner presented himself immediately. His Majesty said, 'Off with the head.' Horror all round! Whose head? – everyone nervously stroked his own. The King dozed a little more, then looked about him and said, 'Where's the head? Where is it?' The executioner folded his hands wretchedly and begged, 'Your Majesty, whose head?' 'You nincompoop!' said the King, 'what do you mean – whose head? Whoever it was who made that abominable sound – *his* head!' There was a sigh of collective relief so deep that the raven suddenly became restless and flew away.

Then the Prime Minister observed to His Majesty that it had been a raven responsible for the sound. The King commanded, 'Summon all the pundits!' In less than five minutes, they stood assembled before him.

The King questioned the group: 'This raven that entered my court and caused a disturbance, can you explain its sound?'

Explain why a raven calls? The pundits looked desperately at each other. One of them, who was almost a boy, answered with considerable embarrassment, 'Sir, perhaps the bird was hungry?'

The King said, 'You are a twit! If it was hungry, why would it come into court? Do we sell puffed rice here? Prime Minister, show this pundit out.' Everyone loudly concurred, 'Yes, yes, quite right, show him out.'

Another pundit said, 'Your Majesty, whatever happens must have a cause – if it rains there must be clouds, if there is light there must be a lamp, hence, if a queer report is emitted from a bird's throat, we may surely presume there is a cause: is there anything odd about it?'

'The only thing that's odd,' said the King, 'is that I pay fatuous fellows like you for burbling like this. Prime Minister, from today stop his salary.' And again everyone chorused, 'Yes, yes, stop his salary.'

The other pundits panicked, seeing the fate of the first two. The minutes ticked by, no one said a word. The King became livid. He ordered that until he had an answer no one would leave the court. And so, by royal command, everyone sat rigid. Some of them became so worried they curried themselves in sweat, others scratched themselves so much they became half bald. In due course everyone grew hungrier and hungrier – except the King, who was never hungry or tired; he carried on dozing.

Just as they had all reached the point of despair, inwardly cursing the pundits as 'idiots, incompetents and useless dolts', a lean-looking fellow gave a monstrous shout and fell down in the centre of the court. The King, the Prime Minister, the courtiers, viziers and all present promptly demanded, 'What's happened? What's happened?'

After much sprinkling of water, waving of fans and wagging of tongues the man sat up with a shiver and said, 'Your Majesty, was there a raven?' They all said, 'Yes yes yes, why do you ask?' The man went on, 'Your Majesty, did it sit above your head and look southwards – and did it incline its head, cast its eyes about and make a sound like "Caw"?' They all said 'Yes yes' with fearful intensity, 'it was just like that.' Then the man began to blubber, saying between sobs, 'Alas! alas! why didn't anyone call me at that moment?'

The King said, 'That's right, why didn't any of you let him know?' No one knew who the fellow was, but they lacked the courage to say so. They said aloud, 'Yes, he should have been told' – though why he should have been told' – though why he should have been told and what information was involved, no one had any idea. Then the man, after much more sobbing, made a strange face and said slowly, 'Crowmagnum.' What was that? They all decided – the fellow's gone off his head.

Said the Prime Minister, 'Cawmagnum, what's that?' The man said, 'Not Cawmagnum – Crowmagnum.' No one was any the wiser but everyone nodded and said, 'Ah!' Then His Majesty himself enquired, 'What's that?' The man replied, 'I'm only a humble man, Sir, I know only this, that since I was a child I have heard tell of Crowmagnum, and I know that when Crowmagnum calls upon a King, he takes the guise of a raven. As he enters the court he finds a place on a pillar to the King's right hand, inclines his head, faces south, rolls his eyes and says, "Caw". That's all I know – perhaps the pundits know more?' The pundits, however, hurriedly dissented, 'No, no, on this matter no more is known.'

The King said, 'But you were crying because you were not informed. What was all that about?' The man said, 'Your Majesty, if I say all I know, people may disbelieve me, so I'm afraid to speak.'

The King said, 'Anyone who disbelieves you will lose his head – now speak without fear.' Everyone vigorously assented.

The man said, 'Your Majesty, I know a mantra: all my life I've known it. If I see Crowmagnum I'm to speak the mantra and then a miracle will occur – no one knows exactly what kind. You see, it has not yet appeared in any book. Now, alas, I may never get the chance!' The King said, 'Tell me the mantra.' The man said, 'Impossible! The mantra may be pronounced before no one but Crowmagnum. I can write it on a piece of paper for you – then you must fast for two days, and on the morning of the third day, upon rising, you may read it. If you spot a raven you may utter the mantra, but beware! no one else should hear it – if they do, or if the raven is not Crowmagnum, this may spell disaster!'

The court was dissolved. They had all listened open-mouthed and now they breathed easy again; they headed home, talking of Crowmagnum, of the mantra and of extraordinary events to come.

The King did as bidden: he fasted for two days and on the third morning opened the piece of paper and read it. It said:

> An orange-green orang-outang
> Sticks and brickbats wham potang!
> Hooray for this gardener fellah –
> Vacant post for office wallah.

68

This the King solemnly committed to memory. Ever since, whenever he sees a raven, he shoos everyone away, speaks the mantra and looks out for strange happenings. But it appears that he is yet to locate Crowmagnum.

(1916)

THE RISE AND FALL OF THE GAMMANS

Rajshekhar Basu ('Parashuram')

The time to which I refer postdates the extinction of the human race by about thirty years. You may be inclined to ask how anyone could still write about it, or for that matter read about it if everyone had been reclaimed by the five elements; returned to earth, water, fire, air and space. If so, you need not worry. Writers and readers exist beyond time and space; they are all-pervasive and all-knowing. All you have to do is sit back and enjoy my story.

For a long time there had been feuding between the heads of the largest nations. Things had gradually reached such a pass that there could be no hope of compromise. Each nation had in effect promoted a nonsense rhyme to the position of National Anthem:

> We are the mighty ayatollahs
> And if you deny it,
> We shall holla.

Eventually each head of state, having consulted his astrological think-tank, concluded that he could never live happily unless he eliminated his rivals and all their followers. He therefore decided to drop an annihilium bomb upon them. This was the very latest thing then; it made the uranium bomb look like pillow-fighting.

The chief bombardiers of each nation cherished the hope that they could finish off their rivals before *their* bombs were ready. Unfortunately for all concerned, all the bombs were ready together. When all the spies delivered this identical information to their masters, the latter launched the ultimate weapons at just the same moment.

No nation – whether civilised, half-civilised or plain barbarous – was spared. Humankind with all its achievements, as well as animals, birds, insects and every kind of plant, was obliterated. But life is very tough, it manages to cling on. In the depths of the ocean, in mountain caverns, on uninhabited islands and in various other impenetrable places, plants and inferior life-forms survived the blast. We need not bother with them; I am going to speak of the creatures that really matter.

In the deep underground drainage systems of metropolises like London, Paris, New York, Peking and Calcutta, lived millions of rats. For the most part they were wiped out by the bombs, but some young males and females were not. They not only survived but altered under the gamma rays emanating from the bomb in ways characteristic of their physiology – or, as biologists put it, they mutated. Within only a few rat generations their fur and tails disappeared; their two front paws became heads; their hind legs grew firmer enabling them to stand up and walk about; their brain-power increased; and, rather than squeaking at each other, they evolved a clear language: in short, they came to resemble human beings. Like Karna of the *Mahabharata*, who came into the world wearing earrings and amulets, boons from the Sun God, the rats acquired a gamma-given intelligence and capacity for progress. Of course in one respect they were already superior to human beings; they could breed faster than them. This faculty too was enhanced.

I do not want to denigrate these new arrivals, brilliant de-tailed bipeds that they were, by describing them as rats. Nor shall I drive the typesetter mad by employing their proper Sanskrit name. Since I regard them as almost human, I shall refer to them as gammans, the blessed progeny of the gamma ray. That should distinguish them sufficiently from us, their human predecessors.

Now I need to introduce a small amount of theory, so bear with me. Historians generally inform us that 25 years may be counted as one human generation. That means 18,000 years equals about 720 generations. What was he like, our ancestor 720 times removed, you may well ask? Anthropologists tell us that he lived in the 'Stone Age': he knew nothing of farming, wore no clothes, did not cook, ate raw meat and lived in caves. Just think – what progress we have made in 720 generations.

Among the gammans one generation consisted of fifteen days, that is, it took them fifteen days to reproduce themselves. So, in the 30 years that elapsed after the extinction of human beings, 720 gamman generations were born. Those 30 gamman years are equivalent to 18,000 human ones. If you doubt me, work it out for yourself.

Over this 30-year era the gammans developed so quickly that they reached the apex of civilisation. They displayed the learning, artistic glory and economic wealth of which their human predecessors had been so proud. Naturally, not all of gamman society reached these lofty heights: they still had a caste system, discrimination between black and white and political differences, as well as large and small nations, empires and subject peoples, commercial competition, hatred and violence and a great many wars. These conflicts eventually induced common sense to prevail in the minds of certain far-sighted gammans all over the earth. What was the point of such strife, they reflected; couldn't all gammans manage to come together and live in peace? Gamman civilisation was without peer: it had analysed the world's deepest mysteries, mastered its most powerful natural forces and put them to work, eradicated the most dreadful diseases and pondered the profoundest questions of philosophy and ethics. Surely, if the gamman political leaders and great minds could act in concert, they could bring the disparate selfish gamman urges into harmonious balance?

With the full backing of geniuses everywhere the leaders convened a grand summit conference. Top politicians, philosophers, scientists and literary figures of many nations attended with enthusiasm. There was a large group of uninvited guests too, of the type who always batten on to such occasions. Since the actual names of the official delegates in the gamman language would be off-putting to readers, I have decided to refer to them by my own names, more convenient to pronounce.

In India, as we know, most conferences customarily begin their proceedings with singing and dancing by gentle maidens. The gammans were less artistically inclined; first, they believed, one should get one's teeth into the agenda; the fun and games could be left until later. What's more, because gamman life-spans were so much shorter than those of human politicians, they kept their speeches strictly to the point. In fact the opening address of the conference by the chairman Chong Ling stated simply that world peace must be attained, by hook or by crook. Otherwise, the gamman race was doomed.

The next speaker was Count Notenough, a gamman from the less-developed world. 'The absence of world peace is a direct result of the absence of equitable distribution of the world's wealth,' he said. 'A few nations have built grand empires by dishonest means. They have grabbed plentiful supplies of raw material and kept millions of victims under their sway in colonies. We have been deprived of our natural growth. If all of us here today truly want to stop wars, the world's riches have to be apportioned fairly.'

Lord Grabearth, representative of the greatest empire on earth, took the floor. 'For the benefit of the whole world we hold custody of our empire,' he remarked. 'Who else has as much experience of running empires as we do? As long as we remain powerful you will all live free from danger. Should someone require raw materials we will of course hand them over to him, provided we get a fair deal. No one should think of casting covetous glances at the uncivilised and half-civilised countries in our care. We are their guardians, and as soon as they are grown-up and able to take care of themselves, we shall lay down our burden. We harbour mischief towards no one. If there is trouble in the offing, it will come from my friend Keepoff's vast state, not from us. He permits neither free trade nor free enterprise; everything is part of the state. The wealthy and the high-born who are the natural leaders of society have no place. Our own work-force is already being corrupted by this ideology. If we don't all watch out, such detestable ideas and shoddy goods will spread throughout the world and undermine social stability and good business practice. If it is world peace we seek, we must first subdue his people.'

General Keepoff stroked his bushy moustache and said, 'My honourable friend Lord Grabearth has just told you an enormous lie, as I am certain you all realise. His own nation, of course, is the one that oppresses us all. He has been trying to foment revolution in our country by bribery for a very long time. All I shall say about that in this forum is this: one day we shall have our revenge.'

Abala Dasji, a nationalist leader from a colonised nation, whose name, translated, would be Feebleji, now spoke up. 'The guardianship of which Lord Grabearth speaks is sheer hypocrisy. If the responsibility for deciding when we are grown-up rests in hands like his, we shall never escape slavery. This conference has one clear duty, to sweep away all empires and grant independence to all subject peoples. Our dependence on others is what breeds hatred and violence.'

The spiritual leader Nishchinta Maharaj, the Maharishi of Meditation, had so far sat motionless, his eyes closed. Now he broke his vow of silence and patted Feebleji soothingly on the back. 'Fear not, friend, do not be agitated, I am here. By virtue of my austerities you will all, at the appropriate time, attain salvation. I am in constant communication with the *rishis* on Mount Gaurishankar, and they unanimously concur with me.'

This set off Dharm Das, a devotee of karma yoga, the way of truth through action. 'Forget all this airy-fairy stuff. We all need our souls purifying before good sense can prevail in national affairs. The solution is straightforward: become vegetarian, avoid all forms of indulgence and for one month [fifty human years, in other words] practise uninterrupted celibacy. In the meantime, the old will die off, none of us will have offspring, our numbers will be halved and there will be no need to think about food and so on. Wars, famines and plagues will all become redundant, and every issue will be settled by uncontaminated moral means.'

Pandit Satyakamji did not agree. 'I have given much thought to this problem,' he said, 'and neither compromise nor miracles can solve it. Vegetarianism, repression of the senses and celibacy are futile; they fly in the face of gamman nature. Further, they cannot be enforced by international law. Our greatest need is to tell the truth. If every member of this conference was willing to open his mind and express his intentions freely, then the way to world peace would easily be negotiated. In science, we have advanced far and enjoyed its fruits. But with the gamman personality we have not made much progress. Science, depending as it does on observation and experiment, permits no deception because matter does not deliberately deceive, and so to reach the truth in science is comparatively simple. But in politics our leaders can barely take a step without uttering a falsehood. Until they are prepared to reveal their secret intentions, the path to peace is blocked. Unless all the symptoms of a disease are known, how can a cure be found?'

Lord Grabearth had become tight-lipped listening to this speech. 'But if someone doesn't want to speak the truth, how can it be extracted from him?' he asked. 'Can he be made to speak?'

'Of course he can,' said General Keepoff instantly. 'With drugs. Haven't you heard of sodium pentathol? Under its influence unruly types soon start blabbing. In our country we give it to traitors to make them confess. Then we shoot them. We don't waste time and money on lawyers and lawsuits, I can tell you.'

74

A world-famous doctor, Bringaraj Nandi, cried out, 'Fools! Fools! Idiots all! People on pentathol become imbeciles. They tell the truth, yes, but they completely lose their power of discrimination. Are we addicts that we sit here blabbering like this? No, we've come to address a complex international problem. For that purpose pentathol is useless; what we need is Veracitin, which I've just discovered. Though an opium derivative, it has no side-effects and is infallible. However experienced or cunning a person is, it will get him in its grip and make him talk. But it will not damage his brain. There are no after-effects at all. Within an hour of taking the drug its spell evaporates, leaving a person happy to tell as many lies as he likes. I have some of it here, and if the chairman allows me, we can have everyone speaking the truth in a matter of moments.'

Count Notenough questioned, 'Have you tested it?'

'Naturally,' replied Bringaraj. 'I've experimented on lots of rats and guinea-pigs.'

There was a roar of laughter from General Keepoff. 'So rats know how to tell lies, do they? I suppose you speak their language too?'

'Oh certainly,' said Nandi, 'it follows from their behaviour. If a rat wags its tail to the left you know it's up to no good; if to the right, you know it's honest. I've also experimented on one of my pupils, and now his wife has filed for a divorce.'

Without further ado, chairman Chong Ling declared that there was no sense in leaving the conference in doubt. 'Why don't we try the drug right here? Whoever wants to volunteer – for the sake of science – let him come forward.'

Dharm Das came up to Dr Nandi, stretched out his hand and said, 'I'm willing. Give me an injection.'

Nandi took a large magazine syringe from his pocket and shot about fifteen drops of Veracitin into the arm of Dharm Das. There was a two-minute delay as the drug took effect and then the Chairman spoke once more: 'Mr Dharm Das, kindly open your mind.'

'I'm a vegetarian. I take no spicy food. I do not indulge in any kind of idleness. I have practiced celibacy for many years. Even so I occasionally fall below my ideal.'

There was another scornful laugh from General Keepoff. 'What's the point in trying the drug on nutcases? When they're normal they don't tell lies: they actually believe what they preach. I will take a shot. I've no objection to speaking either truth or lies.'

Immediately Lord Grabearth sprang to his feet to restrain Keepoff, shouting 'Don't do it! Get a grip on yourself! Don't get mixed up in this. Can any self-respecting leader agree to such a test? We have a legal right to conceal our innermost intentions. We cannot allow a quack doctor to take that away from us. Really gross lies are barbaric, I accept, but lesser lies are weapons of great value. Aimed properly they can conquer the world. That's not something we can just throw away. The carefully refined falsehood protects and shelters society; all our customs and codes of conduct are based upon it. Aren't you ashamed of yourself? Speak your mind freely here – and you might as well stand naked in front of the entire conference.'

General Keepoff was not put off. He extricated himself from Grabearth's clutches and stuck out his arm. Dr Nandi promptly jabbed a needle into it. Then Keepoff turned and gripped Grabearth himself in a firm embrace, calling out 'Give him a jab too and make it a little extra.' Desperately wriggling in Keepoff's fat hairy arms Grabearth exclaimed, 'This is an outrage! You are violating every canon of international law. Mr Chairman, you are totally incompetent. Get up at once and telephone my Prime Minister!'

But Keepoff only shouted, 'Very difficult patient this one, sick to the marrow of his bones, needs a second dose I think.' Without a word Dr Nandi injected Grabearth again and very soon he became peaceable. He said meekly, 'But why only us two? Give that scoundrel Notenough a shot.'

Notenough went for him with raised fists. Keepoff stepped between them saying, 'Hold it! Hold it! Why so scared to tell the truth? We all know each other's secrets anyway, so where's the harm in speaking openly?'

This made Notenough lower his voice to a whisper. 'It's not you lot I'm afraid of, but someone else. Domestic quarrels are far worse than political ones, you know.'

There was an interjection from the visitor's gallery. Countess Notenough shrieked, 'Yes, give him masses. He's the biggest liar of all. He's been deceiving me for years, I know, I know.'

As she spoke, Dr Nandi used the hullabaloo to crawl up on all fours behind Notenough and jab him in his buttock. His wife yelled again, 'Now you'll have to talk. Those women – all of them – who are they?'

Chairman Chong Ling intervened. 'Order, order! The ladies in question will wait, Madam. Now we must keep to the agenda. Lord

Grabearth, Count Notenough, General Keepoff, will you kindly state your political objectives one by one.'

Grabearth kicked off. 'Our objective is straightforward. We believe that the only worthwhile policy is – might is right. Philanthropy is fine if kept within the family, but it has no place between nations. All we want is to grab what we can to the limit of our capacity, from the civilised and the uncivilised, the powerful and the weak. Justice doesn't come into it. Who thinks of the calf when he drinks milk? Do we consider the rights of cows and sheep, tigers, snakes, rats and mosquitoes when we kill them? Plants too are alive. If you want to live a non-violent life you'd better eat stones. We desire all sorts of good things and we are willing to be brutal to get them. Not that we don't have obstacles in our way and some determined enemies – not to mention the business of compassion, what idiots call conscience or religion. Some of us in high places at home and others in foreign parts are weak-willed. We can't bluff them all the time. Sometimes we give ground to keep them quiet. I don't believe this conference can ever fulfil its objectives. Under pressure from our rivals, we may occasionally make a few small concessions, but a lasting settlement – that's out of the question. What it suits us to give today, we may well decide to take back tomorrow. You all know about survival of the fittest: need I say more?'

It was Notenough's turn. 'Our principles are the same. There's not much difference in our practices either, bar one thing. We are the most superior race on earth and in due course we shall become its paramount ruler. We shall employ any means necessary to achieve our heart's desire.'

Keepoff said, 'We also concur, but there is a marked difference in our approach. Fortunately, our country is a large one and we haven't yet felt an overriding need to absorb anyone else's. But our hand is ready to strike in the not-so-distant future.'

Feebleji struck his forehead in despair and said, 'Alas! Lies were better than these stark truths! At least before this we could hope that power had blinded them all and one day their consciences would awaken. Answer me this, Lord Grabearth. We, the oppressed nations, are gradually gaining power. Whatever you may say, some decent gammans all over the earth support us. One day we shall throw off our shackles. Do you have any idea of the hatred that will have poisoned our minds by then? It will mean disaster for you. But if, instead of this, you come to a just agreement with us now and give up much of your power, in the years to come we will not turn against you. Can't you get that simple idea into your head?'

'Easily,' replied Grabearth. 'But why give up the whole cake today in the hope of keeping a piece of it tomorrow? Why should we care what happens to our great-grandchildren when they are old and grey?'

With a deep sigh Feebleji dropped into his seat. The Maharishi patted his back a second time and said, 'Fear not, I am here.'

Dharm Das got up. 'What need for these injections? We knew everything already. Is it not written in our sacred books, our *shastras*?' He launched into Sanskrit, a quotation about the terrible beasts of the epics, the *asuras*:

> I have grabbed this today. I shall grab that tomorrow. I already possess this much wealth. Soon I shall get even more. I have massacred these enemies already. In due time I shall slaughter those ones too. I am God, the Enjoyer, whose every act brings success. I am the mightiest and the happiest. I am the greatest – there is no one to touch me.

This speech completed, the chairman looked at each delegate and said, 'Now that the intentions of each leader are plain, let us discuss ways to world peace.'

Grabearth, Notenough and Keepoff shouted unanimously, 'We like things just as they are. Talk of peace is all ballyhoo. We have no intention of becoming toothless and clawless. We shall carry on as we always have, snatching from our neighbours and fighting with them. It suits us perfectly.'

Throughout the proceedings, one delegate had been sitting quietly at the back. He was Professor Thunderbolt, a scientist and philosopher, whose titles would have filled a ream of foolscap. He stood up and called out. 'Wait. I have discovered the path to world peace.'

'You too offer injections?' queried Dr Nandi.

'One cannot inoculate a race,' replied Thunderbolt. 'The best solution lies with my latest invention; it's a bomb that embraces the entire world and produces peace just like that' – he indicated how with a graceful wave of his hand. 'Instead of cosmic rays, the bomb emits what one might call 'conscious' rays – I really mean unconscious rays – that are a thousand times finer than cosmic rays. Contact with these rays purifies the mind of all lust, anger and greed; they liberate the soul.'

Grabearth protested sharply: 'Watch your tongue, this isn't the place to give away secrets. It's our money behind all that research you're doing. Whatever you have to say, say it to the Prime Minister.'

Notenough sprang angrily to his feet. 'It's we who have paid for it! The bomb belongs to us.'

'You're a damned liar,' shouted Keepoff. We've been supporting this from the beginning. The discovery is ours exclusively.'

Thunderbolt folded his palms together in a gesture of peace and said, 'Gentlemen, none of you should get so worked up. All of you have rights over my bomb, all of you will enjoy its benefits. Mr Feebleji, your conflicts too will be resolved, along with your misery.' So saying, he began to untie the small bundle he had been holding.

The conference became a brawl. Grabearth, Notenough, Keepoff and every other delegate scrimmaged to take charge of the bundle.

'Thunderboltji, why delay?' shouted Dharm Das above the hubbub. 'Release your bomb.'

Thunderbolt in fact needed to do nothing at all. With all the pushing and shoving the bomb fell to the floor and emitted a tiny crackle. There was no bang and no flash. Before any gamman had the slightest inkling, the gamman race had ceased to exist.

For a brief while Grabearth was stupefied. Then he said, 'It seems that the Professor's bomb is good; we have all achieved equality, fraternity and freedom. Notenough, Keepoff, I love you both. Feebleji, you are my bosom companion. I have just composed a National Anthem. See what you think of it:

> Brothers! Let us live together – supernally.
> Let us have no disputes – eternally.
> And now – let us embrace fraternally!

The Maharishi patted Feebleji on the back proudly: 'Isn't this what I predicted?'

Fraternal feelings flew around the conference without reference to caste or religion. After some time Notenough said, 'Come brothers! Let us justly apportion the world's natural resources: its coal, its oil, its wheat, cows, sheep, pigs, cotton, sugar, rubber, iron, gold and uranium.

Let each country have an equal share. Isn't that best?'

Thunderbolt said with a smile, 'There's no need for all that. You have been freed from your mortal coils and are now ethereal beings. You can go to hell, be born again or simply evanesce, just as you wish.'

'You mean to say we've died and become spirits? I don't believe in spirits,' said Keepoff.

'Whether you do or not will make no difference to other spirits,' Thunderbolt reminded him.

Mother Earth must now draw breath after the annihilation of her latest offspring, before girding herself to give birth once more. She feels no emotion at the extinction of useless, sinful children. Time runs on forever, and earth is vast. She can wait: even a few hundred thousand years will not try her patience. Wait in hope, the hope that one day she may conceive progeny truly worthy of her love.

(1945)

THE SWEETMEAT CHILD

Abanindranath Tagore

A Raja had two wives, one forsaken, the other his favourite. The Favoured Rani lived in the royal palace, her every comfort ministered to. She had seven-storeyed chambers and seven hundred maidservants to cherish her, press her feet and paint them with red lac dye, and to preen her hair. She could sit all day plucking flowers from seven baskets and threading flower garlands. The blossoms came from her seven flower gardens. The jewels she wore were kept in seven chests, each worth a Raja's ransom. The Favoured Rani was the light of the Raja's life.

The Forsaken Rani, who was older, received no attention. The Raja viewed her with extreme indifference. The room he had given her was dilapidated, the maid he had given her was deaf and mute. To wear she had torn saris, to lie on a tatty quilt. Once a year the Raja visited her room: he sat down, said one word and left. But the Favoured Rani – she lived in the Raja's apartments all year round.

Then, one day, the Raja called his Prime Minister and said, 'Prime Minister, we shall be travelling to foreign parts – make ready the ships.'

The Prime Minister, at the royal command, made the fleet ship-shape. It took him seven months to prepare the seven ships. The royal retinue was to travel in six of them, the Raja in the seventh, which was made of gold and had a gold sail.

The Prime Minister came and announced, 'Maharaj, the ships await you.'

'We sail tomorrow,' said the Raja.

The Prime Minister retired.

The Junior Rani, the favoured one, was lying on a gold divan in the palace's inner apartments surrounded by seven assistants, when the Raja entered. Seating himself at the head of the bed he said to his Favoured Rani, 'We are leaving for foreign parts. What shall I bring for you?'

The Rani fiddled with the diamond bangles on her butter-soft skin and replied, 'These diamonds are so pale you can hardly see them. If only I had eight pairs of bangles set with the stone that is crimson as blood.'

The Raja said, 'You shall have them, Rani, I will bring back bangles like that from the land of rubies.'

The Rani's dainty feet trembled, her anklets jingled and she said, 'These anklets don't sound nice. If only I had ten pairs of solid gold anklets the colour of fire.'

'I will fetch you such golden bells from the land of gold,' said the Raja.

The Rani fingered her necklace of pearls fit for an elephant's brow and added, 'Look at these, Raja, such small pearls. I've heard tell of a land where the pearls are the size of pigeon's eggs – bring me a necklace like that.'

'The kingdom of pearl is in the midst of the ocean. I'll go there and bring you back a necklace. What else shall I bring, Rani?'

His beloved Rani twitched the gold end of her sari over her golden skin and said, 'Dear me, how heavy these saris are! If only, if only I had a sari as blue as heaven, as light as the breeze and as smooth as water.'

'Yes yes, you poor thing,' said the Raja, 'the gold thread scratches your golden skin and hurts your delicate body. Bid me farewell with a smile, Rani, and I shall certainly return with a sari as blue as heaven, as light as the breeze and as smooth as water.'

The Junior Rani smiled as she bid the Raja goodbye.

He was about to go aboard his ship – when he suddenly remembered the Senior Rani, the forsaken one.

At the door of her dilapidated room he stopped and said, 'Senior Rani, I'm going abroad. For the Junior Rani I'm bringing bangles, necklaces, anklets and saris. For you what shall I bring? Tell me what you desire.'

She replied, 'Maharaj, your safe return is all I desire, that will satisfy me entirely. When once you were mine you lavished affection on me – then I had many desires. To feel the touch of golden saris, to live in a seven-storeyed palace lit by a thousand lamps, seated at the centre of seven hundred servants like a true Rani – that was what I wished for: and to tie golden anklets around the feet of a female popinjay in a golden cage – that too I desired. I had so many wishes then, Maharaj, and many of them came true. Now, what is the use of gold ornaments and saris? Now, who shall I put diamond bracelets on my arms for? Or pearl necklaces around my neck? Or jewels in the parting of my hair? Those days are over, Maharaj. You may give me gold jewellery, but you will not give me back your love! You will not give back the seven hundred servants and the seven-storeyed palace! You may give me a bird from the forest, but Maharaj, you won't give me a golden cage! Here, in this shabby place, won't thieves soon steal gold ornaments, a wild bird soon escape? Maharaj, please go and bestow your bounty on the one you love, there is no use my having wishes.'

'No Rani,' said the Raja, 'it won't do, people will speak ill of me. Tell me what you desire?'

'How can I shame myself by asking for ornaments? Maharaj, bring me only a pink-faced monkey.'

'Achchha Rani, then goodbye.'

The Senior Rani, the Forsaken Rani, fell onto her tatty quilt in a welter of tears. The Raja boarded his vessel.

In the setting sun, golden sails billowing, the gold ship sailed away across the blue water of the infinite deep, floating westwards like a golden cloud.

From her shabby room, lying on her tatty bed, the Forsaken Rani looked out across the ocean – while the Favoured Rani, the beloved one, lay within her seven-storeyed palace, surrounded by seven hundred servants, thinking of her jewellery and listening to the sound of her bird in its golden cage, until she fell asleep on her gold divan.

The Raja, aboard his ship, gave no thought to the Senior Rani; he thought only of the smiling face of the Junior Rani at the moment of farewell – what was she doing now? he wondered. Perhaps her hair? And after her hair, what next? Perhaps the red lac dye would be painted on her feet. And then would she not pick flowers from her seven bowers, and begin to thread each flower in her basket into garlands, while her mind thinks of – me? As she thinks, won't tears come to her eyes and her garland-making lie unfinished? The gold thread, the flower baskets would lie at her feet; all night she would sit there, unable to make her eyes close in sleep.

The Favoured Rani, the Junior Rani, was the sweetheart of the Raja, the one he thought about. The Senior Rani was still mad for him, but he never once gave her a thought.

For twelve months the Raja voyaged from country to country in his ship.

In the thirteenth month he reached the land of jewels.

In this land everything was a jewel. The walls were jewelled, the steps of the ghats by the river were jewelled, even the grit on the roads was made of jewels. Here the Raja had bangles made for his Favoured Rani: eight sets, each studded with eight thousand rubies; when they were worn on the arms, red blood seemed to be shining through the skin.

The Raja took these jewelled bangles and sailed on to the land of gold. Here, at his instruction, the goldsmiths created ten pairs of solid gold anklets. When finished, they flashed like fiery sparks, resonated like the strings of a *vina* and rang like the cymbals of a *mandira*.

Carrying the ruby bangles from the land of jewels and the gold anklets from the land of gold, the Raja arrived in the kingdom of pearls.

In his gardens the Pearl Raja kept two pigeons. Their feet were of pearl, their beaks of ruby; they plucked pearl fruits from trees made of emeralds, and the eggs that they laid were pearls too. The Pearl Rani, at evening time, threaded garlands from these eggs, which she placed in her hair after dark – only to cast them aside, come morning.

Then her maids picked up the pearls, now stale, and bartered them in the market for a ship-load of silver.

And so, in exchange for a ship-load of silver, the Raja bought the pearls he wished to hang about his Favoured Rani's throat.

Bearing the jewelled bangles, the gold anklets and the pearl necklace from the land of pearls, the Raja travelled on, and six months later came to another country. Here, in a princess's grove, blue silkworms fed off the leaves of lapis-lazuli trees, making silk cocoons with threads as blue as heaven, as light as the breeze and as smooth as water. Every night the princess would sit up on the roof, matching the shade of her silk with the sky, spinning a sari. Each sari took six months to weave. Then the princess would put on this heavenly-blue, light-as-the-breeze, smooth-as-water sari for just one day, while performing her *puja* in the temple before Lord Shiva, the Blue-Throated One. After that she would discard it, and her maids would sell the sari in exchange for seven ship-loads of gold. That is what the Raja paid to possess a sari worthy of his Favoured Rani.

84

Six months after that, having crossed the seven oceans and thirteen rivers, bearing the Favoured Rani's jewelled bangles, gold anklets, pearl necklace and sari of her heart's desire, the Raja's ship reached home. And then the Raja remembered – the Senior Rani wanted a monkey.

He confided in his Prime Minister: 'I have forgotten something. I haven't brought a monkey for the Senior Rani. You must go and find me one.'

The Prime Minister went off as he was bidden. And the Raja, mounting his white elephant, passed among his people, carrying to the Junior Rani in the inner apartments the jewellery and the sari of her heart's desire.

In the seventh storey of her seven-storeyed palace the Junior Rani was standing before a gold mirror, parting her hair with a gold comb, tying it up with gold pins and a gold cord, applying a dot of vermilion between her eyebrows with a gold applicator, and decorating her eyelashes with kohl, while her maids hovered around their mistress, painting her feet with red lac dye, handing her flowers from baskets and offering her *pan* from a gold tray – thus did the Raja come upon her.

He sat down beside her in his crystal throne and said, 'Please accept these gifts, Rani. From the land of jewels, where even the ghats and roads are bejewelled – from there I bring you bangles. From the land of gold where even the dust and sand is gold, I give you anklets. In the land of pearls are two birds with feet of pearl and beaks of ruby, which lay eggs of pearl – the Pearl Rani strings the eggs together, puts them in her hair at night and discards them at dawn. Rani, I purchased a necklace of those pearls for you. In another land there is a princess who sits upon her roof and spins seven threads out of one silk cocoon during the depths of the night – she takes six months to spin a sari, but after wearing it one day for her *puja*, she casts it off. Rani, from that land, in exchange for seven ship-loads of gold, I secured one sari woven by her own hand. You've never seen its like! I've searched the world for these jewels and this sari worthy of you, now please try them on!'

So the Rani put on the eight pairs of jewelled bangles. They were too loose – they reached her shoulders.

She tried on the ten sets of anklets. Her dainty feet were too small for them – as soon as she took a step, the anklets slipped off onto the marble floor.

Her face dark with huff, she put the pearl necklace around her neck. But the necklace was too tight – it cut her neck and hurt her.

85

She wrapped the sari of her heart's desire seven times around her body. The blue silk was too short. Now she was in tears.

Then the much-revered Junior Rani pulled the eight pairs of bangles set with eight thousand rubies off her arms, kicked the ten pairs of solid gold anklets off her feet, dropped the pearl necklace and the sari of her heart's desire in the dust, and cried 'Useless ornaments! Useless sari! Which road did they sweep to make these bangles? What kind of dust and sand went into these anklets, Maharaj? A cast-off necklace of cast-off pearls – shame on you! I scorn this princess's second-hand sari! I'm embarrassed to wear such a thing. Take them away, Maharaj, I've no use for someone else's sari, someone else's jewellery!'

The Rani bolted herself inside her boudoir and sulked. The glum-faced Raja picked up the ornaments purchased with seven ship-loads of gold and the sari of heart's desire, and went to his court.

His Prime Minister was waiting next to the royal throne: he had been searching high and low and eventually, meeting a merchant from the land of sorcerers, had bought a baby monkey in exchange for one worthless cowrie with a hole in it.

As soon as he entered the court the Raja said, 'Prime Minister, it's extraordinary! The ornaments and the sari I bought – I took the Junior Rani's measurements – but nothing fits!'

Then the wild monkey bent to touch the Raja's feet in *pranam* and spoke up: 'These things are from the kingdom of magic. No one but the highly fortunate or the deeply pious can wear a sari spun by a divine princess or a garland gathered by a snake maiden. Maharaj, put them in the royal treasury and give them to your future daughter-in-law.'

The monkey's suggestion astonished the Raja. Smiling he said to the Prime Minister, 'Did you hear the monkey? I've no son yet, so how will I give them to a daughter-in-law? Prime Minister, order the goldsmiths to make new ornaments for the Junior Rani, have the weavers loom new saris for her. These ornaments and this sari – deposit them in the royal treasury; when I have a daughter-in-law she shall wear them.'

The Prime Minister went off to the goldsmiths to order new jewellery for the Junior Rani. And the Raja, holding the monkey, went to find the elder Rani.

The ill-regarded Senior Rani, after wiping the Raja's feet gently with the torn end of her sari, bade him tearfully be seated on her tatty quilt in her dilapidated room. 'Maharaj, welcome – though my room is humble, my quilt torn. Have I any other seat to offer you? Alas, Maharaj, after so long you have returned, but I am so unfortunate that still I can offer you but a torn quilt for your seat.'

The Rani's words brought tears to the Raja's eyes. Seated on that tatty quilt in that shabby room he placed the baby monkey in the Senior Rani's lap and said, 'Maharani, your quilt may be torn, your room cracked, but they are a hundred thousand times better than the golden throne and the golden chamber of the Junior Rani. Here is affection, here is concern, here are soft words; there – none of those things. Rani, I spent seven ship-loads of gold on ornaments and a sari, and the Junior Rani rejected them all; for you, with one worthless cowrie I bought a monkey, and you took it with affection. I will not let you stay like this, Rani. I must go now, but I shall return. Careful though, do not let the Junior Rani know of this. If she hears I have been to you she will become a demon! You, and even I, may be poisoned.'

With these words of consolation and warning, the Raja went away. And the Senior Rani retired into her shabby room and began to bring up the monkey child on milk and bananas.

Thus time passed. In the Junior Rani's seven-storeyed palace the seven hundred maids continued to wait; and in the dilapidated room of the Senior Rani, lying on the tatty quilt, the monkey grew up. Day after day went by, month after month, year after year. The trials of the Senior Rani did not lessen, her rice remained coarse-grained, her saris remained coarse-woven. She sat in her shabby room, distressed, with only the monkey for company, and gazed tearfully at the seven-storeyed palace of the Junior Rani with its seven flower gardens. Whenever the monkey looked at her face he saw tears in her eyes, never a smile.

One day he said, 'Now Ma, tell me why you are crying? Why you are suffering so? Whenever you look at the palace, why these tears, Ma? What is there to make you weep?'

The Senior Rani replied, 'Oh little one, my all is there. My seven-storeyed palace is there, my seven hundred servants are there, my seven chestfuls of jewellery are there, so are my seven flower gardens. And, little one, so too is the Raja's Junior Rani, my co-wife. That witch has enchanted the Raja and snatched my palace, my servants and my seven chestfuls of jewellery and now lives blissfully in the golden pavilion in the flower garden; she took away the Raja, my entire treasure, and made me a street beggar. Oh, do you really want to know my woes! I was the daughter of a Raja, and a Raja's wife. I had seven hundred servants, a seven-storeyed palace and a princely husband after my heart. I had all that, but – who knows what curse was upon me – I lost it all, because I did not give the Raja a golden prince. Alas, how many sins I must have committed in previous lives, how many secret plans I must have foiled unknowingly, how many mothers I must have offended to have been reduced in this life to a beggar – all my pride, husbandly affection and hope of a son gone for nothing! Oh little one, I am like a stone now, so much insult and anguish have been my lot!'

Speaking these sad words had brought floods of tears to the Rani's eyes. The monkey crept into his Mother's lap, stood up and wiped away her tears saying, 'Ma, you must not cry. I shall dispel your distress, give you back your seven-storeyed palace, your seven flower gardens and your seven hundred servants, and make you once more a Rani seated beside the Raja in the golden pavilion with a golden prince in your lap – if I don't, I'm no true monkey. Do everything I tell you and you will regain your wealth and honour.'

There were still tears in the corners of the Rani's eyes, but now there was a smile at the corners of her mouth. With a tearful laugh she said, 'O little one, I have said so many prayers in temples, offered *puja* at so many pilgrimage places, but I've yet to hold my prince. Can you, a mere monkey – forgive me – by sheer devotion or divine potions really restore me as Rani, give me a royal child? Let it be, let my Raja live happily as he is, let my co-wife live happily too, I'll remain lost in my sorrows: don't attempt this impossible task. It's late – you must sleep.'

'No Ma,' said the monkey, 'if you don't listen to me, I won't go to sleep.'

The Rani replied, 'You must go to sleep, the night is deep. Clouds have rolled up from east and west, rain is about to split the sky, sleep is stealing over the entire kingdom, you too must sleep. Whatever you want to say will wait until tomorrow, today you must sleep. The door of my shabby room is locked – the storm is rising; look, I have laid out the quilt – it is cold, my little one, come close to me, come to your mother's breast, it's time to rest.'

The monkey nodded his head against the Rani's breast and dropped off to sleep. She laid herself down on the torn quilt and immediately dropped off too.

The night passed. The Junior Rani lay stretched on her divan, surrounded by flowers, the Raja beside her; while the Senior Rani lay on her tatty quilt, surrounded by the noise of the wind and the rain.

Morning came. The palace watchmen signalled the end of the night's final quarter, the palace musicians began to play a dawn raga, and the Raja and Rani awoke.

The Raja washed his face in crystal water poured from a golden pitcher, was dressed in his royal robes and descended to hold court. The Junior Rani lay on her flowery gold bed fanned by flowers, turned on her side and went back to sleep.

And what did the Senior Rani do?

When the golden sunshine peered into her face in that shabby room, she arose. She looked first one way, then the other, in this direction and that – no monkey! The Rani searched every corner of every room, the roof thatch and even the branches of the trees – no monkey! The Senior Rani began to cry.

Where had the monkey gone?

At the end of the night he had left the Rani sleeping in her shabby room and gone to the Raja's court.

The Raja was holding his durbar. The Council of Ministers surrounded him, sepoys guarded each doorway, everywhere people milled. The Rani's monkey pushed through the crowd, slipped through the hands of the sepoys and touched the Raja's feet: 'Maharaj, I am the bearer of great tidings. Ma is to have a child.'

The Raja responded, 'What's that you say, monkey? Is this true? Senior Rani, Forsaken Rani – to have a child? If this is a lie I'm warning you, monkey – I'll have your head and your mother the Rani's head too.'

'That's my worry, Maharaj,' said the monkey. 'Now give me a blessing, I must go back.'

The Raja took off his pearl necklace and dismissed the monkey. The monkey went dancing back to the Forsaken Rani in her shabby room and found her crying.

He wiped away the tears from her eyes and the dust from her body and said, 'Look Mother, look what I have brought you! Though you are the Rani of a Raja you haven't a proper necklace, only some wooden beads – put on these pearls!'

The Rani stared at the necklace in the monkey's hand and said, 'Where did it come from? It's from the neck of the Raja himself! When I was his Rani I threaded it for him – where did you find it? Tell me, monkey, did the Raja discard it, did you pick it up in the grounds of the palace?'

The monkey said, 'No Ma, I didn't pick it up. Are necklaces made for the Raja by the Rani's hands left lying about?'

'Then did you steal it from the Raja's chamber?'

The monkey tut-tutted: 'For shame, Ma – one should not steal! No, I brought good news that made the Raja happy and so he gave me this necklace.'

'But little one, wretched creature, you're just a forest monkey – what tidings could you have found lying here in my lap in this shabby room, that you should run to the palace at dawn to deliver them?'

Said the monkey, 'Ma, I dreamt I had a brother, a baby born to you; and this baby would be enthroned as Raja. I ran to tell the Raja the news – "Maharaj Mashai, Ma will have a child." The Raja felt so happy he took off his necklace and gave it to me.'

The Rani said, 'Oh! Today the Raja hears he has a child, tomorrow he will hear it is a lie! Today the Raja took off his necklace and gave it to you, tomorrow he will order your head to be removed! Alas alack! what have you done? At least before we had a handful of food and a place to sleep, and I saw him once a year – why did you do away with all that? Oh, why have you brought about this ruin? Why did you circulate such a story? Now we're in terrible trouble.'

The monkey said, 'Don't be so worried, Ma. Why worry? Just keep quiet for ten months. Everyone will get to hear about it – the Senior Rani's going to have a child. Then, when the Raja wants to see the child, I will provide you with a golden prince to cuddle which you will show him. Now come, it's time to eat, I'm hungry.'

The Rani said, 'Come then, little one, come along. I've kept you water in a bowl and brought fruit from the trees, come and eat.'

She squatted down on a broken wooden stool and helped the monkey with his meal.

And the Raja went to the Junior Rani's chamber.

The Junior Rani had just woken from a bad dream and was lying on her gold divan thinking about it, when the Raja appeared with the news: 'Have you heard, Junior Rani, the Senior Rani's to have a child! My main worry was, who to leave the throne to, and after all this time the worry's over. If it's a boy I'll make him Raja, if it's a girl, I'll give the kingdom to my son-in-law. What a worry it was, Rani, but now my mind's a bit relieved.'

'What's that to me,' the Rani replied, 'I've got enough troubles of my own, I can't be bothered with those of others!'

90

'What do you mean Rani?' said the Raja. 'Why such words on such a happy occasion? We have a royal child, a future heir for the throne – why be so glum about it? Rani, everyone in the palace is smiling, why are you looking so grim?'

The Rani repeated, 'I can't be bothered! Whose son will be Raja, whose daughter will inherit the kingdom, who'll sit on the throne, I can't worry about all these things. I've got more than enough to cope with, I can't think about whether other people's children are alive or dead. Goodness! there's no sleep with all this babbling in the morning, I've got a headache, I'm going to take a bath.'

Full of anger, her eight bangles and ten anklets ajangle, the Junior Rani stalked off.

The Raja raged too, because the Junior Rani had referred to death in relation to the prince. Gloomily he retreated to the outer apartments. The quarrel between the Raja and the Rani persisted. The Raja stopped seeing the Junior Rani, nor did he go to the Senior Rani's room – if the Junior Rani were to hear about it she might try to poison the Senior Rani! So the Raja stayed alone in the outer quarters.

A month went by – two months – then three: still the Raja and Rani were not reconciled. For four months the quarrelling went on. In the fifth month the Forsaken Rani's pet monkey paid another visit on the Raja. The Raja asked, 'What's up, monkey? What's the news?'

'Maharaj, Ma is feeling very sad! She can't take coarse rice any more, and so she's becoming weak.'

'I had no idea of this,' said the Raja. 'Prime Minister, the best rice and fifty varieties of curry all served on gold plates and bowls for the Senior Rani! From today, whatever I eat, the Senior Rani will eat too. And Prime Minister, present the monkey with a thousand mohurs.'

The Prime Minister paid the monkey and went away to the royal kitchens. And the Rani's monkey went back to the Rani carrying a purse of gold mohurs.

The Rani asked him, 'Where have you been? It's getting late – when shall I take my bath, cook or eat?'

'You don't have to cook any more, Ma,' the monkey said. 'From the palace kitchens, gold plates and gold bowls full of fine rice and fifty varieties of curry are coming – quickly, take your bath.'

The Rani went for her bath. The monkey took a handful of mohurs and went to the bazaar. With sixteen whole mohurs he hired sixteen hut-builders, bought sixteen cart-loads of straw and sixteen hundred bamboos. With these sixteen hundred bamboos and sixteen cart-loads of straw, in the twinkling of an eye the sixteen hut-builders made the Forsaken Rani's shabby hut as good as new. A new quilt lay on the bedroom floor, a new wooden stool stood in the kitchen, while from the palace sixteen Brahmin cooks brought rice for the Rani: everything was covered by the sixteen mohurs.

Then the Forsaken Rani returned from her bath. She stood staring – a new hut! with a new roof! and new straw! and a new quilt on the floor! and a new sari on the rack! The Rani was astounded. She said to the monkey, 'Little one, this was a shabby place when I went to the ghat – coming back, it's new! How is it so?'

The monkey said, 'Ma, Raja Mashai gave me mohurs. With these mohurs I made the room new, got the new quilt and the new stool, and now you can eat hot rice from a gold plate, drink warm milk from a gold bowl.'

The Rani sat down to eat. How long it had been since she ate rice from a gold plate, washed her face in water from a gold pitcher, drank water from a gold bowl – and yet she did not feel happy. She began to eat the royal feast and thought to herself – today the Raja sends me rice on a gold plate, tomorrow perhaps I will be sent to the execution ground.

One month – two months – three months passed by in apprehension. The Senior Rani's new room became older, the thatch in the roof sprang leaks, the straw began to fall out. The monkey went to see the Raja.

'Well monkey, what's the latest?'

'Maharaj, shall I speak in fear or fearlessly?'

'Speak fearlessly,' said the Raja.

'Maharaj, Ma is very unhappy in her shabby room. There are cracks in the doors, holes in the roof and the winter cold gets in. Mother has no quilt to wrap around her and no firewood to burn, she trembles with cold all night.'

'Is that so! Is that so!' cried the Raja. 'I should have been told. Monkey, bring your Mother to the palace. I shall have a chamber decorated.'

The monkey said, 'I'm afraid to do that, Maharaj. The Junior Rani may administer poison.'

'Do not be afraid. I shall put your Rani in a new palace and make a moat all round it with guards at the gates so that the Junior Rani cannot gain entrance. There the Senior Rani will stay, looked after by her deaf-mute nurse and you, her pet child.'

Said the monkey, 'Maharaj, I shall fetch my Mother.'

'Go Prime Minister, get ready the palace,' ordered the Raja.

The Prime Minister hired an army of artisans and soon had the new palace decorated for the Senior Rani.

And so the Forsaken Rani left her shabby room, left behind her shabby quilt, put on a gold sari and entered the new palace. She sat upon a gold divan, ate rice from a gold plate, proffered alms to the poor and afflicted, and there was rejoicing in the kingdom; but the Junior Rani's body burned all over.

The witch Brahmani was the Junior Rani's confidante, her bosom companion, her dearest friend. The Junior Rani gave instructions:'Tell my confidante to come, I must speak to her.'

The Rani had commanded – and immediately the old woman came.

The Rani said, 'Come Bhai, dearest friend, how are you? Have a seat.'

The witch Brahmani sat down beside the Junior Rani and said, 'What is it, Bhai, you called me? Why so glum-faced, why the tears in the corner of your eyes?'

'My whole head's spinning,' said the Rani. 'My co-wife is back, sporting a gold sari, living in a new palace, she's the Raja's favourite Rani! That beggar, that Forsaken Rani, is suddenly the favoured Rani, she's all over the palace! Oh Bahmi! look at me, I'm on fire, get me poison so I can die, I can't bear her having all the affection!'

'Shame! shame on you, dear! How can you say such things! Why should you take poison? The Forsaken Rani may be Rani for today, but tomorrow she'll be a beggar again and you will be Favoured Rani.'

The Favoured Rani said, 'No, Bhai – I've no wish to live like this. Soon the Favoured Rani will have a son and he will have the kingdom! People will say, Oh – what a jewel the Forsaken Rani has borne, she's a true Raja's mother! And look at the Favoured Rani, what an accursed creature she is – she had all the Maharaja's love, still she could not produce a prince! Fie upon her, do not even look at her unlucky face: mention her name and you will have misfortune all day. Bhai, that shame I cannot bear. Get me some poison – either I must take it, or my co-wife must have it.'

'Hush Rani,' Brahmani said. 'Someone may be listening. Don't worry – I shall get you some poison on the quiet and you can give it to the Forsaken Rani. Now let me go, I must go in search of poison.'

'Go Bhai,' said the Rani. 'But remember, it must be strong, so she dies as soon as she takes it.'

'Do not fear, Rani, have no fear! The Senior Rani will take the poison tomorrow, and that will be the end of her life's ambition to give birth, you may rely on it.'

The witch went looking for poison. She went to the forest. Deep inside its thickets, in the depths of the night she enchanted a sleeping snake and extracted from its fangs the deadliest of poison.

The Junior Rani prepared poisoned *moong*-drops, milk sweets and other delicacies. She spread them on a tray and said to Brahmani, 'Here you are, Bhai, take these poisoned sweets and offer them to the Senior Rani.'

Brahmani picked up the tray and made her way to the new palace.

The Senior Rani said, 'Come along, come in, where have you been keeping yourself all this time? Because I was forsaken did you forget me?'

'How could I?' said the witch. 'You fed me and looked after me, how could I forget you? Here, I've brought you some *moong*-drops, some milk sweets and other delicacies.'

The Rani noticed how carefully arranged were the sweets brought by the old woman. Gaily she gave her two handfuls of mohurs as reward: Brahmani smiled and went away.

The Rani ate one of the milk sweets, and lost the taste in her tongue. She ate one of the *moong*-drops, and her throat went dry. She tried another delicacy, and her chest began to burn. She cried out to the monkey, 'Brahmani gave me something to eat! I feel terrible, I think I'm dying.'

'Lie down, Ma, lie down, you'll recover,' said the monkey.

The Rani stood up, and the poison went to her head. She saw darkness everywhere, her head was in turmoil – she fell on the marbled floor.

The monkey cradled the Rani's head in his lap, felt her pulse with his hand, opened her eyelids and looked at her eyes – she was unconscious, insensate!

The monkey lifted his golden goddess on to her gold bed and ran to the forest in search of medicine. Who knows what creepers and roots he collected there? He ground them up together and fed them to the Senior Rani.

The news was sent to the palace – the Senior Rani has taken poison! The Raja jumped up and hurried to his Rani. The Ministers ran after him. After them came the royal physician reciting endless mantras. And after him followed the whole household, guards, bearers, maidservants and all.

'Maharaj,' said the monkey, 'why have so many people come? I am treating Mother, she is all right, she needs rest. Send everyone away.'

The Raja instructed the royal physician to test the poisoned sweets. He deputed the Prime Minister to look after the kingdom. He himself stayed near the Senior Rani.

For three days and three nights the Senior Rani lay unconscious. On the fourth day she opened her eyes.

The monkey came to the Raja and told him the news: 'Maharaj, the Senior Rani has recovered, and you have a baby heir and ruler.'

The Raja took off a diamond necklace and gave it to the monkey: 'Let us go, monkey, and pay a visit on the Senior Rani and the prince.'

But the monkey replied, 'Maharaj, the astrologers have decided that if you look upon the boy's face you will go blind. After his marriage you may see the prince, now let us take a look at the Senior Rani, see what the Junior Rani has inflicted on her.'

The Raja saw that as a result of the poison the body of the Senior Rani was blue, she lay as lifeless as a corpse. He could hardly recognise her!

The Raja returned to his palace and had the Junior Rani incarcerated, and the old witch woman's head shaved and butter milk poured over it: then she was stuck the wrong way around on the back of a donkey and sent trotting out of the kingdom.

That done, the Raja ordered, 'Prime Minister, today is an auspicious day: after many years I have an heir and ruler. Let lamps burn in every home and let alms be donated from the royal treasury to the poor and afflicted – make sure no beggar is left out.'

At the royal command the Prime Minister put lights on every path in the city, gave fireworks to every house and donated alms from the royal treasury to the poor and needy – and there was joy throughout the land.

Thus did the next ten years pass in festive spirit, with *pujas* before the temple of the gods and sacrifice at the feet of Mother Kali.

Then the Raja called the monkey and said, 'Ten years are over, let us see the boy!'

'Maharaj, first find the boy a bride, get him married, then you can see his face! If you look now, you'll go blind.'

The Raja followed the monkey's bidding and sent heralds far and wide. Countless princesses in countless countries were uncovered, but the Raja did not approve any of them. At length, the herald from the kingdom of Patali brought a portrait in a gold casket of a golden girl. Her complexion was lustrous, her eyebrows like twin bows, her eyes large and wide, her lips constantly asmile, and when she dishevelled her hair, it fell right to her feet. This was the girl the Raja selected.

He called the monkey and said, 'I have chosen a wife for my son. The morrow is an auspicious day for a wedding – let them be wed.'

The monkey responded, 'Maharaj, tomorrow evening, send the bridegroom's palanquin and the bearers to my Mother's door and I will accompany them to the wedding.'

'As you wish,' said the Raja, 'I have listened to you for ten years: if I do not see the boy then, there will be hell to pay.'

'Maharaj, do not worry. You must go to the bride's house, tomorrow we shall bring the bridegroom.'

Lest he catch sight of the Rani's son by mischance and make himself blind, the Raja hurried away to the home of the bride.

And the monkey went to the Senior Rani in her palace.

As soon as she heard about the wedding she began to weep, thinking to herself – where will I get the boy from, how will I be able to deceive the Raja!

The monkey came and said, 'Please, Mother, get up. Get a bride-groom's outfit, bring a wedding crown, make me a sweetmeat child and dress it to be wed.'

'O little one, aren't you afraid for your life? How can you dress up a sweetmeat child and marry it? Will a trick like that deceive the Raja? Please, stop this now, deceit has made me the Raja's favoured Rani; for my sins my co-wife poisoned me; with great good luck I survived – how can I think of deceiving the Raja yet again? You must desist, you must not add to the burden of my sins! Please call the Raja here, I will confess everything.'

'Where will I find the Raja now?' said the monkey. 'To reach the bride's house takes two days. The Raja is on his way. Listen to me, make the sweetmeat child. The Raja will be watching the road to see if the bridegroom is coming; if he does not come, the insult will be great. Ma, do not worry, you are sending a sweetmeat child to be wed, but if Shasthi* is merciful, she will send you a blessed child of your own.'

The Rani had faith in the monkey; she made a sweetmeat child after her own heart. She dressed it in wedding finery, placed a crown upon its head and silver-threaded slippers upon its feet.

Without any sound the monkey placed the sweetmeat bridegroom inside the palanquin and drew the coloured curtains: only its two tiny feet, wearing the silver-threaded slippers, were left showing.

Sixteen bearers lifted the palanquin on to their shoulders. With the monkey in a turban and loincloth at the front, flags flying, drums beating and torches flaming, the bridegroom's party departed. The Rani was left alone in her dark room calling out prayers to avert the danger.

The sixteen palanquin bearers, the bearers of the torches, the drummers and the riders accompanying the bridegroom travelled all night, their flutes tooting, their torches flaring, their horses neighing, until they reached the lake at Dignagar.

It was dawn. The torches were finished, the horses were fatigued, the bearers were dead-beat, the drummers had cramps in their hands.

The monkey ordered tents to be pitched at the lakeside. The palanquin he ordered set down before the lake shrine of Shasthi; then he dismissed everyone, saying to the Prime Minister, 'Minister Mashai, Raja's orders – no one to see the bridegroom today, it's most inauspicious.'

The Prime Minister proclaimed the order. And so, once the royal retinue had bathed in the lake, taken their food and lain down inside their tents, no one came near the shrine beneath the banyan tree. When the village women came to pay their respects to Shasthi, the Raja's guards shooed them away.

That day there was no *puja* to the goddess at the foot of the banyan tree, no offerings given. Shasthi became impatient with hunger, her throat began to itch with thirst. The monkey watched and smiled.

Time wore on. Not a drop of water had moistened the goddess's lips, she began to fidget inside her wooden frame while her black cat mewed piteously and vainly. Then the monkey put his plan into action: after opening the curtains of the palanquin, he vanished.

*Goddess of children.

Goddess Shasthi told herself – good riddance! This sun is frying me, I'll step down from my frame and have a look for some holy offerings, some chick peas and bananas. She had a good search and while searching, she saw the sweetmeat child. The temptation was too great for her: immediately she invoked the Lullaby Aunts.

Daytime in Dignagar meant nighttime in the land of sleep. The Lullaby Aunts had been up all night lulling every one of Shasthi's small charges to sleep – it had taken till morning in the case of the bride-to-be – and they were about to close their own eyes for a nap when Goddess Shasthi's invocation reached them. The two Lullaby Aunts, who were sisters, woke up, got up, left the land of sleep and came to Dignagar. *Pranam*ing the feet of Shasthi they asked her, 'Goddess, you've called us at midday?'

The Goddess replied, 'My dears, I know it's rather late, but today I've had nothing to eat. Just be dears, will you, put everyone everywhere in this land to sleep – I want to eat the sweetmeat child sitting inside that dooly.'

At the Goddess's word, the Lullaby Aunts worked their magic, and everyone in the land felt sleepy. The cowherds in the fields, the babies in their houses, the babies' mothers and the babies' elder sisters in their play-houses, all dropped off. The Raja's men around the shrine of Shasthi and the boys and girls in the village school dropped off. The curly pipe of the hookah in the Prime Minister's mouth drooped, so did the cane in the village pundit's hand. Night came to Dignagar in the middle of the day. The Lullaby Aunts brought sleep to every eye – only the foxes and stray dogs on the paths, the Raja's horses and elephants resting beside the lake, the wild birds in the depths of the forest and the Rani's monkey waiting on his tree branch, remained wakeful. Apart, that is, from the wild cats, the water cats, the tree cats and the house cats – they stayed awake too.

Then Goddess Shasthi opened up the palanquin and took the sweetmeat child in her hand. The scent of the sweetmeat pulled the squirrels down from the trees, the wild cats out from the forest, the otters up from the water and the house cats away from their corners. The ten fingers of the sweetmeat child Goddess Shasthi gave to the cats; the sweetmeat hands, the sweetmeat feet, the sweetmeat trunk and head she ate herself; and two sweetmeat ears she donated to the Lullaby Aunts.

The Aunts went back to the land of sleep; and sleep lifted from the bridegroom's party beside the Dignagar lake, lifted also from the eyes of the villagers in their homes. Goddess Shasthi, wiping her mouth, was just hastening back to her frame when the monkey suddenly jumped down from the tree and said – 'Goddess, where are you off to? Give me back my sweetmeat child! If you don't give back what you stole, I'll spread the scandal everywhere.'

The Goddess became frightened and said: 'Off with you, Pink Face, stop chattering, I must be gone; I can't show myself to all and sundry.'

'That's not to be,' countered the monkey. 'Give my boy back, or else. If you don't, I'll drown you, frame and all, in the lake – then you'll know what happens to a Goddess who steals.'

The Goddess was mortified. Quaking with fear she whispered, 'Shsh, dear, there are ears everywhere. I have gobbled up your sweetmeat child – how can I return it? Look there, underneath the banyan tree, look at my children playing – choose any one of them you fancy, take it to the wedding, I will bless it such that its forsaken mother will believe it to be her own. Now leave me alone.'

'I can't see them, Goddess, where are these children beneath the banyan tree? Give me Goddess's eyes, so I can see the children of Shasthi!' Then the Goddess passed her hand over the monkey's eyes, and the monkey received divine vision.

All at once he saw the kingdom of children, where there are only children: children at home, children outdoors, playing in ponds, beside ghats, in the branches of trees, among the green grass – wherever he turned his eyes, the monkey saw hordes of boys, flocks of girls. Some were black, some were fair-skinned, others dark as Krishna. Some wore ankle bells, some had waist charms, some wore gold necklaces around their necks. They were playing flutes, or shaking rattles, or jingling ankle-bells as they stamped their feet, or just dancing around waving their tiny hands. Some wore red shoes on their feet, some wore coloured caps on their heads, others had wrapped themselves in costly *chadars* made of flower-printed muslin. Many were skinny but many were chubby too; some were dare-devils, others were good as gold. One group was dashing and clattering about on wooden horses, a second was fishing in the lake, a third was taking a dip, a fourth gathering blooms from a tree, a fifth plucking fruits from a branch – on all sides there was playful fighting, laughter and tears. What a wondrous land – a realm of dreams! It was always holiday time here, always play-time; there were no schools, no schoolmasters and no schoolmasters' canes.

There was only the lake's dark water, the reed bank at its edge and beyond these, far far away, mango and jackfruit groves with long-tailed parrots in the branches, round-eyed *boal* fishes in the river, and swarms of mosquitoes in the *kachu* hedges. Over there lived the Village Aunties who fashioned sweet cakes out of puffed rice, while in the pomegranate trees beside their homes, Lord Shiva danced. At the riverside grew a *janti* tree loaded with *janti* fruit, in the fields a blue horse roamed and a golden peacock from Gaur strutted and preened. Children, leading the blue horse and the golden peacock, beating a drum and striking a gong, were leading a procession: they were going to the land of Kamalapuli – the land of orange cakes – for the wedding of the Puntu Rani. The monkey joined them.

It was a land of parrots, swarming everywhere: they perched and husked rice, they sat in the trees and chattered, and they constantly played with the children. The people ploughed the earth with cows and bulls, but picked their teeth with diamonds! It was a novel sort of place – morning broke and evening fell in the blinking of an eye: very peculiar, a nursery-rhyme land – where the rhymes were for real. Water shimmered over gently shifting sand and beside it sat a bunch of boys riding in a swing while counting out cowrie shells in sixes. They had been trying to catch fish; some of them had fishbones pricking their feet, others had the sun in their faces. Nearby, the sons of fishermen lay dozing wrapped in nets – when all at once the rain came pitter-patter, the river rose and flooded, and the bunch of boys had to abandon their wooden swing, cease counting their cowries and scatter to their own corners at home. The fishes they left on the path were grabbed by the kites, the fishing-rods were nabbed by large frogs and the boys reached home cross, to be consoled by their mothers with warm milk. And then, beside the water shimmering over the shifting sand, Lord Shiva arrived and moored his boat with three brides on board – one bride to cook and serve, one to sit and eat and a third bride, who got nothing and so went back to her father's house. The monkey followed her there.

As she landed at the ghat, girls were bathing and combing out their long black hair. Two fishes surfaced, a *rui* on one side and a *katla* on the other: one got grabbed by a priest, and the other was grabbed by a parrot sitting in a loaded boat. When an otter saw this he took the parrot by the wing and a fish by the fin and started to dance. A mother, standing by her door, saw everything and began to bounce her baby boy, calling out, 'O Otter, give us a glance, see my Khoka – what a dance!'

What a beauty the boy was! Instantly, the monkey snatched him. In that moment the land of dream, the spell of Shasthi, vanished: the long-tailed parrots flew away leaving the sky greeny-blue; Lord Shiva's boat drifted out of sight; the girls in striped saris turned about and went away; the cat heading the wedding procession to the Puntu Rani put on his cummerbund, picked up his gift of puffed rice brought to please the new mother-in-law and, accompanied by four palanquin bearers and four maidservants, mingled with the darkness of the mango groves; and the otters dancing on the tamarind leaves disappeared inside the foliage. The whole land had sunk below the ground!

The monkey looked about him – where was the Goddess? where had she gone? He was alone beside the lake, cradling a boy in his arms! The monkey called everyone to see the handsome creature and placed him in the palanquin. That evening, with torches flaming and music playing, they left Dignagar.

At the bride's home in the land of Patali, the Raja sat thinking: shouldn't the monkey be here by now? Has he played a trick on me? When I get back I'll have his head. The bride was thinking: what will the bridegroom look like? The parents of the bride were thinking sadly: soon our sweetheart will leave our home! And the palace servants were thinking: now our work's done, perhaps we'll see the bridegroom from the palace roof.

There was a rumbling of drums, a trilling of flutes, a whinnying of horses, a sparkle of lights and the monkey appeared with the bridegroom. The Raja took the boy's hand and led him to the throne, the bride's father joined his daughter's to his son-in-law's hand, the women of the neighbourhood bowed low before the bridegroom in ceremonial welcome and gave ululating voice – and the bridegroom and bride were wedded.

The next day the Raja gathered up his son and the new wife, the flutes played, the horses neighed and they all, including the monkey, went home. Overnight the royal palace of Patali became empty, its darling daughter gone.

In the Raja's kingdom, meanwhile, the Senior Rani had wept for two nights and two days in worry and then fallen asleep in the early morning. She had a dream: Goddess Shasthi herself said, 'Rani, arise!

Go and see, your own son is coming home.' When the Rani awoke, standing at her door she heard her maids call her, 'Get ready, Rani, wear a special sari, your son and daughter-in-law are here!'

The Rani put on the special sari and came out. She saw that the Raja truly had brought a son and daughter-in-law! With a smile on her face she took them in her lap and by the grace of Shasthi her mind no longer dwelt on her sad past life or on the sweetmeat child; in fact, having wanted a child so much, she decided that she must have dreamt the entire story of the sweetmeat child.

As a dowry, the Raja gave his son the kingdom; he also made the monkey Prime Minister and gave his son's wife the eight pairs of eight-thousand-jewelled bangles and the ten pairs of gold anklets from the kingdom of magic. On the arms of the princess the bangles looked as red as blood, while the anklets jingled and sparkled to absolute perfection.

So jealous was the Junior Rani that she died of a burst heart.

(1896)

PRIMORDIAL

Manik Banerji/Bandopadhyay

Bhikhu was having a bad time this rainy season. The very first day, he and his gang had attacked the office of a merchant, Baikuntha Shaha, in nearby Bashantipur, and been caught. Out of eleven men only Bhikhu, nursing a deep stab wound, had escaped.

That night he made his way ten miles to a ruined old bridge and hid himself all day in a reed bank beneath it, his body half-submerged in mud. The next night he went another eighteen miles so as to reach Prahlad Bagdi's house at Chitalpur.

Prahlad did not offer to shelter him.

He looked at the shoulder wound and remarked, 'Looks like a bad one, pal. It's infected. Bound to swell. If people see it, what'll happen to me? If you hadn't gone and murdered – '

'Right now I could murder you, Prahlad.'

'No chance in this life, old pal.'

The forest was not far, only about five miles to the north. Bhikhu had no choice but to go there, to the most inaccessible part. Prahlad himself cut some bamboo and constructed a platform among the thickets. Then he covered it with palm leaves. He said, 'The rain's driven all the tigers up into the hills. Long as a snake doesn't get you, you should be OK, Bhikhu.'

'What about food?'

'I've given you pressed rice and molasses, haven't I? I'll be back in a couple of days with some cooked rice; I can't make it every day – people'll start talking.'

After dressing the wound with leaves and creepers and promising to return, Prahlad went away. That night Bhikhu got fever. The following day he was dimly conscious that Prahlad had predicted right: his

103

shoulder had become septic. His right arm was as tight as a drum and he could no longer move his hand.

There he lay on the narrow platform in that monsoon forest where not even tigers lived, continually soaked by rain, infuriated by mosquitoes and other insects, invaded hourly by leeches in every portion of his body; somehow he survived the battle with pain and fever for two days and two nights. Lashing rain, sultry heat and maddening bites combined without let-up to stifle the very breath from his body. The few *biris* Prahlad had left him to smoke were soon finished. The pressed rice was enough for three or four days, but the molasses ran out sooner. That did not stop red ants, greedy for it, from swarming all over the platform. Disappointed, they took ceaseless revenge on Bhikhu's flesh.

Cursing Prahlad to the foulest of deaths, Bhikhu fought for his life. On the morning Prahlad had said he would return, the water vessel became empty. Bhikhu waited till afternoon and then, tormented by thirst, managed to drag himself and the vessel to the nearest ditch, half-fill the vessel and then drag himself back on to the platform; his suffering was indescribable. When hunger too became intolerable, he chewed some pressed rice. After that he gradually squashed the insects and the ants. He also attached the leeches to his wound, hoping that they would suck the poisoned blood. When once he caught a glimpse of a green snake in the foliage above his head he watched the spot for a full two hours and for another hour or two after that he swatted the leaves around him with a stick, hoping the noise would drive any snakes away.

He refused to die – not here, in this rotten place. A wild animal might not endure it, but a human being must.

Prahlad had gone to visit his relatives. He did not return the day he said he would. He drank so much toddy at a wedding feast he became oblivious of everything. During those three days he did not once think how Bhikhu was surviving in the forest.

Bhikhu's wound meanwhile festered and began to ooze red pus. His body became swollen. The fever abated slightly, but the pain was so excruciating he was stunned, as if stupefied by drink. Hunger and thirst no longer bothered him. The leeches feasting on his body became so gorged they dropped off voluntarily, and he did not notice. He kicked the water vessel over by mistake and it broke; his pressed rice inside his bundle became soaked and started to decompose; and at night hyenas, lured by the stink of the wound, prowled beneath the platform.

104

Turning up at last in the afternoon, seeing Bhikhu's state, Prahlad shook his head gravely. He had brought along a bowl of cooked rice, some pieces of fried fish and some curry. When Bhikhu had not touched anything by evening Prahlad himself ate the food. Then he went home to fetch a small bamboo ladder and Bharat, his brother-in-law.

They laid Bhikhu on the ladder and took him home. They placed him out of sight on a straw bed resting on a specially built platform.

So tough was his constitution that without any medical treatment or nursing, the moribund Bhikhu, lying in this shelter, within a month defeated death. But his right arm was not in good shape. It had shrivelled like the branch of a dead tree and now it hung insensate, disabled. At first he could move it a bit, but quite soon that power too disappeared.

It was after this that he took to coming downstairs when no one was around, manhandling himself down the bamboo ladder with his good arm. One evening he did something really impulsive.

Prahlad was away, out drinking with Bharat. His sister was at the ghat. His wife was just settling her son down to sleep when she caught sight of Bhikhu, saw the expression on his face and tried to rush out. Bhikhu caught hold of her hand.

Prahlad's wife was a Bagdi however, and Bagdis are fighters. One good hand and a weakened body could not capture her. She jerked her hand away, abused Bhikhu violently and escaped. On Prahlad's return she told him everything.

Drink made Prahlad want to murder his ungrateful swine of a guest there and then. First he gave his wife a hiding with a bamboo stick, then he went in search of Bhikhu, but even he, drunk as he was, could see that to finish this particular job – however desirable – was easier said than done: Bhikhu was waiting for him, flourishing a sharp chopper in his left hand. Instead of trying to murder each other, they exchanged obscenities.

Finally Prahlad said, 'I spent seven rupees for you. Give me the money and get out of my house – scram!'

'Oi – what about the gold armlet I had in my waistband?' shouted Bhikhu. 'You stole it. First give it here, then I'll leave.'

'What do I know about your armlet, eh?'

'Give it back, Prahlad, if you know what's good for you. If you don't, I'll hack your head off with one blow like that fellow at Shaha's. Soon as you hand it over, I'll go.' But Bhikhu didn't get his armlet back. Bharat came in while they were quarelling, together he and his brother-in-law tackled Bhikhu. Apart from biting deep into Prahlad's arm, there was not much that the enfeebled, crippled Bhikhu could do. They beat him till he was half-dead and dumped him outside. Bhikhu's half-healed wound burst open and began to pour blood; he wiped it away with his hand, gasping for breath. No one knew where he got to in the darkness, but in the early hours the whole Bagdi community was thrown into chaos by Prahlad's house catching fire.

Prahlad hit his forehead in despair: 'Disaster! What a disaster! I sheltered that devil, now I'm ruined!'

But he did not inform on Bhikhu, for fear of what a police investigation might lead to.

That night, Bhikhu entered the second phase of his primitive, brutish life. There was a river near Chitalpur. After firing Prahlad's house Bhikhu stole a dinghy and drifted with the current of the river. Rowing was beyond him but by using a bamboo pole as a rudder he somehow kept the boat moving all night. Before it became light, the current had taken him quite a distance.

Bhikhu's main fear was that Prahlad would give his name to the police out of pure revenge, not caring if he incriminated himself. The law had been after him for a long time, and the Shaha murder would scarcely have made things easier for him. It would be dangerous to show his face within the area for at least a thirty miles radius around the spot. Bhikhu was desperate though. He had not eaten since the previous afternoon. His weary body was stiff with pain after its pummelling by two hefty men. Around dawn he managed to anchor the boat at the ghat of the local sub-divisional town. He took several dips in the river and eventually he washed away all trace of blood; then he went into the town. He was so famished his vision was dark. But he hadn't even a single pie coin on him to buy puffed rice. At the first gentleman he saw on the road to the bazaar he thrust out his hand and said, 'Give me two pice, Sir.'

Seeing the matted hair, tangled and dusty with ashes, the filthy and torn loincloth and the emaciated arm swinging like a strand of rope, the man felt pity. He tossed Bhikhu a pie coin.

'Only one, Baba?' said Bhikhu. 'Please give another.'

The man became annoyed: 'I've given you one – enough – push off.'

For an instant Bhikhu wanted to say something nasty. But he refrained. Instead, his reddish eyes glowered and he went straight to

106

a shop, bought puffed rice and started to wolf it in handfuls.

That was his initiation into beggary.

Within days he had picked up all the tricks of this ancient and public trade. The gestures and language of appeal seemed to have been his from birth. He no longer washed his body at all; and he made a sustained effort to knot his hair and encourage lice to breed in it. Often he scratched it with both hands like a madman, but he did not dare to chop it off. He also acquired a torn coat which he wore to hide his wound, never removing it even in the most sultry weather. But then, realising that his withered arm was his most compelling advertisement, he uncovered the limb by tearing the coat's right sleeve up to the armpit. He collected a tin mug and stick too.

From dawn to dusk he sat on the road near the bazaar beneath a tamarind tree, and begged. In the morning he ate a pie's worth of puffed rice; at midday he retreated to a deserted garden not far from the bazaar and under a banyan tree cooked himself some rice in a clay pot balanced on a few bricks, or maybe a little fish or some curry. His belly now full, he leant back against the trunk of the banyan and smoked a *biri* in comfort. After that he returned to his place under the tamarind.

The whole day he moaned piteously, 'Oh Baba! Give me one pie. Give to me and God will bless you. Oh Baba, one pie – '

Like many well-known maxims, 'One should never beg' is not particularly apt. During a typical day as many as a thousand people passed before Bhikhu one way or the other, and on average one in every fifty gave a pie or a half-pie. On the days when half-pies predominated, Bhikhu's income was five or six annas, but in general he earned about eight annas. Twice a week was market day. Then his income was seldom less than a whole rupee.

The rainy season came to an end. Both banks of the river grew white with *kash* grass. Bhikhu took over an abandoned thatched hut near the river, renting it from Binnu the boatman for eight annas a month. He slept in it at night. He had procured a tatty but thick quilt, the former property of a malaria victim, and made a snug bed of it using a heap of stolen straw. By begging from the town's bigger houses he obtained some torn clothes. These he bundled together and made into a kind of pillow. When a damp breeze blew from the river at night, chilling him, he would open the bundle and wrap himself in the rags.

Living in comfort with plenty to eat, Bhikhu did not take long to regain his earlier health. His chest grew broader, the muscles in his back and arms stronger each time he took exercise. His energy and vigour, pent up inside him, made his mood grow insolent and impatient. He still gave the beggar's customary whine, but when alms did not come, his temper flared. If people on the road, preoccupied, passed him by, he would curse them foully. And when the shopkeepers did not serve him extra measure for his single pie coin, he abused them also. When the women went to the ghat to bathe he would stand ogling, pretending to beg. Their alarm delighted him; when they asked him to move on, he stayed put, grinning arrogantly.

At night, in his home-made bed, he tossed restlessly. Never in his life had he been womanless. He yearned for past nights of recklessness.

In those days he caused mayhem swilling toddy in the drink shop, then staggering over to Bashi's for a wild time or going on the rampage in the small hours with his gang, killing and looting and then vanishing. He could clearly see the look of disbelief in a wife's eyes as he battered her husband, plainly hear the wail of a mother as she saw him make a jet of blood spurt from her son in the flickering glare of a torch – what could be more rip-roaring than sights and sounds like these? When, afterwards, he had had to flee the village and conceal himself in the forest he had still been deeply contented. Over the years almost all his gang had been caught and sent to jail but not he, except once. It happened when he and Rakhu Bagdi kidnapped the sister of Shripati Biswas: for that he got seven years, but was inside for only two. One rainy evening he leapt the high wall of the jail. After that he broke into several houses and singlehandedly, in broad daylight, held up various village women at the ghat and made off with their necklaces and bangles, before decamping across the sea to Hatiya beyond Noakhali district with Rakhu's wife in tow. Six months later he deserted her, returned and raided three villages in a row whose names he could not now remember, with three different gangs. Since then, of course, he had hacked the head off Baikuntha Shaha's second brother with a single blow.

What a life it had been; how low he had sunk today! A man who once had struck terror into people now exhausted his passion swearing at miserly passers-by. His stamina was unimpaired. But he no longer had anything on which to expend his energy. Late at night he observed the shopkeepers sitting alone before bundles of banknotes, doing their accounts, and he knew of many women who slept alone while their husbands were away. Instead of threatening them all with a weapon and making himself rich overnight, here he lay, as quiet as anything, beneath Binnu the boatman's thatched roof.

Stroking his wasted right arm in the darkness Bhikhu's frustration boiled over. He was a man of daring action among weak and timid mice, unable to use his strength only for lack of an arm. How could a man be so ill-fated?

He could just about stand this misfortune: there is, after all, some pleasure in self-denial. But he could not endure loneliness.

At the entrance to the bazaar there sat a beggar woman. She was not old and her body was trim. Below her knee, however, right down to the sole of her foot, she had a suppurating sore.

It earnt her more than Bhikhu's arm. Therefore she took special care to preserve it.

One day Bhikhu sat down next to her. 'That sore's not going to heal is it?'

The woman replied, 'Why not! With medicine it'd go.'

Bhikhu said earnestly, 'Then do it, do it quickly. Let it heal and you don't have to beg. I'll keep you.'

'Me with you?'

'Why not? Why shouldn't I? Food, clothes, you'll be better off. How can you say no to a man who wants you?'

The woman was not so easily charmed. Stuffing a tobacco leaf into her mouth she remarked, 'And when you chuck me out, will I get my sore back?'

Bhikhu vowed lifelong fidelity and tempted her with visions of happiness. But the beggar woman was unmoved. Bhikhu had to retire disappointed.

The season moved on: the moon waxed and waned, the tide ebbed and flowed, the air drowsed in the gentle winter sun. Clusters of bananas ripened all around Bhikhu's hut. The boatman Binnu bought his wife a silver waistband from the proceeds of selling the fruit. Slowly but surely the palm toddy became dark and thick with fermentation. Bhikhu's passion burnt away any vestige of shame: he could no longer restrain himself.

One morning he got up and went to the beggar woman. He said, 'Achchha, let's go, the sore doesn't matter.'

'Where've you dropped from, eh? Go hang yourself, stuff your mouth with ashes.'

109

'Ashes! Eh, what're you saying?'

'You think I'm sitting here just waiting for you, is that it? I'm with that man – over there.'

Bhikhu followed her gesture and saw a stout, bearded fellow, lame like himself, but in the leg. He sat some way off. His right leg was withered below the knee, carefully displayed before him as he whined for alms in the name of Allah.

Beside him lay a short artificial leg.

The beggar woman said, 'Still sitting here, are you? Get away now before he notices and does you in.'

'What! Any blasted rogue can talk about killing. I can deal with ten of him – want to see?'

'Then go and fight him. But leave me out.'

'Leave him! I'll take you.'

'Oh sweetheart, have some tobacco, lover boy. Look, don't forget – what makes you think I'll give you a welcome? You can't earn even half as much as he does. You have a house, I suppose? Clear off, or I'll give you a real lashing.'

Bhikhu retreated for the time being. But he was not defeated. When he saw the woman alone he approached her again. He tried to chat her up: 'What's your name?'

The two of them were such nonentities that neither had yet asked this question.

The woman bared her tobacco-stained teeth. 'You back! Better you go over there – to that old woman there.' Bhikhu squatted down. He had a small sack on his shoulder to carry the rice people often gave him these days instead of coins. Reaching into it he took out a large banana and held it in front of the woman. 'Take it. I stole it for you.'

The woman promptly peeled her lover's filched offering. 'Want to know my name, then? Panchi's what they call me – Panchi. So you've given a banana, and I've given my name – now off with you.'

Bhikhu did not shift. He was not so generous as to accept a name in place of a first-class banana. As long as he could he squatted beside Panchi and tried to become acquainted. People at this level have no notion of how to introduce themselves. Other people hearing them might think they were abusing each other rather than chatting. Panchi's partner turned out to be called Bashir. Bhikhu tried to approach him.

'Salaam, Mister.'

110

'Why're you hanging about here?' said Bashir. 'Salaam Mister! – what rubbish! I'll crack your head if you don't get out!'

They had a filthy squabble. There was a stick in Bhikhu's hand and a stone in Bashir's – otherwise they would have had a real fight.

Before retiring to his patch beneath the tamarind Bhikhu shouted, 'I'll finish you off, I'm warning you.'

'You come back and mess with her again and I'll kill you, I swear by Allah,' replied Bashir.

About this time Bhikhu's earnings began to decline. New people did not use his path everyday. Their number over the course of two months could be counted on the fingers of two hands. Having given once to Bhikhu, most did not feel obliged to give again. The world did not lack for beggars.

Somehow he scraped by. Except on market days there was hardly any money coming in. He began to be worried. It would be tough, come winter, to continue living in the derelict shack. By hook or by crook he must get a proper roof over his head. Without somewhere for her to rest herself and two meals a day no beggar maid would agree to live with him. Yet, the way his income was dwindling, this winter he would not be able to fill even his own stomach.

He must find a way to boost his income.

In his present condition Bhikhu could foresee no way of doing so. Robbery was out, so was labouring, and without murder snatching cash was impossible. What's more, without Panchi he would not leave. Reflecting thus on his cruel fate, he became mutinous. Binnu's small domestic world nearby provoked him to jealous brooding. There were times when he wanted to set fire to Binnu's house, so agitated was his mind. He would wander along the riverbank possessed by a maddening urge to seize all the women and everything edible in the entire planet, to satisfy his cravings.

This state of ravening discontent persisted a while longer. Then, one midnight, slinging his worldly goods into his sack and stuffing his few rupees into his waistband, Bhikhu left. Not long before, walking beside the river he had come across an iron spike. He had sharpened its tip on a stone at his leisure. This weapon he added to the sack.

The moonless sky was studded with stars. God's earth was profoundly peaceful. Stepping out into such emptiness after so long, ready to roam freely, Bhikhu found himself gripped with awful, unspeakable excitement. He whispered, 'If only, Master, you had spared my right hand not my left.'

He walked half a mile along the river and entered the sleeping town by a narrow alley. Leaving the bazaar on his left he reached the far edge of the town via a maze of small lanes. There the pukka road out of town began. The river, meandering, followed it for a mile or so, and then turned south.

Some way along the road a few houses could be seen dotting the land on either side. Beyond them lay paddy fields and patches of fallow land gone to jungle. In one place, in a clearing, five or six huts had been thrown up by various wretches to form a small shanty village. In one of these lived Bashir. Each day at dawn he would get up and clatter his way into town to beg, and at the evening time return. Then Panchi would light some leaves and cook rice, and Bashir would smoke tobacco. At night she would wrap a few dirty rags around her sore. Then they would lie down together on their bamboo charpoy, mutter to each other in their crude manner for a while and fall asleep. A fetid odour would seep from their nest and from the bed and its two occupants, pass through the pores in the roof and mingle with the midnight air.

Tonight Bashir was snoring, Panchi mumbling in her sleep.

Bhikhu knew where to find them because he had once followed them home. In the darkness he went stealthily behind the hut, stood in the vegetation there and glued his ear to the gaps in the wall. Then he moved back in front. It was only a beggar's hut, the door could not be closed, only pulled to by Panchi. With great care Bhikhu opened it, lifted the iron spike from his sack and gripped it.

He entered the hut. Outside was starlight, inside there was no light. He had no hand to light a match, it was not easy to discern Bashir's heart. If he struck with his left hand and missed, Bashir would raise hell. That would be really awkward.

He paused for several moments, then moved to the head of the charpoy and plunged the sharp instrument into the sleeping man's brain, driving it in to a depth of about three inches. Without being able to see he could not know if he had pushed far enough to be fatal. He felt that the spike was well inside the skull, but he was not absolutely sure. He grabbed Bashir's throat and throttled him.

To Panchi he hissed: 'Not a sound, or I'll kill you too.'

Panchi did not scream, but she groaned.

112

Bhikhu repeated his threat: 'Not a squeak, unless you want to be quiet forever.'

When Bashir became still Bhikhu released his hand. He said, with a sigh of relief, 'Light the lamp, Panchi.'

She did so, and Bhikhu admired his handiwork with deep pleasure. Using only one hand he had slain a grown man: his pride was boundless. Looking at Panchi he said, 'See? Who's the real killer then? See! So many times I told him – careful, Mister, don't come between a horse and the grass. Did he take any notice? He said – I'll smash your head. Come on then, Mister, do it now, smash my head!' Bhikhu bowed before the corpse, swayed his head from side to side and laughed raucously. Then, all of a sudden he became enraged, shouted, 'Why're you standing like a dummy! Say something, or d'you want me to murder you too, eh?'

Panchi said feebly, 'What happens now?'

'Wait and see. Where's his money kept, tell me first.'

It had taken Panchi a long time to locate Bashir's cache. She tried to plead ignorance. But when Bhikhu seized her by the hair she at once confessed.

Bashir's life savings were not small, no less than a hundred rupees in half-rupee coins. Bhikhu had killed for much more in the past. Nevertheless he was satisfied. He said, 'Pack your stuff, Panchi. We're going while it's dark. Soon there'll be a moon and we'll see the path.'

Panchi obeyed. Then, holding Bhikhu's hand, she limped out of the hut and on to the road. Bhikhu glanced at the eastern sky and said, 'The moon's just coming up, Panchi.'

'Where do we go?'

'Town. I'll steal a boat at the ghat. In the morning we'll hide in the jungle on the way to Shripatipur, reach there in the night. Let's go, Panchi dear, we've miles to walk.'

Because of her sore it was difficult for Panchi to walk fast. Bhikhu stopped unexpectedly and waited. 'Your leg's painful, is it, Panchi?'

'Yes, it's bad.'

'Want a ride?'

'How can you?'

'Come, you'll see.'

So Panchi put her arm round Bhikhu's neck and clung to his back. Stooped beneath her weight Bhikhu set off as fast as he could go. The paddy fields on either side lay lifeless in the shadows. Above the trees beyond a village ahead of them, a nearly full moon came up. God's earth stretched everywhere, profoundly peaceful.

That moonlight might or might not have been shining on the dark earth since its history began. What was certain, and perpetual, was the darkness within Bhikhu and Panchi; a darkness fed to them umbilically, carried by them clandestinely and transmitted by them in due time to the very fibre of the offspring of their flesh. It is a primordial darkness; no earthly ray has yet lightened it, nor can it do so.

(1933)

BRAVO TO THE BOSS

Bibhuti Bhushan Banerji

Firms in Calcutta regularly got their supplies of plants, medicinal and otherwise, from all kinds of people living in the villages. Their names were recorded in the accounts, but very seldom their addresses. The transactions were petty ones, carried out in cash by an assistant clerk, the seller not permitted to meet even that person's immediate superior, let alone the chief clerk, the big boss himself.

For the first time Haripada decided to dispense with his usual middleman Nagu and take his plants direct to the company offices. Saleable plants were in good supply in Haripada's village. Nagu was the one who had first suggested to Haripada that he gather them. Shanti, the local physician, had guided him as to which plants to pick. But Haripada's profit, what with having to pay Nagu two rupees per maund towards lorry hire, no longer sufficed him. That was why this year he had stockpiled the plants instead. Nagu had inquired about them several times. 'Look here,' he had said, 'you're letting all this merchandise rot. *Apang shimul* roots and white *parpati* won't last more than six months – they spoil. Even if you sell two for the price of one, people won't buy them. Send it to Calcutta, let me send the whole lot to the godown there.'

But Haripada was not as green as all that. He didn't much care for the journey to the godown of the Mukherjis at Beliaghata. Not that he didn't receive a welcome there; in fact he could go any time he liked. The godown cook knew him: all Haripada had to say was, 'Hey, Kuber, let's have some food!' Still, he wanted to avoid that particular place. 'Nagu doesn't do the gathering, so why should he get the lion's share of the profit?' Haripada told himself.

Now, arriving alone in the city, Haripada heard that the Hindusthan

Chemical Company was purchasing plants. He went straight to their offices. The sight that greeted him was a formidable one. Everywhere he looked he saw employees, lifts, doormen, revolving doors and electric lights burning in daytime. Telephones rang constantly. Perhaps, after all, he should have left everything to a middleman like Nagu? How could a rustic fellow like himself ever sell anything? In the end, though, he found an enquiry office and took directions.

The clerk in charge of purchasing was not very old. As soon as he had inspected the goods he quoted a price at least eight annas per maund higher than the price paid at Mukherji's warehouse in Beliaghata.

Weighing the plants took quite a while. 'Do you want a cheque or cash?' the clerk asked. 'Come tomorrow if you want cash. I'll do the needful today. Bring this receipt with you and get it signed by the chief clerk. Then take it to the counter over there.'

The following day there was a big crowd around that counter. It was pay day. On each sealed envelope the payee's name was typed. The clerk called out, 'Name? Ram Sharan Pal? Take it.' The pile of envelopes gradually diminished. Some people opened theirs and checked the notes inside them, before going away.

The clerk handed an envelope to Haripada. He could recognise the letters H. P. B. He was slightly embarrassed to open it right there and count his forty rupees. In such a large establishment where was the scope for mistakes? Particularly when they had taken the trouble to type his name on the outside of the envelope.

But by the time he reached Sealdah station Haripada felt he should open the envelope and take a look at the money. He got such a shock he had to sit down. With a glance about him he hastily stuffed the notes into his pocket, almost ran along the platform and jumped aboard the train. Though it was winter, there were beads of sweat on his forehead. What a disaster! – the envelope was full of hundred-rupee notes, eleven in all. Instead of forty rupees he had been given eleven hundred!

Haripada could not understand the error. Perhaps in the rush they had given him an envelope intended for a big creditor? He must be H. P. B. too. In that crowd the clerk must have handed the other man Haripada's envelope.

Eleven hundred rupees – it was an enormous sum. He was just an ordinary man, a simple plant collector. This must be God's doing, truly a god-send! If he were to sell plants for the rest of his life he would never amass eleven hundred rupees. And hadn't the cash dropped into his hand? Clearly, it was his lucky day.

The train chugged along and in its cool breeze Haripada's agitation subsided somewhat, but it would not disappear altogether – not until he could break the news to his wife. The train was definitely not moving fast enough. To be unable to share his joy! – only God knew how intolerable the agony was.

He noticed an elderly gentleman sitting in one corner of the compartment, wrapped in a scarf. Should he let on to him? 'Look here Sir, something marvellous has happened. I went to an office to get forty rupees and they gave me eleven hundred in error. Here it is.' Would he then go on and tell the man the name of the company? No, not a good idea: the man would immediately inform the police.

The people in the office would surely detect their error and begin a search for him. But search as they might, there was no way for them to find his address. Nevertheless, he ought to dispose of the eleven notes. His uncle at Sirajgunj who worked in a jute mill – he would help, he could convert the notes into miscellaneous lots of ten rupees. Tomorrow morning he would get the train to Sirajgunj.

Ashalata, Haripada's wife, gazed at the bundle of notes with incomprehension, then looked at her husband. At last she said, 'But don't they have a record of payments to avoid mistakes like this?'

'It's easy for this to happen in a big office,' said her husband. 'The more rules there are, the more loopholes there are. Fifty or a hundred people work in that department and there are many checks. First you go to the boss, the chief clerk, then you take a signed note from him to the cashier, then you get it signed again. But even so, despite everything, all the formalities, things slip through.'

'Don't notes have numbers?' Ashalata persisted. 'What if the police circulate details of them? How will you get rid of them? That's what I'm afraid of!'

'Don't be afraid. First, I don't think they number hundred-rupee notes nowadays. Second, they wouldn't record such ordinary notes in such a big office. Anyway I will change them with my uncle at Sirajgunj tomorrow. But the real thing is, they don't have my address – with only my name, they can't catch me.'

Haripada's wife was now convinced. 'Well let's hope you can change everything into good notes. Then we'll make an offering to Lord Satya Narayan next full-moon night. He must be smiling upon us.'

117

Haripada had no difficulty changing the money at Sirajgunj. The crafty fellow divulged nothing to his uncle; he told him he had sold some land from his Brahmin's inheritance in order to start a business. He also forgot to make an offering to Satya Narayan.

A month went by. There was no bother from any direction, but Haripada was in a state. His mind was in turmoil. Was it right to keep the money? By now the people in the office must certainly have detected the blunder. They would have started an enquiry, even though they had nothing to go on. The entire blame would surely have fallen on the shoulders of that clerk. Very likely he would have lost his job.

As time went on Haripada's uneasiness increased. As long as he had been afraid of the police or the firm snatching the money back from him, the idea of keeping it had not struck him as wrong or sinful. But now that he felt relieved of that particular anxiety his mind fell prey to a new one: that he had no right to the money and had stolen it from someone.

Six months passed like this. Often he considered returning the cash; but the next moment he thought what a fine grocery shop he could open in the village with eleven hundred rupees. Wasn't it the Almighty who had noticed their sad state and provided the capital? Better to keep it, keep the cash.

The strongest resistance to returning it came from Haripada's wife. The moment she heard her husband was considering giving it back, she created a huge fuss. To a daughter of poor parents, married to a poor man, eleven hundred rupees was a vast sum.

Haripada tried to reason with her: 'Don't you see, this is money obtained by deception! I've only just realised this myself, and ever since then I'm having sleepless nights. It can't go on. Eleven hundred rupees won't last us forever anyway. Let's give it back.'

Ashalata replied, 'Why call it deception? Isn't God behind the error? When Goddess Lakshmi enters our house should we turn her away? Listen to me, dear, don't lose your head. You haven't deceived anyone; they made an error, is that your fault? Anyway, the money doesn't belong to any one person, it's company money, from a big company. What's eleven hundred rupees to them? But to us it's a great deal. It'll keep us for the rest of our lives. I'm not thinking solely of myself. Have you taken a look in the mirror recently? All this grubbing around for plants in the jungle, has it made you glow? With that money we could open a shop and really get settled.'

118

This notion of his wife's became a dreadful burden on Haripada's mind. Why had he mentioned the business to her at all? he wondered. But when he looked at her face and saw her suffering, and when he listened to the distress in her appeal he thought to himself, I must keep it, what's the use of my scruples? I have never been able to bring happiness to this unlucky woman, let me spend the money on a business and solve all our pressing needs. These scruples are really selfishness in disguise, extreme selfishness. Ashalata is still young, she's tasted none of life's pleasures. For her sake let me sin against myself.

Or so he thought during the daytime. But in the watches of the night, when the village lay hushed and Ashalata slumbered, he reflected that what he had actually done was to find excellent reasons for becoming a thief. Fraud was fraud, whatever you chose to call it; that was the fact of the matter. If he returned the money he would no longer be cheating himself.

Gazing at his sleeping wife he sighed and thought, women are peculiar creatures! They don't seem to think about anything but rupees, jewellery and domestic matters.

In due course, Haripada recognised that he had started to despise his wife. His cherished Ashalata! Looking at her now gave him no pleasure. How could such thoughts have entered his mind?

Then their calf suddenly died.

Haripada felt no surprise. It was only to be expected with such a woman in the house! Her evil influence would be his ruin.

This idea in time became firm conviction. A bitterness towards his wife took root in his thoughts. He snapped at her in ordinary conversation and scolded her for trifling matters. The bond between them imperceptibly weakened. Ashalata was puzzled: why had her husband altered so much? how had this rift arisen? why does he neglect me? what have I done wrong? From sunrise to sunset I toil away but instead of kind words he finds fault with the slightest thing, if I forget to put lime in his *pan*, for instance.

During that past month Haripada had started to draw upon the office money. He had spent thirty or forty rupees. Ashalata had been thinking: 'He hasn't been looking too well lately with all that tramping around in the jungle under the hot sun. I must take more care of him.' So she started to fry him *luchis* almost every night. Sometimes she cooked other delicacies. Once she said, 'You must keep an eye on your feet, dear. Don't you think you should get a pair of shoes? Otherwise your feet will rot in all that swampy water.'

One evening Haripada was sitting eating as usual and Ashalata brought him a bowl of warm milk. Abruptly, as he bit into a *luchi*, he snicked his tongue and yelled in pain. Ashalata, standing with the bowl of milk in her hand, said, 'What's the matter?' But Haripada only held his cheek grimly with his left hand, his face contorted, and said nothing.

She asked again in a concerned voice, 'What's happened, dear? Why are you so upset?' This was too much for Haripada, who burst out, 'Because of you, of course. From the moment your shadow fell upon this house you've brought nothing but calamity. That's the real reason why the calf died, and why – ' He broke off, shoved the *luchis* violently aside scattering them all over, jumped to his feet and went out. Ashalata stood stunned, clasping the bowl of milk.

Haripada returned very late. As he approached the house he saw his wife sitting quietly on the verandah. His tongue had ceased to hurt and he regretted his harsh words: he wanted to be pleasant, now that the anger had left his mind. He stepped in, came towards her and said softly, 'Please get up. I suppose you're angry? Have you eaten?' Tears trickled down Ashalata's face and she remained quiet.

He gently picked up her hand. She wiped her eyes with the corner of her sari and finally spoke: 'Please, sit down. I want to say something.'

'What?'

'Give the money back. Whatever we've spent can be made up by pawning or selling what's left of my bangles. That will be enough. The moment that money entered this house, peace went out the window. As long as we hang on to it, it will mean trouble. Take it tomorrow, give it back.'

After a short sleep, Haripada found that he was about a hundred rupees short of the original sum. Carrying his wife's bangles he left for Calcutta and sold some of them at Podders the goldsmiths. When he reached the Hindusthan Chemical Company office he decided not to entrust the money to a petty clerk – it was not properly recorded in the first place. He went instead straight to the office of the chief clerk.

'What do you want?' the boss asked.

Haripada came out with the whole tale. No one else was present. The chief clerk was astounded. The vanishing of the cash had caused a rumpus in the office. The error had come to light two days after

Haripada's visit. They had made big efforts to trace his whereabouts, without any success. The clerk in question had had his monthly wages docked by thirty rupees and had lost his annual bonus.

Now, more than two months later, the absconder had returned with the money! Extraordinary! In all his fifty-two years the chief clerk had seen nothing like it.

He questioned Haripada, 'Will you give back the full amount? Have you brought it all? Why didn't you come before?' And Haripada replied that when he left the office with the envelope in his hand he had no idea how much was in it. He realised only on his way home. 'After that my greed got the better of me, Sir. We are poor people. So much money – it was not easy to avoid temptation.'

The chief clerk said, 'I see. Let me see the cash.'

Once it had been counted, Haripada simply went away. But in the meantime word had gone round the whole office. Everyone crowded into the chief clerk's room to hear the details. Was it true that after so long the money had been returned?

The boss gave a chuckle. 'You don't know the half of it,' he said. 'The way I toil for this company has never brought me name and fame. That fellow who was here just now probably planned to make a further sale. After two or three months he probably thought nobody would recognise him. Then I asked him, "What's your name? Didn't you come here selling once before and get overpaid?" I saw his signature on a chit, you see, and I thought I recognised it – had to be the same fellow. Well, when I asked him, he went pale. So I told him to give me the money or I'd call the police. He was a business type, you know, selling a lot of stuff, that's probably why he had such a lot of cash on him. Anyway he was really frightened when he handed over the money. What a situation! When he stepped in here, he had no idea what he was letting himself in for.'

'Bravo! Bravo to the Boss!'

(1937)

UNACCOUNTABLY

Bibhuti Bhushan Banerji

I was feeling in an off mood. It happens sometimes. I didn't want to read, I didn't want to think, I didn't want to talk to anyone. My mind seemed to have run out of fuel – its wheels, lacking oil, to have gradually become dry. All of a sudden, they had ground to a halt.

I was in my old haunts at the time, in Jelepara, playing cards but not enjoying the game. Another time, winning at cards would have had me jumping with excitement: today I thought only – if I win, so what? I wasn't enjoying the usual gossip much either. In fact everything seemed meaningless: the room in which we played with its low ceiling; the walls with their patches of peeling plaster; the cheap and hackneyed oleographs hanging on them – depicting The Slaying of Serpent Kaliya, Goddess Annapurna Offering Alms, how incongruous!; and the chit-chat that I seemed to have been hearing since the year dot – suddenly I felt dull and dispirited, found myself thinking how pointless it all was. I asked the person next to me, 'Are you having a good time? You don't seem to – '

He looked at me in surprise: 'Why? aren't you? Why do you ask?'

That made me really irritable. I invented some excuse to do with my work, and pushed off. It was about four in the afternoon. Hawkers were busy shouting in the lanes – children were coming back from school clutching their books – the splash of water from running taps could be heard somewhere – and at the street corners and on the terraces in front of houses little *addas* of people were already congregating to idle away the rest of the day.

One of these lanes was especially dark and narrow. It ran next to a municipal bathing area. I often used the lane, which meant my walking past a tiled shed beside the bathing area. The occupants of the shed never ceased to fascinate me. It was about eight feet long and the same in breadth. In it was a family; husband, wife and two young children. Without having seen the place it's hard to believe so many living beings could inhabit so small a space – with their belongings too. But even more amazing was the fact that in one corner of this eight-foot-square room there was a kitchen. Whenever I passed by, I would see cooking going on. The wife of the family, her baby son in her lap, would be frying something or heating some milk. Her age was difficult to guess. She could have been 23, or 30 – or even 40. There was a rip in her sari near the veil, and the sari was dirty. At her wrists were the typical married woman's bangles. Her eyes were lacklustre, her whole face struck me as dim: she was probably married to some factory worker; once or twice, coming home at night, I had seen a sooty-faced man stepping into the bathing area with a small bucket in his hand.

I saw the family today, as usual. The wife was squatting in the doorway dandling the baby boy. She gazed at me with a stupid expression. The room was like a pigeon-hole, its walls made of mud smeared on to bamboos and plastered in old newspapers yellowing with time; on a rope hanger soiled clothes were hanging.

My mind became further depressed. How could these people find any pleasure in such a rut? How could they exist there? What a pointless existence! Why persist with it at all? That boy – what would he turn into? Another factory worker most likely, living in a tiled shed with a wife and offspring, plodding through day after meaningless day in the same shabby, ugly, gloomy conditions, towards a degraded death. And yet the way the mother was embracing and cuddling the child, how many hopes and cherished dreams she must have – but here I became a sceptic again. Did the woman really have the brains for such dreams? Could she dream? Could she think herself out of her present state into some future one, and make herself believe in it – give form to her inner longings? Was she capable of losing her cramped and unlovely present in some radiantly imagined future?

At the corner of the main road I stopped to look at books. There were heaps of second-hand ones, and magazines. Most were trash, the product of idle and immature minds. There were vacuous foreign novels in glamorous covers, and film magazines. Another day I would have browsed, looking for something good. Today I lacked the patience. My mind felt dulled, like a tarnished coin or a leaden sky – neither heavenly blue nor monsoon black, brooding with rain – yes, it was exactly like a tarnished coin.

I wondered whether to go to the pictures. Or maybe for a stroll at Outram Ghat? Or should I sit down somewhere for a cup of hot tea? Or walk towards the Lakes? . . .

In front of the church at Dharmatola a crowd had appeared. A man in European clothes was lying obliviously on the footpath, his torso and head at such an odd angle to each other I thought he might be dead. Two police sergeants were present. The word was, the man had been found in a bathroom on the ground floor of the house opposite; the doorman of the house had somehow manoeuvred the immobile body outside, in order to put it in a taxi and take it somewhere.

The figure aroused my sympathy. I didn't have any sympathy for the stupid wife – but for this insensible drunk, I did. The fellow was in search of some pleasure and had found his path – whether true or false only the quality of the pleasure could determine – and who could say what he had experienced? or what it meant? He alone knew. And he was insensible!

I reached Curzon Park. A number of servants and ayahs looking after the small children of sahibs, to avoid the rain were squatting on the footpath below some garage verandahs. The rain was getting heavier, so I stood underneath too. A small boy with curly golden locks and blue eyes – perhaps a year and a half or two years old – was in the process of picking up his guardian's cap from the ground, toddling uncertainly towards him, then somehow, with enormous effort, reaching the servant's head and placing the cap upon it. The moment the cap was on, he waved his hands, jiggled his whole body and was convulsed with toothless laughter. But the cap was not properly attached, a moment later it slipped off, and then the little boy, with equally enormous effort, had to put it back again . . . and this was then followed by the same gurgles of laughter, the same waving of limbs and the same dancing with delight . . . No one was watching him, but he didn't wait for anyone to: his guardian was completely unaware of him, engrossed as he was in conversation with the ayah squatting next to him, not in the least concerned as to what the little boy was or was not doing; and everyone else nearby was truly a baby – so the little boy went on playing the put-a-cap game all by himself.

I watched as if spell-bound. What rhythm there was in the movement of those soft and tender limbs – what animation of attitude, what unguarded gladness, what unparalleled beauty! With superabundant happiness the little boy tilted forward, his whole mouth laughing, lifted his fists as high as he could and then dropped them again; the entire eager joy of early childhood was expressed in a diverse and distinct conversation – without any words.

I could not tear my eyes away. Unaccountably, I seemed to have stumbled upon some novel, unimagined source of grace. I stood for a long while. Then suddenly the servant sensed my watching him: he broke off talking to the ayah, turned to the little boy, snatched the cap from his hand and dropped it in the perambulator. The boy's face darkened. He toddled to the pram and stopped beside it, but it was too tall for him, his small hands were unable to reach inside. He looked helplessly from side to side, then sat down abruptly. His guardian was once more absorbed in talk.

Inside the park I sat down on the bench by myself. The sun was setting. Across the Ganges, the sky had turned red.

I found that the meaningless delight in the mind of the little boy had imperceptibly infiltrated my own mind. The woman in that tiled shed seemed stupid no longer.

(1937)

125

FAREWELL

Samaresh Basu

The hushed watches of the night were shattered by a military patrol vehicle tearing past Victoria Park.

Section 144 and a curfew were both in force. There were riots between Hindu and Mussulman. Each was at the other's throat with billhooks, pokers, knives and sticks. Everywhere assassins were at work, striking clandestinely under cloak of darkness. Looters were on the rampage too, and the shades were haunted by their yells of deadly delight. The *bustees* were burning. Sporadic screams from dying women and children added to the monstrous atmosphere. On top of everything came the panicky soldiers on patrol: they fired blindly in any direction to maintain a semblance of law and order.

At a particular spot two lanes converged. A dilapidated rubbish bin lay overturned there. Behind it, using it as a shield, crouched on all fours was a man. He dared not raise his head. For a while he lay as if lifeless, as he tried to distinguish the cries in an uproar some way off. 'Allah Ho Akbar!' or 'Bande Mataram!'? He could not be sure which they were.

All of a sudden the rubbish bin seemed to move slightly. Every nerve in the man's body tingled. His teeth were clenched, his limbs stiff with apprehension and dread. Several moments passed . . . The night remained still.

Maybe it was a dog. To drive it away, the man shifted the rubbish bin slightly. The silence deepened. Then the bin moved again, and this time the man's fear became mixed with curiosity. Extremely slowly, he raised his head – and opposite him there rose another head. A man! From either side of the bin the two creatures stared at each other, stunned. Their hearts had almost stopped, their eyes were locked in a

126

violent contagion of fear. Neither could afford to trust the other. Each thought the other was a murderer. Their eyes were narrowed, expecting an attack; but no attack came. In both their minds the same question reared its head: Hindu or Mussulman? Depending on the answer, the outcome might be fatal. Neither creature had the courage to ask aloud, but nor could he turn and run, in case the other man jumped him with a knife.

Minutes passed. Both men fidgeted with doubt and discomfort. Finally one of them shot the question, 'Hindu, or Mussulman?'

'You say first,' came the reply from the other side.

Neither was willing to reveal his identity. Their minds were riddled with suspicion. They let the first question lie, each having thought of another one. 'Where's your home?' called one.

'This side of the old Ganges. Shubaida. Where's yours?'

'Chashara, near Narayangunj. What d'you do?'

'I've got a boat. I'm a boatman. You?'

'I work in a cotton mill.'

Once more, silence. Peering through the gloom each tried to see the other, scrutinize the clothes he was wearing. The rubbish bin and the darkness obscured the view. Then the uproar burst out again – and this time it was much closer. The frenzied shouts were clearly audible. The mill worker and the boatman trembled in terror.

'They're not far now,' cried the mill worker in a state of panic.

'Yes, let's go, let's get away from here,' called the boatman in a voice that was equally strained.

But the mill worker objected, 'No. Don't get up, whatever you do! Want to die?'

The boatman's suspicions were refreshed. What evil designs did this other fellow have? The boatman stared hard into the eyes of the mill worker, who stared back and said, 'Just stay where you are, just as you are.'

The boatman felt pricked by these words. Why was this man trying to stop him? Grave doubts clouded his mind. 'Why should I wait?' he called.

'Why? You need to ask?' replied the mill worker in a low, charged voice. 'I've just told you. D'you want to die?'

The boatman did not care for the tone of the question. All kinds of unpleasant possibilities jostled in his mind and made him resolute. Why hang about in this dismal alley for a moment longer?

127

His obstinacy alarmed the mill worker. 'I don't like your behaviour,' he called. 'You haven't yet told me what you're doing around here. Suppose you go off and bring your lot to finish me?'

'What the hell do you mean?' the other man shouted, momentarily forgetting where they were.

'It's the truth. You don't seem to understand how people's minds work.' Something in the mill worker's tone reassured the boatman slightly. He heard him add, 'If you go, d'you think I want to stay here alone?'

The racket of the crowd receded. The lethal hush returned. As time went by, the two men imagined they were awaiting death. Crouched on opposite sides of the rubbish bin in this dark alley they brooded, thinking of their homes, their wives, their children; whether they would ever get back to them in one piece, and whether, if they did return, those faces would still be there to greet them. These riots had come from nowhere, out of the blue, without the smallest warning. Overnight, the gossip and banter of the market place had turned into killing and bloodshed; enough blood to make Mother Ganges herself red. How could men turn so merciless so suddenly? The human race was truly cursed! The mill worker let out a deep sigh. The boatman followed suit.

'Have a smoke?' said the mill worker, taking a *biri* from his pocket and holding it out. The boatman, out of sheer habit, pinched the rolled-up tobacco a few times, twirled it in his ear and only then stuck it firmly between his lips. The mill worker tried to light a match. He had not realised that his clothes were soaked, likewise his matches. He threw the dud stick away in disgust.

'Damned matches are wet,' he said, and pulled another one out of the box.

The boatman impatiently got up and crouched beside the mill worker. 'I'll light it. Give me the box,' he said. He virtually snatched it from the mill worker. After a couple of failures he got a match to go.

'Allah be praised! Here you are, quickly, take it.'

But the mill worker sprang up as if he had seen a ghost. The *biri* between his lips drooped and fell. 'You-are-a . . .'

The match flame died. Both pairs of eyes widened with mistrust and anxiety in the darkness. There was a profound pause.

The boatman stood up abruptly. 'Yes, I'm a Mussulman,' he said. 'What of it?'

The mill worker replied in a frightened voice, 'No – nothing, it doesn't matter. I was only . . .' Glancing at the bundle beside the boatman he asked, 'What's in there?'

'Some clothes for my children and a sari. Don't you know, tomorrow is Id?'

Was that really all there was? The mill worker's doubts persisted.

'You think I'm lying? You don't have to believe me. See for yourself.' He held out the bundle.

'No need for that. Sorry, friend. It's all right. But you never know these days, do you? You can't trust anyone. Don't you agree?'

'That's true. I hope you're not carrying anything?'

'I swear to God I haven't even a needle on me. All I want is to reach home with my life.' The mill worker shook his clothes as if to prove his words.

Both men sat down again next to each other. For some while they inhaled their *biris* deeply, and did not speak. 'Tell me,' the boatman said reflectively, as if chatting with one of his family or friends. 'Tell me what all this killing's about?'

The mill worker kept up with newspapers and had some notion of politics. With some warmth he replied, 'The fault's with those League types of yours. They've started all this in the name of freedom struggle.'

The boatman was stung. 'I don't know anything about all that. I'm only asking, what's the point of all this killing? Some of your people die and so do some of ours. How can it benefit the country?'

'That's what I'm saying. The whole thing's not worth a damn' – the mill worker made a hopeless gesture with his thumbs. 'You may die, I may die, our families may become beggars. In last year's "riot" they hacked my brother-in-law into four, so my sister became a widow and landed on my shoulders with all her children. To me it looks as if the leaders give the orders from the comfort of the top floor, and leave us to do the fighting and the dying.'

'It's as if we're not human beings at all, but stray dogs. Why do we snap at each other and bite like this?' The boatman wrapped his arms round his knees and sat hunched in impotent rage.

'You're right.'

'Does anyone ever think of people like us? Are the fellows who started this riot going to provide my meals? Will I get my boat back? It's probably sunk at Badamtoli Ghat by now. That rich zamindar Rup

Babu – his manager used to get into my boat everyday to cross the river to the courthouse. That man was as generous as Hazrat: five rupees for the fare and five for the tip, ten in all. He covered my entire monthly expenses. Will a Hindu *babu* like him ever step into my boat again?'

The mill worker was about to say something when they heard the march of heavy boots. There was no question, the boots were about to enter their alley from the road. The two men eyed each other with dread.

'What do we do?' The boatman had grabbed his bundle.

'We must escape. But where to? I don't know the city very well.'

'Anywhere to get away,' said the boatman. 'We don't want to be beaten up by the police for nothing. I don't trust those bastards.'

'I don't either. But which way? They're coming.'

'This way.' The boatman pointed towards the southern end of the lane. 'Let's go. If we can get to Badamtoli Ghat we don't need to worry any more.'

Their heads bent, they ran without stopping to catch breath, crossing numerous lanes until they reached Patuatuli Road. It stretched deserted beneath bright electric lights. They peered out anxiously from their side street; could someone be lying in wait for them? Too bad – even if someone was, they could not delay. Scanning both ends of the road they ran straight on in a westerly direction. They had not gone far when they caught the clip-clop sound of a horse's hooves behind them. Glancing back they saw a mounted policeman some way off riding towards them. They darted into a narrow lane used by sweepers.

The horse swept by at a fast trot, its rider's revolver at the ready, each hoof-beat jerking at their hearts. Only when the sound had become faint did they dare to peep out.

'Stick to the edge of the road,' said the mill worker.

And so, clinging to the walls of houses and buildings, they advanced in spurts as fast as they could.

'Stop!' whispered the boatman. The mill worker pulled up, taken aback.

'What is it?'

'Over here.' The boatman took the mill worker behind a *pan*-shop. 'Look over there.'

The mill worker followed the boatman's finger and saw a shed about a hundred yards off with a single light burning in it. Adjacent to it on a high verandah ten or twelve policemen with rifles stood at attention. A British officer was addressing them, gesticulating through a haze of pipe smoke. Below the verandah a policeman held the reins of a horse which tattooed the ground restlessly.

'That's the Islampur outpost,' said the boatman. 'If I go a bit further down the lane to the left of it, I reach Badamtoli.'

The mill worker's face was grey with fear. 'What then?' he mumbled.

'You stay here. There's no point in your going to the ghat. This is a Hindu area, the ghat's in Islampur, Mussulman territory. Spend the night here, go home in the morning.'

'And you?'

'I have to go,' said the boatman in a voice choked with worry and fright, 'I can't stand it any longer, friend. It's eight days since I heard from my family. Only Allah knows how they are. Somehow, I have to get into that lane. If I can't find my boat I can still swim across.'

'Are you mad?' cried the mill worker. He held the boatman's shirt. 'How will you ever make it?' His voice was passionate.

'Don't try to stop me. Don't. You must understand, tomorrow is Id. By now my children and their mother will have seen the new moon. They'll be looking forward so much to new clothes and hugs from their father. My wife will be pining for me. I have to go, brother, I can't wait.' His voice faltered.

The mill worker too was agonised. His grip on the boatman's shirt slackened. 'What if they catch you?' His voice was hoarse with fear and pity.

'They won't, they won't get me. Stay here, don't get up. I'm going. I won't forget tonight. If Fate wills, we two will meet again. Farewell.'

'I also will never forget it. Farewell.'

With a few stealthy steps the boatman was gone.

The mill worker stood up and waited, stock still with suspense. The thumping of his heart refused to slow. He was all ears, praying that God would keep the boatman from peril.

Minutes passed in strained silence. The boatman had been gone some while. How his children would be delighted by their new clothes, and how that would please the poor fellow! The mill worker sighed. The boatman's wife would probably fall upon his chest and weep tears of fond relief. 'You have escaped the jaws of death,' she would say. A

131

small smile played upon the mill worker's lips thinking of the reunion. And what would the boatman do then? Then he would –

'Halt!'

The mill worker's heart missed a beat. Men in heavy boots were running nearby. They were shouting something.

'The bastard's trying to get away!'

The mill worker edged out far enough to glimpse a police officer with a revolver leaping down and running into the lane: he fired twice, splitting the night. The mill worker heard both reports, saw the blue sparks of both bullets. He was so tense he bit his finger. Then he saw the officer jump on his horse and race down the lane. And he heard the death cry of the fugitive.

In his dazed imagination a picture of the boatman floated up. To his chest he was clutching the new clothes and sari for his children and wife. Gradually they turned crimson with blood. He heard the boatman's voice speak to him: 'I couldn't reach them, brother. My darlings will drown in tears on their festival day. The enemy reached me first.'

(1946)

WINTER IN CALCUTTA

Amitav Ghosh

Soon our brief Calcutta winter set in. The lakes were wonderful in that season and my grandmother took to accompanying me when I went out in the evening for my game of cricket. To my relief, she had the good sense to leave me and go off by herself once we were through the gates, but sometimes, when I was fielding at fine-leg or deep-square-leg, I would see her, a little white daub on the far side of the lake, walking briskly, stopping every once in a while to exchange a few words with the other elderly people who came to walk there in the evenings. My parents were pleased about her walks. I overheard them saying she had become easier to cope with now that she was going out of the house regularly and meeting people her own age. Soon she took to staying on in the park till long after our cricket game. I'd often look for her before going home and usually I would find her sitting on a bench, under one of the lake's huge trees, chatting with her new friends. At dinner, my father, smiling good-humouredly, would ask her what they had talked about: did they have any views, for instance, on the recent war with China?

Oh, we're not interested in anything as current as that, my grand-mother would reply. The past is what we talk about.

It turned out that many of the elderly people who went to the park had come across the border from the east too, during or just before Partition. Most of them had settled, just as my grandmother had done, in our part of Calcutta, which was then still undeveloped. So it was not really much of a coincidence that my grandmother often ran into people she had known or heard of in Dhaka, when she went on her walks by the lake.

On one of those evenings my father came home exhausted after a series of long meetings at his office. It was not often that he came

133

back as tired as that, and every time it happened a pleasurable sense of crisis would invade our house. It often seemed to me later that those were the moments in their lives that my parents most looked forward to: my father because it was at those times, tired, fussed over and cared for, that he tasted most fully and richly the subtle rewards of a life that had never strayed from convention by so much as a displaced hair; my mother because it was then that she could best display her effortless mastery of the household arts – for instance, her ability to modulate the volumes and harmonies of our house down to a whisper, while making sure that its rhythms kept ticking over, in perfect time, in much the way that a great conductor can sometimes produce, within a vast tumult of music, one perfect semibreve of silence.

On evenings like those my mother would read the tell-tale signs upon my father's drawn face as soon as he stepped out of the car. She would usher him at once to their room upstairs, and then she would come down again and tiptoe swiftly around the house: the servants would be told to turn off the transistor in the kitchen, the windows of the rooms that faced the traffic would be quickly and silently shut and I would be warned not to play with my cap guns. When silence had fallen on the house she would go back upstairs and lay out a clean, fresh *kurta* and a pair of pyjamas, and gently nudge him into the bathroom. While he was bathing she would hurry down again to the kitchen and make a cup of tea, exactly as he liked it, hot, sweet and milky, take it upstairs to the verandah that looked out over the garden, and put it on a table beside his easy chair. Then, when he came out, bathed and cool, she would sit beside him while he drank his tea, and talk to him in a quiet, soothing monotone about everything that had happened in the house that day.

It was on an evening such as that that my grandmother burst in upon us and cried: 'You'll never believe who I met in the park today!'

My mother was not pleased by this intrusion, and she tried to indicate that, whatever it was, it would keep till dinner-time. But there was no stopping my grandmother.

'I met Minadi,' she said breathlessly. 'You don't know her; her family used to live down the lane from us in Dhaka. She's always up on all the news about the whole world; she's been like that since we were schoolgirls. Anyway, we were talking about this and that, catching up – it's the first time I've met her in years – and suddenly she slaps my hand and says: "Do you know that your cousin, one of your Jetha Mashai's sons, is living right here in Calcutta with his family? Somewhere in Garia if I'm not mistaken?" Of course she knew I wouldn't know; she knows everything about everyone. But anyway, I said no, we had lost touch, I had no idea where he was; and how had she found out? She said her maidservant had mentioned the name once, a long time ago – about a year or so. So naturally, being Minadi, she'd asked her a few questions and she'd found out soon enough that it *was* him – my cousin, Jetha Mashai's son. But it's lucky for me that she's such a walking daily gazette of other people's affairs, because now she's going to find out exactly where he lives so I can go and visit him.'

Running out of breath she stopped to give us an eager sparkling look.

My father, at a loss to know what she wanted him to make of this, remarked mildly that after all those years they probably wouldn't even recognise each other.

My grandmother frowned. 'That's not important,' she snapped. 'It doesn't matter whether we recognise each other or not. We're the same flesh, the same blood, the same bone, and now at last, after all these years, perhaps we'll be able to make amends for all that bitterness and hatred.'

Then, in that particular tone of hers which nobody argued with, a voice we had not heard for some time, she said to my father: 'Don't forget to have the car ready on Sunday. Minadi's promised to send her maidservant to lead us to his house.'

At that, my mother gave a little cry of surprise and opened her mouth to say something, but my father shook his head at her, and she sat back in silence.

It was not as though she disapproved of what my grandmother was planning to do. On the contrary, she would have done the same herself, only she would have done it sooner, because for her, relatives and family were the central points which gave the world its shape and meaning; the foundations of moral order. But my grandmother on the other hand had never pretended to have much family feeling; she had always founded her morality, schoolmistress-like, in larger and more abstract entities. On the whole, for all but a few exceptions, she was extremely wary of her relatives; to her they represented an imprisoning wall of suspicion and obligations. Usually when she spoke of them, it was to remind us that it was all very well for Uncle So-and-so to smile and grin at us whenever he saw us now, but we ought not to forget that he had been

135

quick to turn the other way during her hard years. She chose to forget that in those years it was she who, in the fierceness of her pride, had severed her connections with most of her relatives, and had refused to accept any help from them at all, even from Maya Devi, her own sister; that she, being, as she was, too formidable a woman for people to thrust their help upon without being asked, had never had the generosity to ask of her own will. The price she had paid for that pride was that it had come to be transformed in her imagination into a barrage of slights and snubs; an imaginary barrier that she believed her gloating relatives had erected to compound her humiliation.

It was only natural that my mother was surprised at this sudden onrush of family feeling in her. Nobody had ever heard her speak of any of her relatives – not even Maya Devi, whom she loved – with the missionary warmth that she had in her voice now, while speaking of the children of a man whom her parents had hated more than anyone else in the world.

'I don't know what's got into her head now,' my mother said later, worriedly; 'but I'm sure it's nothing to do with her cousin – there's something else inside her, rattling around.'

Duly on Sunday the car arrived, and soon afterwards so did the woman who was to lead us to my grandmother's cousin's house. She was dumpy and middle-aged with a large round face and prominent eyes.

'What's your name?' My grandmother said, looking her up and down without enthusiasm.

'Mrinmayi,' said the woman, shifting a wad of *pan* from one cheek to the other.

'Oh, "Mrinmayi" is it?' mimicked my grandmother, thrusting her chin forward – she was always savagely cutting maidservants who had names which struck her as being pretentious for their station.

But now my father, intervening hastily, broke in to ask Mrinmayi whether she was sure she knew exactly who we were looking for. He said the name aloud, watching her closely.

Mrinmayi nodded, chewing slowly on her *pan*. 'Yes,' she said, in a thick Noakhali accent. 'Yes, that's the one. Nidhu Babu they used to call him – he used to be a ticket clerk at the Shonarpur railway station near where my brother lived. But after he retired he went off to Garia.'

She stopped and gave my father a long, considering look. 'Of course,' she said, 'you must know that he died last year, of a pain in the chest?'

My grandmother gasped and sank into a chair, stunned; but it was clear that she was less grieved than disappointed. She was silent for a while, covering her eyes with her hands. Then she stood up and announced: 'It doesn't matter – we'll go anyway. Maybe his wife will be able to give us some news of the rest of the family.'

'No, Ma, listen,' my father began, but she cut him short.

'Yes, I've decided,' she said, leading us out. 'Come on, let's go.'

So my father reluctantly started the car and we all climbed in.

We turned off Southern Avenue at Gole Park, and found, inevitably, that the gates of the railway crossing at Dhakuria were down. We had to stew in the midday heat for half an hour before the gates were lifted again. We sped off past the open fields around the Jodhpur Club and down the tree-lined stretch of road that ran along the campus of Jadavpur University. But immediately afterwards we had to slow down to a crawl as the road grew progressively narrower and more crowded. Rows of shacks appeared on both sides of the road now, small ramshackle structures, some of them built on low stilts, with walls of plaited bamboo, and roofs that had been patched together somehow out of sheets of corrugated iron. A ragged line of concrete houses rose behind the shacks, most of them unfinished.

My grandmother, looking out of her window in amazement, exclaimed: 'When I last came here ten years ago, there were rice fields running alongside the road; it was the kind of place where rich Calcutta people built their garden houses. And look at it now – as filthy as a *babui's* nest. It's all because of the refugees, flooding in like that.'

'Just like we did,' said my father, to provoke her.

'We're not refugees,' snapped my grandmother, on cue. 'We came long before Partition.'

Mrinmayi suddenly thrust her head out of the window and pointed to a two-storey concrete building. 'That's the one,' she said. 'That's where they live.'

My father brought the car slowly to a halt, inching it carefully off the narrow road and on to the gravel. He opened his door to climb out, but then, glancing suspiciously at the shacks and shanties on either side of the road, he announced that he was going to stay in the car; he had heard that cars were often stripped down to their chassis in places like this.

137

Turning to me he said: 'Stay here with me. I don't want you to go up there.'

There was a harsh, insistent note in his voice; I knew that he was angry with himself for having brought me there. But now I was determined to go too, so I slipped out quietly when he wasn't looking.

Mrinmayi led us into the building and up two dark flights of stairs. We had to stop several times to make way for groups of children who went swarming past us, chasing each other up and down the staircase, their shouts and laughter booming down the stairwell. The stairs were slippery with dirt, the bare cement walls blackened with soot and wood smoke, the wiring strung up in bright festoons, the copper exposed at the joins where the insulating tape had worn off. It was a long, matchbox-like building, not large, although it was evident from the barrack-like partitions that divided its corridors that dozens of families inhabited it.

Mrinmayi led us to a door on the second floor and called out: 'Anybody in?' We heard feet shuffling inside, and a moment later the door swung open.

My mother and grandmother were taken aback by the appearance of the woman who stepped out. They had been expecting someone very old, with a bent back perhaps, and a face like a raisin. The woman standing in front of us was no more than middle-aged, with thick spectacles, a broad chin, and very black hair – so black, my grandmother said later, that she must have used an industrial dye.

She looked at us in surprise, recognised Mrinmayi, and raised a puzzled eyebrow in our direction.

They wanted to meet you, Mrinmayi said placidly, and my grandmother quickly broke in and explained that we were relatives.

The woman understood at once who we were and how we were related to her dead husband. She smiled and patted me on the head when, in response to my mother's proddings, I bowed down to touch her feet. But then she glanced at her crumpled sari and, gesturing with her thumb and forefinger, she said: 'Just one minute.'

She disappeared inside, shutting the door behind her. When she opened it again, five minutes later there was a thick layer of powder on her face, and she had changed into a brilliantly white nylon sari.

She ushered us into the room, apologising loudly for its smallness, the lack of chairs, explaining that she was soon going to move out,

138

with her son, to a much bigger, better flat, it was a pity we had come at exactly this very moment, we had caught her in the middle of her packing . . .

The room was so dark there was neon light glowing inside although it was midday. A large framed picture of Rabindranath Tagore hung on one of the walls. Under it, on a length of rope, strung up between the corners of the room, hung a dishevelled curtain of drying saris, dirty petticoats and unwashed trousers and underwear. My mother and grandmother seated themselves gingerly on the edge of a bed that was pushed up against the far wall. Our relative sat down beside them and motioned to Mrinmayi to squat on the floor.

There was no place for me to sit, so I slipped back outside to the long, verandah-like corridor. Raising myself on tiptoe, I leant on the low railing that ran along it and looked down. I could not see the road; the corridor faced in the other direction. There weren't any more houses behind the building we were in. The ground fell away sharply from the edges of the building and then levelled out into a patchwork of stagnant pools, dotted with islands of low, raised ground. Clinging to these islands were little clumps of shanties, their beaten tin roofs glistening rustily in the midday sun. The pools were black, covered with a sludge so thick that it had defeated even the ubiquitous carpets of water hyacinth. I could see women squatting at the edges of the pools, splashing with both hands to drive back the layers of sludge, scooping up the cleaner water underneath to scrub their babies and wash their clothes and cooking utensils. There was a factory beyond, surrounded by a very high wall. I could see only its long, saw-toothed steel roof and its chimneys, thrusting up smoke that was as black as the sludge below. Running along the factory wall was a dump of some kind; small hillocks of some black and gravelly substance sloped down from it towards the sludge-encrusted pools. Shading my eyes, I saw that there were a number of moving figures dotted over those slopes. They were very small at that distance, but I could tell they had sacks slung over their shoulders. They were picking bits of rubble off the slopes and dropping them into their sacks. I could only see them when they moved; when they were still they disappeared completely – they were perfectly camouflaged, like chameleons, because everything on them, their clothes, their sacks, their skins, was the uniform matt black of the sludge in the pools.

Our relative spotted me leaning on the railing and ran out.

'Don't look there!' she cried. 'It's dirty!' Then she led me back inside.

I went willingly: I was already well schooled in looking away, the jungle-craft of gentility. But still, I could not help thinking it was a waste of effort to lead me away. It was true, of course, that I could not see that landscape or anything like it from my own window, but its presence was palpable everywhere in our house; I had grown up with it. It was that landscape that lent the note of hysteria to my mother's voice when she drilled me for my examinations; it was to those slopes she pointed when she told me that if I didn't study hard I would end up over *there*, that the only weapon people like us had was our brains and if we didn't use them like claws to cling to what we'd got, that was where we'd end up, marooned in that landscape: I knew perfectly well that all it would take was a couple of failed examinations to put me where our relative was, in permanent proximity to that blackness: that landscape was the quicksand that seethed beneath the polished floors of our house; it was that sludge which gave our genteel decorum its fine edge of frenzy.

Our relative made us tea and served us Thin Arrowroot biscuits, prettily arranged in a flower pattern on a plate.

While we were sipping our tea she and my grandmother had a long conversation. She told my grandmother that her late husband had gone back to Dhaka a few years before he died in the hope that he would be able to persuade his father to move to India.

'You mean he was still there then?' my grandmother cried, leaning forward.

She nodded. 'Yes,' she said. 'Still living in the old house.'

Her husband had tried to get his brothers and sisters to go back to Dhaka with him, to bring the old man to India, but they hadn't shown much interest. They were scattered all over anyway – one of them was in Bangalore, one in the Middle East, and the other God knew where. So her husband had gone back to Dhaka alone. He had thought they might even make a little money by selling the house if their father could be persuaded to move to Calcutta. But when he went there he found that the whole house had been occupied by Muslim refugees from India – mainly people who had gone across from Bihar and U.P.

My grandmother gasped in shock.

'Our house?' she said. 'You mean our house has been occupied by refugees?'

140

'Yes,' said our relative, smiling benignly. 'That's what I said. The house was empty after Partition, everyone had left but my father-in-law, and he didn't even try to keep the refugees out. What could he have done anyway? As soon as he got to Dhaka my husband realised that he wouldn't be able to reclaim that house – no Pakistani court was going to evict those refugees. And the old man didn't care anyway – there was a family living there who looked after him, and that was enough as far as he was concerned. He was – you know – not quite all there; he didn't really care what happened.'

'Poor old man,' my grandmother said, her voice trembling. 'Imagine what if must be like to die in another country, abandoned and alone in your old age.'

'Oh, he may not be dead yet,' our relative said brightly. 'Didn't I say so?'

'What do you mean?' said my grandmother. 'Are you saying he may still be alive? But he'd be over ninety . . .'

Our relative smiled and bit into a Thin Arrowroot biscuit, decorously covering her mouth with the back of her hand as she chewed.

'Well he was certainly alive last month,' she said. 'He wrote to me, you see – just a postcard, but it was definitely in his handwriting. I'd written to him after my husband died, just in case, at the old address – although we hadn't heard from him in years. But that was months and months ago, and when we didn't hear from him I just thought, well . . . But then, last month, there it was, a postcard . . .'

'Can I see it?' my grandmother said eagerly.

Our relative nodded, picked a postcard off a shelf and handed it to my grandmother.

My grandmother stared at it as it lay in her open palms, like an offering.

'There's the address,' she mumbled to herself; '1/31 Jindabahar Lane – it's still the same.'

She had to raise her hand to wipe away a tear that was rolling down her cheek.

'I can read his handwriting!' she said. 'He's written: "He should have stayed."'

Taking a deep breath, she handed the postcard back. Then she rose to her feet, thanked our relative and said it was time for us to go now, my father would be waiting. Our relative insisted politely that we stay a while longer, but my grandmother declined, with a smile. So then our relative said she would come down with us to see us off, and on the way down she took my mother's arm and they hung back, whispering. It was a while before they came down and my father was beginning to get impatient. But before starting the car he thanked our relative profusely and asked her to visit. I turned back to look as we pulled away, and saw her, framed by the concrete doorway, waving.

'What was she saying to you on the stairs?' my grandmother asked my mother.

My mother laughed in a puzzled kind of way, and explained that evidently she'd known all about us, even though we'd never met her before – she'd known exactly what my father did and where we lived. She had talked about her son: he was twenty-five now and had passed his matric, but he hadn't been able to find a job. He was going to the bad, she'd said, doing nothing all day long except hanging around the streets with gangsters. Could my father find him a job? she had begged.

'Poor thing,' my mother concluded. 'We should do something to help her.'

'Why?' retorted my grandmother. 'Did anyone do anything to help me when I was living like that? Don't get taken in by these stories. Once these people start making demands it never ends. Anyway she looks quite capable of managing by herself.'

My mother kept quiet; she knew better than to argue with my grandmother on that subject.

'It's not *her* I'm worried about,' my grandmother said with a vehement shake of her head. 'I'm worried about *him*: poor old man, all by himself, abandoned in that country, surrounded by . . .'

She allowed the sentence to trail away. When she spoke again we were almost home, and her voice was soft and dreamy.

'There's only one worthwhile thing left for me to do in my life now,' she said. 'And that is to bring the old man home . . .'

And her eyes grew misty at the thought of rescuing her uncle from his enemies and bringing him back where he belonged, to her invented country.

(1988)

142

REBIRTH

Abul Bashar

The dwelling-place of the household goddess had a circular thatched roof like a miniature barn. When such a roof showed signs of leaking, Jugin of Bhatshala village would be summoned to repair it. Jugin was an old hand at shrine building, famous for his workmanship over many years. Five years ago he had constructed the frame for the tiles on the cowshed near the shrine, using rafters made of palmyra wood. Now, though his eyes had become a little dim, there was still no one to match his handiwork. It was always Jugin who created the showy crown of thatch atop the deity's humble abode. He was an artist as much as a craftsman. Who else but he could fashion such a crucial thing? People's faith in him went deeper still. The lady of the house, Shudharani, believed that Jugin's crown was so splendid that Goddess Lakshmi's auspicious owl perched on it at night. The source of her faith was her life-long devotion to Lakshmi.

At her shrine, the *puja* offered to Lakshmi was straightforward. A brass pitcher full of water stood permanently by the outer step of the temple door. Every Thursday, in the evening, Shudharani in company with five other married women performed the *puja*: they ululated fittingly, smeared vermilion on each other's partings, and then Shudharani herself distributed to the others flowers and food offerings – the *prashad*. Everything was done correctly: a lamp burned, incense smouldered as the women, saris hooding their heads, prostrated themselves before the goddess. The sandalwood and vermilion marks on the mango leaves tied to the branch in the pitcher gradually dried up in the warmth; and the air lay heavy with the perfume of sprinkled Ganges water. No bell sounded though; theirs was a silent *puja*, like a meditation. Neither was the image of the goddess sacrificially immersed.

143

Each aspect of the ritual was simple, timeless and sacred. Jugin had observed it countless times; he knew its every gesture.

As well as being a shrine builder, Jugin was a folk poet, an accomplished one. He liked to compose songs and rhymes for the boys to sing at the Paush festival in winter. Which people chose to sing them there, or at the autumn harvest festival Nabanna, had never for a moment bothered Jugin Sheikh. He saw nothing wrong in the Muslim boys of Bhatshala singing his songs at a Hindu festival and collecting aubergines, pumpkins, bananas and other fruits and vegetables from house to house. Even when he was building an abode for Lakshmi in the courtyard of Shudharani's house, he never thought of the fact that though his first name was Hindu, his surname revealed him to be a Muslim. And yet today, somehow, he felt everything inside him was being partitioned, all his true feelings being uprooted.

While watching him as he wove together straws Shudharani had suddenly remarked, 'Jugin, your name is not right for you, Jugin.'

The remark's unexpectedness puzzled Jugin. He said respectfully, 'But Didi, which of us really has the right name – is Bhatshala rightly named? The village is full of poor Muslims but it hardly has a grain of *bhat* – and yet it has a fancy name, Bhatshala, "full of rice". I composed a funny song about it once, some twelve years back. "The rice pot sounds boom-boom: *bhat* in Bhatshala – no room. Poets are out of verse, they hang their heads and curse; a noose is hardly worse." Ha ha! That's why we rely on you, Didi. With a lot of struggle I can make ends meet building shrines – even today, when work is scarce.'

As Shudharani began to reply, a loudspeaker started up at the Brahmapada temple in nearby Shivkalitala. Despite the earliness of the hour, a voice began to sing *kirtan*, devotional songs to Krishna, constantly and shrilly. Jugin had heard something about this the night before on his way to Shudharani's. A group of *kirtan* singers had come from Maheshpur, led by a certain Bashab Chandra Das. Once upon a time, Jugin knew, Das had played young heroes in itinerant theatre troupes; now, recognising an opportunity, he had formed a *kirtan* group of his own. Nowadays religion was no longer the benign expression of exalted ideals, no longer a matter of graceful contemplative behaviour – it was a whirlwind of intoxication, a furious blast of emotion like a desert *simoom*. Jugin, in his simplicity, had not grasped what lay behind the change, but he had certainly felt its impact. He began to regret his name, his Hindu name. The loudspeaker was pouring forth, blaring its insane

144

sound in every direction like the wind. Why, Jugin did not comprehend. He thought to himself: Didi's correct, my name isn't right for me. And yet, hadn't his hand built the crown of the divine abode, shaped it like the *shikara* of a temple? Would anyone know that, once he had finished? – that a Sheikh had designed the shrine, that its pinnacle was the labour of a poor Muslim poet? Lakshmi's owl, her golden vehicle, perched there, didn't she? How could the owl be so foolish as to disobey the commandment not to touch anything Muslim? Surely the owl did not believe in it. But did Shudharani believe in it? This year, Jugin felt, Shudharani had changed. This year he ought not to have worked for her, he found himself thinking.

Climbing to the crest of the roof he set about plaiting the straw with slips of bamboo, parting it and tying it with knotted string as if it were hair. As his hands worked, his eyes strayed to the road. A gang of boys in khaki shorts and white cotton shirts were running towards the market carrying sticks and swords. Jugin knew what they were up to. In the courtyard of the Temple of the Twenty-two Goddesses at Chakkalitala they would practice with these weapons. A couple of boys from Shudharani's house, having just finished some rice left over from the previous night, ran out after the others. They carried an ominous tin falchion. The adult men of the house were yet to return from their night-time visit to Brahmapada. There, in the dead of night, the bald-headed ochre-clad swami, the *mahant* of the temple, would have given them secret mantras. There was holy war – *jihad* – in Hinduism too: this fact Jugin had only recently perceived. Never before had he seen Hindus brandishing their weapons like this, like Muslims at Muharram. Whom would they fight? The Muharram procession? The idea made Jugin's sweet old face ashen with concern. What was really afoot among the Hindus? They seemed besotted, as if they had taken leave of their senses.

Various kinds of rumour had been reaching his ears. Things had been said on the radio and printed in the papers. Those who were in the know were talking. The incident at the Babri mosque-cum-temple had raised the temperature of such talk. Mr Jirat, the schoolmaster at Shankarpur, had explained things at length the other day in the mosque. Now it was being said that Emperor Shahjehan had built the Taj Mahal on top of a ruined temple. What did that matter? Everything was once Hindu, all right – but why were Hindus suddenly wanting to remind everyone of that fact? Were they trying to tell Muslims to leave their country? Jugin

145

at last grasped the truth. But if he left Bhatshala, where would he go? If the Hindus could provide him with a land of rice and curry, that would be fine! It was only because there was no *bhat*, no food, to be had in Bhatshala, that he came to his Didi's village Gouripur. But see her now, how grim she looked! His throat felt dry. Where can I go, tell me that? All these sticks and swords threatening us all day, trying to scare us away, and at night who knows what kind of conspiracy being hatched? How can you want to send us away, Didi, when we've lived together so many years? Is that what you want in your heart, Didi – Jugin to go?

His train of thought brought his hands to a stop, so complex was his agony. A shaft of pain was boring into him. He said aloud, 'Why blame my name, Shudha Didi? Everything springs from my birth. When I was born, my mother's cord was found wrapped around me – like a sacred thread! My mother and my aunts were awestruck. Other people looked and were the same. I was a Brahmin, reborn. A Hindu baby had floated into my mother's womb, either in error or on some mysterious current. Take special care of your new-born, they all advised my mother, as long as he lives. Didi, whether you think such a sign is auspicious or not, you must admit I make beautiful straw crowns for your temple. My mother certainly believed I was the son of a Hindu.'

'How can that happen, Jugin! It's just one of those stories. There's no rebirth for Muslims, you know that,' Shudharani said.

'Not for Muslims,' said Jugin, 'but for Hindus there is. I cannot explain these mysteries, Didi. No God – Hindu or Muslim – will come and vouch for my being a Hindu: and yet we all know, don't we, that who gets born in which womb is God's will. Tell me this, do all new-born babies come with sacred threads around them?'

'You should not speak such things. In your religion it is really immoral. I don't believe a word!' Shudharani had become solemn.

Jugin replied, 'No one can control our beliefs, Didi! To me your eyes look like the eyes of Suleyman, but you will definitely rebuke me for saying it. I've never seen such eyes anywhere.'

'What kind of eyes?' Shudharani frowned.

'The eyes of Suleyman. Sweet, dark-brown as catechu. How did you come to have such eyes?'

'Who? Suleyman? Who is he?'

'A Muslim emperor. A prophet. The eyes of your Goddess are black –

146

I wonder where your brown eyes come from? Allah must be responsible,' Jugin concluded contentedly.

Shudharani was sceptical: 'More of your stories! I don't believe any of them.'

'Believe them or not, Didi, but you will never come across anyone who is totally Hindu or totally Muslim. You have Muslim eyes and I have Hindu hands. Otherwise – how could I make crowns for shrines like this? If the crowns are not Hindu – how could Lakshmi's owl perch on them: he'd get wind of the difference! Ponder what I say; we are in the hands of Allah at birth. We are all of mixed race, Didi.'

Having spoken, Jugin went back to his work, interweaving the straw with renewed energy. But Shudharani began to grumble. 'Eyes of Suleyman – fancy! Who says so! How absurd! I will not give you any more *prashad* from today, Jugin. I'm warning you. And no water for your midday prayer either – you can go to the mosque for it. You've been cheating me all along, asking for wages just when you feel like it. And taking advantage of a woman's generosity to get *prashad*, pretending to be Hindu. No more! I won't help you any more. I won't call you any more after this, I'm telling you. I don't need you after this. You can leave, go away!'

The uttering of these words pained Shudharani strangely. Unable to restrain herself, she retreated inside the house and gave a muffled sob. Hers was a patriarchal household, and this year her sons had made strong objection to employing Jugin. People were saying it was a profane act to let a Muslim build the dwelling-place of a goddess. The sons had berated their mother, flashed angry looks at her; in their eyes the Muslims were barbarians and intruders. Not only that, hadn't they once slaughtered Hindus in such numbers that the weight of dead Hindu sacred threads had come to 74½ maunds? That was why Hindus inscribed 74½ at the head of a letter. How could this fact be forgotten? Shudharani had attempted to reason: 'Was that Jugin's fault? He's never killed a Hindu. He's a poor man, he's almost dying of hunger – rather than killing anyone! You're making a scapegoat of him: don't rob Udo to pay Budo.' A war of words had followed. Finally, Shudharani had rolled her eyes in mockery and said to her son, 'This business of 74½ – why revive an ancient story? You should be writing the names of gods on letters – not the weight of some old sacred threads. Your culture's sunk rather low, hasn't it, Kailash?'

Her obstinacy had prevailed, and they had kept off Jugin. But what

147

further arguments and disputes would follow, God only knew. For the time being, Shudharani had ceased to speak to Jugin in her usual pleasant way, ceased now to give him *prashad* or water for his prayers.

At midday, silent and glum, head bowed down, Jugin went helplessly to the local mosque and said his prayers. When he returned, he got on with the job singlemindedly.

Thursday evening came. The *puja* was performed in front of him. He received no *prashad*. Why should he? Are my eyes Muslim eyes that I should take pity on him? Shudharani told herself. I'm a Hindu through and through, from the nails on my toes to the tips of my hair. That's what I want to be, a good Hindu, just as our priests – our *mohants* – have instructed us. Jugin doesn't know that's what we are here. He must not come here any more. I must make this absolutely clear to him.

Jugin did not eat well that night. He lay down, but sleep would not come, instead he lay brooding as if he was about to die. Didi would not call him again. The affection had gone out of her eyes. And affection is the essence of everything. When it goes, men become stones. Clearly she no longer trusted him. He thought: she sees designs in every word I say. My only motive for coming to her is to get some handfuls of food – nothing else. Oh well, I shan't go there any more. But it really is too bad that she did not believe the word of my mother.

A tear welled up quietly in Jugin's eye. He remembered a rhyme he had known since he was a child; it told the one hundred and eight names of Lord Krishna. He began to mutter it:

> His father Shri Nanda named him Nander Nandan –
> Paradise-born One.
> Yashoda his mother named him Jadu Bachadhan –
> Darling Sweet Son.

'That was out of her affection for him, Didi.' Jugin continued:

> His teacher Upananda named him Thakur Gopal –
> Lord of the Cowherds.
> The boys of Braja named him Shundar Rakhal –
> Most Handsome Cowherd.
> His friend Shubal named him Thakur Kanai –

148

Noble Lord Krishna.
His friend Shridam named him Rakhalraja Bhai –
Brother Cowherd King.

'The faith of the cowherds – it has been usurped by the priests, by the *mohants*; that's what's wrong, Didi.' Jugin muttered on:

The sage Kanva named him Dev Chakrapani –
Lord of the Universe.
His guardian Banamali named him Baner Harini –
Fawn of the Forest.

'Yes, Didi; the forest fawn, the owl, the peacock – vehicles of the gods and goddesses – they are all good creatures. Theirs, theirs is the true religion.'

(1988)

MATILAL, PADRE

Kamal Kumar Majumdar

The *shal*-wood cross at Hanshadowa could be seen from far off. It was visible from the Nimra hills, from the slopes of distant Shagarbhanga and from countless cowsheds, pastures and villages. That was because the church was elevated above the surrounding cultivated land.

The ancient geometrical symbol was etched against the blue of the sky; whether lit by the moon or by the ferocious tropical sun, it inspired awe and calm. Who was to know that within its abstract form pain was locked that bore down eternally upon the sweetness of life?

Standing between rows of lanky eucalyptus trees, the little church seemed almost like an English thatched cottage, fittingly neat and pure, but for the fact that the walls had been expertly painted red, the windows were made of bamboo and on the floor inside, in the holy corner, mats lay rolled. Every Sunday and special day these mats would be spread out below the sacred picture and there, before it on a low table, many coloured candles would be kept burning, along with an incenser and flowers scattered here and there. To one side stood an altar flawlessly fashioned by local Santhal people. Outside, on either side of the church, tidy rows of canna lilies grew among green lawns – a most unexpected sight in such an area. And there was a bell, hanging from a pillar entwined in greenery. The bell-rope trailed beside it. The whole verdant scene was most pleasing to the eye in a land rugged for miles around. Matilal the padre had been able to maintain it like this only through endless toil.

Visitors came with circumspect steps, moving timidly and anxiously lest they sin, their clothes restrained by church. Truly, Matilal had made a pious place. Water was scattered there every day, drawn from the well nearby: if no volunteer came forward to fulfil the task then

150

Matilal himself, despite his age, would water the lower-lying parts where croton bushes thrived between shallow gravestones. These graves carried crosses made of red leaves. The sole exception was the grave of Matilal's mother, which had a cross made of jackfruit wood. Although this spot was the resting-place of departed souls, birds such as wagtails and Chinese nightingales, not to mention crows and hawks, liked to perch there. At first this had bothered the padre and he had considered constructing a scarecrow on his mother's grave. But then he had thought how ugly this would be. He had asked advice from his assistant Phulal, who had said, 'I'd use a catapult to scare them off.' But while making this from a piece of guava-wood Matilal had decided it was not the labour of a Christian: suppose the birds really got hurt? The idea had saddened him, and the catapult had soon been abandoned.

Matilal was a man who wanted for nothing, not even peace of mind. The day of judgment caused him no anxiety. He cherished only one desire, to be a true, a full-fledged Christian. The words conveyed to him an ancient feeling of great love, rather than great repentance. There was nowhere for many miles around the church where he had not at some time paused to dwell upon this emotion. Not an inch of soil lay untouched by his austere devotional spirit.

His body seemed to have been carved from a log of *shal*. He was bald at the front, with long hair at the back down to his shoulders. Layers of grime coated the back of his ears, and his ancient black habit was in tatters. Filled with longing to be a true Christian, he tramped the hills in a state of perpetual prayer.

His own meagre thatched hut was set back some way behind the church. On its verandah stood his easy chair, looking ready to collapse if sat upon. Here Matilal sat in the mornings examining tongues and eyes and taking pulses, enriching the poor and the sick with the merest hint of the blessings of civilisation. Sometimes, while they sat on stools, he told them moral tales and stories of the faithful, to soothe their fevered souls. Other times, when he paced up and down his little front garden with a collection of hymns in his hand, his body felt as if it had tendrils, like a creeper. At such moments the sight of some distant old woman wearily resting beside her bundle of firewood made Matilal alert to her yearning for grace, and he would imagine himself transported to where she sat in the wilderness, consoling her misery with the message of Christ.

151

Now *Asharh* had come, the month of showers and storm-bursts. Water had penetrated even the most intimate spaces. Tonight the lightning was incessant, the outdoors as dark as Krishna. The flame in the lantern flickered. Matilal lay on his bed, his Bible open, but his mind lay elsewhere. His eyes were drawn to the lantern on the table and above it, on the wall, to His image. Matilal's lips seemed to mutter.

Then Bhulua, the cook, showed up, his head covered in a wide-brimmed *peka*. Overdoing his shivers a bit he said, 'What a downpour! It's so cold.'

Matilal was listening intently to another sound. He looked past Bhulua through the open door and into the lightning-torn night.

'What rain! Ready for food?'

'Why is that dog barking so much?'

'It's always looking for trouble. Probably seen a cat – I'll give it a kick.'

'How about shining the torch at it?'

'You do it, otherwise my rice'll burn. I'm off.'

Bhulua's reply did not seem curt: the padre was like a mother to them all.

He tightened the string around his waist, slipped the clogs on his feet and went into the verandah. When the lightning flashed he saw the dog darting in and out of the church. His torch was on but the dim beam picked up only streaks of rain. There was a glimmer of light visible in the church and its door could be heard banging.

Matilal went back indoors, paused for thought, grabbed his umbrella and set out fighting into the stormy gusts. When he got to the church he tried to peep through a gap in the window. He saw only the holy picture swaying gently, below it the agitated flame of its candle and to its side a lantern wavering as if about to fall asleep. But above the uproar – rumbling thunder, beating rain and wind, the door banging – his ears caught a fitful whimpering. He pressed his face so hard against the sill that he bruised his chin.

Helped by the lantern, and particularly by the lightning, he could make out what appeared to be a Santhal woman, miry hands braced against the earth of the church floor, legs and feet mired too and thrust forward, her sturdy nearly-naked body arched in pain like a bridge. On one part of her body her sari still clung gracelessly, swollen like an angry hen. Saliva issued from the corners of her mouth, along with frightful

152

groans. These were enough to drown even the racket of Nature, to obliterate all thought.

Of one thing the padre was certain: this was not the rattling of death. Some sort of rawness, incomprehensible to a man, was in it. There was also joy, like the furrowing of a plough in new ground. The deep mysteries of leaves and creepers, storms and showers, earth, stones and the vast inanimate world were all wrapped up in it. Now the dog too was trying to reach the window. Matilal pushed the animal away and somehow reached the side entrance of the church.

The black door was suddenly flung open by the wind. The vision of truth vouchsafed through the swirling downpour made the padre's skin crawl. Grander than a thunderbolt smashing a mountain, more overwhelming than an ocean inebriately swamping a tiny river, it surpassed imagination. Sun, moon and stars were not witnesses, only blood – radiant and supernal. In the soft candlelight it looked red rather than black. A fleshy seedling was bursting from its pod like a blow against darkness – or perhaps it was a tree, giving shelter and shade and bringing rain? Or was it really one more dubious burden, as usual? It must be that. The door banged shut, and then again flew open: there was the holy picture, and there, beneath it, indistinctly illumined by the flashes, was the woman! She was like some billow of dark cloud torn out of the monsoon sky and funnelled into this sacred building.

The padre could merely stare. His umbrella fell from his hand. In a feeble attempt at normalcy he bent to retrieve it. But the umbrella danced frenziedly away among the leaves of the canna lilies. The dog leapt after it. Matilal remained by the door, bewitched, and his hands folded together in a spontaneous *namashkar*, as if in greeting. He might have been standing gravely in some Arabian encampment, some scribble in the desert of Palestine beneath a vast cerulean solitude. His gesture seemed quite in character, nothing odd about it.

Suddenly he returned to reality; water was streaming down his habit. He rinsed his beard, jumped up and began to run – a difficult feat for an old and weary body housed in a soaking garment – but he made it through the graveyard and over the fields below for several hundred yards.

As he stood gripping the fence the dog continued frantically to bark. Matilal shouted hoarsely, 'Phulal! Phulal!'

His assistant was on his verandah. He came at once, his *peka* shoved over his head, and said, 'What's going on, Father?'

'The church, inside the church . . .'

'What, what exactly?'

'Something awful . . . I don't understand.'

'What d'you mean?'

The padre stopped to get his breath, blurted out everything as far as he was able, then stared at Phulal, wide-eyed.

Phulal stared back. 'The woman's in labour is she, Father? She's giving birth?' He ran inside to fetch a *peka* for the padre.

Matilal clasped the fence and shivered. His eyes seemed to open even wider in the lightning flashes. All he said was, 'What now?'

'We're ruined! The church . . .'

The padre tightened his grip and said, 'What to do . . .' He seemed as alarmed and ashamed as if he were guilty.

'We must go and call Bina, the midwife,' cried Phulal, and at once they set off along the dark inundated path. The padre followed behind, his *peka* pressed to his head. Dogs pursued them and had to be shooed away. On and off Phulal cried out, 'We're ruined.'

Then, Bina's house. She sat in her verandah, flashed by lightning, smoking tobacco. Phulal leant against a wooden post and her body bent down to listen. By the time the padre reached them, she had heard everything. She rose, took her few bamboo instruments from their space beneath the thatched roof, chained the door and stuck a *peka* on her head.

The three of them walked fast. At some point the padre's *peka* slipped from his head; he noticed it fall but there was no time to stop.

In front of the church the dog was still barking for all it was worth. The instant it saw them it wagged its tail. Bina washed her instruments in the water streaming from the roof and said loudly to Phulal, 'What's a grown man hanging around for? Haven't you any shame, any manners – d'you want me to give you a kick?' She made the appropriate gesture.

Phulal moved away in embarrassment. The padre wrung his beard and wiped his face. Bina shook the water off her instruments and requested, 'Fetch me a pot of fire, a lantern, some straw and hot water.'

She touched the instruments to her forehead and said softly, 'Durga, Durga, Mother Shasti.' Divine blessings thus invoked, she entered the

154

church, glanced around, went to the wall, picked up a discarded cloth and wiped the instruments, all the while keeping an eye on the sprawled figure of the woman. Her face became visible when the lightning lit it, showing her hair curled about it by the wind. After muttering further incantations Bina circled the woman thrice, genuflected and was ready to begin. When Phulal returned with the pot of fire, the lantern and the straw, he averted his gaze and said only, 'Here they are.'

'Shut both your eyes and hand them to me . . . Then find a way to keep that damned door shut.'

Phulal did as he was bidden, then joined the padre on the steps outside the church door. Bhulua appeared and was about to peep inside when the padre warned him off.

'Achchha, I'll go and roast some onions and come back later,' he said, and took himself off.

Speechless, the two of them held on to the door knockers. The wind pushed the doors so hard that they had to hold one knocker each.

There came the sound of crying, blown on the wind in fits and gusts. For the padre, it brought an image of cranes flying against a black monsoon sky, or of pigeons soaring in the azure depths of the firmament. It was more than the instinctive craving of a human spine to stand erect, it was like a ray of light, weak but refulgent. The padre tingled with excitement.

A sudden clap of thunder and dazzle of lightning. The world shuddered under the monstrous onslaught. The silence that succeeded seemed almost ominous and then, the next moment, came the sound of Bina's watchful words: 'Eh! Oh! A boy. It's a boy.' To her listeners her words seemed to fall from on high.

The men exchanged glances. Phulal expected the padre to speak. When he didn't, Phulal giggled a little and said, 'A boy . . .'

Matilal's grasp on the knocker had gradually slackened, and Phulal all of a sudden had to grab both knockers. The padre crouched forward, elbows on his knees, head in his hands and appeared to fall into profound contemplation: an old man suddenly feeling the strain. Stroking his beard with his fingers he murmured, 'What did you say?' as if speaking to himself: though he had heard Phulal clearly, he seemed to feel an urge to be thoroughly certain of his statement.

Phulal's lips moved, but no sound emerged. The crying rose above the noise of the storm as if wanting to drown it, to harry Nature,

155

vast and ageless though she was, into submission. The new situation both thrilled and bewildered the padre – what an incredible event to have occurred in the dead of night! Of all the places where it might have happened, his church had been selected! His mind searched turbulently for the meaning of the marvel, the underlying significance of the cry, and as it searched the old padre's mental state gradually altered. He went falteringly into the garden, knelt down in the water and with hands folded uttered only, 'Lord!'

The prayer did not spring from stupidity or derangement. Years of devotion lay in its heart. Who was this creature born into this humble house on such a night of enraged skies terrifying to ordinary mortals, when the world was like a cave, the forest ravished and tormented? The rain was whipping the padre's body; but his mind saw only radiant colours. Immediately after, the thought struck him: was it this for which he had been waiting so long? Had the reward for his piety finally come?

Phulal stared at the padre like a clown. As Matilal's mind had drifted off, his hold on the door had loosened further and he had almost let it fly open. Phulal had grabbed it and shouted at the top of his voice, 'What a wind!'

Now Bina tugged the doors from the inside and Phulal slowly released them. She spoke solemnly: 'Go and get something to dispose of the afterbirth, and bring a spade . . .' Then she added, 'And give me a smoke.'

Phulal extracted a *biri* from the fold in his dhoti and held it out. Having washed her unclean hand in the roof-water and shaken it, Bina took the *biri* and disappeared again for a minute.

Phulal stood waiting for clarification. When she returned Bina gave it, standing on the steps of the church, sucking contentedly at her *biri*, having knotted together the two door knockers with the end of her sari. As Phulal splashed away through the mud like a frog to fetch the required items, Bina puffed strongly, blinked to catch Matilal's attention and said, 'Eh, Padre.'

The lightning revealed the padre still motionless in prayer. He had left behind his corporeal body and travelled incorporeally to an ancient time, the age of the earliest gospel. His mind was full of the words of Him whose dust still greened men's thoughts.

'Eh, Padre!'

Bina raised the pitch of her voice to bring him back to his surroundings. The padre was in a state of inspiration; the world was one of purity and sacredness – of this he had never had doubts – and today his faith had been confirmed. He picked his way back to the door and faced the midwife.

She pulled hard on her *biri* and said, 'He's arrived, the creature. Quite a basketful! Looks a real prince, as fair as a prince.' She rolled her eyes in amusement.

Just then Phulal came back at the double, head down, back bent against the storm. Bina looked at him and remarked, 'You old dimwit, you think a small pot like that is big enough for all this earth? Better get another one . . .'

'Blasted woman – why didn't you say so before?' Phulal retorted. Although the padre was watching them both he seemed to be somewhere else. His lips were trembling with mantras. Phulal went off again and after a while returned with the items. Bina nipped the end of her *biri*, stuck the remainder behind her ear, picked up the things and went inside.

She had turned the newly-delivered mother on her side. The baby boy lay on a pile of straw, mewling ceaselessly. With some effort Bina dug up the soiled earth and put it in the pot. Carrying this in one hand and the basket in the other, she kicked open the church door and came out. The two men had their eyes elsewhere. Bina stood on the steps and said, laughing, 'He's all yours, Padre, you've got a real god in there. You can give me a sari, now go and take a look at your little lotus.' With that she walked off into the rain, her head swaying from side to side, calling back once, 'God knows where the woman's from. She says she has no one.'

Bina's words – 'a real god in there' – flooded the padre with divine light.

Neither man knew what he should do. One held the left knocker, the other the right one, together they stood and gazed within. Their strange posture made them look like figures in a triptych. Matilal felt deprived of the power of speech by the palpitating rose-coloured thing; but this did not surprise him. The woman lay further away, cloud-like, while in the foreground, as Bina had said, lay the basket of divine grace. There was some kind of fragrance too.

The padre climbed a few steps to the verandah of the church and sat there with folded hands and unblinking gaze. He smiled a little in a prayerful way.

'Right now!' said Phulal severely. 'All this is fine but where's the woman from?'

Matilal heard what was said but continued to stare at the infant with tears in his eyes. Meanwhile the door flew open and banged shut several times.

Phulal suggested eagerly, 'It looks as though the baby takes after the father, don't you think so, Father?'

The padre gave him a stern glance and said, 'Phulal.' His tone was admonitory. It was most unusual for him, but his intention was simply to preserve the decencies, rather than to show he could bite when provoked.

The people of the area regarded the padre as a gangling child, even imagined picking him up and putting him in their laps. So, although the padre's rebuke slightly embarrassed Phulal, he was not put off. He ran his tongue over his lips, shrugged and said, 'You think I'm imagining it? It's true what I say . . . I don't talk in riddles.'

Matilal shook his head emphatically: 'Later.'

'All right, I'll hold my tongue. But the fact is, you know many things but, being a padre – you don't know the ways of the world. The church is impure now, it's defiled. Let Bina find out the truth.'

Matilal just shook his head impatiently once more: 'You don't understand, Phulal. Cast up your eyes and say a prayer of thanksgiving.' Then in a low voice he added, 'Please go and get my Bible as quick as you can, I seem to be forgetting what must be done.'

Phulal was fatigued. The padre's mention of the Bible disgusted him. He was a Christian but he became annoyed and said, 'Are you about to die! Now the boy's born why not go and change your clothes. Where's she from, who knows? Get up.'

'No no, go and fetch it – and bring a lantern too.'

'Oh Father! On a night like this, with all the bother of this damned birth, d'you really need a Bible? Are you out of your mind, Father?'

'Please go, there's a good fellow . . .'

Phulal had no choice. After some time he came back with the Bible and stood waiting, lantern in hand.

As the padre took the book he asked, 'Hold the lantern up.' Phulal obeyed. The padre opened to the appropriate page, stroked his beard a couple of times and felt his mind become composed. His lips quivered with mumbled sentences. A dung-beetle settled suddenly upon the page; Phulal, seeing the padre's absorption, simply brushed it away with

158

his free hand. The padre reached the end and said, 'Amen.' Phulal immediately repeated the word, lowered the lantern and muttered, 'Bitch!'

The padre looked weakly at him.

Phulal was a bit disconcerted. He changed tack. 'Well, I mean she seems to have all the time in the world and no sense. How long's she been gone? No sign of her . . . Ah, here she comes . . . Where've you been, bitch!' Bina's reappearance was a chance to vent his irritation.

'Oh, just having a screw before killing myself,' she snapped and looked straight at the padre. 'Father, I'm back only for your sake. This man here, this bastard idiot Phulal, tell him to treat me with some respect – casteless Christian fellow!'

'Hey, listen to her, a low-caste woman – lowest of the low.'

The padre was ill-prepared for such spitefulness. It was agony to hear. He felt like a rabbit trying to reach its hole. His mood of meditation was buckling. Bina, fixing her gaze on him, perceived his suffering. She said, 'I swear to you, Father – I have not touched drink, I've brought only some food, I must stay here all night, but I need a smoke.'

'My dear, this is a church, it's not permitted. Come to my house . . .'

'How can I keep on leaving the child and this woman? Here she lies – family unknown, caste unknown, village unknown, having her baby – nothing wrong with that, I suppose? Well well . . .'

Phulal seconded Bina and looked at the padre.

Matilal felt that vile and clammy arms were trying to embrace him and he shrank back, saying helplessly, 'Bina, you don't realise who he is . . .'

She put down her bundle while the padre was speaking, and gathered herself for a retort. Throwing out her hands like a typical rustic actor she challenged, 'Many places and much business have I seen, but I have never clapped eyes on her, whoever she is – the lady herself says she's got no one. But she can have a child here and I can't have a smoke?'

'I agree, it's not at all fair,' said Phulal.

The padre was troubled. The conversation was polluting his mind. He thought of saying, 'There's a small child here – smoking isn't good for him.' but instead he found himself blurting out, 'This one who has just been born, you do not know who – '

'How about that!' Phulal butted in, with a smile in the direction of Bina.

159

'Yes, is that so?' said Bina. 'I delivered him, I cut his cord, I nursed him, and I don't know . . . but you do?'

Like an innocent child, open-eyed with faith, the padre simply repeated, 'The one who is just born you do not know.'

Bina had a streak of mischief in her. She stuck her arms akimbo on her waist, flung out her elbows and danced around like one of Lord Krishna's play maidens. 'Hearing your words makes me dance like mad . . . Now I must give up my caste and become a Christian!' she simpered.

Phulal shouted his disapproval. The padre, for his part, might have been expected to detest the whole exhibition, but he did not. He remarked with a helpless grin, 'Bina, if you live long enough you will understand. I am certain my prayers have not gone unanswered.' So saying he took a long look into the room. The sacred picture still hung above the candles, the ground below was still ploughed up, and in front of it there still lay the struggling pink creature. The whole scene made the padre wild with excitement. All at once he ran off towards the bell-rope, untied it from its post and began forcefully to pull it. The bell rang out like a rejoinder to the thunder-claps in the sky.

Bina said to Phulal, 'Oi, old man, the Christian has gone crazy. You call yourself a Christian – go and save him, save him you wretch.'

A noise of absolute disgust came from Phulal. He had put up with being soaked all this time and now his reward was an outburst of lunacy: it was intolerable. Yet he felt obliged to bear it. Bina's behaviour had provoked the Christian in him; he knew that any task performed in the church, especially one done for the padre, was blessed.

When Phulal reached Matilal he found him tugging haphazardly at the bell-rope as if possessed. In the lightning's glare he was a ghastly sight and Phulal was alarmed. But he pulled himself together and stepped forward to take the rope from the padre who cried, 'Pull, pull well!' and clapped his hands like a child. 'The rain will cease, Phulal, they will come, and I will tell them – look who has come among you . . .'

'It won't stop, I'm telling you,' said Phulal. He wanted the storm to rage without respite, and so give him a break. Then he added with angry conviction, 'You are here. Who else do we need?'

Strangely, the rain did fizzle out. It was a common event in these parts. The clouds vanished, the hills became visible and the moon shone clearly through the gaps in the gently moving eucalyptus trees. In ones

160

and twos people began to pick their way through the mud. A group of conical straw hats – *pekas* and *tokas* – assembled. Their owners came from the lower depths of poverty but each was hell-fearing, each desired to be virtuous as they gathered quietly in the field beside the church. The padre nodded his head joyfully and called out, 'Today a golden being has been born.' The glad news announced, the padre said, 'Phulal, the Bible please – '

Phulal brought both Bible and lamp and stood waiting. The padre read and then they sang the hymn: 'You light the world and bring new life, scattered all around'. It was followed by a prayer: 'He who has come will cause you to see . . .'

Then everyone crowded beside the church and tried to peer through the windows or through the door. Though old they still knew how to cry and how to respond to others' crying. They listened to the baby's sound intently; each thought his crying no ordinary cry.

Bina appeared and said, 'Look, all these fellows'll suffocate the child, make him sick. Send them packing before they finish the boy off.'

Somehow Phulal was able to restrain the people. All were anxious to see the child's mother but the padre stood guard, reminding them this was a church: they did not have the courage to press their claims.

Next to Matilal's house stood another hut. It was allotted to the mother and the new arrival for the time being. They moved in.

One evening soon after, the hermaphrodite Badan turned up. The padre was sitting in his easy chair. Lifting his eyes from the Bible in his hands he asked, 'Where have you been these days?'

'Father, I went away to my sister. Then I did this and that for a while. And then the news reached me that heaven had delivered a small *babu* to your house and so I thought – I must go and see this little lord with my own eyes.'

Matilal was thrilled. Keen to hear more he watched astonished as Badan's body began to undulate with excitement.

'I must sing a song to charm this little heavenly messenger, this Dut Babu. Maybe he'll be true to his name and carry a message for me and then I'll be born again as a man and have a son! This life has been a rotten one.' Badan wiped away a few tears with a corner of sari.

Matilal wanted to speak some words on the subject of rebirth but did not because he knew they would be wasted; besides, he felt pity

161

for Badan's distress. He said only, 'Hold on, Badan . . .' and then got up and called Bhamar.

She, the child's mother, was by now well-versed in such displays. Balancing the child in her lap she came and sat on the charpoy on the verandah. The way she sat made her look like an icon. Badan was highly impressed by the whole picture. With the usual affected gesture Badan said, 'Father, I understand only how to get bread, not to give reverence, but I must say that though I have not seen heaven, I can feel its grace here.'

The words transported Matilal. Badan meanwhile took the opportunity to study Bhamar. The healthy glow of her body was disturbing. Badan felt compelled to pull away, go to the small courtyard, clap hands and begin to sing:

> What's to worry, why worry.
> Heaven has found a home.
> Why should I worry . . .

Warming to the rhythm Badan danced round and round. Some typically salacious words came to mind, but after one or two probing glances at the padre, Badan omitted them: the more the hermaphrodite twirled, the more devotional in tone the song became.

Bhamar sat gazing at Badan without feeling able to display her curiosity; she let herself show only the wonder of a child.

Badan told the baby, 'Why do you look at me like that, do you recognise me? You smile? Oh Dut Babu, I have sung through so many former births.' Badan glanced once at the padre, then winked suggestively at Bhamar.

She initially did not comprehend the gesture and continued to look child-like. Badan went on dancing and on the next round again flicked an indecent look at the woman. This time Bhamar felt herself flush and at the next moment felt a sense of alarm. She bent down and glanced askance at the padre. He appeared tranquil. She became distinctly uneasy, fixed her gaze on the baby's head and watched its pulse throb. The hermaphrodite danced, shadow circling the charpoy. Fear prevented Bhamar from lifting her head, but neither could she find any excuse to get up. She gave the child a small pinch and immediately it began to cry.

162

The padre got up and came over: 'Why is he crying? You had better feed him.' Then he added to Badan, 'Well Badanchand, perhaps you should go now.'

'I'm leaving, Father, but first bless me Father, so that in births to come I can be a father and a virtuous man.' Then Badan bowed several times.

Days passed. Ploughing continued on the spreading slopes of Sharendi. Small shadows passed back and forth across the water lying in the furrows as the big bull buffaloes ambled to and fro. Badan too ploughed. The land belonged to Jadu, who was a labourer. Badan so far had felt unable to voice suspicions, because people would certainly object; in fact they would be outraged. But eventually Badan said to Jadu, 'You know, I think that woman's passed through quite a few hands . . .'

Jadu pretended to rebuke him: 'Eh, go to hell, wretch!' He turned the plough and went off again, but the next time around he said, 'Shame on you . . .' and stopped to question Badan.

'Listen, I'm telling you, she's taking advantage – taking us all for a ride.'

The idea seemed to please Jadu, and he called everyone together. Most were Christians and they were rather proud of the boy-child. There was no such compulsion in Jadu because he owned land, and besides, he was a Hindu. Unlike the others he was also partial to drink and singing. When everyone had dragged his plough to Jadu's land beneath the ridge Jadu unexpectedly lashed the water with his whip and loudly proclaimed, 'Here's this good-for-nothing eunuch! Now listen to him – '

'Old Jadu here has listened to me, do me the honour of listening too,' Badan began.

'What rubbish are you talking, son-of-a-bitch!' someone called out. 'If people hear, what will happen?'

Most of those assembled could not follow what was being said, so they shifted uncomfortably and looked from Jadu's face to Badan's and back again. They were simple folk, looking forward to enjoying a bit of fun.

'If you've got the guts, tell them all you told me,' said Jadu.

'I'm not scared. I look after myself!' Badan tightened his shoulder wrap and said, 'If I tell a lie what do I have to gain? Tell me that . . .' Then, in a sombre voice Badan slowly said, 'The mother of the little messenger *babu* – she's a whore.' Lashing his buffalos, he departed.

The congregated Christians stood wide-eyed and open-mouthed for a moment, then dissolved into hubbub while Badan, twisting the tails of the animals, pulled gradually away. But soon fear of sin and a sense of shock jerked them back to their work; Badan's buffaloes promptly panicked and Badan was deposited in the water. Many of the crowd were clearly over-excited by the hermaphrodite's remark; the little copper bells that hung hidden between their loins as luck charms, were all at once glittering in the sun's rays. They went back to their ploughs and Badan was left lying in the water, staring at the sky.

With the field almost empty again Jadu shouted, 'Why should the bugger lie? He's powerless – he's just an impotent fellow.'

The ugly story did the rounds. Consequently anyone who so much as set foot on the path towards the church fell under suspicion. But no one yet had the courage to crack jokes about it.

A few days later Jadu suddenly turned up at the padre's leading a large goat. He had put kohl on his eyes and wore a clean wrap around his shoulders.

The padre had for some time been thanking the Lord for the way that the baby boy's reputation had spread. The event had given everyone fresh faith; it was thrilling verification of the seriousness of their fundamental beliefs.

Jadu said, 'Father, we ploughed well and now we are ready to reap.' He handed over the goat, adding as he did so, 'It's a fine harvest . . . we expected that, when the heavenly messenger, Dut Thakur, came among us.' After that he had an audience with the baby and mother, and then with a pang departed.

Pataki, a local ruffian, came next. With tears in his eyes he said, 'Please, help me to be good.'

Bhulua, who lacked common sense, got worked up and said to Pataki's face, 'Father, these *badmash*-fellows have bad eyes – like cobras.'

The padre was mortified. When Pataki had gone he said, 'Bhulua, there is no such thing as bad . . .'

'No such thing! If I buy a brinjal and don't look out, won't I get gypped? Even a *biri* costing half a pie – if you don't look sharp, it comes broken . . .'

'Wherever the Lord's name is, there is nothing bad.'

164

'Eh? Nothing bad! So who steals my *biri* every day then? Nowadays I have to keep it round my waist.' He showed the padre.

The gross laughter of Bhulua bothered the padre. It brought back a dim memory: Bhamar, sitting on the charpoy, the child in her lap, and as she tightened her sari around her waist three *biris* dropped out, one of them half-smoked. The padre had ignored them but later returned to them, saying 'You shouldn't smoke those things . . .'

'Bhulua gave them to me to look after.'

Without giving way to his true feeling Matilal said, 'You shouldn't keep them.' He paused. 'Bhamar, you don't know whose mother you are. You must stay pure.' Then he touched his forehead to the feet of the child.

Bhulua's words about *biris* brought the episode back. But Matilal's joy at the baby's new fame swept all before it.

The gossip continued. One day Phulal went to the padre and said, 'Father tell me – how do we answer these people?'

The padre simply patted Phulal on the head and said, 'God's will.'

Questions were constantly being asked of Phulal or of the less-than-brilliant Bhulua, who was the most curious of them all. Wherever his work took him Bhulua interrogated people without getting any firm answers. His opinion remained fixed by his reaction on the very first day: the woman was a bad lot. And the blame for this opinion, it should be said, was Bhamar's: to Bhulua she had said 'I'm from Raina'; to Phulal 'I'm from Sharenga'; and to someone else it was 'Belpahari'.

Phulal brought visitors – village watchmen and others – from distant villages, announcing to all and sundry, 'Men have come here from far away to see the prince.'

Matilal never understood such tricks. Bhamar would sit, baby in lap, with the look of a frightened mouse, praying that the padre would not get up. If he did, the visitors would turn on her with hard eyes and demand of her in Phulal's presence, 'Where's your man? Where are you from?' Bhamar would only look frightened and weep.

In this way time passed but no one became any the wiser about Bhamar's identity.

She seemed to be losing her mind. One evening, when the padre was kneeling absorbed in prayer, Bhamar brought her tall, beautiful body near him and stood like a statue. He was not conscious of the precise moment when she fell and clasped his feet, but her face touched his soles, her hair was dishevelled and the ground was moist with her tears.

Their warmth deepened the padre's composure – until finally he turned his head. He withdrew his feet and stood up.

A flustered Bhamar somehow lifted her eyes and said questioningly, 'Father . . .'

'In church you should not touch a person's feet, Bhamar.'

'Father, what's to become of me?'

'A person can get new life through repentance, my dear. Through repentance a new life has come to you – you must come to know the one who has been born: he is a great saint . . . a preacher whose name will spread far and wide.'

Evening, night and morn the padre prayed before the boy-child. He used no words, simply concentrated his mind. Sometimes the child lay on its mother's lap, sometimes in her arms, sometimes at her breast. He also prayed on the hillside in the middle of the night.

Late one night he was on the verandah, getting ready to go out, when he caught sight of Bhamar leaving her room in an odd fashion: her eyes seemed white in the darkness, as if lacking pupils. When she noticed him she ran up. Her voice was slurred: 'Father . . .'

Stroking her head the old man reassured her, 'Give thanks to God for your new life. Just look at the child, what a beauty he is.'

As he spoke Matilal suffered for Bhamar, and yet he was pleased because he knew that without trials, there can be no redemption.

Another night a slim moon hung low in the sky. The hillside was deserted – only piles of rock kept the padre company. He finished his prayer, rose and suddenly observed Bhamar, her clothes in disarray. She saw him and grabbed his feet, apparently startled: 'I've been searching for you, Father. See how the thorns have cut my feet . . . What's to become of me?'

The padre told her, 'Adore him – and all will be well.'

The padre soon got into the habit of taking the child with him during his prayers. In one place a hill stream called Sharnado flowed within the shadow of tall *shal* trees, forming pools and eddies in the darkness. As the padre stood on one bank he glimpsed on the opposite bank someone as still as a stone. He called out, 'Who are you?'

'It's me, Father.'

He paddled over the sandy bed and queried, 'You're here?'

'I wanted to weep . . . If I weep there, you'll be upset.'

'Please, do not weep. Let me give him to you.' He placed the child in the woman's lap.

For once Matilal called to mind what the gossips said. But then he thought, 'How rare to discover purity such as Bhamar's on this earth!'

The child now lived with the padre constantly. Every detail of its appearance and behaviour was stored in his mind. From his place in the padre's lap the child saw many a midnight, cried on many a hillside and was constantly watched by Matilal and the vast sky for the slightest signs of childish restlessness. How many fields he trod, carried by the padre, and how many ailing foreheads his small feet brushed in blessing! That was how he spent his early life. He called the padre Father, and out of naughtiness he sometimes opened the Bible; an action the padre liked to invest with deep meaning. What was really extraordinary, a matter for real pride, was that the boy never tore a page. Whenever the padre called out, 'O heart, sweetheart', he would come toddling in.

One day the padre, with the boy on his shoulders, was returning from Nimra through the *shal* forest and *mahua* groves at Sharata when suddenly he came across a little party.

A coarse mat was spread out; on it sat Jadu, Jahar, Badan the hermaphrodite, Bhola the messenger and Pataki. There were bottles and Jaga was skinning a *titi* bird. When they caught sight of the padre they hid the bottles, except the one in Jadu's hand which he covered with his palm.

The padre was put out. He stood still, they bowed. He said, 'What's this?'

'Well, it's kerosene for the evening.'

'Kerosene?'

'Well, if we don't drink it our wicks won't burn.'

'Give up all this drinking. Come and see the visitor.'

'Don't we already know him? He's our deliverer – from all the sins we commit in this birth.'

'Shame on you. Do you prefer to lie in the gutter?'

'If we don't lie there how can he deliver us?'

None of the Christians present argued, only Jadu. The padre went sadly away. Later, he knew, they would open the vat of fermenting liquor.

That night he remembered the party they had mentioned. He now felt

167

he had spoken too bluntly about 'lying in the gutter'; that he was in the wrong. It seemed to him that he should ask forgiveness. He dithered for a while but soon became resolute and set forth.

At Jadu's house he found Jadu was not back. Neither was Jahar at home. So, walking over the rough and rolling ground, the padre headed for Nimra. The month of *Phalgun* was then at its peak and the *mahua* trees were in bloom. The main grove was over the summit of a rise. As Matilal neared the top he heard a voice say quickly, 'Oi, eh, padre's coming', as if telling others to beware.

Not far away, between the gaps in the foliage glinting in the moonlight, a few faces were furtively visible, bottles lay strewn about and a dog was licking the vat; closer still the padre's gaze fell upon the body of a well-developed young woman. It sprawled on the ground, her face half in shadow. She was stark naked, her hair fluttering gently in the breeze, a few plucked *titi* feathers scattered around her body. Someone called out, 'Eh Bhamar, padre's here.' The body was the same one that he had once compared to a monsoon cloud.

Bhamar managed to prop herself up in the mire and said, 'Father, what's to be my fate?'

He had not anticipated such an abominable scene. His own voice seemed to speak in his ear, 'You have received new life. You do not know whose mother you are!' He felt insulted, swindled, grossly humiliated by the sight: his chest ached and his forgiving old eyes filled with tears. His whole being was transfixed, only his beard blew in the wind; someone seemed to have hit him hard in the back with a heavy stick and broken his spine. Anger and shame were choking him. Fighting back his tears he strode to the church and wept like a child before it. But once inside he was bewildered. He could not bring himself to stay there.

On the path home his hands wanted to rip apart the leaves of the canna lilies. In his room he turned up the lamp, opened the Bible – but his thoughts would not collect themselves. He felt an urge to ask Bhulua – where's Bhamar? Entering the verandah and gazing at the sleeping figure of Bhulua, his eyes shifted across to the window of Bhamar's room and he got gooseflesh – it was pitch dark. He sat down abruptly in his chair and gripped the arms, his face running with sweat in the dark. To control his jerky breathing seemed all but beyond him.

Standing in the field beside the church he wanted to offer a prayer, but his mind, like his spine, seemed to have shattered. And yet if he, Matilal, a padre, were to forget the Holy Father, even for an instant, wouldn't that destroy his very existence? Horses' hooves seemed to be galloping between his ribs: where was his heart? his compassion? was the soul just a line of words in the Bible after all? Without faith a man might as well use the sacred page as fuel to heat milk for his infant.

A whole jungle of beastliness seemed to have entered him. He was not tired – the day's events had robbed him of fatigue – but the distant call of a nightingale could not move him, he felt so indifferent to such perfect sweetness of creation. Unexpectedly he found himself thinking – my devotion means nothing, I'm just a coward.

When nostrils flare, breathing quickens, brows furrow and teeth become bared, a person's thoughts charge down one narrow path. Matilal could think only, 'I've been cheated' – between tantalising flashes of the body of a woman in the bloom of youth, lying in a *mahua* grove.

His mind went back to the time when he had first heard the name of the Lord; he had felt himself more blessed than the angels themselves – triumphant in his victory. Now he was simply one of the duped. The harsh fact is, padres are more easily deceived than day-labourers.

Wretched Matilal. The harder he clung to the pillars on the verandah and bit his knuckles, the more the tears welled out of his eyes, blurring his vision. Then he caught the sound of another cry: it seemed to approach him in a mass of smouldering colour. He eyed it intensely. Through his misty gaze, the rays of the lantern were like carved lines in a woodcut in which the child stood in the centre-ground, rose-hued like a lovely Persian pomegranate. Hastily the padre averted his eyes.

Then he looked again – but this time stealthily; and the scene transformed him. A normal human being never wears the kind of look that Matilal now wore, lacking as he does either claws or fangs. Matilal was now truly terrifying to see. His head was spinning, his garb chaotic; like a giant bat he flew into the room and swooped upon the child. His mind was snapping but his resolve was swift and fanatical. The child was simply baffled, otherwise he would have burst into tears.

He gazed at the padre and sensed the familiar lap. The padre glanced once at the boy and looked away.

With long strides, often unsteady but firmly intent, he set out. His feet slipped on the ridges of the fields but always he found the path again and then, leaving it, a new path; and after that, yet another path.

The sky turned pearl. Light crept down from the hilltops and spread over the hills. Shadows appeared, long and deep. Birds darted up, uttering cries. The baby boy came to with a giggle.

Matilal's sweating face was oddly set as he observed the child, turned away and again looked. His determination weighed upon him like a stone. Then, abruptly, his brows knitted and he halted. He stood rooted to the ground but his legs still shook as if dreading he would revert to being Matilal the padre. He set the child back on his shoulders and started off again. One or two women were out picking up cowdung on the road. They put down their baskets and bowed to the padre. He walked straight past without a glance.

In time he reached the Khondari jungle.

As some birds flew past, he stopped. Around him, despite the night's rain many varieties of tree were in flower. Storm water still dripped from their leaves. The lower reaches of the Ban Dhoyani waterfall were swollen and gushing, but higher up everything was hushed.

He came to a neat clearing. A creeper had twined itself around a *shal* tree surrounded by dense bushes. The padre lifted the child down from his shoulders and looked away from him. He brought his hands together, prepared to pray, but instead cracked his finger joints in futility, letting the prayer float up unspoken, out of the mundane mortal world.

He gazed about him, absorbing the isolation, sensing the drops of water falling through the breeze. The child was not frightened by such solitude, he knew its eeriness well. He stood holding the padre's habit without alarm, excited by the drops of water, from time to time calling 'Father-Father.'

The pitter-patter of water on the leaves and the trickling of the waterfall might have reminded the padre of lips trembling in church, anxious to repent. But his thoughts were as unbending as an axe, as taut as a bowstring. Without thinking at all he pulled a rattle from his pocket and seemed as if about to hand it to the child – when he suddenly hurled it away. The boy toddled off like a baby elephant to fetch the rattle from among the feebly shivering leaves of the bushes.

One of the bushes shook violently. An animal seemed to pass through it. Its thorns tore at Matilal's habit, but somehow he got through.

170

On the spot where the child now stood, two or three flowers were seen to fall from the agitated tree above. Matilal watched them through a gap in the bushes. The boy was obviously thrilled by the rustling leaves.

A sickly sigh escaped Matilal's throat. His hands slipped slowly downwards from his eyes as if to pray, but hung shaking. The old man's forehead had been scratched by thorns. He saw the child, unblinking, stretch out his hands. Raindrops splashed on his palms. He was extremely happy, his tiny teeth gleaming in his open mouth. Catching hold of the rattle he began to shake it. The rain spattered; the leaves quivered; the toy tinkled. Then the child's second hand started to grope for the habit of the padre: soon it was searching desperately while all the time the first hand continued to shake the rattle. Not finding any trace of another hand the child swung round, looked about him and then, his mouth creasing, yelled 'Fa-ther!' The cry was wild, like his cry on the day he was born.

It did not move Matilal: he ran a short distance as if chased by a snake and hid himself in a hole the size of a man. But though he was caked in mud, the sound of crying still reached him. Raising himself up gingerly like a thief, he peered in the direction of the sound.

Now he could see. The child was walking forward crying, tripping over the hard ground, crawling a bit, then somehow getting to his feet. There was grit and blood on his tender knees.

The endless wilderness, the towering forest lords, the slanting sunbeams gave an air of mystery. The child's frightened eyes were still searching for someone; his face had become dirty as he constantly wiped his tears.

His crying seemed to pierce the sunlight. Birds flew by, leaves eddied down and several bright-red *shal* flowers fluttered earthwards like feathers. The little boy tottered forward.

The padre sprang up as if kicked, ran towards the child. He fell at his feet, rubbed the small body with his face, saying faintly 'My heart, my sweetheart.'

His face touched the wounded knee and his tears washed it clean. 'I am not a true Christian, Father,' he murmured.

(1958)

171

WATER

Mahasweta Devi

The village of Bakuli lay at the centre of a basin in the red earth of the uplands. That was how it struck the leaders of Operation Bakuli when viewing the village by helicopter. The word 'basin' was used in their report to describe the shape of the land-surface with the village at the bottom of it, encircled by high ground. About a mile and a half to the east was a canal. Nineteen families were resident in the village, which had a total population of 109 persons. Their crop was paddy. All the cultivated land lay beyond the basin's rim. Apart from it there was a spreading tamarind tree, several mango trees and some jackfruit, *shirish* and *palash* trees. There was also a famous shrine of Dharma Thakur. The owner of the land in its entirety was Lakshman Shamanta; the other eighteen families were his sharecroppers. Water was acutely short. The two hand-drawn wells and a deep tubewell lay within the perimeter of Lakshman's house. The village's ancient tank had silted up and become dry in recent years. It required a four-and-a-half-mile walk to the west to reach the Khartora river. At the point when we encounter the village, the smoke of evening is coiling up from Lakshman's house and paddy store.

That was when Operation Bakuli began, descending from the sky. The whole business had been fixed in advance by telephone and radio-signal.

Gokul, Nirapada and Tarini were dragging sacks of paddy out of Lakshman Shamanta's store and stacking them beneath the tamarind tree at the time, while Gokul's father Nirbharasha stood cursing his son.

Gokul said to Sharaju, the woman with him, 'Night or day, it doesn't matter which, we've got to get away from here. See if you can find a path.'

'It's dark. I'll go now.'

She left and was swallowed by the darkness.

A while later she returned, tight-faced. She said, 'No way out in any direction. Everywhere's blocked. E-v-e-r-y-where!'

That was because now the command of Operation Bakuli had passed to other hands. With the village surrounded the orders came, 'Don't let a fly get out.'

By morning the eighteen families saw that they were encircled on all sides, caught in a human net that was gradually contracting.

Sharaju could remember little beyond that: many men closing in on them, advancing, dreadfully determined, iron in their wills, soundless except for the crunch-crunch of grit beneath their boots as if the very stones were protesting – crunch, crunch, crunch; and meanwhile the village boys watching the men slowly falling silent, the babies staring in wonderment and Gokul mumbling, 'Sharaju! Can't you hide in those bushes beside the tank?'

No. Her feet would not move. The crunching of the boots continued and then – 'Halt' – an order – followed by, 'Which one is Gokul Das?' A voice like a machine. And after that a black curtain over her mind: unresponsive, rigid, unyielding. 'Which one is Gokul Das?' Down came the curtain.

It fell down and stayed down. Several times Sharaju attempted to lift it, see through it and understand 'Which one is Gokul Das?' But she got no further than the question. The curtain would not move from her memory. It continued unyielding, rigid, impervious to protest. Her mental recall had become like a letter inked by a censor. Some of it was there and could be grasped. The rest was black, a blot on the mind. When, after this dark chapter, she could once more think, when the earth and Bakuli returned to her consciousness, the village wore a different face.

Twenty-two people remained, all old men, women and infants. Every house was gone. Their ashes floated in the sky. Both wells were plugged with brick and grit. The deep tubewell had been ripped from the earth and lay like an abscess. All the trees, bar the tamarind, were reduced to cinders. It was the dry season, and the area was an arid one.

Operation Bakuli had proved 'successful'.

Over on the east rim of the basin, blocking the way to the canal, a temporary aluminium hut now stood. The sun rose behind it, shining

173

angrily like a white eye. Heat poured out of its millions of Fahrenheit. To Sharaju and the rest of them the aluminium glowed like pure silver. At the hut's window, fair-skinned, glorious as a god, a young man sat. At his eyes was a pair of binoculars.

Beneath the hut was a tubewell. Around them both barbed-wire was coiled. Coolies had laboured secretly all day to instal everything: water was now flowing. Above the aluminium roof stretched a second roof, a thatched awning lifted from Gokul's father's house. About ten times a day the coolies hosed it with water: there was no other way to keep the hut cool. This year's drought was a severe one. No rain had fallen since the month of *Phalgun,* four months previously. Now it was *Asharh,* the rainy season month, but all day the sun poured forth from its millions of Fahrenheit. By eight a.m. the horizon was already blurred with heat, the air gyrating like a host of goblins. It had picked up grit and made the colour of the sky ashen, malignant.

Beside the young man sat landlord Lakshman Shamanta's son Sharadindu, known as Sharat. He was running through an account of the village's affairs for the benefit of this temporary deity of Bakuli.

'All the land here near the canal is now ours. Father did that.'

'It's farmed?'

'This year no. Where's the water?'

'What about the canal?'

'Who'll use canal water?'

'They will, won't they?'

'But which of them has even as much as three *bighas* of land in one spot? Will they pay for water for so little land? They've got maybe five tiny *kathas* and then a *bigha* or two a mile or two further on. That's how it is here.'

'Couldn't your father have paid for it, got the water?'

Sharadindu shook his head. No. His father had the land, and the money, but he would not get the water. Why not? Recently Sharadindu had asked him and his father had answered, 'You too Sharat! You're beginning to sound like that crazy Gokul. Gokul's always making a fuss, now you've started too.'

His father had never wanted the sharecroppers to have water, get a good harvest and pay him a good return per *bigha* of his land – or to become self-sufficient. The officials in the local town didn't want it either: improved cultivation meant the end of famine; and only if famine continued would grant-aid continue.

'I could flood the place with canal water if I wanted to,' Sharat's father had said. 'But what do I want with water? I've got wells. Government's given a tubewell to help cultivation. I got it fixed in my house. Water! What for? Paddy growing? Don't give me paddy, Sharat. If I grow paddy how much do I make? Can I make twenty thousand rupees? I don't need water, I don't want more paddy. Just you wait and see – this year, before your eyes I'll lend twenty-five thousand rupees to the ten villages around here. And I'll lend it with interest. It's that interest that has made me rich. As if I don't know the canal's full of water!'

'So what do I tell them?' Sharat had asked his father.

'Decide for yourself. I'm worried about this drought, I'd better go to town. Will the grant-aid come when Gokul makes the sort of statements he's been making? It's us, the people who matter in this place, we should write the reports – then aid'll come.'

After this, Sharadindu had slowly gone outside. What to say to Gokul? The drought was dire; in neighbouring Poratala it had shrivelled all the young plants. If any water had been available the plants could have been saved. Yet here, the canal was full of water – right in front of people's eyes. They could hear its rumbling at night. And yet there was no cultivation – because water was lacking. Every last *bigha* of ground along the banks of the canal was cracking in agony at its own sterility. How could he explain that to the waiting Gokul?

'Your father – what did he say?' Gokul had queried immediately.

'Getting canal water's a lot of bother.'

'Bother means – a petition to the town, to the B. D. office, and the payment of some canal tax.'

'He said, "a lot of bother".'

'And if everything's dying here or already dead?'

Just then Lakshman Shamanta himself had emerged. 'Who's that? Gokul? What's up, Baba?'

'You won't get water from the canal – why?'

'No power to do so, my friend! If you have the power, go ahead. Write a petition. You wrote one when the tubewell was fixed in my house, didn't you? You write petitions well. After that, just collect the tax and I'll take it to the B. D. office personally.'

'It's your land and we pay the tax?'

'I've no power.'

'Have we any?'

'No power? Haven't you plenty? Didn't I see it when the tubewell was installed? Gokul, my friend! don't you see, it was because it was my land, on which my house stands, that Government installed their machine there? Otherwise there'd have been snags – the canal you know – the B. D. Office would have said: why do you need a tubewell?'

'You're an influential man, that's why Government put the well in your house. All right, you don't need the canal water, but there are people here dying. What about that?'

'Baba! People are dying: what do you mean? Have I ever let anyone in Bakuli die? Have I ever allowed that? Who gives the money here? Who gives the paddy seed?'

'Without water the crops wither. You won't obtain it?'

'Baba, I'm an old-fashioned fellow. My view is different. Don't mind if I ask you a question. When God doesn't send water, can a person use canal water? Have you ever heard of that? Does anyone anywhere do that?'

'It happens in Kurashima.'

'Don't argue for the sake of arguing, Gokul. It may cause offence. Tell me, whenever there's been drought in the past you've offered *puja* at the shrine and it's rained, hasn't it? Why not this time, I wonder?'

'How should I know why not?'

'This time your insolence has offended the deity. You have been rude about Thakur. It's you who has brought sin on Bakuli.'

'That's your final word?'

'It is.'

Gokul had gone off. Then Sharadindu's father had turned on him and said, 'I'm giving you a letter, Sharat. Take it to town. Until I send word, don't come back. I don't like the look on Gokul's face. I've already sent your mother and your wife away. Catch a bus. And write a report to the district office.'

It was while he was in town that Sharadindu had received the news. Lakshman Shamanta was no more: his father's house was ablaze.

Sharadindu paused in his account to the young man in the aluminium hut. Then he added, 'Father was very obstinate. Water was at the bottom of all the trouble.'

'Where do they go at night?' the young man now enquired.

'To the old tank. They dig down deep. Water comes up before daybreak. But don't worry, sir. It soon dries up before the morning's over.'

176

'But why haven't they left the village yet?'

In Bakuli, Sharaju was asking Nirbharasha the same question: 'Why don't we leave?'

'And go where?'

'To the town, to beg.'

'You too?'

'Everyone will beg.'

'So no one gave you any water?'

'No. Over there, in Kurashima, they're terrified of the name Bakuli. The boss-sahib there takes his bath and the water all gets wasted. Even that water they wouldn't give us . . . You used to know how to poke a stick in the ground and get water. Everyone used to call you before a well was dug. You knew then. That tubewell they've just dug, d'you think it will give water? Much water?'

'I never tried over there.'

'Sitting here I can hear it pumping. At night I can hear the water in the canal, I hear it flowing. For thirteen days I haven't put a drop on my head. Everything's on fire inside me.'

Sharaju paused, Nirbharasha closed his eyes and sat down. As he sat, he grappled with his own burning, just as he grappled with it when he slept at night. Before dawn the women would go to the middle of the tank, dig down and find water. They would store it in a pitcher. Today was the thirteenth day he had carefully measured it out, giving a bit to everyone. For food they ate burnt rice, husking each grain with their nails.

Day and night they sat beneath the tamarind tree. Sharaju climbed its branches and broke off some leaves. These she handed out. The sour fibre when chewed brought saliva. It kept their throats moist. But now there was no water in their bodies, and so the saliva did not come.

Nirbharasha said, 'If once we go, will we be allowed to return? Sharat will find new tenants.'

'New tenants, yes, and a bus service – Government's giving him the money.'

'Then what do we do?'

'Do you really believe he'll keep any of us? How can he? Women, old women and infants as tenants? Forget it!'

'If only I could leave the village once and return, then I could sort something out,' Nirbharasha persisted.

'What could you do? Fetch water?'

'I could sort out something.' Nirbharasha was pathetically obdurate.

Sharaju sighed. She said, 'Lochan's family, Chiripadar's mother and Shona the boatman's family, they're going.'

'All going?'

'To the town. They'll simply die here, won't they?'

Nirbharasha shut his eyes and sat down. Then he said, 'Ask them to come tonight.'

'Why?'

'I used to be the one who offered *puja* to Dharma Thakur for all of us. All my life I've never told a lie. Tonight I'll sacrifice for rain. Perhaps Thakur will give us water.'

'Who will give the blood?'

'You will.'

Sharaju felt crucified. A memory of Gokul was torturing her. Hadn't he put great trust in her? Could she tear her breast like this, invoke water?

'Won't you?'

Sharaju heaved a tearless sob. She nodded, yes. Had Gokul definitely told her Dharma Thakur was a lie? Hadn't he always said that any deed bringing good to many should be done without hesitation? But why did she hear that crunch-crunch of boots on the squeaking grit, the moment she thought of him? – followed by that question: 'Which one is Gokul Das?' Why did she think of him like that? And immediately after the question; what was it that pulled the black curtain over her mind?

Nirbharasha was reassured. He said, 'It requires much blood, so I can't ask anyone else.'

Sharaju nodded again: 'I will.'

'After it water will come.'

'It will?'

'It has never failed us.'

Sharaju fell mute. Operation Bakuli had been successful: all around seemed hushed; an age seemed to be passing, a new age coming into being. Hush everywhere. Everywhere, that is, except in the canal where water flowed, and in the pumping tubewell. There, there was water, and more water. Sharaju raised her desiccated, bloodshot eyes to the horizon. It was quivering: the goblins were still gyrating against the grey canvas of the sky. Heat streamed from the million-Fahrenheit sun. It was ten a.m.

Then ten at night. All of a sudden the young man in the aluminium hut sensed that the twenty-two inhabitants of Bakuli were up to something. Were they trying to reach the canal or the river? Both directions were guarded. What were they doing?

He slipped his revolver into his waistband, picked up his binoculars, and descended the steps. Passing through the gap in the barbed-wire he went to the rim of the basin and stood there, binoculars pressed to his eyes.

The moonlight was dim and turbid. But through the lens the view was quite clear. Women, old and young, stood with hands upraised. They looked like skeletons with matted hair. Some of them held infants.

One younger woman stood in the middle. And there was an old man; looked like the father of that Gokul Das. He unwrapped the end of the woman's sari and tied it around her waist.

It was a picture of ruthlessness; the old man poised like a god of old, his hands folded together as he chanted. The young man let out a whistle of excitement. He watched as the old man tore at the woman's breasts with a knife. What cruelty! The breasts trembled. The old man had a pot in his hand. The woman took it with both hands and held it to her wound. Blood must have gushed out. Then she raised the small earthen vessel above her head. Flooding out the moonlight and the rumble of the canal she screamed, 'Water! Give us water! Water, Thakur!'

'Give us water!' She swayed round and round as she cried. 'Our whole world is on fire, Thakur, please send us some water!'

The young man had been briefed against all kinds of contingency. If the villagers made trouble, what to do; if they tried to reach the canal or river, what to do. But what to do if, after thirteen days with barely a cupful of water the fathers of Gokul, Nirapada and Tarini tore dry-eyed at the breasts of Gokul's girl, extracted blood and begged for water? Against that contingency, no briefing had been given.

No briefing and no instructions. Never act without orders from a superior: it had been drilled into the young man's very bones. Halt – charge – stop – advance, those were things he understood and could act upon. But in circumstances like these he was helpless. Orderless, he was powerless, a mere passive observer. He stood all night and watched. And all night, the entire night, the girl cried out, 'Give water!'

Morning came. The sun rose. A white, enraged, heartless sun of a million degrees Fahrenheit. The air burned.

179

And then the people left their village. And the young man went back to the hut. Relieved, deeply relieved. Now Sharadindu could instal new sharecroppers. The existing ones were going on their way: old people, women and children, no youth no man not even one adolescent among them, just as intended.

They walked over the hard, scorched ground and got to the main road. Here the bus would come. If they could get aboard they would go by bus. If not, they would walk the seven miles to the town.

As they waited Sharaju said, 'The one who helped them get Gokul and the others, he's not survived, has he? And I, to get water I tore my breast and spilt my blood, but the water didn't come. Why did they take Gokul, why did I give my blood? Why? Why?'

No one spoke. To this question no one had an answer. They saw a cloud in the distance. The bus was coming, the red dust was rising. The wind was on fire, and with it came the rumble of water, the water flowing in the canal.

(1984)

HOMECOMING

Hasan Azizul Huq

Alef dragged one foot slightly; apart from that he had no impediment. But today he had walked such a distance he was fully aware of his weakness. A leg muscle running from his waist to his heel felt as knotted as a piece of rope; he thought his leg would rupture if he went any further. And yet, earlier on, he had not even noticed the muscle. He knew he had to rest.

He sat down. To remove his boots was the first task. They were clamped to his feet; taking them off left him breathless. As the right one came loose it flew out of his hand. In the darkness he could not see where it landed. Involuntarily clutching the left one he sat on the dry grass and brooded, attempting to recall the events that had made him lame. A bullet had penetrated the flesh just below his knee. Not many days before that, he had been caught in a hail of bullets lasting a quarter of an hour. They had been invisible to him despite it being daytime – he had heard only their piercing whistle. Like a snake, like a cobra flicking out its tongue, they had hissed as they passed him. Fool that he was, he had stroked his forehead with his hand and thought: no blood, they missed me.

And so, strange to say, though the air had been full of flying lead, Alef's body had received not a scratch – until, a fortnight later, he had been hit by a stray shot that he had barely sensed. Dr Osman, irritable, wielding a large blunt knife, had sliced up his flesh and rummaged around for the metal. Alef had not been in much pain. Just prior to the operation, he had been given several injections. With complete clarity he had watched the movement of the knife, the tense muscles of Dr Osman's arms and the sweat dripping from his grim face. 'Eh! – is this meat or wood? – a knife's no good for it, what I need's an axe,' the

181

grumbling, harrassed Osman had said, as Alef plainly recalled. Sharif, his group leader, had stood proudly by with a smile on his face: this image too now loomed out of the darkness. 'Alef has been fighting for his country,' Sharif had observed, emphasising each word.

A month later Dr Osman himself had died. He had required no surgery: a bullet had got the doctor in the skull. Where Sharif had got to now, Alef had no idea. Walking away from the hospital many hours ago, Alef had found himself watching the reddish glow of the afternoon sun lingering on the tops of some tall trees in front of him. Whether those patches of light felt warm he did not know, but having followed the smashed-up road leading out of town along the river thus far, he knew that he was now really cold. He had not felt the chill to begin with because his forehead had been bathed in sweat. Now, sitting in this field beside the river holding his left boot, he began to shiver. He had never before appreciated how vast an expanse the heavens were when seen from a field on a clear winter's night. The darkness was not absolute, it seemed as if some white had been mixed with it, making everything visible but blurred. The heavens looked as distant as the abode of Allah. Alef was suddenly afraid: he felt that he would not make it home. He would perish here in this cold place and no one would find his corpse even in the light of day, so forlorn was he.

'I fought in a war – why?'

Muttering to himself in his rustic southern Bengali he repeated the question twice, as if to drive the thought home: he had fought, yes, but what for? He had not yet let go the boot in his left hand, but instead had pressed it to his knees while stroking his rifle with the right hand and interrogating himself. When people dwell on difficult questions their brows become furrowed, their jaws clench – so did Alef's as he sat tense with concentration. Applying what little education he had received up to Class Eight he tried to grapple with his country, his people and the war and find solutions for all their problems.

Before his discharge that afternoon Alef had not looked at Amin's face. He could not bring himself to, after the hospital staff had covered Amin with a red blanket. Still, he had hung about the hospital for three days waiting while Amin died – it had been his duty. He had to give accurate information to Amin's mother. She was waiting in her village, vainly expecting Amin back: he must give her definite news. The fact was, three days after Amin's right leg had been amputated, his whole body had rotted and begun to stink, and he had succumbed. Where was that right leg and that body now? Alef perceived that he was now a messenger with much to tell to many people – but his mind could not comprehend what words to use or to whom he should speak them.

He got to his feet again. Still bent, he slung his canvas bag over his shoulder and took hold of his rifle. His *lungi* was even now wrapped tightly around his waist, not loosened by his exertions. Then, at last, he became conscious of the boot in his left hand. Putting everything down he crawled about and groped for the right boot. Not finding it, he was struck by the thought that if and when he did locate it, he would have to put it on. The idea induced agony in both his legs. He gave up the search and hurled the left boot towards the river as if his life depended on it. But when at last he stood up, the piece of rope inside his leg pulled him down like a hunchback. In this condition he crouched, his bag over his shoulder, his rifle in his hand, thoroughly perplexed by his next move. Which direction to take?

He had travelled the path from his village to the town and back so many times and had been away from home only eight months – and yet now he could not find his way. He knew he had to follow the right bank of the river, then turn off somewhere to the right down the path to the village. There was a small canal at the appropriate spot; but in his absentmindedness he passed several canals. He looked helplessly about him. His entire sense of direction had gone. Paddy fields ready for harvest lay all around, but no one had begun to cut them. The grass was as dry as straw. Not a sound was to be heard anywhere, not even a breath of wind. Looking upwards at the sky he became scared again. Then he realised it was not fear he felt but cold – he was freezing cold. His chest was constricted with cramp, as if some kind of wave from his guts had got stuck there. He had no notion that walking in cold weather could choke the breath like this. His hands, in fact his whole body, shivered so hard he could not stand still. But somehow, before dawn, he reached the path to the village. He was much later than he had estimated. There was a thick mist that began at the canal and lay over the village. It covered his house, in fact to begin with, he could not even find the entrance. Without boots he was as silent as a cat as he made his way through the yard towards the broken door of the single room. Instead of knocking he called out, 'Ma.'

No response. Alef raised his voice a little and called again, 'Ma.' Dead silence. He did not want to shout. He started to rap on the door. After a few knocks a sound was heard. It went on for a bit, then it became

183

a shuffling noise. A match was being struck inside – or so it seemed. Someone was coming to the door. Who was there? Strangers? Had his mother died? Alef knew his mother would not open her door without first discovering who it was.

His mind a total blank, Alef stood and waited. The door opened, and a woman he did not recognise appeared with a small oil-lamp in one hand. He noticed her veins, the shrunken look of what he could see of her face.

'Who's it?'

'I'm Alef.'

The hand with the lamp shook. From the hasty way in which the other hand tried to pull the dirty sari over its owner's face, Alef recognised his wife. He was extremely surprised. She had not been there when he had left home. Once, she had gone without food for three days. Alef had not been neglecting her, he had been scouring the area for work as a labourer, willing to accept less than the usual rate but still unable to get a job. Finally, in despair he had remained in the market all night long and not returned home. Somehow his wife had come to think that he was trying to do away with her. It had taken three days to persuade herself of this – that he was starving her deliberately. Not that her hungry body had not borne such privation before for a day or two, and even tolerated Alef's affectionate demands at night – but three successive days had proved too much for her faith. When, on the fourth, Alef had finally brought home some rice, he had found her gone. So what had brought her back now? He had heard that she had gone to live with someone in another village. He had even heard a rumour that she was going to marry him.

'Where's Ma?' he questioned. His wife moved away to a corner of the room – there, in the light of the lamp, Alef saw his mother. Without a word he entered, calmly took the bag off his shoulder and leant his rifle against a wall. His wife, also without a sound, somehow woke his mother. Trembling, wide-eyed from broken sleep the old woman asked 'Who's that?' From his corner Alef spoke: 'Ma, it's me, it's Alef.' It took time for his mother to grasp the fact, time for her to get up and more time for her to approach him. He, thinking she might fall before she could embrace him, hugged her first. This did not take long: he felt no stab or blow of emotion. Instead there were his mother's hands, coarse and dry as paper, fussing all over his face, his head and his back as her spittle-flecked mouth came forward to kiss him emitting strange,

184

lachrymose noises. She had not died – the fact pleased him: and all of a sudden the muscle in his leg that had stitched together his waist and his heel seemed no longer to exist, nor did he feel so cold. That was about all he felt.

He was home. His mother nearly hung off him as she hugged him. 'Alef, my darling boy, where've you been all this time, Son?'

'I'm back Ma, and you're still going?'

'Waiting for you, Son, just hanging on for you.'

'That's good.' He smiled. Some mist floated in through the open door. Alef's smile faded, his mother's face was obscured.

'Have you been well Alef?'

'Yes,' he almost grunted.

'Nothing happened to you then?'

Alef was slightly disconcerted. He said, 'No, nothing's happened. Did anyone come looking for me?'

'The military came to set fire to the village.'

'They burnt it?'

'Yes, they burnt it – every house. Soldiers came here and asked about you many times.'

'What did you say?'

'The village was on fire then – I can hardly describe it, Alef – and these young fellows came and questioned me, "Eh, old woman, where's Alef?" I said, "Who knows where Alef's got to? I'm up to my eyes in trouble here – how do I know where that pig has gone." Didn't I say the right thing, Alef?'

'The right thing? D'you know where your Alef's been?'

'You were fighting the battle, Son.' The old woman stood up. Turning to Alef's wife she remarked, 'Your wife's back, Son, did you see?'

'I saw.'

'The day your wife came back' – and the old woman began to babble. Her shoulders swayed with delight; spittle sprayed from her mouth; she did not want to stop. After a while Alef suddenly said, 'That's enough, Ma,' and she fell silent. She went out. Alef's wife retreated into the darkness of her corner. Alef continued to stand still, not speaking. He could not work out what he should do next. He wondered whether to lie down on his mother's messy bed. Outside, the sky was getting light. A chilly dawn breeze blew into the room.

'Shut the door. The wind's cold,' said Alef, glancing at his wife. While she obeyed, he took a look around the room. There was not much to see.

185

To one side lay his bag, and in a corner his rifle, its barrel glinting even in the dim light. With the door shut and his wife back, Alef said wearily, 'When did you return?' He could not follow her mumbled reply. He said loudly, 'Eh?'

'During *Shravan*.*'

'Why?'

'What else could I do?'

'Then why did you leave?'

Even in that murky light Alef could see his wife's eyes were brimming with tears.

'Where did you go?'

'Majampur.'

'Did you eat there? It was food you were after, wasn't it? Did you get enough to eat?'

Alef's chest seemed to burn. He had sat down on his mother's bed. Now he got up again. He came towards his wife and stared her in the face. Women had not occupied his thoughts for a long while. To stand in front of one once more, even his own wife, was a strange feeling. His body was in turmoil: 'Why did you leave this house and go away? You wanted to eat, didn't you? So why are you back again? You think you'll eat here?'

His wife shook her head vehemently. Floods of tears fell to the ground.

'So?'

'I have been back a long time. You weren't here then.'

'And where was I?'

'You were fighting the battle.' Alef thought – just now my mother said exactly the same thing.

'Shut up!' he cried with unusual force. His wife was puzzled. 'I nearly died, you know.' He rolled up his *lungi* above the knee and said, 'Here, the bullet entered here.' His wife crouched on the floor and brought her eyes up close to the wound. Even Alef had not studied it so minutely. Its skin was paler than the skin around it, and where the flesh had been cut and broken and then sewn up, it was lumpy.

'Any higher and it would have broken my knee-cap.'

'What then?'

186

'Then my knee and my leg would have had to go. And I would have gone too.' He laughed as he spoke, thinking of Amin.

'What's it like now? Still painful?'

'The leg has become a little shorter.'

Sleep was overcoming him. He stretched out on his mother's tatty and soiled bedding and at once he was reminded of the rope-like muscle between his heel and his waist. Aloud he said again, 'The leg's become shorter.' Though he closed his eyes he could not sleep: in a thick voice he asked, 'The battle's over now, you know – what's become of our country?'

'Our country has gained independence,' said his wife in parrot-fashion.

Alef was almost asleep but he revived abruptly with a choking sound: 'So now, I suppose we turn into kings and emperors? Do you think we will be so lucky?'

His wife protested, 'Why? Why kings and emperors? At least we won't suffer any more.'

'Meaning?'

'We'll get food and clothes.'

'Is that right?' Alef opened his eyes as he spoke and looked hard at her. Her words did not seem to have sunk in. He said in a monotone, 'The meaning of independence seems remarkably clear to you.' Then he began to snore, half-waking occasionally and talking to himself. Once he mumbled, 'I'll catch prawns in the canal at Lalitnagar, gigantic king prawns, each of them weighs half a seer.'

He was not back long before he realised there was no point in wandering around the village with his rifle on his shoulder. A whole crowd of men were doing the same, all over the place. They came to see him in droves beating their chests, to announce that the battle was won and independence had come. That was all they did: beat their chests and break the news of independence. Consequently, within a few days this news became as stale as the sight of rifles. The villagers had other matters to occupy their minds.

Alef's mother would say, 'Show me where the bullet went in, Son.' And Alef would kneel down, find the spot and start to explain, 'The bullet went in just here. I thought those bastard Khans had already fled. I came out of the forest and while I was standing there, there was a hiss and the bullet got me – '

'Won't the Government send for you now?'

Alef looked surprised. 'Why should the Government call me? Why?'

'If they don't call you who will they call? What if the bullet had hit your head Alef?'

'Yes, but why me?'

'Not you alone, I mean all the people who fought in the battle. I tell you Alef, I'm going to improve this place – when you get a bit of land. Ask for a cow and two bulls too and – '

'Enough. Stop it' – Alef had caught a sudden whiff of Amin's rotting corpse.

He said, 'Give me some food – I must go to Benepur.'

'You'll go there? What for?'

'There's a fellow from Benepur I fought with. He got a bullet in the thigh. In the hospital they cut his leg off. Three days later he was a stinking corpse. I have to break the news to his mother.'

'Did he get a grave, Alef?' his mother enquired anxiously.

'Where you fall is where you stay,' he replied.

He returned from Benepur that evening. While he was there he heard the news. He would have heard it sooner if he had listened to the radio. Government had ordered anyone in possession of a rifle or other weapon of war to hand it in, within three days. Alef's rifle was still leaning against the wall in one corner of the room at home. When he got back he called both his mother and his wife inside. There, in the twilight, he pointed to the rifle and said, 'Ma, this is what you fight a battle with, you know?'

A little frightened she said, 'I know, Baba.'

'You know how it works? Here, I'll show you, this is how you load the bullets.' The rifle made a series of sharp unfamiliar noises, then Alef said, 'There, I've closed it now, it's ready.' He crouched down on the floor. Aiming the weapon at his mother and wife he swung it in a semi-circle while his tongue made a series of staccato sounds. He noticed his wife's face, pale and bloodless; his mother's reaction he could not really see.

'This is the way,' he said, and again he mimicked the sound of firing – tararara! tha! tha! tha! – and then burst into guffaws. The sound of the guffaws mimicked the sound of the bullets. He laughed so hard that he cried.

When he finally stood up he saw his mother hobbling out of the room. Suddenly serious, he picked up the gun and called, 'Bou.'

His wife did not respond.

'Will you get enough food here, d'you think? Perhaps you won't.'

'It doesn't matter.'

'You won't run away again?'

'No.'

'Not even if your stomach is screaming, you feel you're going to die of hunger – you won't go?'

Her head shook violently and a burst of tears scattered over the floor.

Rifle in hand, Alef went to the pond beyond the back of the house. With every ounce of strength in him he hurled the weapon into the middle of the water.

On his way back home he thought: the pond's a small one – I could fish it out again without much bother.

(1973)

THE FUGITIVE AND THE FOLLOWERS

Sunil Ganguli

'It's you!'

Rabi put his fingers to his lips and said, 'Shsh.' For an instant he glanced behind him. Then he took a step forward and said, 'Is Uncle at home? What about Ashokda?'

Jayanti nodded her head twice in the negative, 'Neither's here.'

'What about Aunty?'

'She is.'

Jayanti ran her gaze over Rabi's body. 'So much mud on your feet,' she said. 'Better go and wash them under the tap in the yard.'

She herself turned the tap for him and asked him in a low voice, 'Where've you been all this time?'

'I'm extremely hungry, Boudi. Is there any food around? Some puffed rice will do.'

'Come up.'

He went up the stairs. At the top stood his aunt. She could not see very well. She asked Jayanti, 'Who's come, Bouma?'

'It's our Rabi.'

A pair of hazy eyes turned towards Rabi. He was now a young man, but her eyes saw only the child.

'Come, don't stand there.'

'Aunty, I'm extremely hungry.'

The old lady's feet stood waiting for the young man's *pranam*, but he did not bend to touch them: can a famished man remember to do such things? Glancing at Jayanti he said, 'I'm in a bit of a hurry – '

'You're leaving so soon?' his aunt asked. 'Won't you stay tonight?'

'Till Ashokda comes. I need to talk to Ashokda.'

190

'Your elder brother – how is he?'

'Same as ever.'

'And your mother? I've not received any letter from her lately.'

Rabi became annoyed and said sharply, 'Haven't I told you, I'm really hungry? Can't you give me something to eat, instead of grilling me?'

What a temper the boy had! For how long had he gone without food?

Jayanti brought a bowlful of puffed rice which she had mixed with onion, chili and fried snacks to make it tolerably edible. She passed it to Rabi, saying, 'Now eat. Afterwards I'll fry some *luchis* – '

'This is enough. Don't bother with *luchis*.'

'I'll put some water on to make tea then?'

'Fine.'

'In one month you've become awfully thin. Don't you take any care of yourself?'

'Meanwhile Ashokda gets fatter and fatter. Don't you take any care of your husband?'

'You've become hollow-eyed. How many nights do you sleep?'

'Off you go, make some tea, please.'

While chewing the puffed rice Rabi stood beside the window. It was getting dark. He narrowed his eyes and looked out. Soon he could make out three people walking along side by side, engrossed in talk. When they reached his street they looked up as one. For a moment they stood and stared. Then, they seemed to give a joint sigh and come closer. Towards the house.

Gently Rabi set down the half-eaten bowl of rice. His exit was swift: without a word to anyone he was down the stairs; as soon as he was outside, he began to run.

The three men standing near the house saw the fugitive, recognised the fleeing figure. They did not stir, betrayed no sign of concern.

Follower Number One said, 'We've lost him again.'

Follower Number Two said, 'Yes, too bad.'

Follower Number Three took a piece of paper from his pocket, held it up and said, 'Where to now – Dum Dum or Shrirampur?'

Number One said, 'Dum Dum.'

Number Two said, 'Let's give this one up.'

Number Three stuck his hand in his coat pocket and said, 'It's turned pretty cold. That shop we passed at the crossing – it was selling fried snacks.'

One dipped his hand into the bag hanging from his shoulder, pulled out a bomb and chucked it at the door of the house.

Two said contentedly,'Wah! Great sound!'

Three said, 'We don't need to scramble. Let's have some snacks.'

Rabi stood in front of another house. He called out softly, 'Chandan, Chandan.'

There was no response. It was half past nine at night. The locality was a quiet one in a distant suburb. The ting-ting of cycle rickshaws could be heard occasionally, and the barking of the odd stray dog.

Rabi called more loudly, 'Chandan – '

Above him from a verandah a young girl leaned over and said, 'Who is it?'

'Is Chandan in?'

'My brother's got fever.'

'He can't get up?'

'He's asleep.'

'Can't you open the door?'

'What's your name?'

'Please open the door.'

Rabi turned round abruptly. On the main road, not far away, two cycle rickshaws had come to a halt. Without waiting for the door to open he vanished into the darkness.

The three men approached the house. Number One said, 'He's not here. I've been keeping an eye on the place.'

He said no more and went up to the door. Before he could knock, it opened. A fourteen-or-fifteen-year-old girl stood there in a sari she had not quite learned how to wear.

Number Two enquired in an even tone, 'Has Chandan got a real fever?'

'His temperature is a hundred and four today,' the girl said. 'Where are you all from?'

'We're from Rabi Babu, can we see your brother for a moment?'

'He's sleeping just now.'

'Achchha, leave it then.'

'Any message?'

'Tell him three men came looking for Rabi Babu. He'll understand.'

When Number Two came away, Number Three asked him, 'There's no need to do it here, is there?'

Number One said, 'I don't think it's – '

'My younger brother's got fever,' said Number Three. 'Now I think I'm catching it.'

Number Two felt Three's forehead and said, 'You don't feel hot.'

'I feel it inside though. I wish I could lie down under a quilt for a while.'

One said, 'We'll sign off here. No point in continuing.'

'I haven't slept a wink for nights in a row. And now it's cold. God doesn't seem to be taking care of us,' said Three.

'This particular son-of-a-bitch is really giving us a hard time,' said Two.

From his bag Number One fished out a second bomb and threw it at the door of the house. The deep silence was shattered by the explosion. A dog barked raucously.

Rabi spent the whole night beside the Ganges in the burning ghat. Whenever he felt himself about to doze off he got up and paced back and forth, stopping sometimes beside the funeral pyres. There were four of them, burning non-stop, and a ceaseless flow of people, none of whom were interested in him. His eyes watered constantly in the smoke and he was easily mistaken for a mourner. In fact, it was a long time since he had shed tears over death; especially here, in a burning ghat, where death seemed to him a matter of sheer indifference, unrelated to good or evil. Rabi folded his hands on his bare chest. Suddenly he felt like stroking it. Thinking of it as part of someone else's body, he began to caress it.

When the sky became light he mixed with the crowd of dawn bathers heading for a holy dip, and found his way to Howrah station. From there he went by train to Shrirampur.

Shushanta was about to leave the bazaar with his bag in his hand when Rabi appeared and said, 'I must stay here tonight.'

Shushanta hesitated: My father's due back from Delhi today.'

'One night – that's all I need,' said Rabi.

'You know Khokan's living nearby at Goshai. Shall I tell him you're here?'

'No, not necessary,' said Rabi.

He slept the entire day. He could have slept for several days. Once, he got up to bathe and eat. He took a long while over the bath, much less time over the food.

His shirt and trousers were so filthy that he could not bear to wear them again. Instead he put on a dhoti and *panjabi* borrowed from Shushanta. They made him look entirely different. If only, he told himself, I could change myself as easily as my clothes. With this thought, he fell asleep again. He dreamed about a ship.

When he awoke, he saw it was dark. Evening had fallen. He was offered a small room on the roof as a refuge. Peeping out immediately in every direction he saw no one at all.

Shushanta's wife Rupa arrived with tea. As he sipped it Rabi questioned her, 'You don't have anything like an aspirin, do you?'

'No, I can send someone if you like?'

'Don't bother. I get these headaches after dark, but often they go of their own accord. Is Shushanta back yet from his job?'

'He'll be here shortly.'

'That's all for now. Please ask Shushanta to come up.'

'Will you take some food?'

'No one need fuss over me. If I'm hungry I'll ask. Have you any *moong* dal? Could you cook it later? It's so long since I ate any.'

'In your house – '

'You can leave me now. I need to spend some time alone.'

Leaving the light off Rabi sat quite still, facing the wall. He did not turn round even once. After a long interval he shifted position slightly and placed both hands against his temples.

Shushanta appeared. 'What's this, no light?'

'I've been listening to a dog barking for quite a while. I kept a pet dog as a child – its bark sounded like this one, exactly the same.'

'Where's your dog now?'

'At that time we lived at Shibsagar. The dog was my constant companion, very obedient. Then all of a sudden one day it stopped obeying me and became angry. Everyone was scared. My mother and father said it had gone crazy. I didn't accept that – but they didn't have the nerve to keep it at home any more. After a lot of cajoling they got into a boat and left it on a sandbank in the river. That place often used to flood. Ever since then, in quiet places, when I hear a dog bark, I – '

'From here where will you go?'

'I don't know.'

'You can stay here a few days. This room isn't used much.'

Rabi stared hard at Shushanta. Then, with pride in his voice, he said, 'Whether I have a roof over my head or not doesn't much matter to me. If it did I wouldn't have taken this path – '

194

'But now there should be a change of direction,' Shushanta interrupted firmly. 'This path you've chosen, it's not a road, it's a blind alley.'

'I suppose in your home there is certainly a gramophone?'

'What?'

'Remember the jingle? "Some corner of the happy home, must be graced by a gramophone."'

'That's just your silly pride speaking.'

Rupa entered and said to her husband, 'There are three men asking for you.'

Rabi sprang up and went to the boundary wall of the roof. After cautiously peering over he returned and said calmly, 'Does your house have a rear exit?'

Shushanta grabbed his hand and said, 'Why go?'

'I've no time to lose.'

'Don't go. I'll go and talk to them. Why be afraid?'

'It's not fear, it's contempt. I've no time to lose.'

Rupa said, 'Why must you do this? The neighbours have a telephone, I can call the police.'

Rabi did not even glance at Rupa. He leapt over the wall and shinned down the drainpipe. Not far off a train rumbled by.

Follower Number One said, 'The house numbers round here are in total disorder. 52 comes after 37 – what a mess.'

Number Two said, 'And none of the houses has a number plate.'

Number Three added, 'My feet are aching like hell with all this walking.'

One said, 'I was on the run last year. That was a thrill.'

Two began to say, 'The day Bardhan got killed – '

Three butted in, 'You know, in my mother's uncle's house there's a guava tree – the wood's red inside, you know. When I was a boy I fell out of it and ever since then, one of my feet is not as strong as it should be.'

'The inside of a guava tree's red?' asked Two.

'Yes, you get that kind of guava in Deoghar,' said One. 'I've seen them many times when I went there with my elder brother and his wife.'

'So now we pack this job in,' said Two.

'Then we can go home and have a real sleep,' said Three. 'And some hot rice, *mushuri* dal and potatoes – '

Number One stepped forward towards the door, ready to speak to Shushanta. The other two spread out on either side of the house.

Rabi, running for his life, stopped before a stranger and asked, 'Which way to the station?'

'Why try to get there through the field when it's dark? There you are, there's the road,' the man said, pointing.

'Can't I reach it through the field?'

'You could, but you won't find the path.'

Rabi shouted in exasperation, 'I'll find it. Just point me in the right direction – '

The man remained placid and said, 'If you want to get there through a dark field, you'd better find the path yourself.'

Throwing a dirty look at the man, without another word Rabi ran on. He measured out each breath, conscious that he must not tire too quickly. Now he was really alone – but his breath still mingled with the breath of the world, even that of the departed ones, the breath that hangs in the air forever, never extinguished.

With repeated backward glances Rabi raced on. Though the night was wintry he was covered in sweat. He ran slap into a wall.

Not a real wall – a human wall, made of three men. With skilful hands they grabbed Rabi and pinned him to the ground. He did not struggle much, only covering his face with both hands.

Number One prised them away and said, 'All right, Rabi, do you recognise me?'

Number Two said, 'Three of you killed Bardhan – '

'You've put us to a lot of bother, swine,' said Three.

Rabi said nothing. The thought struck him, 'I haven't sent that box of coloured pencils to my little sister – she's always reminding me about it – '

Three knives accomplished their work without noise. The three men gagged Rabi and sliced up his chest and stomach until they were certain he had drawn his last gasp, had well and truly stopped breathing earthly air.

There was a hubbub in the distance. A group of people were coming. The three men were perplexed. They could not make out: were the voices coming to congratulate them or capture them? Either way the shout would sound the same. The three were taking no chances. They stood up at once, chose three different directions, and split up.

Not long after, the group reached the spot. They stood there gazing upon the fugitive body recently known as Rabi, and then they solemnly vowed revenge.

There were nine of them. Dividing themselves into three groups of three, they went in three different directions.

The man who was once Follower Number One was now Fugitive Number One. Pursuing him, follower Number One said to Follower Number Three, 'Where do we go?'

'Get that paper out of your pocket,' said the new Number Two, 'and have a look.'

(1972)

THE MURDERER

Ashapurna Devi

Not long ago a mad fellow turned up in our neighbourhood. Where he came from, and why he picked our area to stay in, were mysteries to us.

We could not discover any way to get rid of him, even though he was driving us round the bend. His madness made him violent. One day he would pick up a stone and smash the window of a house, another day he would chuck a few bricks at a car. Once, he snatched some containers of food out of a servant's hands, another time he sprinkled dirt over somebody – we had all heard stories of his exploits.

I had personally seen him making faces at people, running after them and hitting them, coming up and biting them, and uttering words of unspeakable abuse. What to do about the children was the biggest problem. With this fellow about they did not want to go out; the girls were unwilling to go to school and the boys were giggling over vulgarities. You see, the filthy piece of cloth attached to the madman's waist, had finally dropped off.

God knows what he ate to survive. We never tried to learn. We often saw him loitering around the dustbins. He strewed refuse all over the place. He also shouted obscenities – who knows at whom!

One day one of his garbage missiles hit my nephew.

How could I stay passive after that? I sent an immediate petition to the police, demanding urgent action. Thinking the petition would be ineffective without the signatures of others, I went round the neighbourhood knocking at all the doors. Some people signed, others declined, for fear of the police.

The ones who did not sign persistently remarked, 'How cruel! What

198

inhumanity! That harmless vagabond never bothers anyone for food, but now people are trying to have him put away – what a shame!'

The ones who did sign constantly enquired of me, 'Well then, how goes your police business?'

As if they were not already well aware of the usual efficiency shown by the police – or maybe they thought me foolish to get involved in something like this. My days passed under two-pronged attack, frequently interrupted by unexpected, inventive contributions from the madman. I gathered that the fact that I was trying to have him dealt with by the police had reached him, and so he was up in arms against me.

First my spectacles fell victim to his desire for revenge, then I began to worry for my life. I was compelled to run to the police once more to register a complaint. After endless pleading, they yielded. They promised to turn up the next day. That was the day before yesterday.

From dawn that day I felt a sense of anticipation. Whenever I heard a vehicle in the road I would run to see if 'they' had arrived and at the same time to keep tabs on the movements of the madman. Suddenly I heard a tremendous hubbub.

They must have come. But why was everyone yelling in this crazy manner?

I rushed downstairs, and immediately I saw why. The police van was indeed there.

When the lunatic had heard everyone in the area shouting, 'Police coming', he had shouted 'See if you catch me' and jumped straight out under the wheels.

The vehicle despatched to take him away therefore took away his crushed body, trailing dust in its wake. And the entire neighbourhood stood and stared in silent scorching accusation – not at the departing policemen but at the 'murderer'. I tried to tell myself: this is unfair, unreasonable, a false charge; but I was not persuaded. The fact was, I agreed with them.

(c. 1970)

A DROP OF MILK

Narendra Mitra

It was Latika who first suggested they do it. She placed an order for an extra half pint of milk for her husband. She was already taking a pint and a half for her baby daughter – only a year and a half old, and needing more than sago and barley water – and from that she removed a few spoonfuls for the family tea. The two cups of tea she was giving her husband in the evenings contained mostly powdered milk, much to his disgust. Then, one morning, after the milkman had called, her husband had said, 'Let's have tea today with a drop of real milk.'

Instead of obliging him she had been irritated: 'What are you saying, eh? Where's the milk going to come from? I suppose we have seers of it stashed away? I'm not going to let you have one drop of the baby's for your tea, you know.'

'All right, all right, don't screech,' Binod had replied.

Two days had passed peacefully. Latika had been watching her husband carefully. With all his hard work he had become quite drawn. And he was only just over thirty. His cheeks were sunken, his jaw jutted; together they made him seem much older than he was. She hardly liked to look at him any more.

Then, early in the morning of that third day, Latika set before her husband his usual cup with a broken handle. Binod looked at it in astonishment; instead of tea, the teacup was brimming with milk!

'What's this! Doesn't baby Khuki have all the milk?' he cried.

Latika reassured him, 'No, no, drink it up. She'll have hers, this is extra, just for you. Give yourself a treat, have it for a week or two. Maybe then you'll look yourself again.'

To Binod the cup standing in front of him was no mere cup of milk, it was a whole ocean of milk, the visible sign of the ocean of

200

love in the secret recesses of his wife's heart. It seemed so long since he had married her, he had almost forgotten the day. Now it came back to him. The pale angular face before him now brought to mind a bride's face decorated with vermilion and sandalwood twelve years earlier. Today's eyes, though lustreless, hollow, did not seem so very different from the sparkling glances of that sixteen-year-old goddess Lakshmi.

'But won't it cost a lot?' Binod asked.

'Let it,' replied Latika. 'You earn the wages, so if the household expenses rise a bit because of you, so be it.'

Without another word Binod sipped up all the milk.

Not far away, near the door, lying on his tummy on a mat on the floor doing his homework, was Shunil. He was Binod's nine-year-old son. Between him and baby Khuki there had been three others, but none had survived; Shunil was now in the fifth class of the local school. By much perseverance Binod had managed to get his son a grant of half his fees. He had also bought him the necessary books and materials.

While continuing to read English grammar, Shunil snatched a look at his father's milk-drinking. He was embarrassed, turned back quickly and raised his voice: 'Lion-Lioness, Lion-Lioness, Fox-Vixen, Fox-Vixen.'

Binod listened to the table of genders for a moment, then called out, 'Would you like some milk too, Shunil?'

His son did not lift his head. 'No, you drink it. I don't like milk. Fox-Vixen, Fox-Vixen.'

Latika had noticed Binod's embarrassment. She said, 'You have it, there'll be some for him when the time comes. At exam time – that's when my precious will need it.'

Shunil, still without looking up said, 'No one needs to keep milk for me. I won't drink it. Dog-Bitch, Dog-Bitch.'

Binod became a bit annoyed. 'You seem to take a long time to memorise a few words. Weren't you reading genders last night?'

Binod's younger brother Bijan was a late riser. He burst into the room rubbing his wet face with a towel. 'What's this, Boudi?' he chaffed Latika. 'Haven't you any tea?'

Bijan had got his BA two years before and had been looking for a job ever since. At first he had fretted a great deal. Now he was resigned; nothing seemed to bother him.

201

Latika said to him, 'Look here Bhai, how often have we had tea without you, hanh?'

With his eyes on his elder brother, Bijan laughed. 'So Dada is sipping air from an empty cup, is he? Doesn't Dada deserve a cup of cha?'

Binod and Latika exchanged looks. Was Bijan really in the know and just teasing them? That would be unlike the boy. Binod shifted a bit and said awkwardly, 'It's not tea, Biju, it's a cup of milk. Your Boudi has given it to me.'

His younger brother glanced mischievously at Latika: 'So Dada's been receiving stolen goods, has he?'

Bijan loved jokes of this sort but the other two, in their neediness, were not in the mood for them. They both became glum.

'Let him have a cup of milk tomorrow,' said Binod.

'I will,' replied Latika.

It was Bijan's turn to feel awkward: he said, 'Achchha, what's the matter with you two? Can't anyone take a joke? Do I ever drink milk anyway? Who says I need milk? Tea's fine for me.'

A little later, while Latika was pouring out two cups of tea from a kettle, Bijan suddenly said, 'Please rinse out that cup which had milk in it, Boudi. I really don't like the smell of milk in my tea you know.'

Latika eyed her brother-in-law for a moment and softly commented, 'I have already rinsed it. I haven't given you the cup your brother used.'

Next day she brought her husband his cup of milk in a somewhat furtive way. He took it off to a corner of the verandah and slowly drank it down, almost on the sly.

Shunil was in his usual place but he was not studying English grammar. He was learning his health and hygiene lesson: 'Milk is beneficial to the human body', he read out, perhaps deliberately, perhaps not. Bijan, instead of bursting into the room, stood outside cleaning his teeth with a twig and having a chat with his sister-in-law. Perhaps he too did not want to embarrass his elder brother. As for Binod, so silently did he drain the cup no one heard a thing.

He remained diffident for a few days only; after a week his embarrassment had virtually vanished. Now he drank milk in front of them all, son, brother and wife. If it was a little late in coming he would even call out quite loudly, 'How's my milk then? I have to be off soon.' This would slightly vex Latika who would call back, 'Coming, coming. Can't you have it when you get back? Nobody else will take it.'

202

Binod's job was casual proof-reading in the Bani publishing house in Potuldanga Street. He was not always in work. Sometimes he gave ten or fifteen rupee tuitions as well. He also sold insurance on commission. He slogged his way round his friends and neighbours for what he could get. But still he netted just three or four thousand rupees per annum.

However lowly Binod Das's status in the outside world might have been, within the confines of 7/3/2 Entally 2nd Lane he was an emperor. King, Lord and Master of his realm. Considering the fact that he was giving his last drop of blood for his family, didn't he have a right to a drop of milk! To drink milk bought with his own money – where was the shame in that?

Binod finished the cup.

Two weeks went by, and then a further week in which Latika expected Binod would say of his own accord, 'That's enough. We'd better stop the extra milk now.' But the idea did not seem to have entered his head.

At the end of the month the milkman delivered his bill of seven and a half rupees.

Latika became anxious: where was she going to keep finding all this cash? When the milkman called two or three days later to collect the money, Latika told him, 'That extra half pint we've been having, we'll stop it now. Please go back to one and a half from now on.'

Binod was reading proofs inside and came out, having overheard. 'No, don't cancel it,' he said, 'That extra half pint has been doing me a lot of good. My body's on the mend. We'll carry on for another month.'

The milkman went off and Latika said, 'Where's your common sense? We don't even know how to pay this month's bill.' Binod took offence and snapped, 'Is it your money that you worry about it so much? Whatever the milk costs, I will pay it. I'm the one who slaves away all day for you all, and you say I'm not even allowed a drop of milk?'

'Why stop there?' Latika retorted. 'With your 70 to 75 rupees a month why have only milk, why not have ghee and meat and pulao? Why bother about the rest of us?'

Binod lost his temper and shouted, 'I'll eat what I like, it's my money, I'll spend it as I like, you hear?'

That morning Binod left without taking his cup of milk. But when

203

he returned that night to take his food Latika set some hot milk in front of him, and he didn't refuse it. All day, between tasks he had felt deprived, as if something was missing from his life. At the end of the day's labour, with its share of disappointments and unfulfilled hopes, he had come back on the bus at about ten and, after munching his way through some dry, gritty rotis and the usual dal and *poi* curry, had eyed the little bowl of white liquid as if it were an answer to prayers, ambrosia itself.

Though the content of the bowl was not large it was thick, with skin floating on top. Binod took a lick. Then he said, 'I'd like two more rotis with my milk. My stomach's still rumbling. I'll take the milk at night from now on.'

Latika gave a small smile: 'Fine, I'll do that.'

But oddly enough, the following night Binod found only a pile of rotis awaiting him on his plate; the bowl of milk was absent. He enquired anxiously, 'Where's the milk?'

Latika told him, 'I've given it to Shunil. Today he didn't get his fish. I had no end of trouble to get him to eat. Every day he asks for milk, so today I gave it to him.'

'Quite right,' said Binod in a solemn voice.

A few days after that again Binod found the bowl of precious fluid absent. Before he could even ask, Latika said, 'I gave your milk to your brother today. He went out after a job and got back late. He didn't feel like eating his usual rice, shrimp and *poi* curry – same thing day after day – so I gave him some mango preserve soaked in milk. You won't believe it – after that he got through half a plate of rice.'

Binod said, 'Well done him, but what about the job? All those recommendation letters I got for him – what use were they?'

'He didn't get it. They said no vacancy.'

Binod was provoked: 'For him there'll never be a vacancy, no matter how much milk and mango preserve he eats.' He left his own food more than half uneaten and got up.

Over the next few days Binod had his milk again. Then it stopped once more.

Latika said, 'It's Shunil up to his tricks. He's very greedy these days. He came back at tiffin time and helped himself to a cup of milk from the saucepan. I don't know what to do with him.'

Binod snorted.

'I've been keeping an eye on him for some days,' Latika added. 'Today I gave him a beating, a real hiding. If he knows what's good for him, he won't visit the saucepan again.'

Binod just said, 'Good. Boys shouldn't be so greedy at his age.'

More days went by. And then, yet again Binod noticed that the bowl was missing. He questioned, 'Has Shunil made off with it again? That boy knows no shame, especially after his mother gave him what he deserved.'

But Latika cut him short with a gentle laugh: 'No, today he's not the thief. The white puss from next door got the milk.'

Binod was incensed. 'The neighbours' cat comes and drinks my milk and you laugh! It's so expensive! Can't you be more careful? Each pint costs four annas. What a story! So it's all gone into the stomach of the cat next door! You don't earn money, that's the trouble. You don't understand the first thing about it.'

Latika replied, 'I know I don't earn. But don't be so upset. It wasn't really next door's cat that took the milk. I'm not that careless. It was your own pet puss who lapped it up.' Latika gave a tiny smile.

Binod did not catch her meaning and replied ill-humouredly, 'It's much too late for this kind of joke. What are you on about now?'

Latika had to be more explicit. She had been suffering from acidity for quite a while. Whatever she swallowed upset her. She belched constantly, and her nerves were always frayed. Earlier that day, after her midday meal, she had actually vomited; she could not keep down what she ate. By evening she had been starving, but what could she take? Whatever she had tried, it had been the same story. The old lady upstairs, noticing her plight had advised her, 'You'd better do this – take some milk. And add a handful of puffed grain to it. That will make you less acidic. You'll soon feel better.'

Latika had followed the advice. But she had not been able to have the milk in peace. Shunil had come back from school and said, 'Ma, what are you hiding there? Can I have some?' She had replied, 'Nothing special, I promise you,' but she had given him a lump.

Binod finished eating, then he banged his glass down on his plate and said, 'So you ate what took your fancy, all right – but why all this preamble? Cats, acidity and what not. What it boils down to is this: you helped yourself because you felt like it.'

Latika had imagined that when her husband heard her tale he would be softened, even make a joke of it. When she saw his reaction, at first she was hurt, then genuinely angry. 'So you actually think I took the milk because I took a fancy to it, do you?'

'Not at all,' he said, 'no doubt someone just happened to be around and poured it down your throat.'

'So what if I drank it! You've had it for a whole month. Can't I be allowed it just once?'

Binod went on rinsing his mouth and hands, then turned away and gave a strange smile. 'Well, that's the real point isn't it? I like to have a little milk now and then and you don't get any, and that gets under your skin. You're dying of jealousy.'

'What! I'm dying of envy because you're drinking milk! You old fool, you should be ashamed of yourself drinking milk day after day in front of everyone else! When you don't get it you behave as if the world has fallen round your ears!'

This fired Binod in earnest. 'Shame? You should feel shame, you bitch. It's your father's money buying the milk, is it? or is it your money? No – it's mine. The shame's yours.'

Bijan emerged from the next door room. 'Eh, what's all this? Do you have to have a fight so late?'

'Some fight!' said Latika bitterly. 'Just because I was hungry and took a bit of milk.'

'Shsh, both of you! Calm down, Boudi.'

The racket had woken Shunil. The minute he heard them arguing he understood what had happened. Quietly he crept up to his uncle Bijan, stood close to him and whispered in his ear, 'I know what's up, Kaku. I wanted a bit of milk too and Ma beat me. Today she pinched some and had it herself. Ha ha!'

Bijan said, 'Hush, stop talking. Go to sleep.'

Shunil at least was able to drop off after a short while, but Binod and Latika could hardly close their eyes all night. What a calamity Fate had dealt them – over a mere drop of milk! As Latika lay there she harped on the entire gamut of her grievances. She touched on everything – from saris, ornaments and general contentment to whether she had enough to eat: no one, she cried, cared or bothered to ask her about any of these things. For hours she lamented, sighing noisily and weeping copiously. Several times Binod called out in a cross voice, 'Look, can't you calm down, I have to get some sleep. Tomorrow I must get up early and go to work.'

His rebuke simply set off a fresh outburst of sobbing. Then Binod made an effort to console his wife, saying 'All for some ordinary milk – '

'Yes, just for a drop of milk you go after me. You almost beat me over your measly milk. Even if I was dying I wouldn't touch a drop of it now.' After a great deal more cajoling, Binod made peace with Latika. By the night's end she could be found lying in his arms, their baby daughter pushed to the left side of the bed.

Next morning the milkman brought the milk as usual. Latika swiftly warmed it and brought it along. She set the cup before Binod. He said, 'Eh, what's this?'

She said, 'Drink it down. I can't guard it from dawn to dusk. You never know who might take a fancy to it.'

Without speaking, Binod put his arm around his wife and raised the cup gently to her lips. Shyly Latika said, 'Enough of this, stop it.'

'Hey, Boudi, how's the tea?' Bijan barged in and stopped. He turned and was about to beat a quick retreat when Latika confronted him with the cup of milk: 'Where are you off to? Go on, take this, today it's all yours. It'll do you good.'

'You're the heroine of the battle. You have it, Boudi.'

'Have it for my sake,' she replied.

Bijan said nothing, took the cup in his hand.

Shunil had spread his schoolbooks on a mat in the east verandah. He was watching what was happening inside out of the corner of his eye. He saw the odd game his father, mother and uncle were playing. Today he was not alone. Sitting near him was a boy from the nearby *bustee*. They were in the same class at school, but Phatik was a lot poorer than Shunil. He couldn't afford to buy the books he needed. He lacked not only a proper notebook but also a complete English textbook; the old one he possessed had three missing pages, probably torn out of it by its previous owner for exam copying purposes. Phatik was in the process of copying this omitted portion out of Shunil's textbook into his own book.

Bijan entered the verandah and beckoned to Shunil. Offering him the cup of milk he said, 'It's for you, Shunil.'

'No it's yours, Uncle, you don't have it everyday.'

Bijan repeated himself, 'Come on, drink up. Have it for my sake.'

Without responding, Shunil took the cup and went back to his place. Below him Phatik's head was visible, busy in copying. Phatik looked really thin. His bones were sticking out, his shoulder blades were like the hunched wings of the mythical eagle Garuda. Shunil watched him briefly, then said, 'Hey, Phatik, listen. Stop copying, have this cup of milk.'

Phatik looked up embarrassed and said, 'No, Bhai, it's for you.'

'Don't be silly,' urged Shunil, 'I have it everyday. Today it's yours. Please have it, for my sake.'

(1953)

THE MOURNERS

Premendra Mitra

The night was unusually wintry, and on top of that rain was falling. All day the sun had been invisible; around nightfall a drizzle had started, and since then there had been no let-up. The world was as chilly as a corpse, shrouded in a damp pall of darkness as if entombed.

Suddenly, inside a house a woman screamed and began to weep. The distress in her cry was enough to pierce the heart. But perhaps it was better than the dreadful ache of uncertainty that had choked the house in daytime.

Rama was a gentle, timid girl, whose whole life had been spent avoiding the gaze of the outside world. A wail of agony, coming from her, sounded more like a suppressed groan.

'Oh Aunty, come and see Khuki!'

Rama's husband was pacing tirelessly inside the room. But at this cruellest of moments Rama totally forgot him.

'Aunty!'

Her aunt had already spent three days and nights beside the sick child and was probably in a doze – but she rapidly roused herself.

Rama's brother Ramesh was in the kitchen sitting down, having brought back medicine from the doctor. He let a handful of rice on its way to his mouth fall back on the plate. The feeling of irritation that crossed his mind filled him with self-contempt.

All the way back from the dispensary, shivering in the rain and wind, wrapped in hardly anything, he had been thinking of his warm bed. And not only of its warmth – something else too had tempted him.

He had been married only two months. His wife had returned from her parents' house just the day before. But because of the calamity in the house they had hardly exchanged glances. He had been eagerly awaiting the chance to be together privately at night all day.

Rama's wail, his own irritation: immediately he had sensed he might have to give up the anticipated pleasures of his bed. For an instant he was disappointed, then thoroughly disgusted with himself. The selfishness of his furtive thought had struck him and made him extremely remorseful.

Next door Rama was moaning, 'Oh Aunty, my Khuki, why can't you save her?'

In the doorway her aunt stood dry-eyed, like a stick of wood. Khuki was only seven years old – but the aunt had witnessed many deaths, some of them even more tragic, since coming to her brother's house as a 22-year-old widow. Her source of tears had dried up long ago.

Everyone stood helplessly as Rama wailed again, 'Can't anyone save my Khuki?' It was her first encounter with death. She had yet to understand about human frailty.

Each person watching was transfixed as Khuki seemed to draw her last gasps.

Rama completely forgot herself. This reticent all-suffering girl suddenly bared her teeth and burst our accusingly, 'Can't any of you fetch a doctor?'

A doctor! Why on earth hadn't he called him? Ramesh looked at his sister's distraught face and could hardly restrain his own tears. But ought a man to cry? He looked at the others. No, it would not do. So as to hide the moistness in his eyes he turned away.

Rama cried despairingly to him, 'Can't you go and get the doctor, Dada! Why are you standing there like that?'

Again the doctor! But if he did call him what could he do? Ramesh quickly left the room. As he went out his aunt made a negative sign. Outside she said to him with quiet deliberation, 'And who are you calling the doctor for?'

Ramesh stopped, unable to respond. With a shock it came to him that Khuki had been dying and he had not grasped it. His aunt's words had broken the spell.

Until now, he had been doing everything mechanically, including the shedding of tears. Only now did the full meaning of Khuki's death sink in: face to face with the ineluctable working of the awful mystery, Ramesh was unexpectedly bewildered.

Death was ancient, but man's will to live was more ancient still. The fact of death was simply stated, but not its significance.

The aunt all of a sudden exclaimed, 'Where has Khuki's father gone?'

This galvanised Ramesh. He sensed instantly what lay behind his aunt's concern and ran outside in a state of high anxiety.

Khuki was the apple of her father's eye. Seeing his abnormal affection for her, people used to look at him and Rama and then joke, 'Which of you is really the girl's mother?'

What if, at this terrible moment, he were unable to bear his loss? – the thought sent a shiver down Ramesh's spine. His mind leapt to the bridge above the canal near their house. Less than a month earlier a young woman had jumped from it to her death.

In an urgent tone he shouted out, 'Prashanna Babu!'

There was no answer.

Ramesh began to run towards the bridge. He was convinced that disaster was lurking nearby. But he had barely covered any distance when he was brought up short by the sound of his name.

'Ramesh Babu, why are you running?'

Ramesh halted. 'So there you are!' he said with relief.

It was Prashanna Babu's turn to show surprise. 'You were after me?'

His level voice brought Ramesh to his senses. There really was no reason to run so anxiously, was there?

But there was death – Khuki dying! How could the world carry on just as it had?

Prashanna Babu had taken out a cheroot. Ramesh, his mind still agitated, watched fascinated as the other man went faultlessly through his meticulous ritual for lighting it, cupping the match in his hands against the wind from the north. He shook the matchstick a couple of times to extinguish the flame and threw it away, precisely as he always did.

There was nothing out of the ordinary here – which was exactly what struck Ramesh as strange. 'Shall we go in now?' said Prashanna Babu.

Ramesh did not fail to catch the slight tremble in the words, and it was not difficult to guess the turmoil inside from what little could be seen and heard on the outside. But all that business with the cheroot – so calm – Ramesh could not easily accept.

The moment they stepped in, Rama's weeping could be heard: it was unbearable. Between sobs she was reciting the entire seven-year history of her daughter. Her mother's tales of happiness and sadness, hopes and fears, large and small, the very centre of her life for seven years, seemed inexhaustible.

Ramesh's bewilderment increased. How could someone inhabit the earth for so long and the next moment sever her embrace as if it had never been!

Rama's tears and words continued to flow: 'Oh Aunty, Khuki wanted to wear a gold chain like mine. I wouldn't let her in case she lost it. Will she ever wear one now, Aunty?'

Her aunt stood silently watching. Some of the neighbours arrived and shrank back. They tried to console Rama. But their efforts were futile.

Looking at Ramesh Rama broke abruptly into another fit of loud lamenting: 'You promised to take Khuki to the Bioscope, Dada. Please go and bring her back, Dada.'

Ramesh thought: human appeals as bankrupt and fantastic as these must give a cruel God somewhere a laugh.

Some words of an uncle in the room brought him back to reality. 'Prashanna Babu, give me some rope please.'

Rama too heard them. With a scream she shouted wildly, 'Never! You'll never tie her up with rope. I'll never let you – never!' She seemed to have lost all sense of shame or fear. But what surprised Ramesh much more than the harshness in her voice, was how unmoved his uncle appeared to be.

He responded at once to her plea, calmly: 'Don't be so upset. I'm not going to tie her with rope. It's her bedding we have to tie, don't you see?' He spoke as normally as ever, almost casually; there was no trace of emotion in his voice.

In her over-excitement Rama had got to her feet. Now she fell back exhausted on the floor, sobbing madly. Her uncle swiftly made the necessary arrangements to take the body to the burning-ghat.

Not even a trifling detail of the rites was to be omitted. Why does man feel the need to invest death, the heart-rending riddle, with mumbo-jumbo? Ramesh reflected as he stood observing, stunned.

When the time came to take the body out, Rama fell upon it in a frenzy. 'Where are you taking my Khuki?'

Her uncle had lifted the body on to one shoulder with one arm and was trying to comfort Rama with the other: 'Please, Ma, try to understand.'

But Rama refused to let go. She fiercely embraced Khuki's body with both arms and cried out: 'Let her stay a bit longer, do! I haven't looked at my treasure properly.' In the end the corpse had to be prised from her arms.

The route to the burning-ghat was a long one, but because the body was that of a child, there was no need for many people to come along. In fact only four went. The drizzle was still descending, and gusts of icy wind seemed to penetrate the marrow of their bones.

Ramesh's uncle shifted the body from one shoulder to the other and called out, 'Eh Akshay, have you got the matches?'

Akshay was a neighbour. He was well-known in the area as a do-gooder. Rumour had it, he never turned down a summons to the burning-ghat.

He produced a box of matches from a cavernous pocket in the folds of the loose shirt he was wearing to keep himself warm, and called back, 'I'm never without matches, Dada! If you don't smoke a *biri* on a night like this, you really freeze. I was in a fix like that the other night when we did the rites for the elder son of the Mukherjis . . .'

Ramesh walked along like an automaton listening to Akshay. He heard him tell an elaborate story of how once he had suffered on the way to the ghat because he had been unable to smoke, because he couldn't find a match. As he listened, Ramesh watched the lantern in Prashanna Babu's hand sway, each swing throwing its monotonous patch of light on the shadowy road ahead.

Before Akshay finished, Ramesh's uncle remarked, 'You've reminded me, Akshay. Ramesh, the shops are still open. Go and buy some packets of *biris*, will you? Make sure they're good ones, all right?' He took a rupee from the waist of his dhoti and gave it to Ramesh saying, 'We'd better lay in some stocks for tonight.'

Ramesh did as he was told. The shopkeeper had no big coins, only pice. These he counted out one by one. Ramesh was very impatient. An urge to fling the pice all over the place seized him, but he mastered it. The shopkeeper called anxiously after him, 'Shouldn't you count them too, Babu?'

Ramesh did not bother to reply. His companions had already gone on ahead a fair way and Ramesh had to hurry to catch them. His uncle told him, 'Give the *biris* to Akshay. What a lot of small change

213

they've given you. You'll have to hang on to it, I haven't room in my dhoti.'

Prashanna Babu remarked, 'In this cold didn't you bring a shirt?'

Ramesh's uncle was wearing nothing on top, despite the weather; all he had on was a length of *chadar* wrapped about his waist as a dhoti. But as he was well fleshed he could probably get away with it. He treated Prashanna Babu's comment with a dismissive laugh: 'Cold? What cold? What's this cold you keep talking about?'

Akshay, by contrast, was quite thin. Though he had warm clothes on, he was shivering. He grumbled, 'All right Dada, so you're made of stone, but I'm already feeling a tickle in my throat. I wish I'd brought my comforter.' Ramesh's uncle said only, 'Winter or summer I don't feel comfortable going to the burning-ghat in restricting clothes.'

'That's as maybe, Dada,' Akshay continued, 'but if you don't dress properly in this kind of cold you'll catch something, real pneumonia. That's what happened to Balai Chatterji's third brother. He accompanied a corpse to the funeral pyre on a Wednesday, and on Saturday he himself was taken there. As fate would have it, he was even placed on the same pyre!'

Akshay's talk had made Ramesh rather uncomfortable. He wondered how those carrying a body could chat in such an unruffled way. Was this the natural attitude of a healthy mind – or was it downright callousness? He pondered on it. Akshay's final sentence had properly shaken him.

To avoid unnecessary laundry, he himself had left behind his warm shirt and had worn only an ordinary cotton one. It would not keep out this cold. Already, in the wind, his nose and eyes were streaming. He felt that a cough was coming on. All at once fear possessed him. He would not be surprised if he had already picked up something serious. And there was still the rest of the night to endure. What if . . .

His thoughts gave him gooseflesh. On the point of setting out he had stolen a glance at Lila. How his wife's eyes had pleaded with him! Not just a single night's absence but an eternal separation had seemed to make them dull with pain. The thought crossed his mind, if Khuki had died on another night he would now be lying in his snug bed within the arms of that shy creature, listening to her whispered words. There was so much he wanted to tell her. Suppose his desire was never fulfilled! Suppose he really caught something tonight? Why had he agreed to come? Couldn't he have made up some excuse?

But the next moment he thought, I must do everything in my power to banish this selfishness. To think of myself is wrong. He felt he could hear Rama's weeping, feel Khuki's arms as she came up to hug him. Here he was, in the presence of the dead Khuki, thinking of his own comfort – where had this meanness of mind come from? He must make a big effort to do his bit along with the other three.

He managed to persuade his uncle to let him carry the body. But even then his mind drifted. Lila's eyes, with their pitiful entreaty, kept floating into his head; and the inviting idea of snuggling up in bed in his own tidy room tempted him constantly. So as to shake it off he began to walk faster.

'No point in going so fast, you know,' said Akshay. 'Even if we get there a few minutes earlier we can't go home before dawn.'

It was pitch dark when they eventually arrived. Another group had just finished burning a body. They passed by chanting 'Haribol'. Ramesh's uncle ordered the body set down in front of a hut in the middle of the space. Then he went up to the door, knocked and called out, 'Hello, Mister!'

Hearing no sound at all, he knocked again.

The keeper of the ghat had probably dropped off to sleep. From inside came a disgruntled voice, 'Push hard, Mister. Door's open.'

He was right. With a shove the door came open. A man could be seen within resting awkwardly, his legs on a table, his head on a cushion upon a chair. He showed no sign of wanting to leave his bed. He yawned many times with great determination, stretched himself all over and finally sat upright. When he spoke again his tone was still cross: 'Now you're in you can close the door, Mister – can't you see it's cold out there?'

The whole business made Ramesh angry, but it was not the moment to show his feelings. He silently pushed the door shut. The attendant spent another minute or so rubbing sleep from his eyes. Then he glanced in the direction of the corpse and asked, 'Boy or girl?'

Ramesh's uncle told him. 'Age?' As he spoke the man scribbled the answers on a piece of paper. At length he gave this to Ramesh's uncle, told him the price, pushed the money he was handed into his desk and subsided once more on his makeshift bed. 'Don't forget the door when you go,' he called out.

Outside again Akshay said, 'What a skinflint, eh Dada?' Ramesh's

215

uncle said only, 'What else can he be? He's seen so much death his mind's deadened.'

To accept that human beings could so easily sink so low hurt Ramesh. He wanted to protest against his uncle's statement, but he could not find words to express his feelings.

Then, without warning, he sneezed.

Akshay commented, 'Watch out, careful. This cold is bad! I've also forgotten my comforter.'

Ramesh said hastily, 'No no, it's nothing.' But his words were not much solace to him, standing as he was in the middle of a burning-ghat, surrounded by the shades of death. He felt quite depressed. A few steps further on, and he sneezed again. Now his uncle too became concerned. 'How did you catch so much cold so soon?'

Ramesh lapsed into silence. The story of Balai Chatterji's third brother refused to leave him.

'Let me carry her the last few yards,' offered his uncle. Without any fuss Ramesh transferred Khuki's corpse to his uncle's shoulder and felt immediately relieved. His brooding sadness at her death seemed to lift from his mind.

But when he sneezed a third time his head was in a whirl. In the flickering light of the ghat Prashanna Babu looked at his eyes and said, 'Hey, Ramesh Babu, do you realise, your eyes are red?'

Red! He felt that his insides were shrivelling up. The poignant look of parting in Lila's eyes was like a memory of pain. Had it actually been farewell – forever?

He was consumed with regret. Why hadn't he found an excuse not to come to this place, why? It would have been so easy.

(pre-1946)

216

PRIVATE TUITION BY MR BOSE

Anita Desai

Mr Bose gave his private tuition out on the balcony, in the evenings, in the belief that, since it faced south, the river Hooghly would send it a wavering breeze or two to drift over the roof tops, through the washing and a few pots of *tulsi* and marigold that his wife had placed precariously on the balcony rail, to cool him, fan him, soothe him. But there was no breeze: it was hot, the air hung upon them like a damp towel, gagging him and, speaking through this gag, he tiredly intoned the Sanskrit verses that should, he felt, have been roared out on a hill-top at sunrise.

'*Aum. Usa va asvasya medhyasya sirah . . .*'

It came out, of course, a mumble. Asked to translate, his pupil, too, scowled as he had done, thrust his fist through his hair and mumbled:

'Aum is the dawn and the head of a horse . . .'

Mr Bose protested in a low wail. 'What horse, my boy? What horse?'

The boy rolled his eyes sullenly. 'I don't know, Sir, it doesn't say.'

Mr Bose looked at him in disbelief. He was the son of a Brahmin priest who himself instructed him in the *Mahabharata* all morning, turning him over to Mr Bose only in the evening when he set out to officiate at weddings, *puja* and other functions for which he was so much in demand on account of his stately bearing, his calm and inscrutable face and his sensuous voice that so suited the Sanskrit language in which he, almost always, discoursed. And this was his son – this Pritam with his red-veined eyes and oiled locks, his stumbling fingers and shuffling feet that betrayed his secret life, its scruffiness, its gutters and drains full of resentment and destruction. Mr Bose suddenly remembered how he had seen him, from the window of a

217

bus that had come to a standstill on the street due to a fist fight between the conductor and a passenger, Pritam slipping up the stairs, through the door, into a neon-lit bar off Park Street.

'The sacrificial horse,' Mr Bose explained with forced patience. 'Have you heard of Asvamedha, Pritam, the royal horse that was let loose to run through the kingdom before it returned to the capital and was sacrificed by the king?'

The boy gave him a look of such malice that Mr Bose bit the end of his moustache and fell silent, shuffling through the pages. 'Read on, then,' he mumbled and listened, for a while, as Pritam blundered heavily through the Sanskrit verses that rolled off his father's experienced tongue, and even Mr Bose's shy one, with such rich felicity. When he could not bear it any longer, he turned his head, slightly, just enough to be able to look out of the corner of his eye through the open door, down the unlit passage at the end of which, in the small, dimly lit kitchen, his wife sat kneading dough for bread, their child at her side. Her head was bowed so that some of her hair had freed itself of the long steel pins he hated so much and hung about her pale, narrow face. The red border of her sari was the only stripe of colour in that smoky scene. The child beside her had his back turned to the door so that Mr Bose could see his little brown buttocks under the short white shirt, squashed firmly down upon the woven mat. Mr Bose wondered what it was that kept him so quiet – perhaps his mother had given him a lump of dough to mould into some thick and satisfying shape. Both of them seemed bound together and held down in some deeply absorbing act from which he was excluded. He would have liked to break in and join them.

Pritam stopped reading, maliciously staring at Mr Bose whose lips were wavering into a smile beneath the ragged moustache. The woman, disturbed by the break in the recitation on the balcony, looked up, past the child, down the passage and into Mr Bose's face. Mr Bose's moustache lifted up like a pair of wings and, beneath them, his smile lifted up and out with almost a laugh of tenderness and delight. Beginning to laugh herself, she quickly turned, pulled down the corners of her mouth with mock sternness, trying to recall him to the path of duty, and picking up a lump of sticky dough, handed it back to the child, softly urging him to be quiet and let his father finish the lesson.

Pritam, the scabby, oil-slick son of the Brahmin priest, coughed theatrically – a cough imitating that of a favourite screen actor, surely, it was so false and over-done and suggestive. Mr Bose swung around in dismay, crying, 'Why have you stopped? Go on, go on.'

'You weren't listening, Sir.'

Many words, many questions leapt to Mr Bose's lips, ready to pounce on this miserable boy whom he could hardly bear to see sitting beneath his wife's holy *tulsi* plant that she tended with prayers, water-can and oil-lamp every evening. Then, growing conscious of the way his moustache was agitating upon his upper lip, he said only, 'Read.'

'*Ahar va asvam purustan mahima nvajagata . . .*'

Across the road someone turned on a radio and a song filled with a pleasant, lilting *weltschmerz* twirled and sank, twirled and rose from that balcony to this. Pritam raised his voice, grinding through the Sanskrit consonants like some dying, diseased tram-car. From the kitchen only a murmur and the soft thumping of the dough in the pan could be heard – sounds as soft and comfortable as sleepy pigeons'. Mr Bose longed passionately to listen to them, catch every faintest nuance of them, but to do this he would have to smash the radio, hurl the Brahmin's son down the iron stairs . . . He curled up his hands on his knees and drew his feet together under him, horrified at this welling up of violence inside him, under his pale pink bush-shirt, inside his thin, ridiculously heaving chest. As often as Mr Bose longed to alter the entire direction of the world's revolution, as often as he longed to break the world apart into two halves and shake out of them – what? Festival fireworks, a woman's soft hair, blood-stained feathers? – he would shudder and pale at the thought of his indiscretion, his violence, this secret force that now and then threatened, clamoured, so that he had quickly to still it, squash it. After all, he must continue with his private tuitions: that was what was important. The baby had to have his first pair of shoes and soon he would be needing oranges, biscuits, plastic toys. 'Read,' said Mr Bose, a little less sternly, a little more sadly.

But, 'It is seven, I can go home now,' said Pritam triumphantly, throwing his father's thick yellow *Mahabharata* into his bag, knocking the bag shut with one fist and preparing to fly. Where did he fly to? Mr Bose wondered if it would be the neon-lit bar off Park Street. Then, seeing the boy disappear down the black stairs – the bulb had fused again – he felt it didn't matter, didn't matter one bit since it

219

left him alone to turn, plunge down the passage and fling himself at the doorposts of the kitchen, there to stand and gaze down at his wife, now rolling out *puris* with an exquisite, back-and-forth rolling motion of her hands, and his son, trying now to make a spoon stand on one end.

She only glanced at him, pretended not to care, pursed her lips to keep from giggling, flipped the *puri* over and rolled it finer and flatter still. He wanted so much to touch her hair, the strand that lay over her shoulder in a black loop, and did not know how to – she was so busy. 'Your hair is coming loose,' he said.

'Go, go,' she warned, 'I hear the next one coming.'

So did he, he heard the soft patting of sandals on the worn steps outside, so all he did was bend and touch the small curls of hair on his son's neck. They were so soft, they seemed hardly human and quite frightened him. When he took his hand away he felt the wisps might have come off on to his fingers and he rubbed the tips together wonderingly. The child let fall the spoon, with a magnificent ring, on to a brass dish and started at this discovery of percussion.

The light on the balcony was dimmed as his next pupil came to stand in the doorway. Quickly he pulled himself away from the doorpost and walked back to his station, tense with unspoken words and unexpressed emotion. He had quite forgotten that his next pupil, this Wednesday, was to be Upneeta. Rather Pritam again than this once-a-week typhoon, Upneeta of the flowered sari, ruby ear-rings and shaming laughter. Under this Upneeta's gaze such ordinary functions of a tutor's life as sitting down at a table, sharpening a pencil and opening a book to the correct page became matters of farce, disaster and hilarity. His very bones sprang out of joint. He did not know where to look – everywhere were Upneeta's flowers, Upneeta's giggles. Immediately, at the very sight of the tip of her sandal peeping out beneath the flowered hem of her sari, he was a man broken to pieces, flung this way and that, rattling. Rattling.

Throwing away the Sanskrit books, bringing out volumes of Bengali poetry, opening to a poem by Jibanananda Das, he wondered ferociously: Why did she come? What use had she for Bengali poetry? Why did she come from that house across the road where the loud radio rollicked, to sit on his balcony, in view of his shy wife, making him read poetry to her? It was intolerable. Intolerable, all of it – except, only for the seventy-five rupees paid at the end of the month. Oranges, he thought grimly, and milk, medicines, clothes. And he read to her:

> Her hair was the dark night of Vidisha,
> Her face the sculpture of Svarasti . . .

Quite steadily he read, his tongue tamed and enthralled by the rhythm of the verse he had loved (copied on a sheet of blue paper, he had sent it to his wife one day when speech proved inadequate).

> 'Where have you been so long?' she asked,
> Lifting her bird's-nest eyes,
> Banalata Sen of Natore.

Pat-pat-pat. No, it was not the rhythm of the verse, he realised, but the tapping of her foot, green-sandalled, red-nailed, swinging and swinging to lift the hem of her sari up and up. His eyes slid off the book, watched the flowered hem swing out and up, out and up as the green-sandalled foot peeped out, then in, peeped out, then in. For a while his tongue ran on of its own volition:

> All birds come home, and all rivers,
> Life's ledger is closed . . .

But he could not continue – it was the foot, the sandal that carried on the rhythm exactly as if he were still reciting. Even the radio stopped its rollicking and, as a peremptory voice began to enumerate the day's disasters and achievements all over the world, Mr Bose heard more vigorous sounds from his kitchen as well. There too the lulling pigeon sounds had been crisply turned off and what he heard were bangs and rattles among the kitchen pots, a kettledrum of commands, he thought. The baby, letting out a wail of surprise, paused, heard the nervous commotion continue and intensify and launched himself on a series of wails.

Mr Bose looked up, aghast. He could not understand how these two halves of the difficult world that he had been holding so carefully together, sealing them with reams of poetry, reams of Sanskrit, had

221

split apart into dissonance. He stared at his pupil's face, creamy, feline, satirical, and was forced to complete the poem in a stutter:

> Only darkness remains, to sit facing
> Banalata Sen of Natore.

But the darkness was filled with hideous sounds of business and anger and command. The radio news commentator barked, the baby wailed, the kitchen pots clashed. He even heard his wife's voice raised, angrily, at the child, like a threatening stick. Glancing again at his pupil whom he feared so much, he saw precisely that lift of the eyebrows and that twist of a smile that disjointed him, rattled him.

'Er – please read,' he tried to correct, to straighten that twist of eyebrows and lips. 'Please read.'

'But you have read it to me already,' she laughed, mocking him with her eyes and laugh.

'The next poem,' he cried, 'read the next poem,' and turned the page with fingers as clumsy as toes.

'It is much better when you read to me,' she complained imperti-nently, but she read, keeping time to the rhythm with that restless foot which he watched as though it were a snake-charmer's pipe, swaying. He could hear her voice no more than the snake could the pipe's – it was drowned out by the baby's wails, swelling into roars of self-pity and indignation in this suddenly hard-edged world.

Mr Bose threw a piteous, begging look over his shoulder at the kitchen. Catching his eye, his wife glowered at him, tossed the hair out of her face and cried, 'Be quiet, be quiet, can't you see how busy your father is?' Red-eared, he turned to find Upneeta looking curiously down the passage at this scene of domestic anarchy, and said, 'I'm sorry, sorry – please read.'

'I have read!' she exclaimed. 'Didn't you hear me?'

'So much noise – I'm sorry,' he gasped and rose to hurry down the passage and hiss, pressing his hands to his head as he did so, 'Keep him quiet, can't you? Just for half an hour!'

'He is hungry,' his wife said, as if she could do nothing about that.

'Feed him then,' he begged.

'It isn't time,' she said angrily.

'Never mind. Feed him, feed him.'

'Why? So that you can read poetry to that girl in peace?'

'Ssh!' he hissed, shocked, alarmed that Upneeta would hear. His chest filled with the injustice of it. But this was no time for pleas or reason. He gave another desperate look at the child who lay crouched on the kitchen floor, rolling with misery. When he turned to go back to his pupil who was watching them interestedly, he heard his wife snatch up the child and tell him, 'Have your food then, have it and eat it – don't you see how angry your father is?'

He spent the remaining half-hour with Upneeta trying to distract her from observation of his domestic life. Why should it interest her? he thought angrily. She came here to study, not to mock, not to make trouble. He was her tutor, not her clown! Sternly, he gave her dictation but she was so hopeless – she learnt no Bengali at her convent school, found it hard even to form the letters of the Bengali alphabet – that he was left speechless. He crossed out her errors with his red pencil – grateful to be able to cancel out, so effectively, some of the ugliness of his life – till there was hardly a word left uncrossed and, looking up to see her reaction, found her far less perturbed than he. In fact, she looked quite mischievously pleased. Three months of Bengali lessons to end in this! She was as triumphant as he was horrified. He let fall the red pencil with a discouraged gesture. So, in complete discord, the lesson broke apart, they all broke apart and for a while Mr Bose was alone on the balcony, clutching at the rails, thinking that these bars of cooled iron were all that were left for him to hold. Inside all was a conflict of shame and despair, in garbled grammar.

But, gradually, the grammar rearranged itself according to rule, corrected itself. The composition into quiet made quite clear the exhaustion of the child, asleep or nearly so. The sounds of dinner being prepared were calm, decorative even. Once more the radio was tuned to music, sympathetically sad. When his wife called him in to eat, he turned to go with his shoulders beaten, sagging, an attitude repeated by his moustache.

'He is asleep,' she said, glancing at him with a rather ashamed face, conciliatory.

He nodded and sat down before his brass tray. She straightened it nervously, waved a hand over it as if to drive away a fly he could not see, and turned to the fire to fry hot *puris* for him, one by one, turning quickly to heap them on his tray so fast that he begged her to stop.

'Eat more,' she coaxed. 'One more' – as though the extra *puri* were a peace offering following her rebellion of half an hour ago.

He took it with reluctant fingers but his moustache began to quiver on his lip as if beginning to wake up. 'And you?' he asked. 'Won't you eat now?'

About her mouth, too, some quivers began to rise and move. She pursed her lips, nodded and began to fill her tray, piling up the *puris* in a low stack.

'One more,' he told her, 'just one more,' he teased, and they laughed.

(1978)

SUNDAY

Amit Chaudhuri

On Sundays, the streets of Calcutta were vacant and quiet, and the shops and offices closed, looking mysterious and even a little beautiful with their doors and windows shut, such shabby, reposeful doors and windows, the large signs – DATTA BROS., K. SINGH AND SONS – reflecting the sunlight. The house would reverberate with familiar voices. Chhotomama was at home. Chhordimoni, Sandeep's great-aunt, and Shonamama, his eldest uncle, had also decided to spend the day here. If you overheard them from a distance – Sandeep's uncle, his mother, his aunt, Chhordimoni and Shonamama, all managing to speak at the top of their voices without ever making a moment of sense – you would think they were having a violent brawl, or quarrelling vehemently about the inheritance of some tract of land which they were not prepared to share. And, indeed, they *were* engaged in an endless argument (about what, they did not know) beneath which ran a glowing undercurrent of agreement in which they silently said 'Yes' to each other.

Much of the talk concerned relatives scattered all over India and all over the world. Much of it was about money and the cost of living. Chhotomama's business ran in fits and starts, like his car. It had to be pushed before it worked; it was unreliable. There was no demand for this and no demand for that; this supplier had let him down; that partner was unscrupulous and lazy; the times were not conducive to . . . In short, money was short. 'Today the palm of my left hand's itching,' said Mamima. 'God, God, I wonder – it means I'll have to spend more money – on what, I wonder.' If the right hand itched, it meant one was going to get money – but it seldom itched, and when it did, money seldom followed. Someone was not playing the game.

The subject would switch from money to people 'who need money

225

more than we do', and these people were usually poor relations, or, to be more accurate, poorer relations, old men and widows whose sons were too young to earn or who themselves had lost interest in working for a pittance. The second case was more frequent among men: there seemed to be something masculine about giving up one's job and dignifying one's idle hours by speculating about existence. So they had to be helped and supported, while constantly being assured that they were not being helped and supported, to which they would reply, with different degrees of sincerity, that of course they were and how could they forget it? They were helped and supported, not necessarily because they deserved it, but because money was meant to flow from the hands of one member of the family to another.

This kind of talk, whether at the dinner-table or in the bedroom, did not become too oppressive: it was too full of metaphors, paradoxes, wise jokes and reminiscences to be so. It was, at bottom, a criticism of life. And there were unpredictable breaks, when Sandeep's mother and Mamima would begin to murmur conspiratorially about the colour of a sari. And there were unpremeditated instants when everyone would suddenly stop talking, perhaps to think, each one about something different, and there would be a gap of hushed clarity, in which a crow cawed outside. And the children would be arrested in whatever they were doing at that point of time: one swinging by the window, one lying on his stomach reading a comic, and one sitting on the ground, listening and comprehending nothing. And then they would resume their argument, very loudly, as if they were early twentieth-century actors in some green, neglected village in Bengal, where there were no mikes and no electricity, and every actor had to bellow his speech melodramatically before the large village audience would hear and applaud what he was saying. One would have almost expected Sandeep's uncles and aunts to have been attired in the splendid vibrant costumes that folk-artists wore in keeping with the dramatic excessiveness of their gestures. Yet his uncles wore white pyjamas and nothing else, and the women were draped in faded, handwoven cotton saris – their bodies cool even in the cumulative heat of conversation.

Sometime during the day, probably not too late, nor too early, as on weekdays, Chhotomama would take a bowl of water and other equipment to the verandah, place them on a chair, perch himself on a stool, and shave. This was one of Sunday's simple-minded pleasures and self-indulgences: to shave at what time one pleased, and as long as one pleased, with the children nearby, watching, convincing one that a morning stubble was an amazing thing, and that the shaving instruments were holy tools, and that the act of sprinkling water on the face was somehow profound. When he would look up from the mirror, he would sense the stillness of the street around him, the endless, enduring world of pigeons and crows, the perpetual movement of pariahs, beggars and vendors, and he would feel, simultaneously, the warmth of the sunlight and the coolness of the brush on his cheek. The boys would stand around, noting his movements the way passers-by in Calcutta break their journey to work to stare at acrobats or a monkey-show on the pavement. With curiosity and envy, they followed the determined attentiveness with which he put the cream on his brush, and then swished the lather with a flourish on his face, white and frothy, till it gained a rich uniformity that looked both ornamental and delicious, and then carefully ploughed it with his razor in primitive agricultural fashion.

Later, he would enter the toilet, armed with an ashtray, a newspaper and a pair of reading-glasses. The toilet was his study. Here, filling the room with cigarette smoke, he read the significant news of the day; he pondered on 'world affairs' and 'home affairs'; he pontificated to himself on the 'current situation' from a Marxist angle. He was a water-closet thinker.

This part of the daily ceremonies over, he would enter the bathroom to have his pre-luncheon bath, humming a small tune to himself. He would turn on the old, ineffectual shower and, suddenly elated, begin singing aloud to himself. He had a resonant tenor voice, a voice both strong and delicate. When he sang in the bath, the notes echoed in the four enclosing walls like rays of trapped light darting this way and that in a crystal, a diamond. He usually sang old, half-remembered compositions that had been popular thirty or forty years ago in a Bengal where the radio and the wind-up gramophone were still new and incredible machines breaking the millennial silence of the towns and villages:

> *Godhulir chhaya pathe*
> *Je gelo chini go tare*

Roughly translated, this meant

> In the hour of cow dust, on the shadowy path,
> Who passed by me? I felt I knew her.

227

Knocking on the bathroom door, Sandeep made a pest of himself by asking: 'Chhotomama, what does *godhuli* mean?'

Lost in the general well-being of cleansing himself, his uncle replied patiently: 'The word *go* means cow, and the word *dhuli* means dust. In the villages, evening's the time the cowherds bring the cattle home. The herd returns, raising clouds of dust from the road. *Godhuli* is that hour of cow-dust. So it means dusk or evening.'

As Chhotomama explained, his voice emerging from behind the steady sound of water, Sandeep saw it in his mind like a film being shown from a projector – the slow-moving, indolent cows, their nostrils and their shining eyes, the faint white outline of the cowherd, the sense of the expectant village (a group of scattered huts) and the dust, yes the dust, rising unwillingly from the cows' hooves and blurring everything. The mental picture was set in the greyish-red colour of twilight. It was strange how one word could contain a world within it. Quite unexpectedly, Chhotomama now began a song by Tagore:

> *Bahe nirantar ananta anandadhara.*
> *Baje ashima nabhamajhe anadiraba.*

In an unsatisfactory translation, this meant

> Endless and unbroken flows the stream of joy.
> Its timeless sound resonates beneath the great sky.

It was a song of praise, a prayer-song. Sandeep did not understand a single word of it, but he thought that the tune and especially the sound of the difficult words communicated with him in an obscure way, and he was aware that the repetitive sound of the language had mingled with the sound of the water falling in the bath, till they became one glimmering sound without meaning. Whether the bath ended first, or the song, Sandeep could not tell. A cool spell of remote, waterfall-like music was woven and broken at the same time, as if the words of the song could not endure existing a hundredth of a second after they had been uttered. Chhotomama unlocked the door noisily and came out, smiling, a towel wrapped around his loins and thighs. Pottering about for his new pyjamas and vest, he looked like the chieftain of some undiscovered, happy African tribe. His wet hair stuck out in all directions from his head, like a black, untidy porcupine. The bath, the inner temple where he had performed his last sacrosanct ritual and offered his songs for the day, was now empty and without music, except the sound of a single drop of water falling on the floor with a tone and perfect pitch of its own. Every few seconds, it seemed to repeat that exact pitch without alteration or variation.

At about six o'clock in the evening, the lights went out. The power-cuts had got more frequent with the heat, and the two servant-girls and their little brother who had come downstairs and plopped shyly on the floor to watch the Sunday film on television had to be disappointed and sent home.

'I'm sure they'll show us a better film next Sunday,' assured Sandeep's mother.

'It's not me,' said the girl with the unwashed hair and incredibly clean hands. 'It's Syed,' nodding at the boy, who had worn an imbecilic, puzzled expression ever since the lights had gone off. 'He's never seen a film.' The girl's name was Runa. She was a Muslim janitor's daughter. Sandeep was sorry to see her leave: he had often fantasised about marrying her one day. He noticed, from the corner of his eye, how her bright and ragged body ran impulsively down the stairs, and listened to her slightly hoarse, illiterate voice calling to her brother and sister to follow. The stairs were dark, and a gulf seemed to separate her from him. Then, two minutes later, he forgot she ever existed.

Saraswati brought lanterns into the room each with a strong, yellow yolk of flame. Then she bent to light the candles, and used the dripping wax to stick them onto chipped tea saucers.

'Doesn't Saraswati look like a witch?' whispered Sandeep to Abhi. Indeed, wavering shadows from the candle flame falling and shifting on her face gave her ordinary features a preternatural fluidity. Her cheek-bones and jaw seemed to flow and change with the changing light, as if she were shedding her old face for a new one.

'Saraswati, you look like a witch.' said Abhi.

'Be quiet, you little monsters,' she replied.

She had set down the candles in their saucers at intervals on the floor: one in the room, one in the corridor, one near the staircase. It made it look like there was a festival being celebrated, some esoteric myth in the process of being retold by symbols. As Abhi leaned forward perfunctorily to blow a candle out, and Saraswati rushed towards him – her intention, she said, was to drag him out of the room by his hair – Chhotomama called from the corridor: 'Enough mischief, boys. Come on, let's go out for a walk.'

So they went out for a walk. They went through narrow, lightless lanes, where houses that were silent but gave out smells of fish and boiled rice stood on either side of the road. There was not a single tree in sight; no breeze and no sound but the vaguely musical humming of mosquitoes. Once, an ancient taxi wheezed past, taking a short-cut through the lane into the main road, like a comic vintage car passing through a film-set showing the Twenties into the film-set of the present, passing from black-and-white into colour. But why did these houses – for instance, that one with the tall, ornate iron gates and a watchman dozing on a stool, which gave the impression that the family had valuables locked away inside, or that other one with the small porch and the painted door, which gave the impression that whenever there was a feast or a wedding all the relatives would be invited, and there would probably be so many relatives that some of them, probably the young men and women, would be sitting bunched together on the cramped porch because there would be no more space inside, taking eloquently about something that didn't really require eloquence, laughing uproariously at a joke that wasn't really very funny, or this next house with an old man relaxing in his easy-chair on the verandah, fanning himself with a local Sunday newspaper, or this small, shabby house with the girl Sandeep glimpsed through a window, sitting in a bare, ill-furnished room, memorising a text by candlelight, repeating suffixes and prefixes from a Bengali grammar over and over to herself – why did these houses seem to suggest that an infinitely interesting story might be woven around them? And yet the story would never be a satisfying one, because the writer, like Sandeep, would be too caught up in jotting down the irrelevances and digressions that make up lives, and the life of a city, rather than a good story – till the reader would shout 'Come to the point!' – and there would be no point, except the girl memorising the rules of grammar, the old man in the easy-chair fanning himself, and the house with the small, empty porch that was crowded, paradoxically, with many memories and possibilities. The 'real' story, with its beginning, middle and conclusion, would never be told, because it did not exist.

The road ended, and it branched off, on one side, to a larger road, and on the other side to two narrower ones that led to a great field, a maidan, with a pair of poles at either end which were supposed to be goalposts. As they came closer, they noticed that the field was full of people whom they had not been able to discern at first in the darkness: now they came slowly into focus in the moonlight, like a negative becoming clearer and clearer as it was developed in a darkroom. There were all kinds and classes of people – college boys, schoolboys, couples, unemployed men, families, hawkers, groups of girls. The clammy heat had made them leave their houses or hovels in search of a breeze. It was a strange scene because, in spite of the number of people who had congregated together, there was scarcely any noise. The shadowiness of the place made them speak in low voices, as if they were in a theatre or auditorium where the lights had been dimmed meaningfully, and a film or a play were just about to begin. If there had been no power-cut, or if it had still been light, the maidan, needless to say, would have throbbed with its own din and activity. But the darkness had brought a strange lethargy and even peace to these otherwise highly strung men and women, and there was a perceptible sense of release, as if time was oozing by, and the world happening elsewhere.

Just as Chhotomama and the boys were preparing to join the others in the maidan, to settle on the cool grass and pull the grass out luxuriously with their fingers, the lights came back. It was a dramatic instant, like a photographer's flash going off, which recorded the people sprawled in various postures and attitudes, smiles of relief and wonder on their faces. Each day there would be a power-cut, and each day there would be the unexpected, irrational thrill when the lights returned; it was as if people would never get used to it; day after day, at that precise, privileged moment when the power-cut ended without warning as it had begun, giving off a radiance that was confusing and breathtaking, there was an uncontrollable sensation of delight, as if it were happening for the first time. With what appeared to be an instinct for timing, the rows of fluorescent lamps glittered to life simultaneously. The effect was the opposite of blowing out candles on a birthday cake: it was as if someone had blown on a set of unlit candles, and the magic exhalation had brought a flame to every wick at once.

(1988)

THE LITTLE WORLD
OF SHADANANDA

Satyajit Ray

I am feeling quite cheerful today, so this is a good time to tell you everything. I know you will believe me. You are not like my people; they only laugh at me. They think I am making it all up. So I have stopped talking to them.

It is midday now, so there is no one in my room. They will come in the afternoon. Now there are only two here – myself and my friend Lal Bahadur. Lal Bahadur Singh! Oh, how worried I was for his sake yesterday! I couldn't believe he would ever come back to me. He is very clever, so he was able to escape unhurt. Anyone else would have been finished by now.

How silly of me! – I have told you my friend's name, but not my own.

My name is Shadananda Chakraborty. Sounds like a bearded old man, doesn't it? Actually, I am only thirteen. I can't help it if my name is old-fashioned. After all, I didn't choose it myself; it was my grandma who did.

If she only knew how much trouble it would cause me she would surely have called me something else. How could she have known that people would pester me by saying, 'Why are you so glum when your name means "ever-happy"?' Such fools! As if laughing like a jackass was the only way to show that one was happy. There are so many kinds of being happy when one doesn't even smile.

For instance, suppose there's a twig sticking out of the ground and you find a grasshopper landing on its tip again and again. It would certainly make you happy to see it, but if you burst out laughing at it, people would think you were out of your mind. Like that mad uncle of mine. I never saw him, but I was told that he laughed all the time. Even when they had

232

to put him in chains, he found it so funny that he almost split his sides laughing.

The truth is, I get fun out of things which most people don't even notice. Even when I am lying in bed I notice things which make me happy. Sometimes a cotton seed comes floating in through the window. Small wispy things which the slightest breath of air sends wafting hither and thither. What a happy sight that is! If they come floating down towards you, you blow on them and send them shooting up into the air again.

And if a crow should come and settle on the window, watching it is like watching a circus clown. I always go absolutely still when a crow comes and sits nearby, and watch its antics out of the corner of my eye.

But if you ask me what gives me most fun, I would say – watching ants. Of course, it is no longer just funny, it is – but no, I mustn't tell everything now or the fun will be spoilt. It's better I begin at the beginning.

Once, about a year ago, I had fever. It was nothing new, as I am often laid up with fever. I catch a chill rather easily. Mother says it's because I spend so much time out of doors sitting on the grass.

As always, the first couple of days in bed was fun. A nice, chilly feeling mixed with a feeling of drowsiness. Added to this was the fun of not having to go to school. I lay in bed and was watching a squirrel climbing up the *madar* tree outside the window when Mother came and gave me a bitter mixture to drink. I drank it up like a good boy and then took a glass of water, drank some of it and blew the rest out the window in a spray.

I wrapped the blanket around me and was about to close my eyes when I noticed something.

A few drops of water had fallen on the window sill, and in one of these drops a small black ant was trying desperately to save itself from drowning.

I found it so strange that I propped myself up on my elbows and leaned forward to bring my eyes up close to the ant.

As I watched intently, the ant suddenly seemed as if it was not an ant any more but a man. In fact, it reminded me of Jhontu's brother-in-law who had slipped down the bank into a pond while fishing and, not being able to swim, wildly thrashed his arms about to keep himself afloat. In the end he was saved by Jhontu's elder brother and their servant Narahari.

As soon as I recalled the incident, I had a wish to save the ant.

Although I had a fever, I jumped out of bed, ran out of the room, rushed into my father's study and tore off a piece of blotting paper from

233

his writing pad. Then I ran back into my room, jumped on to the bed and held the blotting paper so that its edge touched the drop of water. The water was sucked up in no time.

The suddenly rescued ant seemed not to know which way to go. It rushed about this way and that for a while, and then disappeared down the drainpipe on the far side of the sill.

No more ants appeared on the sill that day.

The next day the fever went up. Around midday Mother came and said, 'Why are you staring at the window? You should try and get some sleep.'

I shut my eyes to please Mother, but as soon as she left, I opened them again and looked at the drainpipe.

In the afternoon, when the sun was behind the *madar* tree, I saw an ant poking its head out of the mouth of the pipe.

Suddenly it came out and started to move briskly about on the sill.

Although all black ants look alike, I somehow had the feeling that this was the same ant which had nearly drowned yesterday. I had acted as his friend, so he had come to pay me a visit.

I had made my plans beforehand. I had brought some sugar from the pantry, wrapped it up in paper and put it beside my pillow.

I now opened the wrapper, took out a large grain of sugar and put it on the sill.

The ant seemed startled and stopped in its tracks. Then it cautiously approached the sugar and prodded it with its head from all sides. Then it suddenly made for the drainpipe and disappeared into it.

I thought – that's odd. I gave him such a nice grain of sugar and he left it behind. Why did he come at all if not for food?

The doctor came in a short while. He felt my pulse, looked at my tongue and placed the stethoscope on my chest and back. Then he said I must take some more of the bitter mixture and the fever would go in a couple of days.

That didn't make me happy at all. No fever meant going to school, and going to school meant not watching the drainpipe in the afternoon when the ants came out.

Anyway, as soon as the doctor left, I turned towards the window and was delighted to see a whole army of black ants coming out of the drainpipe onto the sill. The leader must be the ant I knew, and he must have informed the other ants about the grain of sugar and led them to it.

234

Watching for a while I was able to see for myself how clever the ants were. They all now banded together to push the grain towards the drain-pipe. I can't describe how funny it was. I imagined that if they had been coolies pushing a heavy weight, they would surely have shouted, 'All together, heave ho! A little further, heave ho! That's the spirit, heave ho!'

After my fever had gone, school was a bore for a few days. My thoughts would go back again and again to the window sill. There must be ants coming there every afternoon. I would leave a few grains of sugar on the sill every morning before going to school and when I returned in the afternoon, I would find them gone.

In the class I used to sit at a desk towards the middle of the room. Beside me sat Shital. One day I was a little late and found Phani sitting in my place. So I had no choice but to sit at the back of the class in front of the wall.

In the last period before recess we read history. In his thin, piping voice the history teacher Haradhan Babu was describing how brave Hannibal was. Hannibal had led an army from Carthage and had crossed the Alps to invade Italy.

As I listened, I suddenly had the feeling that Hannibal's army was in the classroom and was on the march very close to me.

I looked around and my eyes travelled to the wall behind me. Down the wall ran a long line of ants – hundreds of small black ones, exactly like a mighty army on the way to battle.

I looked down and found a crack in the wall near the floor through which the ants were going out.

As soon as the bell rang for recess, I ran to the back of our classroom and spotted the crack. The ants were coming out of it and making their way through the grass towards a guava tree.

I followed the ants and found, at the foot of the guava tree, something which can only be described as a castle.

It was a mound of earth with a tiny opening at the base through which the ants entered.

I had a great urge to look inside the castle.

I had my pencil in my pocket, and with its tip I began carefully to dig into the mound. At first I found nothing inside, but digging a little further, I had the surprise of my life. I found there were countless small chambers inside the mound, and a maze of passages leading from one chamber to another. How very strange! How could the ants build such

235

a castle with their tiny arms and legs? How could they be so clever? Do they have schools where they are taught? Do they also learn from books, draw pictures, build things? Does that mean they are no different from human beings except in looks? How is it that they can build their own house while tigers, elephants, bears, horses can't? Even Bhulo, my pet dog, can't.

Of course, birds build nests. But how many birds can live in a single nest? Can the birds build a castle where thousands of them can live?

Because I had spoilt a part of the mound, there was a great flurry amongst the ants. I felt sorry for them. I thought: now that I have done them harm, I must make up by doing them a good turn, otherwise they would look upon me as their enemy, which I was not. I was truly their friend.

So the next day I took half of a sweetmeat which Mother gave me to eat, wrapped it up in a *shal* leaf and carried it in my pocket to school.

Just before the bell rang for classes to begin, I put the sweetmeat by the ant hill. The ants must have to travel far for food; today they would find it right at their doorstep. Surely that was doing them a good turn.

In a few weeks the summer holidays began and my friendship with ants began to grow.

I would talk about my observation of how ants behaved to the elders, but they paid no attention to me. What really put my back up was when they laughed at me. So I decided not to tell anybody anything. Whatever I did, I'd do alone, and keep what I learned to myself.

One day, in the afternoon, I sat by the compound wall of Pintu's house watching a hill made by red ants. People will say that you can't sit near red ants for long because they bite. I have been bitten by red ants myself, but of late I have noticed that they don't bite me. So I was watching them without fear when I suddenly spotted Chhiku striding up.

I haven't mentioned Chhiku yet. His real name is Shrikumar. He is in the same class as me, but he must be older than me because there's a thin line of moustache above his lips. Chhiku is a bully so nobody likes him. I usually don't meddle with him because he is stronger than me.

Chhiku saw me and called out, 'You there, silly ass, what are you doing squatting on the ground?'

I didn't pay any attention to him. He came up towards me.

I kept my eyes on the ants. Chhiku drew up and said, 'What are you up to? I don't like the look of it.'

I made no attempt to hide what I was doing and told him the truth.

Chhiku made a face and said, 'What d'you mean – watching ants? What is there to watch? And aren't there ants in your own house that you have to come all the way here?'

I felt very angry. What is it to you what I do? Why poke your nose into other people's affairs?

I said: 'I'm watching them because I like doing so. You know nothing about ants. Why don't you mind your own business? Why come and bother me?'

Chhiku hissed like an angry cat and said, 'So you like watching ants, eh? Well – there! There! There!' Before I could do or say anything, Chhiku had levelled the ant hill with three vicious jabs of his heel, thereby squashing at least five hundred ants.

Chhiku gave a hollow laugh and was about to walk away when something suddenly happened to me. I jumped on Chhiku's back, grabbed hold of his hair, and knocked his head four or five times against Pintu's compound wall.

Then I let go of him. Chhiku burst into tears and went off.

When I got home, I learnt that Chhiku had already been to complain against me.

But I was surprised when at first Mother neither scolded nor beat me. Perhaps she hadn't believed Chhiku, because I had never hit anyone before. Besides, Mother knew that I was scared of Chhiku.

But when Mother asked what had happened, I couldn't lie to her.

Mother was very surprised. 'You mean you really bashed his head against the wall?'

I said, 'Yes, I did. And why only Chhiku, I would do the same to anyone who trampled on ant hills.'

This made Mother so angry that she slapped me.

It was a Saturday. Father came back from the office early. When he heard from Mother what had happened he locked me up in my room.

Although my cheeks smarted from the slaps, I wasn't really sorry for myself; I was sorry for the ants. Once in Sahibgunj where cousin Parimal lives, there was a collision between two trains which killed three hundred people. And today it took Chhiku only a few seconds to kill so many ants!

It seemed so wrong, so very wrong.

As I lay in bed thinking of all that had happened, I suddenly felt a little chilly and had to draw the blanket over me.

And then I went off to sleep.

I was awakened by a strange noise.

A thin, high-pitched sound, very beautiful, going up and down in a regular beat, like a song.

I pricked up my ears and looked around but couldn't make out where the sound came from. Probably someone far away was singing. But I had never heard such singing before.

Look who's here! – An ant had come out of the drain pipe while I was listening to the strange sound.

This time I clearly recognised him – the ant I had saved from drowning. He was facing me and salaaming me by raising his two front legs and touching his head with them. What shall I call this black creature? Kali? Krishna? I must think about it. After all, one can't have a friend without a name.

I put my hand on the window sill palm upwards. The ant brought his legs down from the head and crawled slowly towards my hand. Then it climbed up my little finger and started scurrying over the criss-cross lines on my palm.

Just then I gave a start as I heard a sound from the door, and the ant clambered down and disappeared into the drainpipe.

Now Mother came into the room and gave me a glass of milk. Then she felt my forehead and said I had fever again.

Next morning the doctor came. Mother said, 'He was restless the whole night, and kept saying "Kali" again and again.' Mother probably thought I was praying to the Goddess Kali, because I hadn't told her about my new friend.

The doctor had put the stethoscope on my back when I heard the song again. It was louder than yesterday and the tune was different. It seemed to come from the window, but since the doctor had asked me to keep still, I couldn't turn my head to see.

The doctor finished his examination, and I cast a quick glance towards the window. Hullo there! It was a large black ant this time, and this one too was salaaming me. Are all ants my friends then?

And was it this ant which was singing?

But Mother said nothing about a song. Did that mean she couldn't hear it?

I turned towards Mother to ask her, and found her staring at the ant with fear in her eyes. The next moment she picked up my arithmetic book from the table, leaned over me and with one slap of the book squashed the ant.

The same moment the singing stopped.

'The whole house is crawling with ants!' said Mother. 'Just think what would happen if one crawled inside your ear.'

The doctor left after giving me an injection. I looked at the dead ant. He was killed while singing a beautiful song. Just like my great-uncle Indranath. He used to sing classical songs, which I didn't understand very well. One day he was playing the *tanpura* and singing when he suddenly died. When he was taken to the crematorium in a procession, a group of *kirtan* singers went along singing songs in praise of the God Hari. I watched it and I still remember it, although I was very small.

And today a strange thing happened. I fell asleep after the injection and dreamed that, as in the funeral of great-uncle Indranath, a dozen or so ants were bearing the dead ant on their shoulders while a line of ants followed singing a chorus.

I woke up in the afternoon when Mother put her hand on my forehead.

I glanced at the window and found that the dead ant was no longer there.

This time the fever kept on for several days. No wonder, because every one in the house had started killing ants. How can the fever go when you have to listen to the screaming of ants the whole day?

And there was another problem. While the ants were being killed in the pantry, hordes of ants turned up on my window sill and wept. I could see that they wanted me to do something for them – either stop the killing or punish those who were doing the misdeed – but since I was laid up with fever, I could do nothing. Even if I had been well, how could a small boy like me stop the elders from doing what they were doing?

But one day I was forced to do something.

I don't exactly remember what day it was, but I do remember that I had woken up at the crack of dawn and right away I heard Mother announce that an ant had got into Phatik's ear and bitten him.

I was tickled by the news, but just then I heard the slapping of brooms on the floor and knew that they were killing ants.

Then something very strange happened. I heard thin voices shouting, 'Help us! Help us, please!' I looked at the window and found that a large group of ants had gathered on the sill and were running around wildly.

Hearing them cry out I could no longer keep calm. I forgot about my fever, jumped out of bed and ran out of the room. At first I didn't know what to do. Then I took up a clay pot which was lying on the floor and smashed it.

Then I started to smash all the things I could find which would break.

It was a clever ruse because it certainly stopped the killing of ants. But it made my parents, my aunt, my cousin Shabi all come out of their rooms, grab hold of me, put me back on my bed and lock the door of my room.

I had a good laugh, and the ants on my window kept saying, 'Thank you! Thank you!' and went back into the drainpipe again.

Soon after this I had to leave home. The doctor examined me one day and said I should be sent to hospital for treatment.

Now I am in a hospital room. I have been here for the last four days.

The first day I felt very sad because the room was so clean, I knew there couldn't be any ants in it. Being a new room, there were no cracks or holes in the walls. There wasn't even a cupboard for ants to hide behind or beneath. But there was a mango tree just outside the window, and one of its branches was within reach.

I thought: if there is a place to find ants it will be on that branch.

But the first day I couldn't get near the window. How could I, since I was never alone? Either the nurse, or the doctor, or someone from my house was always in the room.

The second day too was just as bad.

I was so upset that I threw the medicine bottle on the floor and broke it. It made the doctor quite angry. He was not a nice doctor, this new one. I could tell that from his bristling moustache and his thick glasses.

On the third day, something occurred.

There was only a nurse in my room, and she was reading a book. I was in bed wondering what to do, when I heard a thud and saw that the book had slipped from the nurse's hand and fallen on the floor. The nurse had dozed off.

I got out of the bed and went to the window on tip-toe.

Leaning out of the window and stretching my body as far as it would go, I grabbed hold of the mango branch and began to pull it towards me.

This made a noise which woke up the nurse – and then the fireworks started.

The nurse gave a scream, came rushing towards me and, wrapping her arms around me, dragged me to the bed and dumped me on it. Others, too, came into the room, so I could do nothing more.

The doctor promptly gave me an injection.

I could make out from what they were saying that they thought I wanted to throw myself out of the window. Silly people! If I had thrown myself from such a height, all my bones would have been broken and I would have died.

After the doctor left I felt sleepy. I thought of the window by my bed at home and I felt very sorry. Who knows when I shall be back home again?

I was nearly asleep when I heard a thin voice saying, 'Sepoys at your service, Sir – sepoys at your service!'

I opened my eyes and saw two large red ants standing with their chests out beside the medicine bottle on the bedside table.

They must have climbed onto my hand from the mango branch without my knowing it.

I said, 'Sepoys?'

The answer came, 'Yes Sir. At your service.'

'What are your names?' I asked.

One said, 'Lal Bahadur Singh', and the other said, 'Lal Chand Pandey.'

I was very pleased. But I warned them, they must go into hiding when people came into the room, or they might be killed. Lal Chand and Lal Bahadur salaamed and said 'Very well, Sir.'

Then the two of them sang a lovely duet which lulled me to sleep.

I must tell you right away what happened yesterday, because it's nearly five and the doctor will be here soon.

In the afternoon I was watching Lal Chand and Lal Bahadur wrestling on the table while I lay in bed. I was supposed to be sleeping, but the pills and injection hadn't worked. Or, to be quite truthful, I wilfully kept myself awake. If I slept in the afternoon when would I play with my new friends?

Each ant fought gamely and it was hard to say who would win when suddenly there was a sound of heavy footsteps. The doctor was coming!

I made a sign and Lal Bahadur promptly disappeared below the table.

But Lal Chand had been thrown on his back and was thrashing his legs about, so he couldn't run away. And that was the cause of the nasty incident.

The doctor came, saw the ant, and, saying some rude words in English, swept it off the table with his hand.

From his scream, I could tell Lal Chand was badly hurt but what could I do? By then the doctor had grabbed my hand to feel my pulse. Still I tried to get up, but the nurse held me down.

241

After the examination, the doctor as usual made a glum face and scratched the edge of his moustache. He was about to turn toward the door when he suddenly screwed up his face, gave a leap and yelled 'Ouch!' three times in English.

Then all hell broke loose. His stethoscope flew out of his hand, his spectacles jumped off his nose and crashed on to the floor, one of the buttons of his jacket came off as he struggled to remove it, his tie wound tighter around his neck and made him gasp and splutter before he at last managed to pull it free, the hole in his vest showed as he yanked off his shirt, while all the time jumping around and yelling. I was speechless.

The nurse said, 'What is the matter, Sir?'

The doctor continued to jump about and yelled, 'Ant! Red ant! Crawled up my arm – ouch!'

Well, well, well! I knew this would happen, and it served him right! Lal Bahadur had taken revenge on his friend's behalf.

If they saw me now they would know how deliriously happy Shadananda can be.

(translated by the author)
(1962)

THE TENANT

Bharati Mukherjee

Maya Sanyal has been in Cedar Falls, Iowa, less than two weeks. She's come, books and clothes and one armchair rattling in the smallest truck the U-Haul would rent her, from New Jersey. Before that she was in North Carolina. Before that, Calcutta, India. Every place has something to give. She is sitting at the kitchen table with Fran drinking bourbon for the first time in her life. Fran Johnson found her the furnished apartment and helped her settle in. Now she's brought a bottle of bourbon which gives her the right to stay and talk for a bit. She's breaking up with someone named Vern, a pharmacist. Vern's father is also a pharmacist and owns a drugstore. Maya has seen Vern's father on TV twice already. The first time was on the local news when he spoke out against the selling of painkillers like Advil and Nuprin in supermarkets and gas stations. In the matter of painkillers, Maya is a universalist. The other time he was in a barbershop quartet. Vern gets along alright with his father. He likes the pharmacy business, as business goes, but he wants to go back to graduate school and learn to make films. Maya is drinking her first bourbon tonight because Vern left today for San Francisco State.

'I understand totally,' Fran says. She teaches Utopian Fiction and a course in Women's Studies and worked hard to get Maya hired. Maya has a PhD in Comparative Literature and will introduce writers like R. K. Narayan and Chinua Achebe to three sections of sophomores at the University of Northern Iowa. 'A person has to leave home. Try out his wings.'

Fran has to use the bathroom. 'I don't feel abandoned.' She pushes her chair away from the table. 'Anyway, it was a sex thing totally. We were good together. It'd be different if I'd loved him.'

Maya tries to remember what's in the refrigerator. They need food.

243

She hasn't been to a supermarket in over a week. She doesn't have a car yet and so she relies on a corner store – a longish walk – for milk, cereal, and frozen dinners. Someday these exigencies will show up as bad skin and collapsed muscle tone. No folly is ever lost. Maya pictures history as a net, the kind of safety net travelling trapeze artists of her childhood fell into when they were inattentive, or clumsy. Going to circuses in Calcutta with her father is what she remembers vividly. It is a banal memory, for her father, the owner of a steel company, is a complicated man.

Fran is out in the kitchen long enough for Maya to worry. They need food. Her mother believed in food. What is love, anger, inner peace, etc., her mother used to say, but the brain's biochemistry. Maya doesn't want to get into that, but she is glad she has enough stuff in the refrigerator to make an omelette. She realises Indian women are supposed to be inventive with food, whip up exotic delights to tickle an American's palate, and she knows she should be meeting Fran's generosity and candour with some sort of bizarre and effortless countermove. If there's an exotic spice store in Cedar Falls or in neighbouring Waterloo, she hasn't found it. She's looked in the phone book for common Indian names, especially Bengali, but hasn't yet struck up culinary intimacies. That will come – it always does. There's a six-pack in the fridge that her landlord, Ted Suminski, had put in because she'd be thirsty after unpacking. She was thirsty, but she doesn't drink beer. She probably should have asked him to come up and drink the beer. Except for Fran she hasn't had anyone over. Fran is more friendly and helpful than anyone Maya has known in the States since she came to North Carolina ten years ago, at nineteen. Fran is a Swede, and she is tall, with blue eyes. Her hair, however, is a dull, darkish brown.

'I don't think I can handle anything that heavy-duty,' Fran says when she comes back into the room. She means the omelette. 'I have to go home in any case.' She lives with her mother and her aunt, two women in their mid-seventies, in a drafty farmhouse. The farmhouse now has a computer store catty-corner from it. Maya's been to the farm. She's been shown photographs of the way the corner used to be. If land values ever rebound, Fran will be worth millions.

Before Fran leaves she says, 'Has Rab Chatterji called you yet?'

'No.' She remembers the name, a good, reliable Bengali name, from the first night's study of the phone book. Dr Rabindra Chatterji teaches Physics.

'He called the English office just before I left.' She takes car keys out

244

of her pocketbook. She reknots her scarf. 'I bet Indian men are more sensitive than Americans. Rab's a Brahmin, that's what people say.'

A Chatterji has to be a Bengali Brahmin – last names give ancestral secrets away – but Brahminness seems to mean more to Fran than it does to Maya. She was born in 1954, six full years after India became independent. Her India was Nehru's India: a changed, progressive place.

'All Indian men are wife beaters,' Maya says. She means it and doesn't mean it. 'That's why I married an American.' Fran knows about the divorce, but nothing else. Fran is on the Hiring, Tenure, and Reappointment Committee.

Maya sees Fran down the stairs and to the car which is parked in the back in the spot reserved for Maya's car, if she had owned one. It will take her several months to save enough to buy one. She always pays cash, never borrows. She tells herself she's still recovering from the U-Haul drive halfway across the country. Ted Suminski is in his kitchen watching the women. Maya waves to him because waving to him, acknowledging him in that way, makes him seem less creepy. He seems to live alone though a sign, THE SUMINSKIS, hangs from a metal horse's head in the front yard. Maya hasn't seen Mrs Suminski. She hasn't seen any children either. Ted always looks lonely. When she comes back from campus, he's nearly always in the back, throwing darts or shooting baskets. 'What's he like?' Fran gestures with her head as she starts up her car. 'You hear these stories.'

Maya doesn't want to know the stories. She has signed a year's lease. She doesn't want complications. 'He's all right. I keep out of his way.'

'You know what I'm thinking? Of all the people in Cedar Falls, you're the one who could understand Vern best. His wanting to try out his wings, run away, stuff like that.'

'Not really.' Maya is not being modest. Fran is being impulsively democratic, lumping her wayward lover and Indian friend together as headstrong adventurers. For Fran, a utopian and feminist, borders don't count. Maya's taken some big risks, made a break with her parents' ways. She's done things a woman from Ballygunge Park Road doesn't do, even in fantasies. She's not yet shared stories with Fran, apart from the divorce. She's told her nothing of men she picks up, the reputation she'd gained, before Cedar Falls, for 'indiscretions'. She has a job, equity, three friends she can count on for emergencies. She is an American citizen. But.

*   *   *

Fran's Brahmin calls her two nights later. On the phone he presents himself as Dr Chatterji, not Rabindra or Rab. An old-fashioned Indian, she assumes. Her father still calls his closest friend, 'Colonel'. Dr Chatterji asks her to tea on Sunday. She means to say no but hears herself saying, 'Sunday? Fiveish? I'm not doing anything special this Sunday.'

Outside, Ted Suminski is throwing darts into his garage door. The door has painted-on rings: orange, purple, pink. The bull's-eye is gray. He has to be fifty at least. He is a big, thick, lonely man about whom people tell stories. Maya pulls the phone cord as far as it'll go so she can look down more directly on her landlord's large, bald head. He has his back to her as he lines up a dart. He's in black running shoes, red shorts, he's naked to the waist. He hunches his right shoulder, he pulls the arm back; a big, lonely man shouldn't have so much grace. The dart is ready to cut through the September evening. But Ted Suminski doesn't let go. He swings on worn rubber soles, catches her eye in the window (she has to have imagined this), takes aim at her shadow. Could she have imagined the noise of the dart's metal tip on her windowpane?

Dr Chatterji is still on the phone. 'You are not having any mode of transportation, is that right?'

Ted Suminski has lost interest in her. Perhaps it isn't interest, at all; perhaps it's aggression. 'I don't drive,' she lies, knowing it sounds less shameful than not owning a car. She has said this so often she can get in the right degree of apology and Asian upper-class helplessness. 'It's an awful nuisance.'

'Not to worry, please.' Then, 'It is a great honour to be meeting Dr Sanyal's daughter. In Calcutta business circles he is a legend.'

On Sunday she is ready by four-thirty. She doesn't know what the afternoon holds; there are surely no places for 'high tea' – a colonial tradition – in Cedar Falls, Iowa. If he takes her back to his place, it will mean he has invited other guests. From his voice she can tell Dr Chatterji likes to do things correctly. She has dressed herself in a peach-coloured nylon georgette sari, jade drop-earrings and a necklace. The colour is good on dark skin. She is not pretty, but she does her best. Working at it is a part of self-respect. In the mid-seventies, when American women felt rather strongly about such things, Maya had been in trouble with her women's group at Duke. She was too feminine. She had tried to explain the world she came out of. Her grandmother had been married off at the age of five in a village now in Bangladesh. Her great-aunt had been burned to death over a dowry problem. She herself had been trained to speak softly, arrange flowers, sing, be pliant. If she were to seduce Ted Suminski, she thinks as she waits in the front yard for Dr Chatterji, it would be minor heroism. She has broken with the past. But.

Dr Chatterji drives up for her at about five ten. He is a hesitant driver. The car stalls, jumps ahead, finally slams to a stop. Maya has to tell him to back off a foot or so; it's hard to leap over two sacks of pruned branches in a sari. Ted Suminski is an obsessive pruner and gardener.

'My sincerest apologies, Mrs Sanyal,' Dr Chatterji says. He leans across the wide front seat of his noisy, very old, very used car and unlocks the door for her. 'I am late. But then, I am sure you're remembering that Indian Standard Time is not at all the same as time in the States.' He laughs. He could be nervous – she often had that effect on Indian men. Or he could just be chatty. 'These Americans are all the time rushing and rushing but where it gets them?' He moves his head laterally one, twice. It's the gesture made famous by Peter Sellers. When Peter Sellers did it, it had seemed hilarious. Now it suggests that Maya and Dr Chatterji have three thousand years plus civilisation, sophistication, moral virtue, over people born on this continent. Like her, Dr Chatterji is a naturalised American.

'Call me Maya,' she says. She fusses with the seat belt. She does it because she needs time to look him over. He seems quite harmless. She takes in the prominent teeth, the eyebrows that run together. He's in a blue shirt and a beige cardigan with the K-Mart logo that buttons tightly over the waist. It's hard to guess his age because he has dyed his hair and his moustache. Late thirties, early forties. Older than she had expected. 'Not Mrs Sanyal.'

This isn't the time to tell about ex-husbands. She doesn't know where John is these days. He should have kept up at least. John had come into her life as a graduate student at Duke, and she, mistaking the brief breathlessness of sex for love, had married him. They had stayed together two years, maybe a little less. The pain that John had inflicted all those years ago by leaving her had subsided into a cosy feeling of loss. This isn't the time, but then she doesn't want to be a legend's daughter all evening. She's not necessarily on Dr Chatterji's side is what she wants to get across early; she's not against America and Americans. She makes the story – of marriage outside the Brahminic pale, the divorce – quick, dull. Her unsentimentality seems to shock him. His stomach sags inside the cardigan.

247

'We've each had our several griefs,' the physicist says. 'We're each required to pay our karmic debts.'

'Where are we headed?'

'Mrs Chatterji has made some Indian snacks. She is waiting to meet you because she is knowing your cousin-sister who studied in Scottish Church College. My home is okay, no?'

Fran would get a kick out of this. Maya has slept with married men, with nameless men, with men little more than boys, but never with an Indian man. Never.

The Chatterjis live in a small blue house on a gravelly street. There are at least five or six other houses on the street; the same size but in different colours and with different front yard treatments. More houses are going up. This is the cutting edge of suburbia.

Mrs Chatterji stands in the driveway. She is throwing a large plastic ball to a child. The child looks about four, and is Korean or Cambodian. The child is not hers because she tells it, 'Chung-Hee, ta-ta, bye-bye. Now I play with guest,' as Maya gets out of the car.

Maya hasn't seen this part of town. The early September light softens the construction pits. In that light the houses too close together, the stout woman in a striped cotton sari, the child hugging a pink ball, the two plastic lawn chairs by a tender young tree, the sheets and saris on the clothesline in the back, all seem miraculously incandescent.

'Go home now, Chung-Hee. I am busy.' Mrs Chatterji points the child homeward, then turns to Maya, who has folded her hands in traditional Bengali greeting. 'It is an honour. We feel very privileged.' She leads Maya indoors to a front room that smells of moisture and paint.

In her new, deliquescent mood, Maya allows herself to be backed into the best armchair – a low-backed, boxy Goodwill item draped over with a Rajasthani bedspread – and asks after the cousin Mrs Chatterji knows. She doesn't want to let go of Mrs Chatterji. She doesn't want husband and wife to get into whispered conferences about their guest's misadventures in America, as they make tea in the kitchen.

The coffee table is already laid with platters of mutton croquettes, fish chops, onion *pakoras*, *ghugni* with *puris*, *samosas*, chutneys. Mrs Chatterji has gone to too much trouble. Maya counts four kinds of sweet-meats in Corning casseroles on an end table. She looks into a see-through lid; spongy, white dumplings float in rosewater syrup. Planets contained, mysteries made visible.

248

'What are you waiting for, Santana?' Dr Chatterji becomes imperious, though not unaffectionate. He pulls a dining chair up close to the coffee table. 'Make some tea.' He speaks in Bengali to his wife, in English to Maya. To Maya he says, grandly, 'We are having real Indian Green Label Lipton. A nephew is bringing it just one month back.'

His wife ignores him. 'The kettle's already on,' she says. She wants to know about the Sanyal family. Is it true her great-grandfather was a member of the Star Chamber in England?

Nothing in Calcutta is ever lost. Just as her story is known to Bengalis all over America, so are the scandals of her family, the grandfather hauled up for tax evasion, the aunt who left her husband to act in films. This woman brings up the Star Chamber, the glories of the Sanyal family, her father's philanthropies, but it's a way of saying, *I know the dirt*.

The bedrooms are upstairs. In one of those bedrooms an unseen, tormented presence – Maya pictures it as a clumsy ghost that strains to shake off the body's shell – drops things on the floor. The things are heavy and they make the front room's chandelier shake. Light bulbs, shaped like tiny candle flames, flicker. The Chatterjis have said nothing about children. There are no tricycles in the hallway, no small sandals behind the doors. Maya is too polite to ask about the noise, and the Chatterjis don't explain. They talk just a little louder. They flip the embroidered cover off the stereo. What would Maya like to hear? Hemanta Kumar? Manna Dey? Oh, that young chap, Manna Dey! What sincerity, what tenderness he can convey!

Upstairs the ghost doesn't hear the music of nostalgia. The ghost throws and thumps. The ghost makes its own vehement music. Maya hears in its voice madness, self-hate.

Finally the water in the kettle comes to a boil. The whistle cuts through all fantasy and pretence. Dr Chatterji says, 'I'll see to it,' and rushes out of the room. But he doesn't go to the kitchen. He shouts up the stairwell. 'Poltoo, kindly stop this nonsense straightaway! We're having a brilliant and cultured lady-guest and you're creating earthquakes?' The kettle is hysterical.

Mrs Chatterji wipes her face. The face that had seemed plump and cheery at the start of the evening now is flabby. 'My sister's boy,' the woman says.

So this is the nephew who had brought with him the cartons of Green Label tea, one of which will be given to Maya.

Mrs Chatterji speaks to Maya in English as though only the alien language can keep emotions in check. 'Such an intelligent boy! His father is government servant. Very highly placed.'

Maya is meant to visualise a smart, clean-cut young man from south Calcutta, but all she can see is a crazy, thwarted, lost graduate student. Intelligence, proper family guarantee nothing. Even Brahmins can do self-destructive things, feel unsavoury urges. Maya herself had been an excellent student.

'He was First Class First in BSc from Presidency College,' the woman says. 'Now he's getting Master's in Ag. Science at Iowa State.'

The kitchen is silent. Dr Chatterji comes back into the room with a tray. The teapot is under a tea cosy, a Kashmiri one embroidered with the usual *chinar* leaves, loops, and chains. '*Her* nephew,' he says. The dyed hair and dyed moustache are no longer signs of a man wishing to fight the odds. He is a vain man, anxious to cut losses. 'Very unfortunate business.'

The nephew's story comes out slowly, over fish chops and mutton croquettes. He is in love with a student from Ghana.

'Everything was A-Okay until the Christmas break. Grades, assistant-ship for next semester, everything.'

'I blame the college. The office for foreign students arranged a Christmas party. And now, bap-re-bap! Our poor Poltoo wants to marry a Negro Muslim.'

Maya is known for her nasty, ironic one-liners. It has taken her friends weeks to overlook her malicious, un-American pleasure in others' misfor-tunes. Maya would like to finish Dr Chatterji off quickly. He is pompous; he is reactionary; he wants to live and work in America but give back nothing except taxes. The confused world of the immigrant – the lostness that Maya and Poltoo feel – that's what Dr Chatterji wants to avoid. She hates him. But.

Dr Chatterji's horror is real. A good Brahmin boy in Iowa is in love with an African Muslim. It shouldn't be a big deal. But the more she watches the physicist, the more she realises that 'Brahmin' isn't a caste; it's a metaphor. You break one small rule, and the constellation collapses. She thinks suddenly that John Cheever – she is teaching him as a 'world writer' in her classes, cheek-by-jowl with Africans and West Indians – would have understood Dr Chatterji's dread. Cheever had been on her mind, ever since the late afternoon light slanted over Mrs Chatterji's drying saris. She remembers now how full of a soft, Cheeverian light Durham had been the summer she had slept with John

250

Hadwen; and how after that, her tidy graduate-student world became monstrous, lawless. All men became John Hadwen; John became all men. Outwardly, she retained her poise, her Brahminical breeding. She treated her crisis as a literary event; she lost her moral sense, her judgement, her power to distinguish. Her parents had behaved magnanimously. They had cabled from Calcutta: WHAT'S DONE IS DONE. WE ARE CONFIDENT YOU WILL HANDLE NEW SITUATIONS WELL. ALL LOVE. But she knows more than do her parents. Love is anarchy.

Poltoo is Mrs Chatterji's favourite nephew. She looks as though it is her fault that the Sunday has turned unpleasant. She stacks the empty platters methodically. To Maya she says, 'It is the goddess who pulls the strings. We are puppets. I know the goddess will fix it. Poltoo will not marry that African woman.' Then she goes to the coat closet in the hall and staggers back with a harmonium, the kind sold in music stores in Calcutta, and sets it down on the carpeted floor. 'We're nothing but puppets,' she says again. She sits at Maya's feet, her pudgy hands on the harmonium's shiny, black bellows. She sings, beautifully, in a virgin's high voice, 'Come, goddess, come, muse, come to us hapless people's rescue.'

Maya is astonished. She has taken singing lessons at Dakshini Academy in Calcutta. She plays the sitar and the *tanpura*, well enough to please Bengalis, to astonish Americans. But stout Mrs Chatterji is a devotee, talking to God.

A little after eight, Dr Chatterji drops her off. It's been an odd evening and they are both subdued.

'I want to say one thing,' he says. He stops her from undoing her seat belt. The plastic sacks of pruned branches are still at the corner.

'You don't have to get out,' she says.

'Please. Give me one more minute of your time.'

'Sure.'

'Maya is my favourite name.'

She says nothing. She turns away from him without making her embarrassment obvious.

'Truly speaking, it is my favourite. You are sometimes lonely, no? But you are lucky. Divorced women can date, they can go to bars and discos. They can see mens, many mens. But inside marriage there is so much loneliness.' A groan, low, horrible, comes out of him.

She turns back toward him, to unlatch the seat belt and run out of the car. She sees that Dr Chatterji's pants are unzipped. One hand works hard under his Jockey shorts; the other rests, limp, penitential, on the steering wheel.

'Dr Chatterji – *really*!' she cries.

The next day, Monday, instead of getting a ride home with Fran – Fran says she *likes* to give rides, she needs the chance to talk, and she won't share gas expenses, absolutely not – Maya goes to the periodicals room of the library. There are newspapers from everywhere, even from Madagascar and New Caledonia. She thinks of the periodicals room as an asylum for homesick aliens. There are two aliens already in the room, both Orientals, both absorbed in the politics and gossip of their far-off homes.

She goes straight to the newspapers from India. She bunches her raincoat like a bolster to make herself more comfortable. There's so much to catch up on. A village headman, a known Congress-Indira party worker, has been shot at by scooter-riding snipers. An Indian pugilist has won an international medal – in Nepal. A child drawing well water – the reporter calls the child 'a neo-Buddhist, a convert from the now-outlawed untouchable caste' – has been stoned. An editorial explains that the story about stoning is not a story about caste but about failed idealism; a story about promises of green fields and clean, potable water broken, a story about bribes paid and wells not dug. But no, thinks Maya, it's about caste.

Out here, in the heartland of the new world, the India of serious newspapers unsettles. Maya longs again to feel what she had felt in the Chatterji's living room: virtues made physical. It is a familiar feeling, a longing. Had a suitable man presented himself in the reading room at that instant, she would have seduced him. She goes on to the stack of *India Abroads*, reads through the matrimonial columns, and steals an issue to take home.

Indian men want Indian brides. Married Indian men want Indian mistresses. All over America, 'handsome, tall, fair' engineers, doctors, data processors – the new pioneers – cry their eerie love calls.

Maya runs a finger down the first column; her fingertip, dark with newsprint, stops at random.

Hello! Hi! Yes, you *are* the one I'm looking for. You are the new emancipated Indo-American woman. You have a zest for life. You are at ease in USA and yet your ethics are rooted in Indian tradition. The man of your dreams has come. Yours truly is handsome, ear-nose-throat specialist, well-settled in Connecticut. Age is 41 but never married, physically fit, sportsmanly, and strong. I adore idealism, poetry, beauty. I abhor smugness, passivity, caste system. Write with recent photo. Better still, call!!!

Maya calls. Hullo, hullo, hullo! She hears immigrant lovers cry in crowded shopping malls. Yes, you who are at ease in both worlds, you are the one. She feels she has a fair chance.

A man answers. 'Ashoke Mehta speaking.'

She speaks quickly into the bright-red mouthpiece of her telephone. He will be in Chicago, in transit, passing through O'Hare. United counter, Saturday, two p.m. As easy as that.

'Good,' Ashoke Mehta says. 'For these encounters I, too, prefer a neutral zone.'

On Saturday at exactly two o'clock the man of Maya's dreams floats toward her as lovers used to in shampoo commercials. The United counter is a loud, harassed place but passengers and piled-up luggage fall away from him. Full-cheeked and fleshy-lipped, he is handsome. He hasn't lied. He is serene, assured, a Hindu god touching down in Illinois.

She can't move. She feels ugly and unworthy. Her adult life no longer seems miraculously rebellious; it is grim, it is perverse. She has accomplished nothing. She has changed her citizenship but she hasn't broken through into the light, the vigour, the *bustle* of the New World. She is stuck in dead space. 'Hullo, Hullo?' Their fingers touch.

Oh, the excitement! Ashoke Mehta's palm feels so right in the small of her back. Hullo, hullo, hullo. He pushes her out of the reach of anti-Khomeini Iranians, Hare Krishnas, American Fascists, men with fierce wants, and guides her to an empty gate. They have less than an hour.

'What would you like, Maya?'

She knows he can read her mind, she knows her thoughts are open to him. *You*, she's almost giddy with the thought, with simple desire. 'From the snack bar,' he says, as though to clarify. 'I'm afraid I'm starved.'

Below them, where the light is strong and hurtful, a Boeing is being serviced. 'Nothing,' she says.

He leans forward. She can feel the nap of his scarf – she recognises the Cambridge colours – she can smell the wool of his Icelandic sweater. She runs her hand along the scarf, then against the flesh of his neck. 'Only the impulsive ones call,' he says.

The immigrant courtship proceeds. It's easy, he's good with facts. He knows how to come across to a stranger who may end up a lover, a spouse. He makes over a hundred thousand. He owns a house in Hartford, and two income properties in Newark. He plays the market but he's cautious. He's good at badminton but plays handball to keep in shape. He watches all the sports on television. Last August he visited Copenhagen, Helsinki and Leningrad. Once upon a time he collected stamps but now he doesn't have hobbies, except for reading. He counts himself an intellectual, he spends too much on books. Ludlum, Forsyth, MacInnes; other names she doesn't catch. She suppresses a smile, she's told him only she's a graduate student. He's not without his vices. He's a spender not a saver. He's a sensualist: good food – all foods, but easy on the Indian – good wine. Some temptations he doesn't try to resist.

And I, she wants to ask, do I tempt?

'Now tell me about yourself, Maya.' He makes it easy for her. 'Have you ever been in love?'

'No.'

'But many have loved you, I can see that.' He says it not unkindly. It is the fate of women like her, and men like him. Their karmic duty, to be loved. It is expected, not judged. She feels he can see them all, the sad parade of need and demand. This isn't the time to reveal all.

And so the courtship enters a second phase.

When she gets back to Cedar Falls, Ted Suminski is standing on the front porch. It's late at night, chilly. He is wearing a down vest. She's never seen him on the porch. In fact there's no chair to sit on. He looks chilled through. He's waited around a while.

'Hi.' She has her keys ready. This isn't the night to offer the six-pack in the fridge. He looks expectant, ready to pounce.

'Hi.' He looks like a man who might have aimed the dart at her. What has he done to his wife, his kids? Why isn't there at least a dog? 'Say, I left a note upstairs.'

254

The note is written in Magic Marker and thumb-tacked to her apartment door. DUE TO PERSONAL REASONS, NAMELY REMARRIAGE, I REQUEST THAT YOU VACATE MY PLACE AT THE END OF THE SEMESTER.

Maya takes the note down and retacks it to the kitchen wall. The whole wall is like a bulletin board, made of some new, crumbly building-material. Her kitchen, Ted Suminski had told her, was once a child's bedroom. Suminski in love: the idea stuns her. She has misread her landlord. The dart at her window speaks of no twisted fantasy. The landlord wants the tenant out.

She gets a glass out of the kitchen cabinet, gets out a tray of ice, pours herself a shot of Fran's bourbon. She is happy for Ted Suminski. She is. She wants to tell someone how moved she'd been by Mrs Chatterji's singing. How she'd felt in O'Hare, even about Dr Rab Chatterji in the car. But Fran is not the person. No one she's ever met is the person. She can't talk about the dead space she lives in. She wishes Ashoke Mehta would call. Right now.

Weeks pass. Then two months. She finds a new room, signs another lease. Her new landlord calls himself Fred. He has no arms, but he helps her move her things. He drives between Ted Suminski's place and his twice in his station wagon. He uses his toes the way Maya uses her fingers. He likes to do things. He pushes garbage sacks full of Maya's clothes up the stairs.

'It's all right to stare,' Fred says. 'Hell, I would.'

That first afternoon in Fred's rooming house, they share a Chianti. Fred wants to cook her pork chops but he's a little shy about Indians and meat. Is it beef, or pork? Or any meat? She says it's okay, any meat, but not tonight. He has an ex-wife in Des Moines, two kids in Portland, Oregon. The kids are both normal; he's the only freak in the family. But he's self-reliant. He shops in the supermarket like anyone else, he carries out the garbage, shovels the snow off the sidewalk. He needs Maya's help with one thing. Just one thing. The box of Tide is a bit too heavy to manage. Could she get him the giant size every so often and leave it in the basement?

The dead space need not suffocate. Over the months, Fred and she will settle into companionship. She had never slept with a man without arms. Two wounded people, he will joke during their nightly contortions. It will shock her, this assumed equivalence with a man so strikingly deficient. She knows she is strange, and lonely, but being Indian is not the same, she would have thought, as being a freak.

255

One night in spring, Fred's phone rings. 'Ashoke Mehta speaking.' None of this 'do you remember me?' nonsense. The god has tracked her down. He hasn't forgotten. 'Hullo,' he says, in their special way. And because she doesn't answer back, 'Hullo, hullo, hullo.' She is aware of Fred in the back of the room. He is lighting a cigarette with his toes.

'Yes,' she says, 'I remember.'

'I had to take care of a problem,' Ashoke Mehta says. 'You know that I have my vices. That time at O'Hare I was honest with you.'

She is breathless.

'Who is it, May?' asks Fred.

'You also have a problem,' says the voice. His laugh echoes. 'You will come to Hartford, I know.'

When she moves out, she tells herself, it will not be the end of Fred's world.

(1988)

THE CONCLUSION

Rabindranath Tagore

1

Apurba Krishna had just passed his BA examination in Calcutta and was returning to his village. On the way his boat had to cross a small river. Later in the year, after the close of the rainy season, it would have been almost dry. Now at the end of *Shravan*, the monsoon month, it had reached the edge of the village and was lapping at the roots of the bamboo grove. But after days and days of heavy rain, the sun shone in a cloudless sky.

Apurba's thoughts as he sat in the boat were brimming too. Had we access to the pictures in his young mind we would have seen them dancing like the sun's rays on the wind-ruffled water.

The boat drew up at the usual ghat. From the riverbank Apurba could see the tiled roof of his house through a gap in the trees. No one there knew of his arrival, and so no one had come to meet him. The boatman offered a hand with the luggage, but Apurba refused it and stepped gaily ashore. His feet touched the mud of the ghat, and he fell over, luggage and all. At that instant a melodious peal of high-pitched laughter came from somewhere and startled the birds in a nearby peepul tree.

Extremely embarrassed, Apurba quickly recovered his balance and looked about him. On top of a pile of bricks in course of being unloaded for the local money-lender, a girl sat doubled up with giggles. Apurba recognised her as Mrinmayi, daughter of their recently-arrived neighbours. He knew they had previously lived by a big river some distance away, but when the river had swallowed their land they had settled in the village two or three years previously.

Apurba knew much about the girl's reputation. The men of the village referred to her affectionately as Pagli – 'Madcap' – but their wives were in a constant state of alarm at her wayward behaviour. All her playmates were boys, and she had vast scorn for girls her

257

own age. In the ranks of biddable children she was regarded as a scourge.

Being her father's favourite made her all the more unruly. Her mother never stopped grumbling about it to her friends. Yet because her father loved Mrinmayi, her tears would have hurt him deeply if he had been at home. That fact, and natural deference to her absent husband, kept the mother from imposing too strict a discipline.

Mrinmayi was dark-complexioned with wavy hair that straggled over her shoulders. Her expression was boyish. Her enormous black eyes held no shame or fear, and not the slightest coyness. She was tall, well-built, healthy, strong – but of an age people found hard to estimate; otherwise they would have criticised her parents because she was still unmarried. If the boat of some distant zamindar arrived at the ghat, the villagers became impressively alert. As if at a signal, the women pulled their veils down to the tips of their noses, thus concealing their faces like curtains on a stage. But Mrinmayi would arrive holding a naked child to her chest, her unbound hair hanging free. She would stand like a young doe gazing inquisitively in a land where there is neither hunter nor danger. Eventually she would return to her boy playmates and give them elaborate descriptions of the new arrival's manners and mores.

Our Apurba had set eyes on this untamed creature several times during holidays at home, and had occasionally thought of her in a casual way, and sometimes in a not-so-casual way. In the course of life one sees a great many faces, but only a few become fixed in the mind, not for their external appeal but for some other quality – a transparency perhaps. Most faces do not give away much of the personality; but the transparent face – the face in a thousand – clearly reveals the mystery behind it and immediately impresses itself on the mind. Mrinmayi's face was one of these. Her eyes held all the wilful femininity of a nimble, unfettered fawn. It was a face that, once seen, was not easy to forget.

Of course its melodious laughter, however charming it might have been to others, sounded rather painful to the unlucky Apurba. Hastily handing the suitcase to the boatman, he set off red-faced towards home.

And so the scene was beautifully set, with the riverbank, the shady trees, the birdsong, the morning sun, the joy of being twenty – no need to mention a pile of bricks: but as for the person sitting on top of them, she bestowed grace even on that dull and solid heap. How cruel of fate to have turned poetry into farce at the first entrance of the first act.

2

The peal of laughter from that pile was still echoing in Apurba's ears when he picked up his mud-smeared case and *chadar*, took the path beneath the trees, and arrived at his house. His widowed mother was ecstatic at his unexpected arrival. She sent out at once for rice-pudding, curds and *rui*-fish and caused a bit of a flurry in the neighbourhood. Once the meal was over she introduced the subject of marriage. Apurba had expected it. He had already received many proposals, and in keeping with the slogan of the day had obstinately insisted 'BA pass before bride'. But now he was a BA, and his mother had been expectant for so long that he knew further excuses would be useless. He said, 'Very well, first let me see the girl then I'll decide.'

His mother said, 'I've seen her. You needn't give it a thought.'

Apurba was quite prepared to give it a thought himself and said, 'Bride must be seen before marriage.' His mother thought she had never heard anything so outrageous, but she consented.

That night, after Apurba had put out the lamp and lain down to sleep in his solitary bed, he caught a sound from beyond the patter of midnight rain and the stillness of the village, the sound of sweet high-pitched laughter. His morning downfall bothered him very much, and he pondered how to rectify the impression he had created. The girl doesn't know that I, Apurba Krishna, am an erudite fellow, he thought, who has spent long periods in Calcutta – not a village bumpkin to be dismissed with a laugh because of a trifling slip in some mud.

The next day Apurba had to inspect the potential bride. She was not far away; the family lived in a neighbouring village. He dressed with some care. Discarding his usual dhoti and *chadar*, he wore a long silk *chapkan*, a puggree on his head, and his best varnished shoes, and set out at dawn with a silk umbrella in his hand.

The instant he entered the prospective father-in-law's house, he was received with pomp and circumstance. In due time a trembling creature painted and polished, tinsel round the bun in her hair, and wrapped in a fine colourful sari, was produced before him. She was led silently to a corner, where she remained with her head bent almost to her knees and an elderly maidservant at her back to give her courage.

Her small brother Rakhal now concentrated his total attention upon this latest intruder into the family and scrutinised its puggree, gold watch-chain, and newly-sprouted beard. After stroking this a few times, Apurba finally asked with a solemn air, 'What have you read?' The dumbfounded ornamented bundle made no response. After a few more questions and some encouraging prods in the ribs from the maid, the girl blurted out in a faint voice, '*Charupath* Volume Two Grammar Volume One Descriptive Geography Arithmetic History of India.' Simultaneously there came a sudden series of repeated thuds outside the room, and a moment later Mrinmayi raced breathlessly into the room with her hair flying. Without so much as a glance at Apurba Krishna, she grabbed the brother of the bride-to-be by the hand and began to pull him out of the room. But Rakhal refused to cooperate, so absorbing was the situation indoors. The maid did her best to retrieve this by berating Mrinmayi as sharply as propriety permitted. Apurba Krishna meanwhile preserved his own dignity as best he could by sitting bolt upright in his lofty turban and fiddling with the watch-chain across his stomach. When Mrinmayi finally grasped that she could not distract Rakhal, she slapped him loudly on the back, whipped the veil off the girl's head, and dashed out like a whirlwind. The maid growled in fury, and Rakhal tittered at the sudden sight of his sister minus her precious veil. The slap on the back he did not object to at all, for such exchanges often took place between them. Mrinmayi's hair, for instance, once hung half-way down her back, rather than to her shoulders. One day Rakhal had sneaked up behind her and snipped off a handful with a pair of scissors. She had grabbed the scissors from him in anger and finished the job with a few slashes. Waves of hair had fallen to the ground and lain there like clusters of black grapes. This was the system of discipline between them.

The inspection session fell silent and did not endure much longer. Somehow the girl uncurled herself, regained a perpendicular position and returned to the inner rooms escorted by the old maid. Apurba, still stroking his sparse moustache, rose as solemnly as possible and prepared to depart. But when he reached the door he saw that his new pair of varnished shoes had vanished, and no one could find them. Everyone in the house was frightfully put out and hurled endless reproaches in the direction of the culprit. Eventually a desperate Apurba borrowed an old, torn and flapping pair of slippers belonging to the master of the house. With this additional touch to his fancy *chapkan* and puggree, he very gingerly set out along the village path.

By the edge of a pond, at a deserted point on the path, the high-pitched laughter caught him again. It was as if some fun-loving nymph in the forest had seen the slippers and could not suppress her giggles. While Apurba stood hesitating, she emerged brazenly, placed his new pair of shoes on the path, and was about to take to her heels when Apurba managed to grab both her hands and capture her.

Twisting and turning, Mrinmayi tried to free herself but could not. A stray sunbeam slanted through the trees on to her full, mischievous face. Like a curious traveller stooping to see the sunlit bed of a moving stream through clear water, Apurba gravely gazed on Mrinmayi's upturned face with its sparkling eyes, very gradually loosened his grip on his prisoner, and released her. If he had struck her in anger Mrinmayi would not have been at all surprised, but this gentle sentence of punishment in this empty glade quite baffled her.

The whole sky seemed to ring with laughter like the sound of celestial ankle bells. Lost in thought Apurba Krishna plodded home.

3

All day Apurba made up excuses for not joining his mother in the inner rooms. He had an invitation elsewhere; he ate there. The fact is – though it may be hard to swallow – that even someone as erudite, serious-minded and original as Apurba was remarkably eager to regain his lost dignity in the eyes of this simple village girl. What did it matter if she had momentarily reduced him to a laughing-stock, then ignored him in favour of some ignoramus named Rakhal? Must he prove to her that he reviewed books for a magazine called *Vishvadip* and carried in his suitcase cologne, shoes, Rubini's camphor, coloured letter-paper, and a book on how to play the harmonium, not to mention a note-book awaiting future publication like the dawn in the womb of night? Nevertheless, whatever common sense might say, Mr Apurba Krishna Ray was definitely unprepared to admit defeat at the hands of this flighty rustic girl.

When he appeared in the inner rooms that evening, his mother asked, 'Well Apu, you saw the girl. Do you approve?'

Somewhat awkwardly Apurba replied, 'I saw the girl, Mother, and there was one I liked.'

261

Astounded, his mother cried, 'You saw *girls*!'

Then, after much shilly-shallying, he revealed that he had selected Mrinmayi, daughter of their neighbour. What a choice after so much education and study!

At first Apurba was considerably abashed, but he was no longer so when his mother began to object vehemently. He sat there insisting doggedly that he would marry no one but Mrinmayi. The more he thought of the dolled-up kind of girl, the more repulsive became the idea of marrying one.

Battle was joined between them, in the form of tiffs, sulks, fasts and sleepless nights, and after two or three days Apurba was victorious. His mother managed to convince herself that Mrinmayi was still immature, that her own mother had been unable to bring her up properly, but that if taken in hand after marriage Mrinmayi's nature would change. Gradually, she came to believe that the girl had a pretty face. It was when she thought of the girl's cropped hair that her heart filled with despair. Yet even that, she hoped, if tied up firmly and thoroughly soaked in oil, might in time respond to treatment.

To the village people Apurba's choice of bride quickly became labelled *apurba* – original. Many of them rather liked 'Pagli Mrinmayi', but not, it must be said, as a possible daughter-in-law.

Her father, Ishan Majumdar, was informed. He was a clerk in a steamship company, responsible for the correct loading and unloading of goods and the sale of tickets from a decrepit tin-roofed hut at a distant riverside station. When he heard the news, he shed tears of sorrow and joy, mingled in proportions unknown. He petitioned his boss, a head-office sahib, for leave of absence to attend his daughter's wedding. The sahib considered this insufficient grounds and turned down the request. Then, expecting a week's holiday at Puja time, Ishan wrote home to postpone the wedding. But Apurba's mother said, 'The auspicious days fall in the present month, and the wedding cannot be put off.' Twice rejected, the distressed father protested no more and went back to weighing goods and selling tickets.

Whereupon Mrinmayi's mother and all the older women of the village assembled and began to instruct Mrinmayi day and night in her future duties. Their stern prohibitions against playfulness and frolicking around, loud laughter, gossip with boys, and eating when hungry succeeded in making marriage sound like a nightmare. An alarmed Mrinmayi thought she had been sentenced to life imprisonment with hanging at the end of it. Like an unbroken pony she stiffened her neck, reared back, and said, 'I'm not going to get married.'

4

Nevertheless, she did.

Then her lessons began. Overnight, Mrinmayi's world contracted to the confines of her mother-in-law's inner rooms. Her mother-in-law began the task of correcting her. Assuming a minatory expression, she said, 'Look, dear, you're not a little girl any longer. We don't tolerate disgraceful manners in our house.' Mrinmayi did not grasp what she meant. If my manners are not tolerated here, I'd better go elsewhere, she thought. That afternoon she was missing. A thorough search was launched. Finally the traitor Rakhal led them to her secret hideout, the abandoned old chariot of the village deity Radhakanta under a banyan tree. It is easy to imagine how the mother-in-law and willing well-wishers set upon the girl.

That night the clouds gathered and rain began with a pattering sound. Apurba Krishna edged a little closer to Mrinmayi as she lay in bed and whispered in her ear, 'Mrinmayi, don't you love me?'

'No!' she said violently, 'I will never ever love you!' And then she unleashed all her rage and humiliation on Apurba's head like thunderbolts.

In a wounded voice he said, 'Why, what have I done?'

'Why did you marry me?'

A satisfactory counter to this accusation was tricky. But then and there Apurba decided he must win her over.

The next day the mother-in-law saw all the signs of rebellion and locked Mrinmayi in. At first and for some time she fluttered about the room like a newly captured bird. When she could not escape she shredded the bedsheets with her teeth in futile anger and then, lying prone on the floor, pined for her father and wept.

In time someone slowly came and sat beside her. Affectionately he tried to lift her hair off the floor and away from her face. Mrinmayi shook her head vigorously and threw off the hand. Then Apurba bent down to her and said softly, 'I've opened the door. Come, let's get away to the back garden.' But Mrinmayi's head shook vehemently and said, 'No.' Apurba tried to lift her chin and said, 'Just look who's here.' Rakhal, bewildered at seeing Mrinmayi prostrate on the floor, stood at the door. Without looking up she pushed away Apurba's hand. 'Rakhal's come to play with you. Won't you go with him?' In a voice loud with irritation she repeated 'No!' Rakhal realised he had chosen the wrong moment and fled with a sigh of relief. Apurba sat on in silence. Mrinmayi wept and wept, until she exhausted herself and fell asleep. Apurba tiptoed out and fastened the door behind him.

The next day she received a letter from her father. He grieved over his inability to attend his darling's marriage, and he sent the newlyweds his heartfelt blessings. Mrinmayi went to her mother-in-law and said, 'I want to go to my father.' The astonished woman exploded at this outlandish request. 'Who knows where her father lives, and she wants to go to him! A fantastic notion!' Mrinmayi went away without replying. She went to her room, bolted the door, and in utter hopelessness began to pray to her father as if to God: 'Father, come and take me away. I have no one here. I'll die if I stay here.'

In the dead of night, while her husband slept, Mrinmayi very carefully opened the door and left the house. Clouds passed over now and then, but the paths were plain in the moonlight. How to choose one leading to her father was beyond her. She assumed that if she followed the route of the mail-runner it would take her to any address in the world. She set off on this familiar path. After walking quite a way she grew weary, and night was nearly over. As a few birds uncertain of the time began to give tentative chirps, she found herself on a riverbank in a place like a large market. She paused to think, and then recognised the 'jham-jham' of the mail-runner's ankle bells. Then he himself appeared, out of breath, with the mail-bags on his shoulder. Mrinmayi rushed up to him and begged, 'I want to go to my father at Kushiganj. Will you take me?'

'I don't know where Kushiganj is.' With barely a pause for breath he roused the boatman on the mail-boat tied up at the ghat, and the boat cast off. He was not allowed time to answer questions.

By and by the market awoke. Mrinmayi went down to the ghat and called to another boatman, 'Will you take me to Kushiganj?' Before he could reply, someone in the next boat called out, 'So it's you, Minu Ma? What are you doing here?' Bursting with impatience she called back, 'Banamali, I'm going to my father at Kushiganj. Can you take me in your boat?' Banamali was a boatman from their village and knew this wilful girl very well. 'You're going to your father? That's good. Come on, I'll take you.' Mrinmayi jumped in.

The boatman cast off. The clouds descended and a torrential downpour began. The boat tossed in a current swollen with the rains of *Bhadra*. Mrinmayi was overwhelmed with fatigue. She spread the loose end of her sari, lay down, and went tamely to sleep, rocked by the river like a baby in Mother Nature's arms.

She awoke in her bed in her married home. Seeing her eyes open the maid began to scold. This brought the mother-in-law and a stream of harsh words. Mrinmayi, wide-eyed, stared at her. But when she made a dig a Mrinmayi's father's bad training, Mrinmayi got up, went to the next room, and bolted the door.

Apurba forsook his usual timidity, went to his mother and said, 'What harm is there in sending her to her father for a few days?'

His mother turned on him: 'She's bewitched!' and then she took up an old theme: with so many girls to choose from, why had he brought home this bone-burning good-for-nothing?

5

All day the downpour continued, and the atmosphere indoors was equally foul. That night in the early hours, Apurba woke Mrinmayi and said, 'Do you want to go to your father?' Suddenly alert, she clutched his hand and said simply 'Yes!' Apurba whispered, 'Come then. We'll escape very quietly. I've arranged a boat.'

Mrinmayi looked at her husband with profound gratitude. She got up quickly, dressed, and prepared to leave. Apurba left a note to allay his mother's anxiety, and the two of them stepped out. In the dark, without a soul or a sound nearby, she first put her hand in her husband's of her own free will; the tingle of her excitement thrilled his every nerve.

The boat moved out into the night. In spite of her ecstasy Mrinmayi fell asleep almost at once. The next day, what freedom! what delight! On both banks were so many villages, markets, fields of grain, forests, other boats passing back and forth. Soon she was plying her husband with a thousand questions about the tiniest and most trivial of sights. What is in that boat? Where have those people come from? What is the name of this place? Questions whose answers could not be found in any of Apurba's college books or extracted from his Calcutta experience. His friends there would have been embarrassed to know that he answered every one of them and that most of his replies did not tally with the truth. He asserted for instance, that a boat carrying

265

sesame carried linseed, and he called a magistrate's court a zamindar's warehouse and confused the town of Panchberia with that of Rainagar. His wrong replies did not impede in the slightest the satisfaction in the heart of his trustful questioner.

The following evening they reached Kushiganj. In a tin-roofed hut half-lit by an oily old lantern Ishan Chandra sat bare-chested on a stool, bent over a huge leather-bound account book resting on a small desk. The newlyweds entered and Mrinmayi said, 'Father!' in a tone of voice quite alien to that room. Ishan wept. He could not think what to say or what to do. His daughter and son-in-law were standing in his hut like the princess and prince of an empire, and all he could offer them for thrones were some bales of jute. He was absolutely disoriented. And what about food? As a poor clerk he cooked his own dal and rice – but this was a joyous occasion. Mrinmayi said, 'Father, today we'll all cook.' Apurba agreed with alacrity.

The room was without space, servants, and food, but joy sprang in abundance from the constricted circumstances of poverty, as a fountain gushes with increased force from a tiny aperture.

Three days went by. Twice the river steamer appeared on schedule with many passengers and much hubbub; but by evening the riverbank had emptied, and then the three of them were at liberty once more. They cooked together, making mistakes, and ended up with meals not quite what they had intended, which Mrinmayi, now the devoted wife, served to son and father-in-law, while they teased her about a thousand shortcomings in her household arrangements and she jingled her bangles in pretended pique. At last Apurba said they really had to leave. Though Mrinmayi pleaded with him for a few more days, her father said, 'Better not.'

On the last day he hugged his daughter, stroked her head, and said in a choked voice, 'Darling, you must be a Lakshmi to brighten your husband's home. Let no one find fault with my Minu.' A sobbing Mrinmayi bade farewell and departed with her husband. Ishan turned and went back to his hut, now twice as cramped and cheerless, and resumed weighing goods, day after day, month after month.

6

When this guilty couple returned home, Apurba's mother wore a long face and said nothing. She blamed no one, and they did not try to exonerate themselves. Unspoken reproof and reproach sat sternly upon

266

the house like a stone. At last the atmosphere became unbearable, and Apurba said, 'Mother, college has opened, and I had better return to start my law degree.'

His mother said indifferently, 'What will you do with your wife?'

'She'll stay here.'

'No, son, it won't work. You must take her with you.' She did not employ the usual affectionate form of address.

Apurba in a mortified tone said, 'All right.' He began to prepare. On the night before his departure, he came to bed and found Mrinmayi in tears. Sorrowfully he asked, 'I suppose you don't want to go with me to Calcutta?'

'No.'

'Don't you love me?' There was no answer. Sometimes an answer comes easily, but other times the psychology of it is so complex that a shy girl can only keep silent. Apurba asked, 'Will you mind leaving Rakhal?'

'Yes,' said Mrinmayi without hesitation.

A pang of jealousy as piercing as the point of a needle passed through this Bachelor of Arts at the thought of the boy Rakhal. He said, 'I won't be able to return for a long time.'

No reply.

'I think it could even be two years or more.'

'When you return, bring a Rogers three-bladed knife for Rakhal,' Mrinmayi ordered.

Apurba, who had been reclining against a bolster, rose a little at this and said, 'So you really do want to stay here.'

'Yes, I'll go and stay with my mother.'

Apurba sighed and said, 'All right, that's that. I won't come back until you write me a letter. Does that make you very happy?'

Mrinmayi felt that this question did not require reply and dropped off to sleep. But Apurba did not sleep. He propped himself up with a pillow and remained alert.

Late at night the moon rose, and moonlight fell across the bed. Apurba looked at Mrinmayi and thought he saw a fairy princess put to sleep by the touch of a silver wand. If he could only find a wand of gold he could awaken her and exchange a garland of love. But he knew that such a wand would only bring him heartache instead of happiness, while the silver wand had turned her into a blissfully sleeping beauty.

At dawn he woke her and said, 'Mrinmayi, it's time for me to go. Let me take you to your mother's house.' She got out of bed and stood there, and Apurba took her hands. 'Now I want you to grant me a wish. I have helped you many times. Now that I am going will you give me a reward?'

Mrinmayi was puzzled. 'What?'

'Give me one loving kiss.'

Apurba's ridiculous request and earnest voice made Mrinmayi burst into laughter. Then she pulled a long face and prepared to kiss him. She came close and could not, giggled and began to laugh again. Twice she tried, and at last gave up, muffling her hilarity with her sari. Apurba pulled her ears as a punishment but made a stern vow: he must not lower his dignity by snatching his reward by force. It must come spontaneously, as a sacred offering – or not at all.

Mrinmayi laughed no more. They set out together for her mother's house in the hush of early morning. When he returned he said to his own mother, 'I thought it over and decided to take her to her mother. Having a wife with me in Calcutta would restrict my studies. She'd have no company there. You don't seem to want her here, so I left her with her own mother.' In deep resentment, mother and son parted.

7

In her mother's house Mrinmayi found that she could not settle to anything. The entire house seemed to have altered. Time dragged. What to do, where to go, whom to see, she could not decide. It was as if the house and the village had been obliterated by a total eclipse of the sun at midday. And another thing: the desire to go to Calcutta that overwhelmed her now – where had that been last night? Only a day ago, she had had no conception that the life she loved could completely lose its savour. Today, like a mature leaf ready to detach itself from a tree, she effortlessly rejected her former existence.

There is a tale told of a swordsmith so skilled he could make a weapon keen enough to slice a man in two without his feeling a thing; only when he moved would the two parts divide. Mrinmayi was unaware when the Creator's sword severed her childhood from her youth. She looked around her, astonished and bruised, and saw herself anew. Her bedroom in her old home was no longer familiar.

The girl who had lived there had disappeared. Now all her memorable moments gathered around another house, another room, another bed.

No one saw Mrinmayi out of doors any more. No one heard her peals of laughter. Rakhal was afraid even to look at her. Games together were out of the question. She said to her mother, 'Take me back to my mother-in-law's house.'

There Apurba's mother had been grieving, remembering her son's face at farewell. She agonised over his going away angry and leaving his wife with her own mother. Then the mournful Mrinmayi, veiled with due respect, came to touch her mother-in-law's feet. No wonder the old woman wept, embraced the younger, and in a moment was reconciled. Then the mother-in-law looked into the newly-married girl's face and was amazed. The Mrinmayi she had known was no more. Could ordinary beings be so transformed? Such an enormous change would require enormous strength. The mother-in-law had intended to correct Mrinmayi's faults one by one, but an invisible Rectifier had taken charge of her and in one fell swoop had moulded her anew. Now Mrinmayi could understand her mother-in-law, and her mother-in-law Mrinmayi. They intertwined as one household like the branches and twigs of a tree.

A profound sense of womanhood filled every fibre of Mrinmayi and made her feel as tender as heartache. Tears of contrition welled up in her like the inky-black rain-clouds that herald the monsoon. They cast deep shadows beneath her eye-lashes. She kept thinking to herself: I didn't know my own mind. You could see that. So why didn't you make it up for me? Why didn't you punish me? I didn't want to go to Calcutta with you and behaved like a witch. Why didn't you make me go? You shouldn't have taken any notice of me and my obstinacy.

She thought of that morning when Apurba had captured her on the lonely road by the pond, had said nothing, only looked at her. She saw the path, the spot beneath the trees, the morning sunbeams, the expression in his eyes and all of a sudden she sensed their full meaning. The half-kiss she had given him before he went away now tormented her like a thirsty bird in the desert darting forward and hesitating before a mirage. Over and over again she thought: I wish I'd done that then, I wish I'd said that, if only it had been like that!

Apurba was similarly despairing. He was telling himself: Mrinmayi has never seen my best self. While Mrinmayi was asking herself: what

269

must he think of me? What must he take me for? A difficult, thought-less, silly girl, not a mature woman capable of returning his love from an unquenchable heart. She felt sick with shame and remorse and began to repay all her debts to Apurba with kisses and caresses on his pillow.

When he had gone away he had said, 'If you don't write, I won't come home.' When she remembered that, she shut the door and began a letter on the gold-bordered coloured paper that he had given her. Very care-fully she drew some lines and then, after smudging her fingers, without bothering to address her husband with a formal salutation she wrote: 'Why don't you write to me? How are you?' and 'You come home.' What more could she say? Everything worth saying was now surely said, but not perhaps with quite the flair for expression to which humans are accustomed. Mrinmayi understood that and racked her brain for ways to put some new words together. 'Now write me a letter, and write how you are and come home, mother is well, Bishu and Puti are well, yesterday our black cow had a calf.' With this she ended the letter. She put it in an envelope and in drops of love inscribed each letter: Shrijukta Babu Apurba Krishna Ray. But even so much love could not make the lines straight, the letters neatly formed, the spelling faultless. And on an enve-lope, besides the name, something else is required. This Mrinmayi did not know. To keep the letter private she gave it to a trusted maid for posting. Needless to say, nothing came of it. Apurba did not come home.

8

His mother knew that he had a holiday, yet Apurba had not returned. She and Mrinmayi assumed that he was still angry, and when Mrinmayi thought of her letter she was overcome with shame. It had conveyed nothing she really wanted to say, and Apurba would think her even more immature and even less worthy of his efforts. She was transfixed with anxiety. Again and again she asked the maid, 'That letter, did you post it?' A thousand times the maid reassured her, 'Yes, I dropped it into the box myself. The master should have got it days ago.'

A day eventually came when Apurba's mother called Mrinmayi and told her, 'Daughter, Apu has been gone a long time, so I am thinking of going to Calcutta to see him. Will you come?' Mrinmayi nodded in agreement, went to her room, shut the door, fell on the bed, embraced the pillow with all her might, and shook with silent laughter. Then all her pent-up emotion spilled out and she became serious, gloomy and apprehensive. Finally she started to cry.

With no prior warning these two repentant women set out for Calcutta to plead with Apurba for absolution. There they stayed at the home of his married sister.

That evening Apurba, who had given up hope of a letter from Mrinmayi, broke his vow and sat down to write to her. No words came. He groped for one to convey mingled love and hurt. Not finding it, he became contemptuous of his mother-tongue. Just then a note arrived from his brother-in-law: 'Mother is here. Come at once and have your meal with us. All is well.' In spite of this assurance, Apurba went along in a mood of gloomy apprehension. As he entered his sister's house he promptly asked, 'Mother, is everything all right?'

'Everything is perfectly all right. You didn't come home for the holiday, so I have come to fetch you.'

'You needn't have troubled,' Apurba said. 'You know I have to prepare for law exams . . .' And so on.

When it was time to eat his sister asked, 'Dada, why isn't your wife with you?'

'My law studies, you know . . .' her brother said solemnly.

His brother-in-law laughed. 'All these feeble excuses! You were afraid of us.'

The sister said, 'You look ferocious enough to frighten any young person.'

The banter continued, but Apurba remained downcast. Nothing made him feel happier. All he could think was that since his mother had come, Mrinmayi could easily have come if she had wished. Perhaps his mother had tried but been turned down. It was hardly something that he could question her about: one must simply accept that all human intercourse, in fact all creation, was a maze of deception and error.

After the meal a blustery wind arose and heavy rain came down. Apurba's sister proposed, 'Dada, do stay with us tonight.'

'No, I must get back. I have to work.'

'What can you achieve at this hour?' asked his brother-in-law. 'Stay. You're not obliged to anyone. Why worry?'

After more urging Apurba acquiesced. His sister said, 'Dada, you look tired. Don't stay up. Go to bed.' That was Apurba's wish as well. He wanted to be alone in bed in the dark and away from all this chatter. At the bedroom door he saw that the room was dark.

His sister said, 'The wind has blown out your lamp. Shall I bring another?'

'No need. I sleep without a lamp.' His sister left.

Apurba began to feel his way towards the bed. He was about to climb into it when with a sudden sound of bangles, a soft arm took him in its embrace, and a pair of lips like a flowering bud smothered him with a flood of passionate kisses that left no space to express surprise. He was startled only for a moment. Then he knew that the half-kiss interrupted by fits of laughter was at long last being concluded among uninhibited tears.

(1893)

GLOSSARY OF BENGALI/INDIAN WORDS

achkan	kind of long coat worn by men (originally Persian)
adda	leisurely gossip in a group ranging over every conceivable subject; the group itself
alap	introductory phase of raga, with no measured rhythm and very slow tempo. It expresses and then unfolds characteristics of raga (phrases, important notes and tone range of its melody)
annaprashana	literally 'initiation to eating of rice'
arati	worship of deity by waving lamp, fan etc before his or her face
Asharh	third month of Bengali year corresponding to mid-June to mid-July
Baba	father
babu	someone from leisured class or someone with pretensions to it, depending on context. Attached to a name, e.g. Bibhuti Babu, it is rough equivalent of 'Mr'
babui	weaver-bird, widow-bird
baiji	professional dancing girl and singer
Bhai	brother; friend (both male and female)
bhat	boiled rice
bigha	land measure, approximately third of acre
biri	cheap cigarettes wrapped in tobacco leaf and tied by thread
Bou	wife
bustee	huts in poorest quarters of Calcutta, virtually synonymous with slums
chadar	length of cloth wrapped round upper body; folded and placed on shoulder for decoration or when not in use
chapkan	long, loose robe for men, chiefly used as part of official dress

273

Dada	elder brother, but also sometimes used to address strangers
darshan	act of seeing or visiting in order to pay homage
devi	goddess. Attached to a name, e.g. Maya Devi, it is honorific used to address married woman
Didi	elder sister; elder woman
esraj	four-stringed instrument with sympathetic strings, played with bow
ghat	flight of steps leading to river landing-place, often used for bathing, collecting water etc
Kaka	paternal uncle
katha	land measure twentieth part of bigha (also spelt cotta)
kirtan	devotional songs in honour of Lord Krishna
luchi	thin circular kind of fried bread prepared from refined flour and water so that it blows up like a balloon
lungi	length of cloth wrapped once or twice round hip and tucked in at upper edge, worn by men
Mahabharata	one of two ancient epics, the other being Ramayana
mahant	chief priest of temple
maidan	open space in town; parade ground (Calcutta's Maidan is equivalent to London's Hyde Park)
Mashai	master, teacher; respectful form of male address
maund	Asian measure of weight, equivalent to about 82 lbs in India
pan	mildly addictive preparation of areca-nut, catechu, lime paste and other condiments, wrapped in leaf of betel tree; chewed all over India, especially as digestive after meals. Combination of ingredients produces blood-red juice
panjabi	loose shirt worn in hotter regions of north India, possibly imported into Bengal from the Punjab
Paush	ninth month of Bengali year corresponding to mid-December to mid-January
Phalgun	eleventh month of Bengali year corresponding to mid-February to mid-March
pranam	form of greeting to respected older person in which one 'takes the dust' from the feet, or to divine image in which worshipper prostrates himself

prashad	offerings to Hindu gods, usually in form of sweets
puggree	light turban
puja	Hindu worship; Durga Puja is Bengal's main annual festival, in honour of goddess Durga
puri	small and thin saucer-shaped brown bread fried in ghee
sarangi	three-stringed instrument with as many as eighteen sympathetic strings, played with bow
shastra	sacred Hindu writings and laws
Shravan	fourth month of Bengali year corresponding to mid-July to mid-August
tabla	best-known Indian percussion instrument
tanpura	four-stringed instrument with sympathetic strings, used as drone accompaniment for sitar and other instruments
toka	conical hat of straw or split bamboo
Vedas	earliest and most sacred Hindu texts
vina	oldest Indian stringed instrument, with four strings for playing and three for rhythm, and twenty-four movable frets

NOTES

The publication details of each story give the Bengali title of the story (if it is in Bengali), the title and date of the book in which the story first appeared (in Calcutta, unless otherwise indicated), or the date of the story's first publication in magazine form if the story was not anthologised until long after its first appearance in print. Many of the stories appeared initially in a magazine or journal: this date of publication, if known, is the date given in the Introduction. Other dates in the Introduction are those of first book publication.

These notes are not intended to be exhaustive, only to answer the occasional vital question that may arise in the mind of a reader unfamiliar with Bengal or Bengali.

The Raj Seal (Rabindranath Tagore, 1861–1941)
Publication: 'Rajtika' in *Galpa Guchchha*, 1901.

p. 1   'Rai Bahadurship' Rai Bahadur was a minor title given from the middle of the nineteenth century to Hindu civil officers, such as deputy magistrates, for distinguished government service: it was a rough equivalent of OBE, Order of the British Empire.

p. 6   'Indian National Congress' The Tagore family was actively involved in the organisations that preceded the founding of the Indian National Congress in 1885. The opening session took place in Bombay with Tagore absent, the second session in Calcutta in 1886, when he composed and sang the inaugural song. He attended several later sessions, gave speeches, but never became actively involved in Congress politics.

p. 8   'Fort William' The cantonment of Calcutta, around which the European city grew.

p. 8   'Anglo-Indian class' Before 1947, 'Anglo-Indian' usually denoted the Britisher serving in India, especially officialdom; after 1947 the term came to mean those of mixed British-Indian parentage (who were generally known as Eurasians pre-1947).

p. 10   'Babu . . . idiot.' This sentence is in English in the original.

p. 12   '*Englishman* and *Pioneer*' A daily newspaper, the *John Bull in the East*, was published in Calcutta from 1821; in 1834 it became the *Englishman*, which was partly funded by Tagore's grandfather Dwarkanath Tagore. This later became a notably reactionary paper. The *Pioneer*, published from Allahabad, is famous for having employed the young Rudyard Kipling in the 1880s.

Natunda, Babu (Sharat Chandra Chatterji, 1876–1938)
Publication: 'Natunda' in *Shrikanta*, 1917.

p. 13   '*Mister* Kanta' 'Shri' is the equivalent of 'Mr', but in Shrikanta's case, it forms an actual part of his name: Natunda does not twig this fact and hence mocks Shrikanta for being so apparently formal.

p. 16   'Darjipara' This was originally the tailors' quarters of Calcutta (*darji* means tailor). Natunda's joking reference to 'Dirtypur' is made in English, not in Bengali: an example of the many small problems facing the translator of Bengali - especially Bengali humour - into English.

The Goddess (Prabhat Kumar Mukherji, 1873–1932)
Publication: 'Devi' in *Nabakatha*, 1900.
In 1982, Satyajit Ray wrote of his film *Devi*:

> The western critic who hopes to do full justice to *Devi* must be prepared to do a great deal of homework before he confronts the film. He must read up on the cult of the Mother Goddess; on the 19th century renaissance in Bengal and how it affected the values of orthodox Hindu society; on the position of the Hindu bride in an upper-class family, and on the relationship between father and son in the same family.

277

Those interested enough may turn to *Hinduism* by Nirad C. Chaudhuri, *Ramakrishna and His Disciples* by Christopher Isherwood, and *Satyajit Ray: The Inner Eye* by Andrew Robinson.

The Music Room (Tarashankar Banerji, 1898–1971)
Publication: *Jalshaghar*, 1937.
For a detailed account of a major Bengal zamindar's way of life, see *A Bengal Zamindar: Jaykrishna Mukherjee of Uttarpara and His Times (1808–1888)* by Nilmani Mukherjee (Calcutta, Firma K. L. Mukhopadhyaya, 1975).

The Adventures of Goopy and Bagha (Upendrakishore Ray Chaudhuri, 1863–1915)
Publication: 'Goopy Gyne', 1915 (republished in the autumn issue of the revived *Sandesh*, 1961, as 'Goopy Gyne Bagha Byne').

Crowmagnum (Sukumar Ray, 1887–1923)
Publication: 'Drighanchu', 1916.

The Rise and Fall of the Gammans (Rajshekhar Basu, 1880–1960)
Publication: 'Gammanus Jatir Katha' in *Galpakalpa*, 1950.
p. 70   'Ayatollahs' Rajshekhar's original reads 'Kazis of the land of Iran'.
p. 73   'Grabearth' The names are all in English (though written in Bengali script) in the original: we have simply preserved them.

The Sweetmeat Child (Abanindranath Tagore, 1871–1951)
Publication: *Kshirer Putul*, 1896. A large-format edition with illustrations by Satyajit Ray was published in 1944.
Kshir is a milk solid made by boiling milk and condensing it; *putul* means doll. One might compare a *kshirer putul* with a gingerbread man.
p. 100 There are a number of references here to Bengali nursery rhymes reminiscent of Edward Lear's Jumblies.

Primordial (Manik Banerji/Bandopadhyay, 1908–56)
Publication: 'Pragaitihashik' in *Pragaitihashik*, 1937.

Bravo to the Boss (Bibhuti Bhushan Banerji, 1898–1950)
Publication: 'Barababur Bahaduri' in *Janma o Mrityu*, 1937.

Unaccountably (Bibhuti Bhushan Banerji, 1898–1950)
Publication: 'Akaran' in *Janma o Mrityu*, 1937.

Farewell (Samaresh Basu, 1924–88)
Publication: 'Adab', 1946.
p. 126 'Allah Ho Akbar/Bande Mataram' The first cry means 'God is
Great'; the second 'Hail to the Motherland'. 'Bande Mataram'
was a song written by the Bengali novelist Bankim Chandra
Chatterji (1838–94), which became a rallying cry for Hindu
nationalists.

Winter in Calcutta (Amitav Ghosh, 1956–   )
Publication: This is an extract (pp. 124–34) from *The Shadow Lines*,
London, Bloomsbury Publishing, 1988.
p. 133 'the recent war with China' The 1962 Indo–China war, which
provoked strong feelings in Calcutta.

Rebirth (Abul Bashar, 1951–   )
Publication: 'Janmantar' in *Anya Nakshi*, 1989.
p. 145 'Babri mosque-cum-temple' Since the 1940s, controversy has
surrounded a mosque in Ayodhya in north India, said by Hindus
to be built on the site of the birthplace of Lord Rama. From the
late 1980s there have been violent clashes between Hindus and
Muslims over this issue.
p. 148 'names of Lord Krishna' For details of the Krishna story
see *Krishna, The Divine Lover: Myth and Legend Through
Indian Art* (no author or editor, London, Serindia Publications,
1982).

Matilal, Padre (Kamal Kumar Majumdar, 1914–79)
Publication:'Matilal, Padre' in *Nim Annapurna*, 1963.
p. 161 'hermaphrodite' *Hijras* (hermaphrodites/eunuchs) are common
sights all over India, especially at occasions such as marriage and
birth. They dance and sing and importune people for money.

Water (Mahasweta Devi, 1926–   )
Publication: 'Jal' in *Shrestha Galpa*, 1984.

Homecoming (Hasan Azizul Huq, 1938–   )
Publication: 'Phera' in *Namhin, Gotrahin*, Dhaka, 1975.
For an account of life in a Bangladeshi village today see *Songs by the River's Edge* by Katy Gardner, who lived in one for some months.

The Fugitive and the Followers (Sunil Ganguli, 1934–   )
Publication: 'Palatak o Anusharanakari' in *Mahaprithivi*, 1974.

The Murderer (Ashapurna Devi, 1909–   )
Publication: 'Khuni', c. 1970.

A Drop of Milk (Narendra Mitra, 1917–75)
Publication: 'Ek Po Dudh' in *Kathgolap*, 1953.
Satyajit Ray wrote this of Narendra Mitra in 1967:

> I can say this without hesitation that he is the only modern writer
> in Bengali who has never wholly let me down. This is remarkable
> in an age of mushrooming literary reviews whose editors fling a
> deadline at you, coax you to write at the point of a gun, and
> sometimes even pay you well for it. The urge to compromise must
> be great. But Narendranath Mitra has not done so. This may be
> innate honesty or abundance of invention or both. I like to think
> it is both.

The Mourners (Premendra Mitra, 1904–88)
Publication: 'Sabajatra' in *Mrittika*, 1946.

Private Tuition by Mr Bose (Anita Desai, 1937–   )
Publication: in *Games at Twilight*, London, Heinemann, 1978.
p. 221 'Banalata Sen' This poem is among the most famous poems of
    Jibanananda Das (1899–1954), perhaps the most original of the
    post-Tagore poets.

Sunday (Amit Chaudhuri, 1962–   )
Publication: in *A Strange and Sublime Address*, pp. 49–59, London,
Heinemann, 1991.

The Little World of Shadananda (Satyajit Ray, 1921–   )
Publication: 'Shadanandar Khude Jagat' in *Aro Ek Dozen*, 1976.

The Tenant (Bharati Mukherjee, 1942–   )
Publication: in *The Middleman and Other Stories*, New York, Grove Press, 1988 (London, Virago, 1989).

The Conclusion (Rabindranath Tagore, 1861–1941)
Publication: 'Shamapti' in *Katha Chatushtoy*, 1894. This translation first appeared in Tagore, Rabindranath, *Selected Short Stories*, London, Macmillan, 1991.
p. 260 '*Charupath*' A simple Bengali reader.
p. 261 '*Vishvadip*' 'The Light of the World'.

FURTHER READING

Bengali literature in translation (short stories and novels)

Banerji, Bibhutibhusan, *Pather Panchali: Song of the Road*, trans. by T. W. Clark and Tarapada Mukherji, London, George Allen and Unwin, 1968

Bardhan, Kalpana (trans.), *Of Women, Outcastes, Peasants and Rebels*, Berkeley, University of California Press, 1990 (selection of stories by Rabindranath Tagore, Tarashankar Banerji, Manik Banerji Bandopadhyay, Mahasweta Devi, Hasan Azizul Huq)

Chatterji, Sarat Chandra, *Srikanta*, trans. by K. C. Sen and Theodosia Thompson, London, Oxford University Press, 1922 (Introduction by E. J. Thompson)

Gangopadhyay (Ganguli), Sunil, *Pratidwandi*, trans. by Enakshi Chatterjee, Delhi, Sangam, 1974 (Introduction by Satyajit Ray)

Mitra, Narendranath, *Mahanagar*, trans. by S. K. Chatterji and M. F. Franda, Bombay, Jaico, 1968 (Introduction by Satyajit Ray)

Mitra, Premendra, *Snake and Other Stories*, trans. by Rina and Pritish Nandy, Calcutta, Seagull Books, 1990

Mukherji, Prabhat Kumar, *Stories of Bengalee Life,* trans. by Miriam S. Knight and the author, Calcutta, Chukerverty Chatterji & Co., 1912

Ray, Satyajit, *Stories*, London, Penguin, 1988
   The Adventures of Feluda, trans. by Chitrita Banerji, Delhi, Penguin, 1988

Ray, Sukumar, *Nonsense Rhymes*, trans. by Satyajit Ray, Calcutta, Writers Workshop, 1970
   The Select Nonsense of Sukumar Ray, trans. by Sukanta

Chaudhuri, Calcutta, Oxford University Press, 1987

Raychaudhuri, Upendrakishore, *The Stupid Tiger and Other Tales*, trans. by William Radice, London, Andre Deutsch, 1981

Tagore, Rabindranath, *The Home and the World*, trans. by Surendranath Tagore, Penguin, 1985 (Introduction by Anita Desai)

Selected Short Stories, trans. by Krishna Dutta and Mary Lago, Macmillan, 1991 (Introduction by Anita Desai)

Background books on Bengal

Banerjee, Sumanta, *In the Wake of Naxalbari*, Calcutta, Subarnarekha, 1980

Blaise, Clark and Mukherjee, Bharati, *Days and Nights in Calcutta*, 2nd edn, Ontario, Penguin, 1986

Bose, Buddhadeva, *An Acre of Green Grass*, Calcutta, Orient Longmans, 1948 (review of Bengali literature)

Chaudhuri, Nirad C., *The Autobiography of an Unknown Indian*, London, Macmillan, 1951

Hinduism, London, Chatto and Windus, 1977

Thy Hand, Great Anarch!, London, Chatto and Windus, 1987

Chaudhuri, Sukanta (editor), *Calcutta: The Living City* (Volume 1 The Past; Volume 2 The Present and Future), Calcutta, Oxford University Press, 1990

Gardner, Katy, *Songs at the River's Edge*, London, Virago, 1991

Ghatak, Ritwik, *Cinema and I*, Calcutta, Rupa, 1987

Ghosh, J. C., *Bengali Literature*, Curzon Press, 1976 (reprint of 1948 edn.)

Isherwood, Christopher, *Ramakrishna and His Disciples*, London, Methuen, 1965

Kripalani, Krishna, *Rabindranath Tagore: A Biography*, London, Oxford University Press, 1962 (2nd edn., Calcutta, Vishva Bharati, 1980)

Moorhouse, Geoffrey, *Calcutta: The City Revealed*, 2nd edn., London, Penguin, 1983 (this contains some major errors, especially about Bengali culture, but is nevertheless a lively introduction to the city's history)

Ray, Satyajit, *Our Films Their Films*, Delhi, Orient Longmans, 1976

Robinson, Andrew, *Satyajit Ray: The Inner Eye*, London, Andre Deutsch, 1989 (Calcutta, Rupa, 1990)

Tagore, Rabindranath, *Glimpses of Bengal*, 2nd edn., London Macmillan, 1991 (Introduction by Andrew Robinson)

My Reminiscences, 2nd edn., London, Macmillan, 1991 (Introduction by Andrew Robinson)

A NOTE ON THE EDITORS

From a distinguished Calcutta family, Krishna Dutta is the translator of Tagore's *Selected Short Stories* and a selection of his letters, *Glimpses of Bengal*.

Andrew Robinson is the author of *Satyajit Ray: The Inner Eye* and a study of Tagore's paintings and drawings. He is also the editor of four books by Tagore, including the above.

The editors are currently researching a biography of Tagore.